in case you didn't know

CARRIE ELKS

one

FRANCIE

"You can't wear jeans to a sex club," Charlie says to me, like he's the bastion of all knowledge when it comes to all things carnal.

"It's not a sex club." I roll my eyes. My twenty-six-year-old cousin – who happens to be younger than me by all of ten months – is scrolling through his phone the way he always does. He's almost certainly either checking stock prices or his dating app. "It's an exclusive, luxury adult intimacy venue," I remind him, parroting the description they put on their members only website.

Technically, Charlie isn't my cousin. He's my nephew. Well, half-nephew. The son of Myles, my eldest brother. But 'cousin' is so much easier when talking about our relationship.

We're sitting at a table outside the coffee shop below my apartment building. It's a tad too cold to be sitting out here, but the sun has come out and it's like all of Manhattan has decided this might be our only chance at summer. Like snakes shedding our skins, we've removed our thick parkas and replaced them with thin jackets.

And of course, I'm shivering. Thank goodness for coffee.

Charlie looks up from his phone, smirking, and I roll my eyes, because this whole situation is his fault.

"Okay," he drawls. "You can't wear jeans to an *exclusive, luxury, adult intimacy venue*."

"I'm not wearing jeans to the club," I say, exasperated. I love my cousin to bits, but I wish I'd never confided in him. "But really, it doesn't matter, does it? I'm not going there to do anything."

"Voyeurism is doing something," he says.

"I'm not a *voyeur*. It's research." He's enjoying this situation way too much. From the moment I confided in him about the meeting with my potentially brand-new book editor, panicking because I have to take my writing from zero to sixty in about five seconds, he hasn't stopped grinning.

"You should have just gone out and gotten laid," he says. "It would have been so much easier. And you could have worn jeans."

"Shut up." This is the problem with growing up so close to somebody. They know you far too well. "And women can't have sex in jeans. It's a physical impossibility," I point out.

He finally puts his phone down. A girl at the next table is batting her eyelashes at him, despite the fact that *I'm sitting right here*. He grins at her, and it makes her blush.

"Hello?" I say to him. "Am I interrupting you?" He has this amazing ability to get along with everybody. Man, woman, child, animal. They're all drawn to him.

"Nope." He brings his gaze back to me. "Where were

we? Oh yeah, you were going to tell me what you're wearing to the sex club."

"Exclusive, luxury adult intimacy venue. And I'm wearing a dress."

"Please tell me it doesn't have flowers on it." He wrinkles his nose like there's some kind of etiquette list I have no idea about.

"It doesn't. It's white and it's tight and I won't stand out like a sore thumb." It's one of my only "going out" dresses. Truth is, I'm a bit of a hermit. I'm more often at home interacting with characters I've made up in my head than with real life people.

"Virginal. Nice touch."

"You're not helping." I shake my head, even though a smile pulls at my lips because Charlie has the same effect on me that he does with everybody else. It's impossible to be annoyed with him for long. But the truth is, I'm terrified about going to this place. It's so far out of my comfort zone it's not funny.

But if I get this contract, I'll have to write the most spice I've ever written in a book. Until now I've been self-published, and though it's had challenges – trying to write, work with editors, cover designers, and bloggers has always been a juggling act – the only person I've had to please with my first draft has been myself.

But Alice Duchamps, the CEO and Publisher in Chief of Twisted Publishing is a tour-de-force in the industry. She's swept in like a summer storm, turning the whole traditional book publishing model upside down.

She knows exactly what she wants in a book. It has to be supremely marketable, with all the characters, tropes, and hooks that modern readers love. And she's not afraid to work with authors from the very beginning, pushing them to write their best work, and in return she markets them so hard they hit the top of every chart available.

This opportunity is huge. It's also very scary, because if this book – which I haven't written a word of yet – works, it's going to catapult me into the limelight. Which isn't the most appealing thing to an introverted, pen named author like me.

But still, I'm concentrating on the story, which we workshopped together over the past few weeks. It's a romantasy – since that's what I've been known for in the self-publishing book world – but it has more of everything. More tropes, more buttery scenes.

And way more sex. Including this one spicy group scene that has me shaking in my boots. Alice Duchamps knows this too. She's been completely upfront regarding the steam level she wants, and has suggested I send her a first draft of the first five chapters before we sign any contracts. We both have to be comfortable that I can deliver the kind of book she needs.

Which is why, when Charlie offered to hook me up with his friend who's the concierge at an intimate venue, I agreed for the sake of research.

Charlie's phone starts to vibrate – reminding him that he hasn't checked it for at least five seconds – and he lifts it up, wrinkling his nose. "My car is here," he says, looking up. Sure enough, a black town car is pulling up to the sidewalk next to where we're sitting. "I gotta go." He looks at the carry-on bag beside our table. "Listen," he says, leaning in. "It's going to be okay. Simone is great. She'll take care of you."

His mouth twitches. And that's when I realize that Simone must be an ex of his. I lost count of them after he turned twenty-one. The man flies through women like nobody else, *and* they all stay friends with him.

"She seemed nice when I talked to her," I tell him.

"She's the best." He stands, running his hands through his dark, thick hair. "Message me. Let me know how it goes." He leans down, kissing my cheek. "Love you, cuz"

"Love you too. Safe travels." He's off to L.A. for meetings. He works for his dad and uncle – my much older brothers – in finance.

Grabbing the handle of his aluminum ribbed carry-on, he wheels it over to the driver, who takes it and loads it into the trunk. While he closes up, Charlie smiles at the woman sitting across from me again.

She pulls her bottom lip between her teeth. I'm so going to put an overly flirtatious side-kick cousin into my next book. With a very, very dark ending. Charlie deserves it. Then he climbs into the car and lets the driver close the door, much to the woman's disappointment.

I want to tell her she's dodging a bullet. But I'm pretty sure she wouldn't agree. So instead I finish my coffee and throw my cup into the trash, waving at Niall, the coffee shop owner who's also a friend of mine. Then I walk through the door next to the shop, that leads into a foyer, and up the steps to the apartment that I live in alone, ever since my best friend and roommate got married.

Once situated at the tiny, beaten up kitchen table in my even tinier apartment, I sit down at my open laptop and sigh. I have two thousand words of the first chapter to write today if I want to meet the deadline Alice gave me for the first submission before they offer me a contract. But all I can focus on is the white, strappy dress that's hanging up on the door, ready for me to put on tonight and make what could be the worst mistake of my life.

My only consolation is that the club guarantees anonymity. I'll walk in, see what I need to see – hopefully without needing therapy – and be done.

It's no different to the time I went to the Bronx Zoo to study the Komodos for six hours straight so I could describe the way a dragon moved, even though the one I wrote had wings and averaged about forty feet in height.

Or the time I went to a Renaissance Faire to learn about chainmail and how it feels to run in it, because the heroine in that book was kick ass and would slay the world once she realized her power.

It'll be fine. Nobody but Charlie and I will ever know about this particular piece of research.

Thank goodness.

* * *

I have a habit of being chronically early for any appointment I've made. Probably because my childhood was so chaotic. Coming from such a huge family, I never had any control over where I went or what I did. My dad was mostly absent – he was seventy when I was born, and though he's in his nineties now he still travels south for the winter – and my mom was his constant companion even though she's over thirty years younger than him.

My brothers – I have six of them – took turns taking care of me during school vacations and holidays. They had kids of their own and they spent a lot of time at our dad's estate in Virginia where they all have cabins of their own around a lake. I wasn't neglected. I had a great childhood, all things considered.

But for all intents and purposes, I was an only child with seven fathers. And sometimes it still feels that way.

My Uber pulls up outside a restaurant a block down from the club. It's twenty minutes before my agreed arrival time, and there was no way I was typing that place into an app. The less of a trail I leave the better. But I have plenty of time to walk the rest of the way.

I add a tip to the ride, thank the driver, and climb out, grimacing because either I've put on a bit of weight, or this dress has gotten tighter since I last wore it.

The Ivory Rooms – the exclusive luxury adult intimacy venue Charlie arranged for me to visit – is based in a non-descript three story brownstone at the corner of the block. A simple sign, black serif script on white, is above the door. Nothing to say what it is, or who's allowed to enter. Like Simone promised when we chatted, nobody would ever know you're walking into an erotic club. It's classy and discreet and it makes me breathe a little easier.

Night has already fallen over Manhattan as I press the buzzer on the door. The sky is an inky dark blue, and the streetlights are illuminating the sidewalk.

"Hello?" A low, smoky voice echoes from the speaker.

"Hi. It's Sylph." I was given the code name when Simone registered me. It's their way of giving anonymity. Every member goes through a full check – financial and security. But after that, no names are used.

"Sylph, welcome. Come on in. Turn left and I'll be waiting for you." The smokiness disappears, replaced by a friendly tone.

Sure enough, the door buzzes open and I step through, feeling the rush of a breeze as it clicks closed behind me almost immediately. I turn left as directed, into an open hallway that smells of gentle florals, like they're piping perfume in. The floors are marble, and the walls are painted a soft ivory and the room is well lit. Nothing like I expected at all.

There are no audible sex sounds, no people parading around in the flesh bending each other over in the corridors. It could be the entrance to any upmarket club where rich people come to meet.

At the far end is a woman dressed in black pants and a white sleeveless blouse. Her hair and makeup are exquisite. She smiles at me as I approach.

"Sylph. I'm Simone. It's a pleasure to meet you in person." She holds out her hand and I shake it, warming to her immediately.

"Thank you for everything," I tell her.

"No worries. It's a pleasure to be able to help a friend of Charlie's. How is he?"

Okay, so she's not keeping complete anonymity. Not that I really mind, I'm not here for anything anonymous, after all.

"The same old Charlie. He's in L.A. at the moment."

A dreamy expression comes over her face. "I went to L.A. with him once. Best weekend ever." She turns to the desk next to her, picking up a thick bracelet that has a tiny computerized screen on it. "This is your pass. You'll need to wear it at all times. Anybody found inside the club without one is removed by security."

I slide it onto my wrist, trying not to smile at how much this feels like going to a conference or exhibition. Maybe it's going to be okay after all.

"There's no photography, obviously," she reminds me. "No saying your real name. And if you have any trouble at all, come find me, I'll be here all night."

I take a deep breath. "Where should I start?" I ask. She knows I'm only there to observe, not partake.

"Through that door is the main hall. It's where people go to relax, hang out. There's some beautiful women in there, serving drinks. Sometimes doing more." Her lip quirks. "But it's gentle and a good place to begin."

Charlie has obviously warned her that I'm a novice at this. At all things, pretty much. "That sounds good."

"And then, maybe after a couple of drinks, I'd suggest you go to room five. It's a voyeur room. Watching is very much encouraged in rooms five through seven. You won't stand out, and there's always some interesting things going on in those rooms."

Her eyes twinkle and I try not to blush. Because we both know what interesting means.

"Definitely avoid rooms one to four," she tells me. "Unless you're feeling brave. They're group participation only. No voyeurism"

I nod. "No rooms one to four. Got it."

"And rooms eight to twenty are for private encounters. There's a light on each door. Red means occupied, green means empty. They're accessible with your bracelet. Each participant will need to swipe if they are using the bed."

"I won't be using them," I say firmly. I'm here to research, that's it. I'd probably spontaneously combust if I did anything other than that.

"Okay." She smiles widely. "Any questions?"

"None right now. But thanks for answering the ones I had when we spoke last week. It was really useful."

"Again, anything for a friend of Charlie's." She looks at the door and presses a button. "You're in. Have fun."

"Thanks." Though I'm not sure that *fun* describes it accurately. Fear mixed with the need to run is how I'm feeling right now. If I get through tonight without barfing, I'll be happy.

I take a deep breath and tell myself to woman up. I'll wander around for a couple of hours, take in the sights, smells, and feels that I'll need to write the scenes I've agreed to with my editor, and by midnight I should be home in my fleecy pajamas with a cup of hot cocoa.

Two hours, a few mental notes, and zero interaction.

What could possibly go wrong?

two

ASHER

Looking at the banks of monitors in front of me, I let out a sigh. The security room of the sex club on the corner of Stratton Street is the last place I want to spend my Friday night. And yet here I am, sitting in front of a dozen screens, my laptop linked to the club's security system, trying really hard not to look at the dozen different real-life porn scenes playing out in their full, unexpurgated glory.

"Wow." The owner, a suave suited, bald, sixty-something, leans over me, looking at the interface from my laptop to their security system. "That's a lot of letters and numbers."

The multi-million – soon to be billion – dollar cyber security company we formed straight out of college works mostly with government contracts, not with a damn erotic clubs in the middle of Manhattan, but here I am, thanks to my ex-business partner who tried to throw me down the river.

This was one of his many dodgy fucking deals. I let him run wild last year, mostly because I was neck deep in creating this new security model. But while Nathan might not be my business partner anymore – or at least he won't once he accepts the very generous amount of money I'm offering him and signs on the line – I'm not backing out. He agreed to update their security system to make it state of the art, and that's what I've done.

And as soon as we run the final checks, my job here will be done. I can't fucking wait.

"It will really alert me before anything happens?" the owner asks me. I start taking him through how the newly designed system works.

A woman slowly spreads her legs on one of the screens in front of me and I immediately look away.

"The software is designed to track interactions," I tell him. "It won't record them, but if it sees behavior out of the norm, an alert goes off." Along with a small team, I've worked for years on this software, which has never included Nathan. He was always the smooth talker, businessman, while I worked on the products.

I trusted him. And now I know better. But the events of the past year still leave a bitter taste in my mouth. Bringing my attention back to the man next to me, I give him a short nod.

User and Entity Behavior Analytics is a cybersecurity solution that combines analytics and machine learning to analyze behavior and identify potential threats within systems in real time. We've taken it a step further and made it applicable to human movements.

A place like this is where it could work perfectly. Alert the security team to potential bad actors before they even do anything wrong. It can allow this control room to put the right people in the right place before they're needed.

Most of all, it can protect those who are the most vulnerable.

I look down at the laptop in front of me. The continuous script that I uploaded is running and analyzing. One name keeps coming up.

"Room five." I nod at the screen. "There's a guy there worth keeping an eye on. Code name Panther."

This place only uses code names within their servers. If an investigation was needed, they could track back and find real names, but if you work in this control room or on the floor, you don't have that level of access.

Despite my wishing I wasn't here, I'm pretty impressed by the set up. From a purely professional point of view, of course. If I ever wanted to go to a club to have sex – which I don't in case you were wondering – this place would probably be it. It's exclusive, anonymous, and full of beautiful people. Like the ones coming up on the screen.

There's a huge bed at the center of the fifth room, which is lit by red lights, giving it an edgy vibe. And on the bed, there's a group of naked people. Three guys, one woman. None of them are Panther though.

According to the analytics, he's in the room. "Zoom in by the door," I tell them.

They do, and there he is, his eyes narrow, focused. But not on the bed. He's staring at a woman across the room, like he's trying to decide if he wants to make his move. She's standing by the wall, though all I can see is the back of her head. She's wearing a tight dress, accentuating every curve. Her legs are long, her arms bare, and her hair is dark, the lighting making it look almost red, as it hangs in a glossy curtain down her back.

"Do you have another camera in there?" I ask, leaning forward.

"On it," the man monitoring the cameras says.

"Should I call security?" the owner asks me. "I don't want to spook anybody."

"Just ask them to wait outside the door," I say.

He murmurs into his radio as the camera operator changes the view, giving me a full, face-on view of the woman Panther is so fixated on.

She's beautiful. High cheekbones, wide eyes, and lips that are slightly parted as she watches the sex going on in the bed in front of her. Her chest rises as she inhales and exhales rapidly. Like she can't take her eyes off the scene playing out.

But her eyes aren't what makes my mouth drop open. Nor is the way she looks so stupidly innocent and attractive in that dress. It's the fact that I recognize her.

I know exactly who she fucking is.

Francie Salinger. My baby sister's best friend. What the hell is she doing here?

* * *

FRANCIE

I'm debating whether I can leave the room without anybody noticing. What's the etiquette? Do I say thank you as I leave? Do I say nothing? Nobody prepares you for how to be polite in a club like this.

It's actually been hugely educational. In a sexy kind of way. When I first found out I had to write a group scene before Alice gave me the contract, I'd tried watching porn –

another one of Charlie's helpful suggestions. But there'd been nothing sensual about any of the videos I watched. It was all wham, bam, thank you for pretending to orgasm, ma'am.

But this room is different. There are four people on the bed, one woman and three men. And they're worshipping her. It's actually breathtaking, the way they're so intent on her pleasure. All of them are beautiful. From the moment they walked in – the woman wearing a gorgeous gold silk dress, the men wearing suits and ties that made them look like they'd just come in from a day commanding their businesses – a feeling of sensuality took over the room.

It was in the way they touched her, kissed her, slowly undressed her while making sure she was the center of their attention. For men who looked so powerful, they were determined to serve her.

I've seen enough now. I know I can describe a scene like this without feeling like I'm writing an instruction manual – fit part A into part B, twist part C...

But just as I turn to leave my eyes clash with a man standing in the corner, his face partially shadowed, the rest of it glowing red from the overhead lights. He looks almost devilish, and it sends a shiver down my spine.

He doesn't smile. Doesn't move. Just keeps staring at me. It's unnerving.

Okay. I'm going to go. *Without saying thank you.* Maybe I'll just mouth it. My mom brought me up to be polite, after all. But before I can reach for the switch that unlocks the room from the inside, the door flies open, making everybody in the room stop what they're doing.

Including the poor foursome on the bed.

Whoever it is, they don't quietly step in and close the door softly behind them, like I know is the etiquette for this room. Instead light floods in from the hallway, ruining the whole ambiance of the room.

It reminds me of the time my oldest brother stormed into my bedroom when I was making out with a pillow to practice my kissing.

He'd assumed I had a boy in there. The memory of him frowning in confusion, then turning around and walking out without saying a word still makes my cheeks pink up.

"Can you close the door please?" one of the men on the bed says, his voice unexpectedly high pitched. "We're busy here."

My mouth twitches. I wonder if I can put this in a book.

But instead of closing the door, the rude intruder walks the rest of the way inside. And that's when my heart stops beating.

Because he's striding toward me, his lips pressed together, his expression full of fury as he reaches for my arm.

It's Asher Fitzgerald. Fuck my life. What are the chances of this?

"Francie?" my best friend's much-older brother says, his voice ominously low. "What the hell are you doing in here?"

His fingers wrap around my wrist. Not hard, but firm. They're warm, almost possessive. It's the kind of touch that shoots heat up my arm and settles low in my belly, even as my brain screams danger.

I blink at him, my heart hammering. Because this isn't the friendly Asher I remember from childhood summers. He looks like someone else entirely. Taller, broader, sharper. His face is hard and beautiful, his jaw flexing as he stares at me like he can't quite believe what he's seeing.

Neither can I.

His fingers burn into my skin, strong and tight as I try to get control of my mind, because currently I can't think. I can't speak. I can't do anything, I'm frozen in place.

"I…" My mouth opens and closes like a fish. "We aren't supposed to use real names."

The tension in his hand tightens just a fraction. "You shouldn't be here," he says, his voice low.

"Neither should you."

His brows rise. His eyes are ice. But I see the flicker the second he realizes I'm not backing down. And maybe, just maybe, I'm not the little girl he remembers anymore.

"Can you take this outside?" the high-pitched naked man asks from the bed. "This really is doing nothing for my libido."

Asher shakes his head, like he's as dumbfounded as I am about this whole situation, which is only a small consolation, because pure, unadulterated embarrassment is starting to rush through me.

Oh. My. God. Why does this kind of thing always happen to me? I'm going to kill Charlie, I really am.

"Seriously, I was so close," the woman says, shaking her head.

"I'm sorry." I shoot what I hope looks like an apologetic look at her. Not that I can bring my eyes to the bed right now. "I was just leaving." I pull my wrist from Asher's grasp. "Feel free to continue. Hope you have fun." I pause for a second and then it comes. "Thank you!"

Mortification causes me to practically run out of the room into what is thankfully, an empty hallway. A second later I hear the door click shut, and the sound of footsteps behind me.

"I'm leaving," I huff at him. "I told you that."

"And I'm making sure you're safe." Asher's voice is low.

He still sounds pissed. "Francie, will you just slow the hell down?"

I turn around and my gaze clashes with his stupidly piercing blue eyes. In the cold light of the hallway, I see he's wearing a suit, just like the men who walked into room five. Is that his kink? Does he like men as well as women? My face flushes, because right now I'm imagining his broad, muscled, six-two frame completely naked, pleasing the woman on the bed along with the other men.

My thighs squeeze together.

"We're not supposed to use real names in here," I hiss at him, because I don't like the way my whole body heated up at his closeness. I've known this man for half of my life. Autumn – his sister – and I have been best friends since we both ended up fully clothed in a lake at summer camp as kids, thanks to an initiation prank.

Every summer we'd gone back to the same camp, growing up together. She would invite me to stay with her family in their huge house on Liberty Island, right off the east coast, and I'd invite her to my dad's equally huge house in Virginia.

And yes, Asher was sometimes around, just like Autumn's other brothers – she has four of them – and her younger sister, Eden. But her brothers were older than us. Grown men.

Sure, I had a little crush on each of them in turn. Especially Asher, because like me, he was always reading books. He normally wears contacts, but I remember tiptoeing into the library one night in search of something to read, only to see him at the desk, leaning over a book, wearing a pair of wire-rimmed glasses.

I was eighteen then. He was twenty-eight. He was my first grown-up crush. But he was too old, had a girlfriend, and I knew he never noticed me. Which was fine, because I think Autumn would spontaneously combust if I ever dated one of her brothers. She thinks they're all assholes.

"What on earth possessed you to come here?" Asher growls, his jaw tight. "You shouldn't be in a place like this. It's not for you."

My jaw drops open. Seriously, he thinks he has the right to say that to me? "I'm an adult. I can make my own decisions," I point out. "And maybe you should tell me what you're doing here?" Because I'm not big on double standards. "Did I just ruin your fun?"

He blinks, like he's taking my words in.

"Were you about to join in?" I ask him. "Because you can go back in if you want. I'm sure Princessa would love an extra man on the bed."

He looks appalled. "Princessa?"

"The woman with the three men. That's her code name." I reach for his security bracelet, determined to find out what his is. But there's no name on there. "Why's your pass different than mine?"

"It doesn't matter. You need to leave. *Now*." He reaches for my arm, but I step away.

"Don't tell me what to do," I protest. "I already have six brothers. I don't need another one."

His mouth twists at that.

"Do they know you're here?" he asks, and a shiver rushes down my spine. If they ever found out I'd have to flee to a convent. And black isn't my color.

"Does your girlfriend know you're here?" I counter.

"We're not talking about me," he huffs. "I'm a grown man." He pauses. "And I don't have a girlfriend."

"And I'm a grown woman." I lift a brow, trying to ignore the rush I feel from knowing he's single. The last I heard he was practically living with somebody. "If I want to go to a sex club, I can. If I want to have sex, I can do that too."

His lips part. "Francie…"

"Sylph," I correct. "No real names, remember?"

His jaw ticks. "What the hell are you wearing?"

My cheeks heat. The white dress had felt daring earlier, a little dangerous. Now, under his burning stare, it feels… *wicked*. His gaze drops to my legs, then flicks back up, a second too slow. Just enough to make my pulse skip.

"You need to leave," he tells me. "*Now*. I'll call my driver, he'll take you straight home."

"No thanks." I shake my head. "I'll get an Uber."

His face hardens, like I've just told him I'll catch the subway naked. "No you won't." His voice is low. Commanding. I bet he's a load of fun in this club.

"My driver will be here in five minutes," he says. "Black town car."

The door to room five opens, and amid the loud sounds of moans and grunts – I guess they managed to get back to things quickly – somebody walks out. It's only when Asher manages to look even more pissed that I realize it's the man who was standing in the corner with his eye on me.

"Actually," Asher murmurs. "I'll walk you out." Without any advance notice, he slides his arm around my waist, his touch so soft it sends a shiver down my spine. "*Darling*."

It's my turn to frown. *Darling*? Seriously. And yes, the way he presses his palm against my stomach as he pulls me close is making me tingle in all the right kind of ways, but still.

The man who came out of the room stops in front of us. "You're a very beautiful woman," he murmurs. There's an accent to his voice that I can't quite place. He looks at Asher. "Do you share?"

Asher shoots him the dirtiest of looks. "No, I don't. Fuck off."

"I'd pay good money."

"You couldn't afford her."

Oh my God, they're talking about me like I'm some kind of deal to be made. Like I'm for sale.

"Excuse me," I tell the man. Panther, his security card says. "I wouldn't sleep with you if you were the last man on Earth. That's not how you get a woman. Not by offering to pay for her. I expect at least a nice dinner and a foot rub before I put out."

Asher coughs, like he's trying not to laugh. So I turn around and fix him with a dark stare.

"I'm leaving," I tell him.

I turn on my heel, but I don't get far. Because his hand catches my wrist again. Gentler this time, but no less firm.

"Francie," he says, his voice low, rough.

I look over my shoulder. Panther has gone, thank goodness. There's only Asher behind me, his gaze dark, focused. I can't read his expression at all.

"Dinner and a foot rub," he murmurs. "Good choice."

My breath catches, and then he lets go. "Stay safe." This time his voice is demanding. And I hate the way it makes my skin flush.

So I walk away, my heart racing, absolutely certain of one thing.

I'll never look at him the same way again.

three

ASHER

"Did somebody piss in your cornflakes this morning?" West asks. "You've had a face like a baboon's ass ever since you walked in."

I knew I shouldn't have come here, despite Hudson and West's insistence. My brother and his best friend are both in Manhattan for the night – for their respective businesses. I'd turned down dinner with them because I had to complete the contract at the Ivory Rooms. And to be honest, I didn't want to come to this club to drink with them either.

But the alternative – going home – doesn't feel appetizing anymore.

After making sure Francie got into my car, despite her vow to Uber, I waited until the driver confirmed she was safely inside her apartment before I strode back into the club and demanded that Panther be removed and banned from the place.

Thankfully, the owner agreed.

And then I made a couple of phone calls to our security team, before I left the Ivory Rooms and climbed into the car that came back to pick me up.

"I'm fine," I say to West, taking another sip of whiskey. "It's just been a long day."

"Did you get it done?" he asks. He's aware of my business problems with Nathan. He's the one person I was able to talk things through with when it looked like I was about to lose everything. I know Hudson would have helped, but he has his own problems to deal with. His daughter, Ayda, has had a whole lot of issues after a massive custody battle with his in laws. The last thing he needs are my problems too.

"All done." And that's all I want to say about it. There's no way I'm telling them that I saw Francie Salinger in a sex room.

And I definitely won't be telling them that she looked like trouble in heels. A walking contradiction with her innocent eyes, filthy setting, and her smart mouth that made my blood pressure spike.

God, I need to stop thinking about the way she looked.

The hostess walks over and fills our glasses with the expensive bottle of twenty-five year-old Macallan that West must have bought.

"Thank you," he says, winking at her. She smiles back at him and he leans forward to whisper something in her ear, making her giggle.

Unlike Hudson, who's so straight laced it isn't funny, West is laid back. He lives in L.A., and although officially he's an entertainment lawyer, he's more of a trouble shooter. And his clients get in a lot of trouble.

He's also got the gift of sweet talking. He's never

without company. And from the looks of the way the hostess is nodding at him, he won't be tonight, either.

"Asher," West says when the hostess leaves with a promise to meet him later, "you'll be delighted to know that Mindy has a friend. We're meeting at my penthouse in a few hours." He grins at me and I wrinkle my nose.

"That's okay," I say. "I need to go home and do some work."

"After midnight?" West looks skeptical. "What the hell are you going to do that late?"

Review the security tapes for the Ivory Rooms from the last few months to see if Francie is a regular. "It's been a long day," I tell him. "I'll be sleeping. Alone."

And I absolutely won't be thinking about long lashes and innocent eyes.

"Well you're about as much fun as your brother," he says, wrinkling his nose at Hudson.

"Keep me out of this." Hudson shakes his head. "I've had enough headaches today, thank you. Did you know Eden lost her passport in Peru?" He glances at me, clearly pissed. "I had to pull some strings to get one urgently provided at the consulate."

I roll my eyes, because that's so like our youngest sister. "Yeah, I heard."

West frowns. "Wait, is she okay?

Hudson gives him a sharp look. "Yeah, she's fine. Why?"

West shrugs, too casually. "Just making conversation." But he takes a slow sip of his whiskey, like he's hiding a smile.

"Anyway," West says. "I've bigger fish to fry. Like how to deal with an extra woman coming to my hotel room." He lifts his brow at me.

But my gaze meets Hudson's. We both try not to smile because that doesn't exactly sound like a problem for West.

And that makes me think of Francie again. Of the way she looked in that tight white dress, her dark hair cascading down her back, her hazel eyes large and full of desire.

When the hell did she grow up? My mouth feels dry as I try to remind myself that she's ten years younger than I am. But all I can think about is the way she looked at me through those thick, long lashes.

How soft her skin felt against my palms.

I blink that thought away. She's off-limits. And I don't need any more problems right now.

Especially not ones involving my little sister's best friend.

* * *

FRANCIE

Hysterical laughter echoes down the phone as I recant the sorry tale of my night at the Ivory Club to Charlie two days later. It's midnight here, which means it's only nine o'clock in L.A., and my cousin is getting ready to go out to a bar, that requires clothing.

I, on the other hand, am right out of the shower and ready to get into my pajamas because I've spent the last two days in a writing whirlwind, despite my complete embarrassment at my confrontation with Asher Fitzgerald.

I'm stupidly annoyed with him. But I have to submit these chapters to Alice soon so I need to buckle down and write them. So rather than letting my fury fester, I decided to throw myself into the new world I'm creating.

The anti-hero, the annoyingly sexy War Legate Thane Arcor, is all iron muscle and battlefield calm. One quiet 'Enough' and entire battalion obeys him. He blocks onslaughts with his shields, drags the heroine behind him to protect her, despite her annoyance, and then growls at her for being reckless.

He's controlling, overprotective, and maddeningly hot. He'd be perfect if every time I write a scene with him I didn't see Asher Fitzgerald growling at me to 'stay safe'.

"Why didn't you just tell him you were there for research?" Charlie asks me, sounding delighted at the turn of events. I'm glad I'm entertaining him with the most humiliating night of my life.

"Because he doesn't know I'm a writer," I remind him. When I first started self-publishing I made the decision that I didn't want anybody except my closest friends to know. That's why I chose a pen name and swore to never tell my big brothers about it.

"So you're just going to let him think you're a deviant?" Charlie asks. "Oh this is so delicious. No, sweetheart," he says. "Ten minutes."

"Are you with somebody?" I ask him.

"Just a friend. It's all good." He lowers his voice. "Are you going to tell Autumn about this?" he asks.

"No." I shake my head, even though he can't see me. The towel becomes loose and I have to tuck the end back in. "I can't."

"Why not?"

"Because then she'll know her brother goes to sex clubs."

"I think you'll find it's an exclusive, luxury adult intimacy venue," Charlie says, before he guffaws again.

And I wrinkle my nose because I'd never thought that

somebody like Asher Fitzgerald would frequent a place like that. I'm really trying not to think about what he does there.

And yes, I'm completely failing.

"Listen, I have to go. Try not to do anything stupid until I'm back to witness it," Charlie says. "It'll be okay. It sounds like you both have something to lose if this gets out. If he tells anybody he's seen you there, he'll have to explain why he was there, too."

It's a good point. And another reason why I love my cousin.

He hangs up and I slump back on my bed, not feeling any better about the other night. All I can think about is the humiliation I'll feel the next time I see Asher. And I *will* have to see him. Autumn is my best friend after all.

Before I can think about what the hell I'll say to him, I hear a thud against the door. I tip my head to the side, trying to figure out what it was, since it's after midnight and the only neighbors on this floor are Mr. and Mrs. Penny, a lovely old couple who are both slightly deaf and go to bed at nine o'clock sharp.

After a minute of being on high alert, I start to relax. I'm going to brush my teeth and go to sleep, because tomorrow I have more words to write. It's only as I quietly pad across the hall that I hear the tinny voice. Like somebody talking through a radio.

My heart starts to hammer against my chest.

In bare feet, I tiptoe as quietly as possible, praying the floorboard in the hall doesn't squeak. Because if I'm about to be bludgeoned by a serial killer, I'd like to at least draw my time out on earth for as long as possible.

It's only a short walk through the tiny living room, slash kitchen, slash dining room to the front door. This is

Manhattan, after all, and the rent per square foot is stupidly high. When I get to the door, I roll onto the balls of my feet and press my right eye against the peep hole, only to see an eye on the other side trying to stare in.

"Shit!" I shout loudly, almost falling over in my attempt to back away from danger. My heart starts to pound as I steady myself, putting my hand against my chest to try to control my breathing. A knife, I need a knife. I look around, trying to remember if I've emptied the tiny dishwasher.

I'm going to die with my face in dirty dishes. Nobody will find my body for weeks. It'll be all over social media, what a loser I am, even in death.

"Miss Salinger?" a voice calls softly. "I'm sorry for disturbing you."

He knows my name. Is this targeted? Maybe he's not here to kill me but kidnap me. He'll send a note to one of my brothers demanding a huge ransom, and I'll never hear the end of it.

"Who are you?" I call out.

"My name's Shaun. I'm a security guard."

"How do I know that? You could be anybody."

"I'm putting my ID up against the door. You can look through the peep hole and see it."

"And let you shoot me through the door? Oh no."

"If I shot you through the door it'd make a huge mess," he points out, annoyingly reasonable. "It'd be much simpler to make a fake ID and have you open the door so I could use a silencer."

"You're not making me feel any better about this, Shaun."

"I understand. And you're not supposed to know I'm here. I've only worked for this company for a few weeks," he says.

"So why *are* you here?" If it isn't to kill me, that is.

"I've been asked to guard your apartment after an incident the other night. I've been mostly outside keeping watch on the building. But my boss asked me to make a check inside tonight."

"How long have you been here?" I ask him, frowning.

"The last couple of nights. After the incident on Friday."

The incident on Friday? I frown, because there was only one thing happening on Friday. "Did the club send you?" I ask him.

"What club?"

A little tingle snakes down my spine. "What company did you say you work for?"

He clears his throat. "I can't tell you that."

"Then I'm calling the police." I don't know why I didn't think of that before. I've always thought I'd be calm in a situation like this, but my mind has turned to mush. Still, I pull out my phone and lift it to unlock with facial recognition.

"Don't do that. I'll lose my job. It's Fitzgerald Security, okay?"

I pause for longer than a beat.

"As in Asher Fitzgerald's company?" I finally ask, my voice tight.

"That's correct. Please don't tell him you caught me. My instructions were to be discreet. I really need this job. My wife's having a baby next month."

Letting out a sigh, I stride to the door and wrench it open.

On the other side, a man in a dark suit, white shirt, and dark tie is standing there. He's in his early thirties, I think, and he's looking at me with puppy dog eyes.

"Miss Salinger." He nods at me.

"Shaun." I sigh.

He looks at my body and then I remember what I'm wearing. It's hard to look tough in unicorn pajamas.

"Listen," I tell him. "I don't need protection. I'm fine. You can go home, or go get a coffee somewhere."

"I'm sorry, ma'am. I can't disobey orders."

I take a deep breath. "Thank you for making sure I'm safe, but everything is fine. I'd like to go to sleep now."

He nods. "I'll be outside for the rest of the night. I won't disturb you again."

I blink, a sudden thought coming into my head. "What if I left the apartment?" I ask him. "What are your orders then?"

"I'm to keep you under surveillance at all times. Until I'm told otherwise."

"So do you have a car?" I ask him.

He frowns. "Yes."

"Great. You can give me a ride." I grab a denim jacket from the hook on the wall, and slide my feet into my sneakers.

"You're going out in your pajamas?"

"Yep." I nod. Because I don't have time to think this through.

I storm down the hallway, Shaun following close behind, and when we get outside I give him the address and insist he drives me there in his car.

And less than ten minutes later, I'm in Asher Fitzgerald's very opulent, shiny condo lobby, still in my unicorn pajamas. And ready to tell him exactly where he can stick his protection.

four

ASHER

It's 1:03 in the morning and I should be asleep after forty-eight hours of negotiating with lawyers, drinking a vat load of coffee, and cajoling my ex-partner to sign the company over to me. Instead, I'm hunched over my laptop reviewing security footage from the Ivory Club, running facial-recognition software on two targets: Panther and Francine Salinger.

Panther is a ghost. No hits, no name, nothing. It's frustrating but solvable. Tomorrow I'll ask Brad, my second in command, to find him. And for now I have a guard on Francie's building, which is perfectly reasonable. She is Autumn's best friend, she was followed by a creep and she needs protection. That's it.

I click through the footage from Friday night again. At nine-thirty she steps under the entrance light in that white dress, fabric painted on skin. My pulse trips. She presses the buzzer, bites her lip. Curious, nervous, gorgeous. She walks inside and every head turns. Of course they do.

I track her to the bar. Her hips sway, and my jaw tightens. She orders fizzy water, fends off three men and one very determined woman, then drifts toward the private rooms. I should look away. I do not.

The next camera takes over. She peers through windows, wide-eyed. Panther enters the hallway behind her, eyes locked like a predator. Heat spikes in my chest. The likelihood is he's a coward in real life, but I feel better knowing that one of my guards is keeping watch.

I bring my eyes back to the screen. She walks with uncertainty into a voyeur room, standing in the shadows as bodies tangle on the bed. Her breath lifts her chest, no bra, nipples tight under the silk. She pulls her bottom lip between her teeth and my blood roars.

Enough. I kill the feed. I'm watching this for her safety, not her curves. Focus, Fitzgerald.

I'm about to go through the whole thing again when my phone buzzes with an alert from my intercom.

"Yes?" I say, frowning, because nobody should be pressing my intercom at this time of night.

A soft voice echoes through the line. "It's Francie. Let me in."

Fuck.

I pull up the lobby cam, and there she is, in a pair of pink unicorn pajamas, cheeks flushed, a very nervous security guard hovering behind her.

Perfect. The one woman I am trying not to think about just showed up at my door in sleepwear.

I press the microphone.

"What are you doing here?" I ask.

"I'm sorry, boss," the guard says. "She refused to take no for an answer. Made me drive her here."

He's new. I can't remember his name. And I'll deal with him later. Thankfully he steps back, making it clear he's not coming in.

Not that I'd let him. But still, my mouth quirks at the fact she made him drive her.

"We need to talk," Francie says. And once again, I stare at her through a screen, but this time it's live.

Sighing, I press the code to grant access to the elevator and stairwell.

And then I wait.

* * *

FRANCIE

When Autumn and I left college and announced we were leasing a tiny run-down place in Washington Heights, our brothers threw every fit known to man. They traded cash bribes, guilt trips, one dramatic Hudson meltdown the neighbors still talk about. We kept the apartment anyway, taking only their signatures on the lease.

Waltzing into Asher Fitzgerald's marble-and-waterfall lobby in unicorn pajamas feels like I tracked mud into a Cartier showroom. He deals in billion-dollar contracts while I make up stories about hot warlords and their equally hot dragons, mostly in these pajamas.

"Francie." His jaw is tight as he opens the door. He's wearing his glasses, which makes me think he must be getting ready for bed. He's usually a habitual contact lens wearer.

"Why did you put a security guard outside my door?" I ask.

But he doesn't answer. Instead he gazes at me, the wire rim of his glasses carving neat angles around his cheekbones, making his eyes look dangerously sharp.

There's a tic in his cheek, but his expression is neutral, like he's unwilling to give anything away.

"Because you put yourself in an unsafe situation. And I wanted to make sure you didn't get hurt."

My mouth drops open. "Are you being serious right now?"

He runs his thumb over his jaw, so calm, so unruffled. Ugh, I hate how annoyed I am right now.

He exhales once, slow and controlled. "I'm very serious. I'm still trying to track down the asshole who wanted you. The guard stays on the door until I have a name and address."

I plant my hands on my hips. "Absolutely not. Shaun is done babysitting me. Tell him to pack up or I start charging him rent, and tomorrow morning I file a loitering complaint with the police. Your guard goes tonight, Asher, or the next knock on your door will be a cop asking why your company is stalking your sister's best friend."

For the first time he blinks and a rush of satisfaction bolts through me.

"And you don't punish Shaun for this," I add. "His wife is pregnant, he needs this job."

Asher's brows lift for a heartbeat. "He has a pregnant wife? How do you know that?"

"We talked. I know, it's a crazy concept, talking to the man posted at my door."

He runs his thumb over his jaw, still looking at me. Why

do the glasses make him seem so much more intense? "Okay, I'll take him off the door if you agree not to go to the Ivory Rooms again."

I fold my arms across my chest. I had zero plans of returning but he doesn't know that. But still, it's late and I'm actually feeling tired.

"And Shaun?" I ask.

"He won't be punished."

"Good." I nod, turning to walk away. Because my job here is done, and truth be told, I'm feeling a little sheepish now. "Thank you."

But before I can walk away, his fingers close gently around my wrist, heat flaring where we touch. "One more thing," he says, his voice low enough to vibrate through my body. "If anything feels off. Anything at all, you call the police and then you call me."

I swallow hard. "Even if it's the middle of the night?"

His eyes lock on mine. "Especially then."

"I'm a grown up, Asher. I can take care of myself," I say softly. But the tightness in his jaw doesn't give.

"Please," he requests softly. And that's what does me in.

I nod once, trying to ignore the way his voice pierces my chest. "Okay," I agree. "I'll call if anything happens. But you need to promise that we'll never, ever talk about this again."

"Never," he agrees, even as his thumb grazes the inside of my wrist in a silent promise I feel everywhere, before he lets me go.

I back into the elevator and hit the lobby button, the air crackling between us. He holds my gaze until the doors slide shut and the last sliver of his face disappears.

I exhale and lean my forehead against the cool,

mirrored wall for the moment it takes to reach the ground floor. It's over. Things can go back to normal now, right? I can forget about the Ivory Rooms and the security detail and every other stupid thing that's happened to me over the last few days.

And get back to writing my book.

five

FRANCIE

Two weeks vanish in a blur of word counts and deadline coffee. Theres no sign of Panther or any other club creeps. Just me, my laptop, and two brisk check-ins from Asher that I answer with equal frost.

I send off my opening chapters and *that scene* to Alice, with my fingers crossed and nerves shredded. Autumn demands that I come stay with her to celebrate on the little island of Liberty right off the east coast, where she and her brothers grew up.

"Pack a bag and get to Liberty Island, the mainland can spare you," she tells me. And to be honest, I need the break. A ferry ride, sea air, and zero deadlines sound like the perfect way to stop fretting about how long it will take for Alice to get back to me, and instead spend some time with the friend I love the most.

As the ferry bumps against the dock and I walk off,

Autumn barrels toward me, salt wind whipping her hair. She collides with me in a hug that smells of sunscreen and home.

"Oh my God, it's so good to see you!" she says.

"I missed you," I reply, pulling back to take her in. She's glowing. Married life and salt air agree with her. And even though she's in the middle of planning a full blown Disney Princess extravaganza for her niece's sixth birthday, I don't think I've ever seen her happier.

"Come on, I stole Hudson's car," she says, grabbing my hand and towing me toward the giant black Range Rover. "Ayda's in full Elsa mode, and I'm hanging on by a tiara thread."

I laugh. "How many people are coming to this party?"

"Two hundred or so."

My mouth drops open. "She has *that* many friends?" For a child who's been mute since watching her mother die and recently moved back to Liberty, that's a lot of people to already know.

Autumn shrugs. "We're having an adult party in the evening. This island is too quiet. It needs a little shaking up."

It's warm outside so I press the button to roll down the window as she drives along the country roads that lead to the lighthouse where she lives.

When we were all growing up, it was a shell of a building. The kind of place that you only went to if you wanted to make out with somebody, or scare them. But she's worked magic on it, using her interior design degree to its full strength, creating a home where she and Parker can live for the rest of their lives.

"Speaking of which, I've got a great costume for you." She grins at me. "I can't wait for you to try it on."

"Has your family all arrived?" I ask lightly, because I don't dare ask if Asher is coming.

But I'm determined not to let that spoil my fun.

"Eden can't get away," Autumn says. Her younger sister by two years is in South America right now. She has a degree in environmental science, and is working on a sustainability project there. She's also a huge animal lover and is involved in campaigning against animal cruelty, so that keeps her pretty busy.

"And Wyatt and Zach are busy too," Autumn adds, looking sad. Those are her two other brothers – younger than Hudson and Asher but older than Autumn and me. "But Asher has promised to be here by Saturday morning."

I take a deep breath. So there it is. I try to ignore how it makes me feel, because I'm in way too good a mood to think about that.

Autumn pulls up outside the lighthouse. She's done some more work since I was here last. Vibrant peonies clash with purple lupins in the cottage garden she's planted. There's a vegetable garden too.

"Who are you and what have you done to my best friend?" I ask her. Because seriously, she wouldn't eat anything that wasn't completely processed when we lived together. Her diet was based on pizza, which she would demand covers all the main food groups.

"That's not mine, it's Parker's," she says, climbing out of the car. She opens the trunk and we have a little tussle over who is going to carry my luggage until Parker walks out and takes it from both of us. I grin, because Parker is the kind of gorgeous, tall, laid back ex-NFL player that is perfect for Autumn.

He's the ice to her fire in the best of ways.

"Hi," he says to me, kissing my cheek after he's put my

case in the hallway of the lighthouse. There's a guest suite attached to the tall structure in the back. I have a feeling it won't be very long until they think about either extending or converting the guest room to a nursery.

"Hello handsome." I beam at him. "Thank you for letting me invade your castle."

"Anytime." He winks and leaves me and Autumn to it. Like he knows she needs girl time. Another tick in the *Parker is the Perfect Man* book.

"So," she says, turning on the Keurig because she knows I need coffee like I need oxygen, "how's your love life?"

"Nonexistent." Unless you count me being intimately close to many naked bodies in the Ivory Room a month ago. Which I don't.

She wrinkles her nose. "You should get back on the apps. I want somebody to double date with. Parker's lovely, but I need estrogen in my life."

"The apps are the devil's work. You know what happened the last time I tried."

Autumn has the good grace to look sympathetic. She knows that dating and I don't mix. And yes, I wish we did. I wish I had somebody like she has Parker. But not everybody gets to be that lucky.

She hits the button on the machine and it starts to hiss. My body relaxes in anticipation of the caffeine hit. By the time she adds the cream and hands me the mug, my stomach is gurgling.

We finish our coffees in no time, and follow them up with a glass of wine, which quickly turns into us drinking the whole bottle. So we're all giggly by the time Parker comes back into the lighthouse, looking at us through narrowed eyes.

"Should I leave again?" he asks, eyeing the empty bottle.

"No. Come in." Autumn holds out her hand and he gives her that soft smile that he only seems to have for her. My stomach tightens at the way they seem to communicate through their gazes. "Listen, we need you to find somebody for Francie to date."

My mouth drops open. "What? No."

Parker grins at my obvious dismay. "Like somebody local, or somebody on my old football team?"

"I'm fine," I say firmly. "I don't need you two organizing my love life for me."

"Of course, there's always your brothers," Parker continues, looking at Autumn.

She wrinkles her nose. "Ugh, no way. She deserves better."

"Then we definitely shouldn't hook her up with a football player." Parker grins.

"You were a football player," I point out.

He lifts a brow. "Exactly."

Autumn's phone starts to buzz, and I send a prayer of thanks up to the god of single ladies for interrupting this conversation. "Sorry, I better take this," she says. "It's Asher."

I retract my prayer quickly, trying not to blush at the mention of his name. Oh, I'm going to have to see him at the party. That's not going to be fun.

"Hey," she says, after she swipes to accept the call. "What's up? I'm with Parker and Francie."

Whatever he says next, I've no idea, but I try to keep my expression neutral as Autumn continues her conversation with her brother, oblivious to the fact that the last time I saw him I was dressed in pink unicorn pajamas and he told me I was barred from a sex club.

I'll never tell her about that. Of course I won't.

But that doesn't mean I'm ready to see her brother again. Especially since this time I'll be dressed like a damn Disney princess.

six

ASHER

I'm already regretting this.

Not coming to Liberty. Autumn would've found a way to drag me here regardless. No, what I regret is walking into the Captain's House thinking I could survive the weekend without throwing something. Preferably my ex-business partner through a window.

The bastard has the nerve to demand more money before he's willing to sign his half of the company over, after he was the one who got caught trying to steal from it, and trying to screw me over. My lawyer is working on it, but the entire thing feels like I'm trying to wrestle a rattlesnake into a gift box.

I rub a hand over my face and step inside the house. It smells like old wood, lemon oil, and some kind of citrus cleaner Hudson's housekeeper has probably bulk-bought. The floors shine. Everything's pristine, a far cry from how it looked when our father lost it in a poker game.

Hudson bought it back years ago. Restored every inch. And now it feels like home again, even if that home comes with chaos.

"You're wearing a damn costume and that's final!" Autumn's voice echoes down the hallway.

I walk into the living room to find her brandishing a red velvet robe like it's a saber, a furious expression on her face. Hudson stands across from her, arms folded like a he's a human wall. Parker's watching from the sofa with a grin, clearly enjoying the show. And West – because Hudson's west coast lawyer best friend always shows up for good drama – is sipping whiskey like it's popcorn as he watches my siblings go head to head.

"It's not happening," Hudson says, his voice low.

"It is." Autumn turns and sees me. "Perfect timing. You're wearing one too."

I lift a brow at her welcome. It's completely in character for our family. "Absolutely not."

"Yes you are. For Ayda."

"Still no."

Autumn growls and throws a gold-trimmed crown at me. I catch it easily, turning it over in my hands like it might explode. "You're not getting out of this," she says.

"I'm thirty-six, not six," I point out, keeping my voice even. "The dress-up phase is behind me."

West looks over at Autumn, giving her a wink. "Let the cranky old men wear only the crowns. Parker and I will go full royal. Right?"

Parker shrugs, because he knows which side his bread is buttered. "I'll even curtsy if that helps," he promises her.

Autumn presses her lips together but accepts her partial victory. "Fine. But I get to pick the crowns."

Hudson and I exchange a glance. His says *kill me now*.

Mine probably says *only if you go first*. Oh, and I really need some damn sleep.

I'm about to slip out of this drama and take my suitcase upstairs before she starts measuring us for sceptres when the air shifts.

Or maybe it's just me that changes.

Because that's when I see her.

Francie Salinger is standing in the doorway looking like sin in sneakers and a ponytail. Her cheeks are flushed, and she's holding a half-empty iced coffee like it's a weapon.

Our eyes meet, and for a second, the room goes quiet. Or maybe it just feels that way.

She doesn't smile. Doesn't look away.

And damn it, neither do I.

She's the last person I need to see right now.

And she's definitely a complication I don't have the bandwidth for. Especially not this week. Especially not when every time I close my eyes, I see her mouth on the security feed, whispering my name.

I shift my weight and run a hand along the back of my neck.

Get it together. It's just Francie.

She's here for the weekend. You're here for your niece. Nothing else.

Hudson's phone buzzes on the table, vibrating against the wood with a low, insistent hum. He snatches it up like a drowning man grabbing a life preserver. "Sorry," he says to Autumn, who's holding a crown out to him. "I have to take this."

She narrows her eyes. "Oh no, you don't get out of this that easily." Still gripping the crown, she charges after him. The door swings shut behind them with a thud.

West raises his empty glass, inspecting it like he's just

discovered the tragedy. "I need a refill before she comes back with tiaras."

Parker chuckles. "I'm coming with you."

Their footsteps fade down the hall, silence settling in their wake.

I glance toward the door, then back at Francie, who's turned her back to me, suddenly fascinated by Hudson's bookshelf like it holds the secrets of the universe.

I clear my throat, but she doesn't move.

"You know Hudson hasn't read a single one of those books, right?" I say, just to cut the silence.

She glances over her shoulder, arching a brow. "Let me guess. He bought them in bulk to make himself look intellectual."

I shrug. "Something like that. Pretty sure he thinks Moby Dick is a seafood restaurant."

She smiles, and damn if it doesn't knock the air out of my chest for a second. That smile lights up the room like the first morning rays of sun. It makes my chest tighten.

She turns back to the shelves, running her fingers over the spines like she's trying to buy time. Or steady herself. I get it. Because every cell in my body is aware of her. Her scent. Her shape. The way she's studiously avoiding me while also not leaving the room.

"I wasn't sure you'd be here," she says finally, her voice softer than before.

"I didn't plan to be." I pause. "Work blew up." She doesn't need to know about the shitshow that's been my negotiations with Nathan.

She nods, still not facing me. "That seems to happen to you a lot."

I don't argue. She's not wrong.

A beat passes. I'm not sure if she's going to say anything

else. Or if I should. But then she slowly turns around, arms folded across her chest, like she's bracing herself.

Her eyes meet mine. They're calm. Maybe too calm.

Because then she drops it. The killer line.

"So," she says, one brow lifting, "been to any good sex clubs recently?"

For a second, all I can do is blink at her.

She just stands there, cool as hell, like she didn't light a fuse and toss it in my lap.

And I hate how much I want to laugh.

How fixated I am on her lips, her smile, the way her hair curls down her back. How often I've watched her on that security feed, taking in every inch of those curves in that tight dress.

I push off the wall and head for the door without looking back, before I do something I know we'll both regret.

Let her think I'm pissed. Let her think I'm cold.

It's safer for both of us that way.

seven

FRANCIE

"Seriously," I tell Charlie. "I don't think I should be let out in public."

One sleepless night, a bucket of humiliation, and the lingering image of Asher's face after my sex club comment – and I'd rather be anywhere but Liberty Island.

It's only because Autumn is my best friend that I'm staying here and facing the humiliation I so rightly deserve. Right now I'm in one of the offices in the Grand Liberty Hotel – the hotel that Hudson bought and renovated and Autumn helped decorate – getting ready to show my face at the party in the extensive grounds that stretch down to the ocean.

The second I dropped that sex club line, Asher stared at me like I'd grown antlers and walked out without a word. I stood there, wondering if it was possible to strangle yourself with your own hands, until Autumn came back.

They were the longest five minutes of my life.

"That sex club's the gift that keeps on giving," Charlie splutters. "God, never change."

"Francie, are you in here?" Autumn calls out.

"Gotta go," I tell Charlie.

"Keep me updated if you say anything else completely inappropriate," he tells me gleefully.

"I'm taking a vow of silence," I reply, only half joking. "I'm going to become a Trappist nun."

"Good luck explaining your sex club visit to them." He disconnects before I can reply, and Autumn runs in, her face flushed.

"I need your…" She stops dead in her tracks, her eyes wide. "Oh, wow. You look amazing."

I glance down at the costume she chose for me. She's already in her dress – a pale blue Cinderella costume made of satin, with a tight bodice, heart shaped low neckline, and a skirt that could rival Scarlet O'Hara for its puffiness.

Autumn decided I should be Belle because the yellow gold of the dress matches my tan skin and dark, wavy hair. She was right, damn her.

"That neckline is completely inappropriate. I love it." She grins, taking in the cut that's much lower than hers, and the sleeves that are so far off the shoulder they're halfway down my arms. I've never been known for having ample cleavage, but this dress is working overtime. My boobs are halfway to my chin.

But it's the skirt I love the most. It's full and floaty, cascading in golden ruffles from my hips to the floor. Not as dramatic as Autumn's, but it makes me feel like a Disney heroine with a secret.

"Okay," she says, grabbing my arm. "We need to get this party started."

For the next hour I'm Autumn's servant, running this

way and that, hiking my skirt up with my hands because rushing around in a full dress is way harder than it looks. I have no idea how Victorian women got anything done. No wonder they spent half their lives fainting.

Guests start to arrive, and Autumn gestures me over. "I need you to keep Mylene busy," she hisses, somehow managing to still keep a welcoming smile on her lips. "Because Eileen just walked in."

"I thought Cinderella was the one who got bossed around," I complain, but I say it lightly, because I'd do anything for her and she knows it.

Eileen and Mylene are the sixty-one year old twins who haven't spoken to each other for forty years, even though they live and work less than two hundred yards apart from each other. Nobody knows the reason for their feud, but whatever it is, they've managed to completely ignore each other all this time.

I rush over to Mylene, who takes two glasses of champagne from the server. She's dressed as Queen Victoria, I think, complete with black dress, a blue sash, and a veil over her face to show she's mourning the death of her husband, Prince Albert.

From the corner of my eye I see Autumn ushering Eileen away, keeping her hand on her arm so Eileen doesn't see her twin sister is here, too.

My mouth drops open when I see she's also dressed as Queen Victoria. How the hell are we going to be able to tell them apart?

In fact, how do we even know who is who *now*? The twins get completely tetchy if you call them by the wrong name. And I don't want to be responsible for ruining this party.

"Hi," I say breathlessly when I reach her. "Remember me? I'm Francie, Autumn's friend."

"I know who you are," she says haughtily, her accent sounding suspiciously British. As though she's taken on Queen Victoria's persona along with the dress. "Iced latte, even in the winter when your stomach really would do better with a warm drink."

Okay, it's definitely Mylene. She runs the coffee shop, Brewed Awakenings, at the top of the hill that leads down to the ferry. You can see Eileen's By The Sea – the guest house that her twin sister owns – from the shop. And still they pretend the other doesn't exist.

"You're right," I tell her. "I get terrible gripes in the winter."

For a second she says nothing. And I'm reminded of the silence between me and Asher yesterday.

Don't say sex club. Don't say sex club.

"Autumn's decided to make you the guest of honor," I babble. "Isn't that great?"

"What?" She looks understandably confused.

"Just you. Nobody else. You get to be treated like a VIP." I'm making it up as I go along and it shows. Autumn is probably going to kill me. "Anything you want, you just tell me and I'll arrange it."

"Another glass of champagne would be good."

She's already drained both glasses. *Fantastic.* A tipsy Queen Victoria is exactly what this party needs.

"Of course. But first I need to take you on the tour," I say, offering her my arm like I'm her beau. "It's part of the honor."

"I have a bad leg."

That she does. It takes almost forty minutes for me to

take her around to see the whole spectacle that Autumn has arranged. I show her the candy stalls, the dance floor, the face painting, and everything else that I can think of. I even decide that she has to meet the chef in the kitchen of the hotel.

"I'm getting very tired now. And very thirsty," she tells me as we take our leave from Martin, the Michelin starred chef that Hudson headhunted to run the kitchen here. He seemed as perplexed as Mylene as to what she was doing here, but at least I've kept her out of the way of Eileen.

I send Autumn a message to ask her where Eileen is, because after all this work I don't want them coming face to face as we walk back into the garden.

Eileen's sitting down by the bar. Just stay away from there and we're good. – Autumn.

Mylene wants a drink. What do I do with her? – Francie.

The party has really filled up since we went inside. We have to walk even slower than before to make our way through the crowd.

"Oh look!" I say, my voice way too high and enthusiastic. "There's the carousel. You get to ride on that too."

"I don't want to ride on it," she says.

The carousel is the party's piece de resistance. It's full size, complete with an intricately painted canopy and hand-crafted horses that each have different colors and expressions.

"It's part of the guest of honor's duties," I tell her, sending up a prayer of apology for being such a liar. I'm doing it for the best reasons, mostly because the Carousel is in the children's part of the party, a long way from the bar and her twin sister.

But still, a lie is a lie.

"I guess you could skip it," I muse. "Maybe Autumn could find somebody else to do it. I hear your sister is here."

Mylene's expression turns dark. "I'm the guest of honor, of course I'll do it."

"Great." I beam at her, offering her my arm again right as the carousel slows down to a stop. We walk to the front, and I manage to get her up the step and walk her to a carriage that's painted white and gold. "This one is for you," I tell her, because I think getting on a horse might cause her an injury.

Once she's settled down, I walk over to the operator. "Please run it three times, don't let anybody off."

Because I need a break. And to call Autumn. I'm not sure how long I can keep this up.

I'm back on the grass when the carousel starts up. I grab my phone and pull up Autumn's name. She answers almost immediately.

"Mylene isn't doing as she's told," I tell her.

Autumn gives an annoyed grunt. "You're doing a great job," she reassures me. "But Eileen has decided to take up court in the bar. I've paid the barman to keep her here. Just keep Mylene away and we'll be good. I've arranged for Mylene to leave on the shuttle at five. You only have another couple of hours to keep her busy, then you're done, I promise."

"How do I keep her away from the bar?" I ask plaintively.

Somebody says something to Autumn. "I have to go,"

she says quickly. "Thank you so much for this. You're a star."

"I'm starting to understand why the evil stepmother hated Cinderella," I mutter, as she ends the call.

* * *

ASHER

"Damn, check out Belle," a voice behind me says. "She's practically spilling out of that dress."

My jaw clenches.

I turn to find two twenty-something idiots ogling Francie like she's a side of meat. One is dressed as Prince, complete with purple velvet, eyeliner, and a fake guitar. The other's in an Aladdin costume with a smug grin plastered across his face.

"Who are you here with?" I ask, my voice cold.

They blink at me. "Uh, we're interns. We work for Hudson."

Of course they are.

"Well, consider this your first lesson in not being a complete asshole," I say. "The woman you're talking about is family. If Hudson hears you talking like that, you'd be on the next ferry, if I don't throw you in the ocean first."

They straighten defensively. I take a step forward.

"I'm Asher Fitzgerald," I add. "Hudson's brother."

That does the trick. They back off fast, muttering apologies as they disappear into the crowd.

I exhale through my nose and rub a hand over my jaw.

Francie's barely said two words to me since I walked out on her yesterday, and I'm here playing party cop while my company's hanging on by a thread. Nathan's lawyer emailed twice already this morning, and I have three missed calls from his sister.

The guy who tried to screw me over now wants a buyout clause that's basically a ransom note written in lawyer speak. I should be in Manhattan shutting it down. Instead, I'm stuck at a princess party, trying not to body check toddlers.

Ever since I walked into Hudson's house yesterday, I've been on edge. Even Hudson noticed. And the worst part? I'm not sure if it's the fallout from Nathan's extortion attempt... or her.

Been to any good sex clubs recently?

The line's still echoing in my head. Her deadpan delivery. The look on her face when I walked out.

The way I keep imagining her in that dress.

I shouldn't have left. I should've laughed it off. Hell, I should've asked if she'd gone to more without me.

West appears beside me, handing me a beer. "What'd you say to those two? They looked like you cancelled Christmas."

I grunt. "They were talking about Francie."

His brow lifts. "Let me guess. Something about that dress?"

I don't answer.

He chuckles, clearly amused. "You gonna fight every guy who looks at her?"

I shoot him a look.

"Damn," he says, low. "You've got it bad for her."

"She's a kid," I mutter, though the words sound weaker every time I say them.

"She's not a kid," West says. "She's Belle. And every guy here wants to be her beast."

I scowl. "Are you one of them?" Because God help me, I'd throw him into the fucking ocean too.

He grins. "Relax. She's not my type. I prefer my women slightly less likely to stab me with a tiara."

Before I can bite back, something yellow catches my eye.

Her.

She's walking toward the dance floor with one of the twins on her arm. And yeah, the interns were right, she looks stunning. Too stunning. It's distracting.

I can't keep my fucking eyes off of her.

She glances at me, pulling her lip between her teeth when she realizes I've been watching her. And still I can't look away..

That's the problem. Not that every guy here wants her.

But that I do too.

"Look, Mylene!" Francie's voice is unnaturally bright. "It's Asher and West."

Mylene squints at us. "What does a girl have to do to get a drink around here?" she asks, her voice throaty.

Francie's jaw stiffens. "You still have duties. Remember? As guest of the day?"

"Duties?" I echo, already regretting it.

"You get to dance with all of the Fitzgerald brothers," Francie says to her, cheeks flushing. "Well at least the ones who are here today."

West grins. "Well, who could say no to that? I'm sure Asher would be delighted to dance with you."

"Not me," I mutter, shooting him a look. "You're an honorary Fitzgerald brother, too. You dance with her."

"I've had three knee replacements," Mylene says with a sniff.

West mouths *three?* and glances down like he's

checking for spare limbs. I sigh and hold out a hand, because I know when I'm done for. And I've already pissed Francie off enough this weekend.

"I'll be gentle," I tell Mylene. "And I promise not to shake anything loose."

She latches on with surprising speed and strength. By the time we shuffle onto the dance floor, pushing our way through a bunch of overexcited kids, she's got her arms around my neck and is wiggling like she's at a '60s sock hop.

Over her shoulder, I catch West giving me a smug little wave. I flip him off behind her back.

As the song changes to 'Can You Feel the Love Tonight', Mylene sighs and leans against me. "Mmm. You smell like cedar wood. My favorite."

I blink down at her. "You smell... like funnel cake."

"Francie made me eat half a dozen." She looks up at me, dead serious. "Help me."

"Help you?" I say. "How?"

"I hate being guest of the day. I just want to sit down and drink champagne. She won't let me breathe." She tilts her head toward Francie, who's laughing at something West just said. His hand brushes her arm and something tightens in my chest.

"I'll talk to her," I say, because quite frankly I'll jump on any excuse to be near her.

"Now?"

"If it will help."

She beams. "Okay, but I'll stay here. If I get any closer, she'll drag me to the face-painting table. She's relentless."

By the time I make it back through the crowd, Francie's leaning into West, smiling.

I clear my throat. She looks up, her eyes locking on mine. The shift in her expression is instant.

"Where's Mylene?" she asks, voice low.

"She asked me to talk to you," I say. "She's tired. Wants a break."

"But where is she?" Francie's voice lifts, looking frantically over my shoulder. "She's not on the dance floor."

I glance back. She's right. There's no sign of Mylene.

"You had one job," Francie mutters. "I gave you one freaking job!"

"She's not six," I say. "She'll be fine."

"She's over there," West points toward the bar, where a tiny black-clad figure is bee lining for the champagne.

Francie lets out a strangled sound. "Three hours. I've kept her away from Eileen for three damn hours. If she blows it now—" She shakes her head and hikes up her skirt, chasing after Mylene and yelling something about hair braiding.

West watches her go, grinning. "You really know how to win a girl over."

"I didn't sign up to be Mylene's babysitter."

Hudson joins us. "What happened now?" he asks, frowning at me.

"Francie's mad at him again," West says cheerfully.

Hudson lifts a brow. "What did you do this time?"

"Apparently," I mutter, "I lost the guest of honor."

And before either of them can say anything else, I turn on my heel and head for the bar, needing a drink more than I need air.

eight

FRANCIE

"Are you sure you don't mind keeping an eye on her?" Autumn asks me later that night. We're at Hudson's house, where we brought a partied-out Ayda who's snoring softly upstairs in her princess bedroom.

Truth be told I'm exhausted, too. An afternoon of chasing after Mylene has taken it out of me. All I want to do is go back to the lighthouse and sleep for about a thousand years, but Autumn has to get back to the party to pay the wait staff, and although Parker went to find Hudson, neither of them have come back yet.

"Of course I don't mind," I tell her. "Go. It'll be fine."

She hugs me tightly. We're still Belle and Cinderella, but it's like the Disney luster has worn off us both. We look like princesses well after the happily ever after and the long, unsatisfying marriage, the threat of divorce hanging in the air. Autumn's hair is falling out of her elaborate updo and my makeup is smeared from rubbing my face with panic at almost losing Mylene.

Who, I'm happy to say, made it through the party without ever coming face to face with her twin sister. I feel victorious.

After Autumn rushes out, I make myself a cup of tea and carry it into Hudson's pristine-looking library.

Autumn was responsible for creating this room and as soon as I walk inside I feel my heart get full. It's not quite on the level of the one that the Beast gave to Belle, but it's still full of thousands of leather bound books, the aroma of the binding filling my senses. Then I spot the ladder on wheels, attached to the tall shelves, and my heart tightens.

We have a similar ladder in the library at my dad's house in Virginia, a sprawling mansion in an estate called Misty Lakes, but I've never gotten to climb it while dressed as Belle.

It's an opportunity too good to miss. I feel as giddy as a child as I walk over and kick my shoes off, putting my hands on the higher rung and placing one bare sole on the bottom, using the other to push myself off the floor so the ladder moves.

I let go with one hand as the ladder glides across the shelves, leaning my head back and closing my eyes. I start singing of dreaming of more than this small town life as I ride, and it makes me laugh, because this is so much fun.

It's only as I come to a stop that I hear a throat clearing. And I recognize that low, gruff sound all too well.

Asher Fitzgerald is standing in the doorway. At some point in the evening he's taken off his jacket and tie, and rolled up his sleeves in response to the sultry weather. His hair is mussed, but the rest of him still looks annoyingly put together. His shirt is still crisp, his dress pants unwrinkled.

"Why is it that every time I see you today you're either saying weird shit or flying around a library?" he murmurs.

"I'm not talking to you," I tell him, climbing down. "You almost lost Mylene."

He glances down at my bare legs, visible because I'm holding up the skirt. It takes him a moment too long before he lifts his eyes to look at my face.

"What are you doing here?" he asks, not meanly. Just like he's curious.

"Here in Hudson's house, or life in general? I'm only seeking clarification because I don't have an answer for the latter."

"Here. At the house." At least he sounds amused for once.

"I'm babysitting Ayda. She's asleep in her room."

His jaw twitches. "Well, I'm back so you can go now."

Not gonna lie, his dismissal stings. "I don't have a car. Autumn and Parker are going to pick me up when the party's over."

"I'll take you."

"You can't, we can't leave Ayda." I have no idea why he wants to get me out of this house. It's pretty rude, actually. "It's okay, I'll stay in here and read a book. I won't disturb you."

"You always disturb me."

The way he says it, so low and matter-of-factly shocks me. "That's a horrible thing to say," I tell him. And yes, it's probably the exhaustion and the buzz of the day, but my throat feels tight, like I'm about to well up.

"I didn't mean it like that." He lets out a breath. "I'm going to go before I make things any worse. I'll go change out of these clothes then give you a ride home when Hudson or West gets back."

Before I can ask him how he *did* mean it, he turns on his heel and strides into the hallway. A moment later I hear the sound of his shoes against the polished wooden staircase that leads to the second floor.

I stand there, fuming for a moment, before deciding that either I go talk to him or I'm going to have another sleepless night.

I hate the way things have been between us this weekend. Picking up my skirt once more, I pad up the stairs to the room on the third floor that was always Asher's when we were growing up and where he sleeps when he comes to visit.

The door is closed, so I tap lightly on it, the wood so thick that I can barely hear his reply telling me to come in. Pushing the handle down, I stride inside only to be greeted by his very bare, very muscled back.

Holy shit.

My mouth turns as dry as the Sahara. His back is absurd. Lean, muscled, and unfairly gorgeous. He could rival the fae warriors in my books for sheer buffness.

Honestly, a shirtless Asher could bring about world peace. We'd all be too busy ogling to argue.

"I said wait," he says, turning around. I try to rearrange my expression into something that doesn't look like a salivating dog in heat. But now he's showing me the front of his torso. My eyes can't decide where to look first – his rippled abs, or the deep V where his hips disappear into his pants.

"Francie?" he murmurs, his gaze locking with mine. For a moment neither of us says a word. There's a weird buzzing in the room, or maybe it's in my ears. All I know is I've forgotten how to breathe.

He looks at my mouth then back at my eyes again. And I'm stupidly mesmerized. He's taken his contacts out and put glasses on and damn it, he's just hit my Achilles' heel. My breath catches in my throat.

Hot guys in glasses are my thing. Especially when the hot guy is half naked and staring at me like I'm his favorite kind of food.

"I came to talk to you," I manage to get out. My skin feels like it's combusting. "About the thing."

"*The thing*?" He grabs the t-shirt on his bed and pulls it on. There are a pair of sweat pants next to it. I'm guessing he won't be putting those on in front of me.

"Yeah." I nod, trying to think but my brain is way too scrambled. "The thing we did."

"What did we do?" He tips his head to the side, like he's trying to scrutinize me. "Christ, I can't talk to you when you're dressed like that."

I look down at my golden dress. "Want me to take it off?"

"Absolutely not." He looks almost alarmed at my suggestion. "That would be completely inappropriate. You're just a kid, Francie."

I completely balk at that. "I'm twenty-six," I point out, because this is stupid. "You're only ten years older than me."

"And I knew you when you were twelve and I was twenty-two."

"Then that's your problem," I point out. "Because that was half a lifetime ago. I don't know if you've noticed, but somewhere in the past fourteen years I've grown up."

"Don't worry, I've noticed," he mutters.

"Is that why you were so angry with me for being at that club?" I ask him. "Because you think I'm too young?"

His jaw tightens. "I was angry because you clearly have no concept of how to be safe."

"I know how to be safe. I use birth control, Asher." God, he's annoying. I was feeling so happy earlier. And now he's brought my mood down in a matter of moments.

He pinches his nose, like his brain is hurting. Serves him right for having such a big one. "I didn't mean safe like that, though thanks for putting *that* image in my brain. I meant safe as in being aware of your own vulnerabilities. Taking care of your security." His eyes are narrow as they meet mine. I have no idea what I've done to make him this furious again, but I'm so tired of arguing with him.

"Is this a commercial for your business?" I ask him. "Are you trying to sell me a security package?"

"No," he rasps, like he's on his last nerve. "I'm trying to tell you to stop putting yourself in situations where you can be taken advantage of. Do you know why I was at the club?"

"To have sex?" I say, trying not to wrinkle my nose, because the image of him climbing onto a bed like the one in the room he'd found me in, and having women throw themselves at him isn't exactly welcome in my already-too-full brain. But it's also stupidly turning me on. Would he look mean, like he does now, his mouth all twisted and hard as they lean over him?

Ugh, no, I need to stop thinking about this, before I combust.

"You think I was there to fuck somebody?" he murmurs. And that stupid image comes into my head again.

"Isn't that why people usually go to sex clubs?" I ask

him. "And it's okay, I haven't told anybody if that's what you're worried about."

"Is that why you went to a sex club?" His voice is so low I have to lean forward to hear him. His eyes are trained on mine, like he's hanging on for my answer.

I pull my lip between my teeth. I could tell him the truth. I was going to, I really was. The truth is always so much easier than a lie, after all. I could smooth all of this out by telling him I'm a writer and that I was there to research, but with the way he's acting he doesn't deserve my truth.

He's judging me. And that's really pissing me off. As is the way my body is reacting to him.

"That's none of your business," I tell him. "But the fact that you're judging me, when you were there too? It's hypo-critical, and it makes me feel like you don't think I have the right to make my own choices."

"I was there updating their damn security systems."

The breath wooshes out of me. "What?"

"They're a client. Not of my choosing, I'll add, but they paid their money and they deserved a good product." He lets out a sigh, and shakes his head, like he's as tired of this back and forth as I am.

"What kind of product?" I ask him, more to distract myself from the soft curve of his mouth than anything else. I can remember when he set up his security business. Back then I was a teenager, and he was newly graduated from business school. Before his MBA, he studied physics and computer science. He and Eden are the brainboxes of the Fitzgerald family, not that the others are stupid. But where Hudson is clearly business-smart, Asher is just smart-smart.

He blinks, like he wasn't expecting that question. "It's a predictive software program. Sees problems before they happen."

"How can it do that?" I ask, tipping my head to the side.

"We've built an algorithm that takes in a lot of data. It's proprietary so I can't go into the details, but basically, if somebody is about to do something you don't want them to do, the system identifies them and gives you the heads up."

"You can tell what somebody's going to do before they do it?" My voice lifts an octave. God, that's scary and impressive at the same time.

"Not exactly." There's a hint of a smile on his face, and I prefer it so much more to the anger I've been seeing all too often. "It's very specific. Certain behaviors and certain individuals. Unfortunately I can't tell the future, otherwise I'd be on a beach somewhere living it up."

"That's still amazing, though. How come I haven't heard about this before?"

He runs his thumb across his shadowed jaw. "Because we don't want people to know it exists."

"Your competitors?"

"Among others." He lifts a brow.

"What others?" I ask him. It's only when I look up that I see we've taken steps closer to each other. He's only a foot or so away from me now. I have to lift my head to look at him. "Who else can't know?"

"The people it identifies, for one. Foreign governments. And you. You shouldn't know at all."

"Are you going to have to silence me?" I ask him, aware that I sound all flirty.

"I'm going to have to ask you not to say anything. I should probably ask my lawyer to make you sign an NDA."

"I won't tell anybody," I say to him, and it's true. I mime

a zip pulling across my lips and his own mouth quirks. Why can't it always be like this between us? When he's soft and open, it makes me feel so warm. Hot, even.

And then a thought occurs to me. "Did you see *me* on the software?" I ask him. "Is that what made you come into the room that night?"

The smile disappears from his face. Oops, I probably shouldn't have reminded him that I was there in that room. Watching.

Feeling hot like I am right now.

"No. It alerted me to somebody else."

"The man who was watching me?"

His jaw tightens. "Yes."

My brows pull tightly together. "You were angry because you thought I was going to get hurt?"

"You shouldn't go to places like that. You don't need to. You're a beautiful woman, Francie. Desirable. Men look at you and they want to take. Most men have control, but that guy..."

"What happened to him?" I ask, trying to ignore the way my heart pounds at his words. He thinks I'm beautiful.

Asher looks away, like he doesn't want to answer me.

"You didn't kill him, did you?" I ask with horror.

"Of course I didn't kill him. What kind of business do you think I'm running?" He stares at me like I'm delusional.

"But you did something," I breathe.

"His membership was rescinded." His voice is emotionless.

"And what else?" I prompt, because I'm a writer. I study people like Asher studies equations. And I know there's more to this.

"Once we tracked him down, he got a little visit to

remind him that if he ever thinks about touching you, stalking you, or doing anything else, he'll regret it."

"You sent one of your guards to tell him that?" I ask him. I don't know why that makes my heart tighten.

He glances down at his hands. "Sort of."

"You went to see him yourself?" My mouth drops open. The man runs a multi-billion dollar company. Why would he do the dirty work when he has minions to do it for him?

He shrugs. "I wanted to make sure it was done properly. And it was. You don't have to worry about him. And if you could keep yourself from going to any other clubs, neither of us will have to worry about anybody else messing with you."

"Keep myself from going to any other clubs?" I frown. "Why would that be any of your business?"

"I'm just trying to keep you safe," he says. But there's something in his eyes that I can't quite read.

"I already have six brothers who think that keeping me safe is their full time job. I don't need you doing it too. And if I want to go to a sex club, I'll go to a damn sex club. I'm a grown woman. I can fulfill my needs however I want."

"Jesus." He shakes his head.

"There's nothing wrong with sex, Asher."

His gaze dips to my lips. Then down to my chest, where the dress is still pushing my breasts up like I'm offering them on a plate.

"I like sex," I tell him. "Very much. It would also be nice if every man I know wasn't desperately trying to stop me from having any. Maybe then I wouldn't need to visit sex clubs for inspiration."

"For fuck's sake." He steps closer. "Will you stop talking about sex and looking like that?"

"Ash?" a low voice comes from the hallway. "You here?"

We both snap around to see West appear in his doorway. He takes in Asher's body so close to mine that I can almost feel my breasts brushing against his chest.

"Is everything okay?" West asks.

"Everything's fine," Asher says, his voice strangled. "I was just telling Francie that we need to get her home."

nine

ASHER

"You okay, man?" West asks me the next day. I'm camped out in Hudson's office, trying to deal with a crisis because the minute I try to take a damn day off work everything goes to shit.

"Uhuh." I nod, deleting the swear words out of the email I'm writing to my lawyer.

"It doesn't look like it," West murmurs. "And by the way, you look like shit."

I finally look up from my laptop and meet his gaze. I haven't seen him all day. Haven't seen anybody, even though I specifically promised to spend more time with my family once this damn lawsuit was settled.

"Nathan's pulling out of the agreement," I say tightly. "Wants a cut of any future licensing deals."

"I thought you had that locked down," West says, dropping into the leather chair in the corner.

"We did. Until someone told him a major tech conglomerate's been asking about the software."

West frowns. "You have a mole?"

"Looks like it." My jaw tightens. "I'm working on finding out who."

He smirks. "Poor bastard."

I shrug, but the fury's simmering. Nathan might've coasted through the business, but people liked him. Trusted him. And now one of them is feeding him intel.

The idea of a traitor on the inside makes my blood boil.

If there's one thing I can't stand, it's a liar.

Before I can tell him I'm too busy to talk anymore, Parker walks in with three glasses of whiskey. He passes one to West, then holds one out to me.

"Hudson check in yet?" he asks. Hudson left for the mainland with Ayda this morning.

"Nope." I shake my head.

"So I guess he hasn't mentioned the security upgrade?"

I let out a breath. "The system's a year old. It's solid."

"Tell that to Hudson," Parker says, lifting a brow.

"I will when I get a minute." My voice is sharper than I intend, and Parker exchanges a look with West.

"He's pissed because the asshole he tried to pay off wants more," West explains.

"He didn't sign?" Parker asks, frowning.

"Nope." I take a sip of the whiskey. "He's heard someone big is sniffing around the software and suddenly wants back in."

Parker takes the seat across from me, eyes narrowing. "And you're going to tell him to fuck off, right?"

"That's the plan."

From somewhere down the hall, music starts playing

with a low beat and a steady pulse. It matches the one in my skull, the headache I've had since this morning.

Or since last night, really. Since Francie showed up in that goddamn dress.

I don't have a thing for Disney Princesses, but fuck, my body didn't seem to get the memo.

West offered to drive her home, thank goodness. I didn't trust myself to be alone with her. And yeah, maybe that makes me a coward, but I'm trying to keep this all together.

Then she asked me about my work and... something shifted. I still wanted her, but I also wanted her to get me. Understand me.

And that way lies madness.

But the thing that's been looping in my head since she left is what she said...

I like sex. Very much. It would also be nice if every man I know wasn't desperately trying to stop me from having any.

Twenty hours later, I'm still stuck on it. The flush in her cheeks. The way her lashes dipped. Those lips I can't decide whether I want on my mouth or my cock.

I tried to shake it off. Touched myself to the memory of her. *Twice.* The way she looked at me, full of heat and defiance. The sway of her hips as she walked away.

All it did was make me want more.

I wanted to pin her to the wall, slide my hand between her thighs, and show her exactly how much I like sex too.

I could make her come in seconds. I know that.

But it would ruin me. I know that, too.

West walks over to Hudson's perfectly ordered bookshelf, pulling out a copy of *The Art of War* by Sun Tzu. He holds it up to show Parker, who smirks.

"Is Hudson planning to start his own army now?" West

asks, shaking his head as he puts the book back. Haphazardly, which I know will piss Hudson off. He likes everything in his life perfectly ordered.

"Probably," Parker says. He looks at me. "Seriously, just talk to him about this security stuff. And your problems, too."

"I'm not burdening him with my problems," I tell them. "And as you said, it's easily dealt with."

"What's easily dealt with?" Autumn asks, walking in. She's wearing a silver dress that's pretty much molded to her body, the tiny sequins sparkling as she walks. Parker lifts a brow and lets out a low whistle at the same time.

"I thought you were going out for drinks with the girls?" I say, because she and Francie are heading out tonight – celebrating Francie's last night here on Liberty before she heads home tomorrow. But this outfit doesn't scream *drinks with the girls*, it screams *party like it's 1999*.

"I like to look pretty." Her eyes lock with Parker's and she smiles. West shakes his head. "What are you guys talking about anyway?"

"Nothing important," I say. And it's the truth, yes I'm pissed that I have to deal with business problems, but I try not to bring that to the family.

"That's good. Because I need to talk to Asher alone." Autumn looks pointedly at West, because Parker will pretty much do anything she asks of him when she's wearing a dress like that and she knows it.

"Uh oh," West murmurs, giving me a grin. "Somebody's in trouble."

I shake my head as he and Parker walk out, and Autumn shuts the door and turns to look at me.

"Whatever it is, I didn't do it," I tell her. She has that same expression on her face that she used to get as a child.

Determination mixed with annoyance. I remember trying to teach her how to tell the time when she was five and I was a teenager. Every time she got it wrong she'd wrinkle her nose and pout.

"Why are you being such an ass to Francie?" she asks.

"What makes you say that?"

"The fact that you can't look at her without frowning. I saw you yesterday, glaring at her at the party." Autumn sighs, plopping down in the seat West just vacated. "She's my best friend, Ash. And yeah, she used to have a crush on you. Emphasis on *used to*."

I blink. "No she didn't."

"Don't worry, I think you've pretty much assholed any crush out of her. But she's having a hard time and I hate that you're making it worse."

"What kind of hard time?" I bark out, because this is news. She didn't mention anything last night. There's a weird twist in my chest that I try to ignore.

I hate that I didn't know. That she didn't tell me. That I can't be the one she turns to when things get hard.

"Just stuff." She shrugs. "But anyway..."

"Stuff? What's that supposed to mean?" I glare at her. "Seriously, Autumn, you can't tell me she's having a hard time and not tell me what it's about. How am I supposed to help?"

My sister rolls her eyes like I'm an idiot. "Why are men so stupid?" she asks. "I'm not asking you to solve anything. Women aren't puzzles to be easily put together you know? We can work our own problems out, thank you very much. I'm asking you not to make things worse."

I open my mouth then shut it again, because I have no idea what she's talking about. "Does she have a stalker?" I ask, my voice low. Because if that asshole is harassing her...

"What?" Autumn's mouth drops open. "Why would you say that? Of course she doesn't. Not everything is a security issue, Ash. Even if you wish it would be."

"Why would I wish that?" I frown.

"Because you like solving problems. And if you can't solve them, you feel like you've somehow failed. Which is completely stupid if you ask me. Anyway, I'm not here to talk about your deficiencies."

"My deficiencies?" I repeat, my eyes wide.

"Shut up. Stop making everything about you." She tips her head back, like she's losing her patience. "Just promise me you'll stop being an ass to my best friend. If I didn't have her…"

I rein my annoyance in. I know how important Francie is to my sister.

"What kind of problems is she having?" I ask, my voice gentler this time.

"Just work stuff." She shakes her head. "I told you, it doesn't matter."

"What work stuff?" I ask.

Autumn shifts in her seat. "Nothing." For some reason she won't meet my eye.

"Autumn?" I frown. She's hiding something. And I hate when people hide things.

"It doesn't matter. Just be nice." She stands up, shaking her hair out. "Now let's go grab another drink and listen to some good music. This house is way too quiet for my liking."

* * *

"I'm sorry, I'm sorry, I'm sorry," Autumn wails four hours later, as I lift her into my arms and carry her to my car parked beside The Salty Dog – Liberty's best (and only) beach bar. Her breath is sweet from cocktails, and the hair she probably spent hours styling is a tumbling mess that frames her smeared makeup.

"Let's just get you home," I murmur, shifting her weight in my arms so I can open the backdoor of my car. Francie reaches for the handle, and our fingers brush.

One soft touch and a jolt shoots through me. I ignore it, concentrating on getting Autumn into my backseat. She flops over twice before I can get the belt around her.

"What the hell was in those cocktails?" I ask, mostly to myself.

"It was the speed of drinking them rather than the ingredients," Francie says wryly. I turn to look at her. Unlike Autumn, she's still put together, gold top slashed across her neck, one tan shoulder bare.

She brushes past me. Accidental or not, it works. My body reacts before my brain can stop it. I grit my teeth. Maybe I shouldn't have come. But the moment Francie called, I stepped in like an idiot.

I stride around her, opening the passenger door.

"I was going to sit in the back seat with Autumn," Francie says, giving me a glare.

"I'm not a taxi driver." I flourish my hand at the passenger seat and she gives a huff before she slides inside and I close the door behind her.

I start up the engine. "Did you have a nice evening?" I ask Francie, wanting to cut the silence between us.

"So we're making small talk now?" she asks me.

"I'm trying to be nice," I tell her. "I can make any kind of talk you like." I clear my throat as I back out of the lot and turn right to drive through "downtown" Liberty before we reach the open road to the Lighthouse. Parker is there waiting – he left Hudson's house shortly after the girls went out. Hudson called him to let him know what to expect after Francie's SOS.

"Maybe we should just be silent," Francie suggests. "I'm too tired to argue with you tonight."

"Is asking if you had a nice evening arguing?" I ask her, genuinely interested.

"No, but no matter what I say, it'll end up in an argument."

My chest tightens again. I should probably get my heart checked out. Or stop letting her near it.

"I'm sorry," I say gruffly.

Francie shifts in her seat. From the corner of my eye I can see her looking at me, like she's trying to figure me out.

"What for?" she asks.

I let myself glance at her. Only for a second. But that's long enough for me to take in her wide, expressive eyes and soft-as-fuck lips. "For being an asshole."

She lets out a soft laugh. "Which time?"

This time I chuckle. Mostly because she's right. "Every damn time," I admit. "Work's a mess. And I hear you've got your own stuff going on. I'm sorry if I made it worse."

"What kind of hard time?" she asks, and I'm struck by how she always pushes the conversation away from herself. And by how similar we are in that respect. I don't like talking about myself much either.

"Corporate bullshit. There are lawyers involved. It's a ball ache, but it'll work out." There, I've admitted it. "How about you? What's going on at work?"

"At work..." she trails off. "Oh yeah. No, it's okay. I'm just a little burned out."

She smiles as I pull up outside the lighthouse. My headlights sweep across the lighthouse window. Like clockwork,

Parker opens the front door before I've even turned off the car.

"How is she?" he asks, looking concerned.

"Drunk as a skunk," I tell him.

He walks around to the passenger seat and opens the car door. Autumn is snoring loudly. Parker unclips her belt and softly shakes her, kissing her brow as he does. "Come on, baby. Let's get you to bed."

Her eyes open. "Hello gorgeous," she slurs.

He smiles and pulls her toward him, lifting her into his arms. She loops her arms around his neck and nestles her face against his chest. "I missed you," she mutters.

"Missed you too, sweetheart." He looks at me. "Thanks for picking her up, man." Then he carries her inside, leaving me and Francie alone in the quiet.

I close the car door and circle around to her. The light on the second floor comes on.

"You okay?" I ask her.

"I'm fine." She nods. "Thank you for picking us up."

"You don't need to thank me." I take a breath. "If someone's giving you trouble at work – a customer, co-worker, whatever – you can tell me." I reach out like an idiot and tuck a lock of hair behind her ear. She stares up at me for a moment, and all I can think about is kissing her.

"I didn't go to the sex club to have sex," she blurts out.

My lips twitch. Why is she always so unexpected? "What?"

"You told me the truth, so I should do the same. I didn't go to the sex club for sex."

There's a pulse thudding in my ear. "Then why did you go?"

"I can't tell you."

"Can't or won't?" I ask.

She leans against the car, and I catch the outline of her nipples beneath that gold top. No bra.

"Does it matter?" she asks. There's that ghost of a smile on her lips.

"I could make you tell me," I murmur.

"How exactly do you plan to do that?" she asks, her voice teasing. "Have you invented some kind of truth serum to go with your world changing algorithms?"

"Sadly not. Though it would be useful sometimes." I give her a wry smile and she grins back. She's still leaning against the car, looking up at me, our height difference making her have to angle her head up. I look at her lips again, wondering if they feel as soft as they look.

"Did you really think I was in danger at that club?" she asks, her voice low. A cloud drifts over the half-moon hanging high in the sky, casting a dark shadow all around us.

"Yeah." I nod.

"And you came to save me." Her lips part as she inhales.

"Of course I did."

"Because I'm Autumn's best friend."

I swallow. "I wasn't really thinking about Autumn right then. I just saw you and..." I shake my head. "I don't like people getting hurt."

For a second she says nothing. Our eyes are locked, our breaths synchronized. "You saved me."

Fucking hell. It's like she knows how to hit every damn button in my body.

"I'm not a hero."

"Yeah you are. You fight injustice, just with code instead of a cape."

"You have an overinflated sense of my worth," I tell her. "I'm a damn idiot who can't treat a beautiful woman right."

"And that beautiful woman would be... *me?*" she asks, breathlessly.

"You know you're beautiful," I say. "You have to see it when you look in the mirror."

"If I'm so beautiful, why is it that no man has touched me in four years?" She tips her head to the side. "Not even kissed me?"

For a second there's silence. I try to take her words in. She hasn't had sex since she was twenty-two? *Fuck.*

"What? How is that possible?" I shake my head. "I don't..." Christ, what do I say here? "It's their loss," I tell her. "Maybe you haven't met the right man yet."

"I have." Her eyes don't leave mine. I feel the warmth of her stare pulsing through my body. I can't look away. I don't want to.

"Francie..."

"It's okay, you don't have to say anything. It's my problem, not yours." She pulls her bottom lip between her teeth and my dick throbs. "It'd really help if my brothers didn't intimidate every man who's interested in me."

"If they're intimidated by your brothers, they don't deserve you," I tell her. "You deserve so much more than a dick who doesn't want to fight for you."

Her gaze dips to my mouth then back to my eyes. "Would you fight for me?" she whispers.

There it is. The one question I haven't let myself think about.

This is such a bad idea. I think about stepping back. And yet I can't pull my eyes away from her.

Pushing herself off the car, she steps toward me, closing the gap between our bodies. I don't move, my feet so firmly planted on the ground that I'm not sure even an earthquake could loosen their hold.

"Would you, Asher?" she murmurs, sliding her arms around my neck. The floral sweetness of her perfume envelops me. Her body presses against mine in all the right places. Her soft breasts press into my abdomen. Her belly nestles against the thickening ache between my legs. I try to think but I can't.

My brain decided to clock out for the night. It's my body's turn right now.

She tips her head back, her gaze meeting mine. And I'm well and truly fucked. The control I'm always so proud of maintaining is nowhere to be found. All I can think about is tasting her. Touching her.

Showing her what she's been missing for the last four damn years.

"I'm done being careful," she murmurs. "Kiss me."

I let out a strangled groan. Her lips are right there, parted for me. I drag my tongue along my own, scrambling for one good reason not to do this.

But I come up with nothing.

There's a steady throb between my legs as I angle my head down until my mouth is a breath away from hers. Our eyes are so close our lashes brush together. Cupping her jaw with my palm, I angle her face so it's perfect.

"Francie..." I want to give her an out. But I also don't.

Before I can say anything else, she's the one who closes the gap. Her mouth meets mine and it's so fucking welcoming I feel like moving in there. I kiss her hard, one hand on her face, the other trailing down her side, to the hem of her skirt where it meets her bare flesh.

I dig my fingers into her thigh and hitch it around my hip, turning her around so her back is against the car. When she gasps at the sudden movement, I swallow her low breath with my mouth.

Our lips move as one as I slide my hand beneath her hem, feeling the edge of her panties. She lets out a soft, broken sound, part need, part surprise. She hitches against me again, letting out a sigh like she's almost in pain. "Touch me," she whispers.

I obey, because saying no to her is no longer an option. I trace my thumb down the seam of her, feeling the warmth of desire through her panties. Her eyes widen as she whimpers at my touch. Four fucking years. God, I need to make her come.

"Asher..."

"It's okay," I murmur. "I've got you."

"Don't stop," she says to me. "Please."

I shift my hand, pressing the heel of it against where she needs me the most.

My fingers tease at the lace, and she rocks against me in a quiet, desperate rhythm. Her breath shortens, her kisses become more frantic.

And I've never been more turned on in my life.

"I need your fingers," she begs. "Inside of me."

I'm mesmerized by this woman. If she told me to jump off a damn cliff I probably would right now. But thankfully all I have to do is nudge the lace to the side, groaning as I feel the slickness ready to greet me. As I slide two fingers inside of her I wish it was my cock.

And I know it never can be.

My thumb finds her clit, circling against it as I curl my fingers inside of her, finding the spot I know is going to make her legs buckle. She clings on tightly to me, her head dropping to my shoulders, her cries soft as I bring her to the peak.

Her body tightens around my fingers as I massage the spot inside of her, my thumb echoing the movement on her clit. Then she's gasping, and so tight I feel like my fingers are about to break.

"God... I'm gonna come, Asher. I'm gonna—"

I lift her head with my free hand, determined to taste her pleasure. Our mouths clash, her body stiffens, and she falls to pieces against me, letting out a whimper as she tightens around my fingers again and again.

I hold her as the convulsions subside, my own excitement throbbing in time to her ebbing orgasm. She slowly comes down from the peak, her eyes wide as they meet mine.

"It's safe to come in," Parker calls out as he opens the door to the lighthouse. I immediately jump away from Francie, like I'm on fucking fire, her feet dropping to the ground.

Her mouth opens in shock but she at least has the wherewithal to adjust her skirt so it's hiding the sweetest part of her body, before she adjusts her top so it's not messed up.

"Coming," she calls out. Then she smiles at me and I smile back. Because yes, she fucking was.

Luckily Parker's sudden arrival has cooled any ardor I had, and my erection subsides.

"You heading home?" Parker asks, walking over to the car where I just made Francie come like a fucking steam train. He winks at Francie. "Go on inside, I'll be there in a minute."

She looks at me and grimaces before walking past Parker to head inside.

"Everything okay?" Parker asks me.

"Why wouldn't it be?" I ask him.

He shrugs. "Autumn's worried about you and Francie. She thinks you have something against her."

"I have no idea what you're talking about," I tell him. "Everything's fine. Why wouldn't it be?"

"Okay, no need to bite my head off." Parker grins at me. "Thanks for taking care of my wife tonight. I appreciate it."

I'm still thinking about the way I took care of her friend as I bid Parker good night and walk around to the driver's side of my car, giving him a wave before I climb in and drive away.

But I don't sleep much that night. I'm too busy thinking about my sister's best friend whimpering as she orgasmed, and then, in the early morning clarity, wishing that I'd never touched her. Because then I wouldn't know what I was missing.

Eventually, at four a.m., I decide I'll go over and talk to her in the light of day. Explain that while I find her undeniably beautiful, the two of us are a bad idea and that we should chalk this one up to experience.

But when I pull up to the lighthouse in the morning, she's already gone.

ten

FRANCIE

"I don't hate this part," Alice says, tapping her lacquered fingernail against her laptop screen like it's a metronome of doom as we sit in her Manhattan office, stacks of manuscripts teetering on every flat surface. "But I also don't love it. And with this deadline..." She flips the calendar on her desk and circles a terrifyingly close date. "We don't have time for lukewarm."

I nod mutely, clutching my notebook like a lifeline. Alice is a powerhouse editor. Brilliant, blunt, and allergic to bullshit. She's the reason I signed the contract the day after I got back from Liberty Island. It still smelled like printer ink when the anxiety set in.

It's been three months since I left the lighthouse behind. Three months since I let Asher Fitzgerald touch me like he already owned me. Since he looked at me like I was breakable, beautiful, and his. All in the same breath. And then nothing since.

Now I'm three weeks behind on the manuscript that is supposed to be my big break. I haven't slept, my right eye won't stop twitching, and I can't stop thinking about the way he held me as I came. How gentle his hands were, how wrecked his voice sounded when he said my name.

Of course he hasn't called. Who wants a hot mess who basically dry-humped her friend's brother in the dark then ghosted him the day after like she was allergic to consequences? Because she was too embarrassed to face him, knowing she'd practically begged for him to touch her.

"I can do better," I say, although my voice cracks on the word better. And like she knows I'm on the edge, Alice changes tack, shutting her laptop with a decisive snap.

"Francine, let me explain something." She stands, heels clicking on the polished floor as she walks around the desk. "There are a thousand writers who would kill to have this shot. But I don't care about them."

I blink. "You don't?"

"No," she says. "I care about *you*. Because you're the one with the voice. You're the one who made me laugh, cry, and squirm in the first five chapters of your sample.

She stops in front of me. "But this—" she gestures vaguely toward the pages I recently submitted, "It reads like someone who's writing with one hand tied behind their back."

"I'm trying," I whisper.

"I know you are," she says, and it's not unkind. "But something's holding you back. And I think I know what it is."

My heart stutters. "You do?"

"It's the Commander," she says flatly. "You created this magnetic, emotionally repressed man who practically sizzles on the page. But now it seems like you're afraid of what happens when he finally lets go. Like you don't trust what comes next."

I open my mouth, but nothing comes out. Because how can I tell her that I've based the commander on the same man I ran away from three months ago without a word?

The one who made me see the kind of stars that no woman could ever recover from.

Alice crosses her arms. "Honey, that man wants to wreck her. He wants to protect her. He wants to ruin his life for her and pretend he didn't mean to. But you're keeping him on a leash. Why?"

I swallow hard. Because of who he is based on. And it's making it impossible to write him in the way I want to.

"I don't know," I lie.

She doesn't call me on it. She just gives me that look. The one that made me initially sign the contract and believe I could actually do this.

"Trying isn't enough anymore. Not for this. This is your coming-out party. And the publishing world is full of people who will take one look at you and try to eat you alive."

She gives me a smile that's all teeth and belief. "So show them exactly who you are and how good you can be."

My chest tightens. "And if I can't do it?"

"Then I'll give your slot to one of the other hundreds of authors who asked for it. The ones I turned down because you walked into my office." She tilts her head. "Don't make me regret betting on you, Francine. Make me look like a genius."

I nod, swallowing the lump in my throat. "You're not going to regret it."

Alice watches me for a beat, then nods like she's satisfied. For now. "Good. Because marketing's already moving. And our rights team is on standby."

I blink. "Wait. What?"

She strides back behind her desk and flips open a thick binder with color-coded tabs. "We've got early mockups for the cover. The team's brainstorming titles that'll melt the Amazon algorithm. There's already interest from two streaming producers – big ones – who want first look at the pitch."

My stomach flips. "Before the first draft is even finished?"

Alice doesn't even glance up. "Absolutely. You're hot in the industry right now, Francie. The right kind of hot. The sample you sent blew open doors you don't even know about."

I open my mouth, then close it again. Breathe. Inhale. Exhale. I might be on the cusp of the biggest opportunity of my life.

And not one of my brothers even knows I write.

Alice finally looks up, like she can read my mind. "You've told your family, right?"

My laugh comes out a little strangled. "Um no. Not yet. I just... haven't found the right time."

Alice raises a brow. "You've had months."

"It's complicated," I say weakly.

"It's cowardly," she replies, but not without sympathy. "And it's killing your writing."

The words hit their mark, clean and true. I grip the arms of my chair.

Alice's face softens just a notch. "This book is going to be amazing. Your voice, your vulnerability, your fury, it's all there, ready to be unleashed. But if you keep holding back because you're afraid someone might see too much? This whole thing will fall apart."

I nod. My throat is tight. My skin hot. I feel seen and exposed and, weirdly, grateful.

"Finish this chapter by the end of the week," she says. "The real one. With the leash off."

She picks up her coffee, already moving on to the next thing as I stand up to leave. "Oh, and Francine?" I glance back as I reach the door. "Tell the Commander I said he's allowed to wreck her. That's what we're here for."

My mind is still reeling as I walk out of the building, Alice's words echoing in my ears like a volley of bullets.

Producers are interested. Marketing is already rolling. Your name's going to be big.

I step into the bright Manhattan afternoon, squinting against the glare. The sidewalk is busy, full of honking horns, clacking heels, and food cart steam. And I'm one more heartbeat away from a full-on panic attack when I hear it:

"Francine?"

I freeze. That voice doesn't belong here.

I turn slowly, dread curdling in my stomach like bad milk.

Sure enough, my oldest brother is standing at the curb, one hand adjusting the cuff of his expensive navy suit, the other holding a phone like he's about to launch into a press conference. His gray hair gleams in the sun, and his familiar frown deepens as his eyes lock on me.

"Myles?" I manage, trying to force a casual smile. "What are you doing in the city?"

"I had a meeting. You?"

I falter for half a second. "Just... meeting a friend."

His gaze shifts past me to the building's entrance,

where the publisher's name is etched in a very large, very obvious sign above the door.

"A friend who works in publishing?"

"She's in… marketing," I say. It's technically not a lie. Alice does have a marketing department. *Somewhere.*

Myles gives me a look that probably works wonders in boardrooms, when he wants his minions to fall at his feet. "And does this marketing friend have a name?"

He used to work in publishing. He still has way too many connections for me to lie without panicking. I have to think fast.

"Uh-huh," I say, scrambling. "Jessica. She's new. I was just helping her… settle in."

He narrows his eyes, and I can practically feel the older brother radar scanning me for inconsistencies. "Hmm."

I grip my notebook tighter. "What was your meeting about?" I ask, desperate to change the subject.

"Security." His mouth twitches like he just remembered something funny. "We're upgrading our systems. You should probably get a commission. I'm spending a lot of money with the Fitzgeralds right now."

My brain short-circuits. Fitzgerald. As in Asher Fitzgerald.

"You're working with… Asher?" I try not to sound like I've just swallowed a wasp.

Myles nods. "He's heading up the project personally. I insisted. We've had too many near-misses lately. And his team's the best."

Of course they are.

He glances at his watch. "Listen, I have to run to another meeting, but I'm glad I ran into you. I've been meaning to reach out and spend time with you. Come to dinner with me tonight."

My eyebrows lift. "Dinner?" I say, trying to find an excuse.

He nods, already half distracted. "You and me. Just a catch-up. It's been too long."

"Oh." I blink, thinking about all the work I have to do on the manuscript. "Okay. Yeah, sure."

"Meet me at my club at seven," he tells me.

"Okay," I say again, pasting on a smile. "See you then."

He nods, adjusts his cuff, and strides away like a man late for a boardroom takeover.

My feet stay frozen on the sidewalk long after he's gone.

Great. Dinner at the club. With my oldest brother. While I'm juggling deadlines, dodging questions, and drowning in secrets I'm not ready to share.

And he's working with someone I've been trying very hard not to think about.

What could possibly go wrong?

* * *

I answer Autumn's call right as my Uber swerves around a bus and narrowly avoids a closed up hotdog cart.

"Hey," I say to her, bracing myself against the door as the driver accelerates through the evening traffic, like he's on a mission to get me to Myles' club on time for dinner.

"There she is!" Autumn's voice is warm and bubbly, underscored by the faint sound of waves and distant seagulls. "How's New York? I miss having someone to complain about overpriced lattes with."

I smile despite the nerves churning in my stomach. "Loud. Crowded. Smells like ambition and hot trash."

"So basically perfect." She pauses. "Have you been writing today?"

"Sort of," I hedge. "I had a meeting with Alice."

"Yikes. Is she still terrifying and fabulous?" Autumn asks, because she knows all about Alice's reputation. She was as giddy as I was when she first approached me.

"She might have scared my creativity into hiding. But yeah." I hesitate. "She believes in me. Maybe more than I do right now."

Autumn hums. "Well, I believe in you too. Even if you are terrible at answering my messages."

"Sorry." I wince, because she hit the nail on the head. "I've been... busy."

There's a loaded pause. "Francie. You've been weird ever since you left the island. Did something happen? Is there something wrong?"

I glance out the window. "No." Too fast. "Just work stress."

There's a pause. Then her voice softens.

"You know you can tell me anything, right?"

Guilt prickles under my skin. I hate lying to her. She's my best friend. She'd go to war for me. But what do you say when the one thing you can't talk about is her brother?

The one you kissed like he was yours, then ran from like a coward.

So instead I change the subject. "So what's up? You didn't call just to check on my caffeine intake."

"Okay, fine. I have news. Big news. We're leaving next week."

I blink. "Leaving where?"

"Liberty." She sounds giddy. "Parker signed a deal to commentate the NFL International Series."

My mouth drops open. "Wait, seriously? You're moving?"

"Just for a couple of months. London will be our base, but we'll be traveling to Berlin, Madrid, Rome... It's wild."

"Autumn, that's amazing!" I know how much she loves to travel.

"I know!" Her voice lifts. "But terrifying. I'm still trying to convince myself I won't fall apart on a twelve-hour flight."

I laugh. "You'll be amazing. London won't know what hit it."

"Come with me."

I snort. "Tempting, but I'm three weeks behind on my book and currently heading to dinner with one of my brothers."

"Ugh. Which one?"

"Myles."

"Oh God. Wear armor."

I smile wryly. "Thanks for the pep talk."

"You're going to be fine," she says, her voice softening. "But seriously, Francie... is everything okay? You've seemed a little... off."

"I'm fine. Really," I promise. "And anyway, you've been busy. With everything that's going on."

"Yeah." She exhales. "It's been kind of a whirlwind. Between Hudson falling for Skyler and Ayda starting to talk... it's like everything shifted overnight."

I smile at the mention of Ayda. "She's really talking now?"

"Mostly to Skyler," Autumn says, and I can hear the warmth in her voice. "It's like she cracked some secret code. Hudson's completely smitten with the both of them. Honestly, I think that's the only reason I feel okay leaving the island. For the first time in a long time, they don't need me."

"That's huge."

"Tell me about it," she says. "I've spent so long worrying about Ayda, about Hudson. Now it's like I can finally breathe."

She pauses. "Which is why I really want you to come with us. I want you to breathe, too."

I close my eyes for a moment, resting my head against the cool glass of the window. The city rushes past in a blur of headlights and neon, all too fast, too loud, too everything.

"I love that you want that for me," I murmur. "But right now breathing looks a lot like writing until my fingers fall off."

Autumn sighs. "Okay. But promise me when you're famous and everyone's fighting to turn your books into movies, you'll take a real break and come drink mimosas with me in Europe, on Liberty. Wherever."

"Only if I get to wear a tiara," I say, and she laughs.

"Obviously."

We say our goodbyes right as the car pulls up in front of the old stone building that houses Myles' club – one of those private members' only places with heavy doors, polite doormen, and a wine list that probably costs more than my rent. I thank the driver and step out, adjusting my bag on my shoulder.

The night air is cool and crisp, a shock after the stuffy Uber ride. I pause on the steps, trying to pull myself together.

Dinner with Myles.

I think I'd rather come face to face with a fire-breathing dragon.

eleven

ASHER

Either I'm a glutton for punishment or I take rejection very, very badly. Quite possibly both. Truth is, since the night I felt her come all over my fingers while she devoured my lips with her own like I was some kind of god, I haven't been able to stop thinking about Francie Salinger.

She's too young, I tell myself as my cock hardens.

She's not your type, I remind myself as I fist it, remembering her ragged breaths against my mouth.

She's way too fucking forbidden, I think as I come all over my hand.

Christ, I need to get her out of my system.

It's been months now, and every day I've been a hair's breadth away from storming over to her apartment to demand she explain why she left without saying a word.

But I don't chase. I don't give second chances. And most of all, I don't play games.

If she doesn't want to talk about it, fine. Let her run away.

The next time I see her at a family party, I'll pretend it never happened.

Even if it did something to me. Even if I woke up the next morning, sheets somehow smelling like her, with a hollow ache in my chest I couldn't name.

After a long, cold shower, I pull on my clothes. A Tom Ford suit because his tailoring fits me like a glove – I have five of them in different shades of blue and gray – a Brioni white cotton shirt with French cuffs, and a Kiton patterned silk tie that knots like a dream.

When my driver drops me off at the corner of Ellery and Eighth, the sun is just starting to set, casting a salmon-pink glow over the New York skyline.

"Can you come back at ten?" I ask him. I'm not planning on staying long. Truth is, I'd rather not be here at all.

But Myles Salinger was the one who contacted me, wanting my firm to upgrade his security systems. The actual work will be carried out by one of my top teams, but as a family friend, it only felt right that I had the initial meeting with him.

And since he was staying the night in Manhattan, something he told me he hates doing, he suggested we meet for dinner at his club.

The Langston Club is as discreet as it is imposing. A monument to old money and power. Five stories of brownstone rise up from the sidewalk, with Georgian windows and intricate black ironwork that speak to another era. One where men made deals that industrialized America.

A liveried doorman nods at me as he opens the door. "Mr. Salinger is expecting you," he says. "In the Amber Room."

For a second, I'm reminded of the Ivory Rooms. Same low-level elegance, completely different purpose. That place is about fucking. This one is about fucking people over.

But they're both about money. And lots of it.

"Asher?" a soft voice says. The familiarity of it makes my stomach twist.

A tall blonde in a long black dress walks toward me.

"Annalise." I keep my voice flat. She angles her head like she expects me to kiss her cheek. I don't.

"Are you still salty with me?" she asks, pouting her lips like she didn't try to screw me over in every way possible. "Can't we let bygones be bygones?"

The way she says it – flirty, familiar, like she still thinks she has power over me – makes my blood boil.

"I'm not salty," I say. "I'm just not interested in talking to assholes."

Her eyes flash. "That's not what you used to call me."

I shrug. "You were just a way to scratch an itch, Annalise. Nothing more." I lean down like I'm about to kiss her and feel her shiver. "Tell your brother I said hi. And that he's never getting another penny from me. I won. It's over."

I walk away before she can reply, glad she can't see the fury in my expression.

The deal's done – he finally signed last week – but now he's out there partying on money he didn't earn. Still smug. Still circling like a vulture, only with a bigger bar tab and better drugs, courtesy of me.

I should've known better. About both of them.

He tried to take my company. She handed him the keys. Stole files, read private emails, fed him everything he needed to launch the takeover.

They were a package deal. All charm and betrayal.

And yeah, I won the war. But some victories leave scars.

By the time I reach the Amber Room on the third floor, I've buried the anger. On the outside, I'm calm as I step into the gilded, hush-toned dining room with its gold-leafed walls and ruby carpet.

The maître d' leads me to a round table in the far corner, murmuring that Mr. Salinger and his guest have already arrived.

I nod. Smile. Put on the mask. I'm ready to do business. Ready to be professional.

Until I see her.

She's sitting next to Myles, her inky-black silk dress skimming her thighs and clinging to every goddamned curve. Her hair's swept up, showing off the line of her throat and the slope of her shoulder.

And just like that, I'm pathetically breathless.

"Asher," Myles says, standing up to shake my hand. "I invited my sister Francine to join us. I hope you don't mind."

I can't even pretend to look at Myles. My eyes are locked on her.

She meets my gaze with something that's definitely not surprise. More like... simmering disdain, which is probably fair.

She might have ran far away from Liberty and from me, but I did nothing about it. It's my fault we're sitting down to dinner like we're strangers.

And I have no goddamned idea how I'm supposed to get through the next ninety minutes without doing something very, very stupid.

* * *

FRANCIE

I swear to God I'm going to kill my brother. And Autumn's brother. That's all he is to me now. Just some guy in a perfectly tailored suit who once made me forget my own name.

He might look like a walking wet dream in designer threads, but I know better. I've got the hot flush to prove it.

"Francine," he says, a smile playing at his lips because he knows I hate it when people use my full name. He holds out his hand as though we haven't seen each other in years. And because my brother is here, I have to take it, dammit.

His fingers curl around mine, warm, confident, like they own me. The same fingers that brought me to my knees.

I yank my hand back before the memory finishes replaying.

We sit, and the waiter comes over to fill our glasses with water. Myles orders a whiskey, Asher does the same, and I ask for a cocktail, because if I'm going to get through this meal I'll need sugar and alcohol to do it.

"So how are you?" Asher asks me, his voice conversational. I look at him, but his face betrays no expression.

"I'm fine. How are you?" I ask, equally as politely.

"Never been better," he says smoothly. "Remarkably calm, actually. Peaceful. Quiet." He glances at me. "Almost made me wonder if my phone had stopped working."

Myles frowns. "Have you thought about changing providers?" he asks. "Surely that can't be good for your line of work."

"Maybe you need to improve the service you provide," I say to him, my voice bright. "If you expect repeat business."

His smile cracks a little. And yes, it's a low blow, but if

he's going to start hinting about our tryst, then I'm going to hit him where it hurts.

"I'm sure his service is excellent," Myles says. "He comes highly recommended."

Asher smiles as he looks down at his silverware.

"I guess you're only as good as your last review," I murmur.

"I've had some glowing reviews recently," he says, slow and deliberate.

My smile falters. That shouldn't feel like a slap. But it does.

Because what? He's had sex since Liberty? I have no idea why that hits me right in the chest. It's not like he owes me anything. He's a grown man, he's single. He's entitled to have carnal relations with whomever he desires.

But it still hurts.

"I was telling Francine about our discussion this after-noon," Myles says to Asher, as the waiter discreetly places our drinks in front of us. I pick up my Blackberry French 75 – gin, blackberry syrup, and chilled champagne in a vintage crystal coupe glass, wishing I was anywhere but here.

He watches as I down half my drink. He doesn't say a word, but I feel it, the heat of his gaze. Like he's remem-bering exactly how my mouth feels against his.

"Oh yes?" Asher takes a sip of his whiskey.

"I thought we could discuss her security," Myles contin-ues. "After reading those statistics, and seeing where she lives, it worries me."

"I'm fine," I say, trying not to roll my eyes. "I told you, I'm a grown up, I have it covered."

"You're a single woman in a big city," Myles points out. "And you're rich and beautiful."

"Who said I'm single?" I ask too brightly, like a kid daring someone to call her bluff.

I'm still pissed off that he's moved on so easily. That he's... fine. For a second neither of them say a word. Myles frowns like he's trying to take my words in.

Asher just looks annoyed. Good, now he knows how it feels.

"Do you have a boyfriend?" Myles asks.

I don't reply. Just shrug. That's not lying is it?

"Why haven't you told me about him?" my brother continues.

"It's still pretty new," I say.

Asher stares at me, his lips pressed together.

"He's very big," I tell them, pausing for a beat. "Physically, I mean. I don't need to worry about anything when he's around. So let's not worry about my security. I'm fine." I give them both a broad grin. "Let's talk about something else," I say, turning to Asher with a sugary smile. "Like how to fix a failing rating. You know, before the bad reviews start piling up."

* * *

ASHER

My jaw is tight as I watch her leave the table, her black dress swaying against her thighs like a taunt. She says something to the waiter, probably ordering another cocktail, and then disappears down the hallway.

I shouldn't follow her.

I've told myself that a dozen times since I sat down. Don't look too long. Don't ask questions. Don't care.

But I'm already pushing back my chair.

Myles is mid-conversation with one of the wait staff about how many calories are in the sticky toffee pudding. He doesn't flinch when I tell him I need to take a call and slip away.

The hallway is quiet, lined with gold sconces and heavy wooden panels. Female laughter spills faintly from the powder room. Then silence.

I shouldn't care who she's dating.

She made her choice. She left without a word. That's fine, I can live with that. I'm not my sister's-best-friend's keeper. And from a completely dispassionate perspective, she's better off without me. I'm might be in my mid-thirties but the last year has felt like an overwhelming mid-life crisis.

Being attracted to somebody way too young and way too pretty matches the modus operandi.

But when she steps out of that bathroom and stops short at the sight of me, eyes wide, chest rising, I feel it again.

That pull. Like gravity, like a goddamn weapon. And I keep stepping into the line of fire.

She presses a hand to her chest, like I've shocked her. "What are you doing, skulking around women's bathrooms?" she says softly, her brows scrunched.

I don't answer. Instead, I reach for her wrist before I can think better of it. Her pulse thuds beneath my fingertips, fast and hot and alive.

"Who's the man you're dating?" My voice comes out low, rougher than I intend. "Were you with him when we were together?"

Her eyes flare, and I feel it – the crack in my armor. I

didn't want to say that. I wanted to be cool. Detached. Indifferent.

I wanted to lie. To pretend I don't care that somebody else gets to kiss those lips, gets to see her lose control.

That somebody else gets to watch her smile.

But she's not smiling now. She leans in, defiant as hell. "Of course I wasn't. I'm not a cheater. And you can't exactly judge me. Not with all these reviews you've been getting."

I wince, even as my lips twitch. I deserved that. I'm an idiot. There hasn't been anybody else. Even if I had the time, I have no inclination.

The only woman I've been seeing is her, when I close my eyes in the shower.

"Why did you leave the island without saying anything?" I ask.

She blinks, like I caught her off guard. "I was busy. I had to get back to the mainland for meetings."

"No, you didn't." My fingers tighten slightly on her wrist. "You were afraid." I don't tell her I know that because I was too. Which makes me a dipshit, I'm fully aware.

Her jaw drops. She scoffs. "I'm not scared of you, Asher. Or your fingers. You were good, but you weren't *that* good."

I grin, because she's lying and we both know it. I may be an asshole, but I'm not an idiot. "The way you moaned my name says otherwise," I murmur, enjoying the way her eyes flare.

"I didn't moan your name."

God, I want her.

I want the way she feels against me. I want the fire in her voice, the fight in her eyes. I want to undo her zipper and wreck her lipstick and fall apart as she moans my name again.

But I can't.

"We need to get back to the table before Myles starts wondering why we've both disappeared," she mutters.

I don't move. "Tell me who he is."

Her shoulders rise and fall with a sharp breath. "What are you going to do, take out a hit on him?"

My lips twitch. I'm a sarcastic word away from a full blown smile. "I'm not a killer, Francine."

She used to wrinkle her nose when I called her by her full name. And she still does. Some things never change. "Call me that again and I'll never tell you," she says.

I lift a brow. Of course she's still angry with me. Of course she still makes my heart kick like it's trying to get out.

Her nipples are hard beneath the silk of her dress. I notice without meaning to. My mouth goes dry.

Get out of here, Fitzgerald.

But I don't. I lean in, close enough that my breath stirs the hair near her temple. Her skin smells like citrus and heat as I ask her a third time. "Who is he, Francie?"

She shudders, just barely.

"It's none of your business," she snaps.

This time I grin, but it's not a nice one. It's the one I wear when I'm broken and bleeding. The one I've been wearing way too much lately. "It's a good thing I own a security company," I murmur. "I can find out in ten minutes."

She jerks her chin back. "You'd snoop on me?"

I shrug. "I just want to make sure you're safe."

She knows that's a lie. Even if I'm telling myself it's true.

"No. You want to control me." She steps in closer now, her breath hot against my skin. "If you ever, *ever* snoop on me, I'll never speak to you again. Do you understand? It's a violation. I'm a grown woman. If I need help, I'll ask. But I don't. Got it?"

My gaze drops to her mouth. My restraint frays.

I nod, slowly. "Got it." And truth be told, I wouldn't anyway. I'm just pissed and tired and wishing I'd made better decisions in life.

But I don't move. Because she's still the only thing I want. The one thing I can't have.

And I'm not sure how much longer I can keep pretending that's okay.

* * *

FRANCIE

I stand on the sidewalk, staring at my apartment building in disbelief, as the cab pulls away, leaving me stranded. Surely this isn't happening. Not after tonight's painful dinner – which was already the cherry on top of a very bitter sundae.

Sitting across from Asher, pretending not to notice the way his fingers wrapped around his glass, or the way he looked like he hadn't slept in weeks was awkward as hell.

Pretending I didn't want to throw my cocktail in his face, or climb into his lap – maybe both – was even harder.

And now all I want to do is take a shower, get into my pajamas, spend a bit of quality time with my battery operated boyfriend, then go to sleep so I can wake up early and get to work on the manuscript-from-hell that needs to be with my editor in less than four weeks.

But instead, the whole block is blacked out. There are workmen in bright yellow jackets setting up floodlights and cordoning off sections of the sidewalk in front of Niall's coffee shop.

"What's going on?" I ask one of them.

"Sewer problems," he tells me. "And electricity problems. The two don't mix."

"But I live here," I say, pointing at the door that leads to the apartments. "That's my apartment. I need to go to bed." And maybe scream into a pillow. Or rehash every stupid thing I said during dinner.

And try not to replay the sound of Asher's voice in my ear, low and possessive, like he still had every right to touch me.

"You can go in," he says. "We're setting up a temporary generator so you should have power back on by the morning. For a little while at least."

"The morning?"

He nods. "I'm afraid we may be noisy," he says, right as a pneumatic drill starts up, shattering the air and making me wince. "Nothing some ear plugs won't solve."

"How long will this take?" I say loudly, hoping it will be done in a couple of hours. I may just have to sleep in and work later tomorrow. That'll be okay, I'll manage.

"About a month, we think."

"A *month*?" My mouth drops open.

"The sewer drain collapsed." He shouts as a second drill starts up. "Don't worry, we're diverting your pipes. You should be able to use your water and flush by sometime tomorrow."

Fuck my life. A month. I have to hand in my draft in a month. And yes, I can go to the library, but I need silence to write. I need to be alone.

Fuming, I send a message to Autumn, because she's the

only person that will understand my mental turmoil right now.

A second later, she replies.

Come to Liberty. You can stay in the Lighthouse while Parker and I are in Europe. You'll have more alone time and silence than you'll know what to do with. – Autumn

You're a lifesaver. I'll pay rent. And I promise to keep it clean. – Francie

The only rent I need is for you to send me what you've written so far. I'm desperate to read it. I'm going to need something to keep me warm while Parker is off commentating. – Autumn

It's a deal. – Francie

I put my phone in my purse and look at the disaster that is my apartment building, trying not to think about the disaster that's my life.

Going to Liberty might be the best idea. Maybe some distance will help me concentrate on writing.

Or maybe I'm just fooling myself again.

twelve

ASHER

I've just finished a meeting in the New York office the next day when my phone lights up with a message. I look down, frowning to see a new group chat has been made. It even has a title, *The Fitzgerald Family Group Chat*. And I frown even harder when I see that Hudson made it.

Hudson? The man who hates messaging? I lift a brow, because he's changed a lot since he and Skyler finally stopped dancing around each other and became an item.

It's been a hard time for them both. First Hudson's ex-inlaws tried to steal Ayda and take her back to England with them, and then after she was found, Hudson was an idiot and ended things between him and Skyler.

Luckily, he saw sense, and now they're back together and Skyler's pregnant and the three of them – Hudson, Skyler, and Ayda, are all living together at the Captain's House.

Still, this is out of character, and I can't help but open it right away.

HUDSON:

I have a question for you all. Skyler says it's weird we don't have a family group chat. Is it weird? I don't know. Anyway, she thinks it is, so here we are. This is our new group chat. For family.

ZACH:

It's not weird. It's just us keeping our sanity. Looking at the title of this chat is breaking me out in hives. Only bad things can come from group chats. Although obviously I'm staying.

AUTUMN:

Woohoo! 🎉 I think it's a great idea. And welcome to the twenty-first century big brothers. I'll be able to keep you entertained with my thoughts on Europe. Also, tell Skyler I've tried to create about a hundred family chats and you all never reply.

I let out a sigh. I hate being the voice of doom in this situation, but it's worth reminding them that no chat is fully safe.

ASHER:

Just remember that though this is encrypted, it's still better not to say too much on here.

HUDSON:

I'm not planning on giving you my bank details. Or where the bodies are buried... Jesus, why do you all have to make this so difficult? By the way, Skyler says you're all assholes except for maybe Autumn.

EDEN:

Hey, I haven't said anything. How can I be an asshole? Anyway can you send me a pic of Ayda? I miss her. And hi everybody!

I lift a brow at that. Tracking Eden down is like trying to catch a butterfly. She's always flitting here and there. And she's almost allergic to telling us anything, like she's scared we're going to drag her back home.

She reminds me a bit of Francie. Beautiful, but a pain.

And now I'm thinking about Francie's fucking boyfriend. Who is he, anyway?

HUDSON:

Eden! Where are you right now? Are you safe? Do you have food? A phone charger? Are you inside a building with plumbing?

ASHER:

Does Eden even own a phone charger? Because I've called her five times in the past month and she hasn't answered once.

True story, that. I like to check in on her once a month at least.

AUTUMN:

Haha, the king of ignoring everybody is being ignored for once. I love it. Suck it, Ash.

ASHER:

Thanks for reminding me why I hate group chats.

EDEN:

I'd forgotten how dramatic you all are. Yes I'm alive. Yes I'm fed. No I'm not telling you exactly where I am. I've made that mistake before.

AUTUMN:

See, she's fine. She's an adult. Leave her alone. Or we'll create a sister chat without any of you.

ASHER:

Don't threaten us with a good time.

· · ·

ZACH:

Hey, don't sweat it. Eden will let us know where she is when she loses her passport again and Hudson has to bail her out.

ASHER:

Or when she texts us from a burner phone asking for €5,000 and a blood sample.

EDEN:

That's rude. It was an accident. But also thank you for that one time. Love you, big bro.

HUDSON:

Talking of being ignored, Wyatt? You alive?

That makes my mouth twitch. The only family member less communicative than Eden is our youngest brother. Last I heard from him, he's still working on the ocean, captain of a boat. But he's a man of action, not words.

WYATT:

👍

ZACH:

Well that's more words than he's said all year. It's practically poetry.

· · ·

AUTUMN:

It's his way of showing he cares. I think it's sweet. I'm feeling emotional right now – it's so nice to chat with you all. It's like having us all back together, even though I'm leaving the country. I miss you guys.

ZACH:

Are you going to cry again? Because I don't do tears. Especially not after the last time you sobbed for two hours when you found out Skyler was pregnant.

AUTUMN:

Shut up. I'm a strong independent woman. I can show my emotions any way I want to.

EDEN:

You once cried at an IKEA commercial. Just saying.

AUTUMN:

That was FIVE YEARS AGO! And it was beautiful. It just hit me in the gut, that's all.

EDEN:

It was a kitchen remodel, sis.

· · ·

AUTUMN:

But the family LOVED IT! They were all laughing and eating and... You know what? Skyler's right, you ARE all assholes.

HUDSON:

So this family chat thing is going well. Should I delete it?

EDEN:

No. I like knowing what you idiots are up to. And it takes the heat off me.

ASHER:

We'd just like to know the same, kid. Just saying.

AUTUMN:

Actually, while you're all here, I have an announcement.

EDEN:

Uhoh.

ZACH:

Has Parker done something to upset you? Am I going to have to beat him up?

· · ·

My lips twitch, because Parker wouldn't hurt a damn fly. Of all the men I'd trust to be married to my sister, he's at the top. Still, it's fun to tease her sometimes.

AUTUMN:

NOBODY'S BEATING PARKER UP. I just wanted to let you know that Francie's going to be staying at the lighthouse while Parker and I are away. Her apartment has some structural issues. So – Hudson, can you and Skyler keep an eye on her? And Asher – if you happen to be anywhere in the vicinity of Liberty can you BE NICE, please?

ASHER:

Francie's coming to Liberty?

AUTUMN:

Yes, Please don't ruin it for her.

HUDSON:

Of course we'll take care of her. Let me know her travel details. It'll be nice to see her.

EDEN:

Well as fun as this has been, I need to go. I need to see a man about a Llama. Stay cool, fam. And remember – love not war. And nobody beat Autumn's husband up.

· · ·

I turn off the phone, already feeling exhausted by my family. Damn, I love them, but they're a lot.

And then I turn it on again, just to re-read Autumn's words.

Francie is going to be staying on Liberty.

Because I have a few pieces of unfinished business where she's concerned.

* * *

FRANCIE

"You'll get bored within a week," Charlie's voice echoes down my phone as I haul my suitcases up the steps to Brewed Awakenings, Liberty's resident caffeine dealer. The sun is shining in the sky, the ocean is sparkling like a thousand diamonds, and I don't think I've ever seen the island looking prettier.

"Good," I say as I push open the door, the aroma of coffee and sugar cookies washing over me. "I came here to work, not party."

Charlie lets out a huff. "What am I supposed to do without you to annoy?" he whines. "Manhattan's boring without my favorite auntie sneaking into sex clubs."

"First of all, we don't call it a sex club." I lower my voice on that one, because the coffee shop doesn't need to know about that particular snafu. "Second, don't call me your auntie. Third, there's this magical thing called a phone. You can still annoy me remotely."

"Hah," he says, not even trying to laugh. "Speaking of phones, I downloaded you an app."

I frown. "What app?"

Charlie's always been a pest. In high school, he messaged every guy in my contacts claiming I had a crush on them. He even swapped my yearbook headshot for a rat in a sparkly crown – and the yearbook committee just went with it. Sometimes I wonder how he made it past twenty.

"Just check your screen," he says, sounding smug as hell.

I pull the phone away and scroll through the chaos of apps until I find it. And groan.

"You downloaded a dating app on my phone?"

"Remotely," he confirms. "Open it. You'll love the profile."

I brace myself and tap. It's a photo of me at Misty Lakes, sitting on the dock in a pink bikini, legs dangling in the water. I'm sticking my tongue out at the camera like a six-year-old.

"How old are you?" I mutter. "If you ever get a girlfriend who sticks around, I'm telling her about the time you pooped the bed."

"I was five!"

"Doesn't matter. Your love life is over."

I hang up on his wheezing laughter and step further inside the coffee shop, hoping for caffeine and a little peace before Simon – the island's one and only cab driver – shows up to take me to the lighthouse.

It could take him ten minutes, or ten hours. Simon runs on chaos.

It's quiet in the café. The tail end of tourist season means most people are off exploring the island or drifting on one of the new charter boats the hotel runs. Or maybe they just have better things to do than loiter in a coffee shop. Unlike me.

"If you're here to make me go on another carousel,"

Mylene says, eyeing me from behind the counter, "you can go spin alone. I never want to see one of those again."

I hold up my hands. "No carousels. No fairground attractions. You're officially off duty."

Her shoulders visibly relax. "Thank God. What'll it be?"

"Iced matcha, please," I tell her, then drift over to the big picture window overlooking the dock and a sliver of the Atlantic beyond it.

Between here and the water, Eileen's By the Sea stands primly next to Mylene's coffee shop, their owners still locked in a blood feud that's lasted decades. They live and work within spitting distance of each other – and somehow the island hasn't exploded yet.

Right past that is The Salty Dog, run by Skyler, who has fallen in love with Hudson Fitzgerald. The last time I was here, that whole whirlwind was still unfolding.

It feels weird being here without Autumn. I've never done Liberty solo before. And now I'm moving into the lighthouse like some reclusive author trying to outrun the world.

Maybe that's why I'm glad the cab hasn't arrived yet. Maybe that's why I'm still standing here.

Procrastinating. It's my real talent.

"Hey!" Jesse walks in, grinning when he spots me. "I heard you were coming."

I lift a brow. The last time I saw Jesse was during our chaotic ladies' night. The one Asher had to drive us home from. Since then, he's had a bit of a life change, too, building a relationship with Skyler – the sister who had no idea he existed until a few months ago.

I blink away the memories of that night as Jesse pulls me into a hug. He smells of sea air.

"Let me guess," I say as he lets me go. "Autumn told you to babysit me?"

He smirks. "If she did, I'll never admit it. Not that you need me looking after you. Her big brother's got that covered."

"Hudson?" I ask. "He's too busy being loved up with Skyler and planning world domination to worry about me."

Jesse shakes his head. "Not Hudson. *Asher.*"

Even hearing his name sends a shiver down my spine. I force a shrug.

"I know he's a security genius, but even he can't monitor me from New York."

"He's not in New York," Jesse says casually. "He's here."

My stomach drops. "Here, like... on Liberty?"

Now Autumn's joining Charlie on my imaginary murder list. I'm not sure who ranks higher.

Below, I decide. Because at least Autumn doesn't know there's... something between me and her brother. Or there was. But it's over. Done. History. God, I wish my brain would shut up.

"Here, as in walking into the coffee shop," Jesse says, right as the bell above the door jingles.

My skin prickles as a warm gust of air hits my back.

No. No no no.

The last time I saw Asher Fitzgerald, I was stomping out of Myles' club, muttering something about a boyfriend I don't have and trying to hang on to the last shred of my dignity.

What the hell is he doing on the island?

I turn slowly, like I'm in a horror movie where the killer is wearing tailored slacks and smells of cedarwood and sin.

His dark eyes meet mine and his unflinching gaze sends a shiver down my spine.

"Francie," he says, like it's totally normal that we're both standing in the same coffee shop on the world's tiniest island.

"Here's your drink," Mylene says, handing me my iced matcha. I blink at her, realizing I never paid.

I double tap my phone, reach for the payment terminal, only to see another phone has beat me to it.

Asher slides his phone back into his pocket.

"I can pay for my own drink," I mutter.

He doesn't acknowledge me. Just looks at Mylene. "Can I have an espresso? To go."

She gives him a warm smile, zero shade. "You don't need to tell me," she purrs. "I know you like your coffee hot and dark."

Kill me now. Seriously, bury my body so deep I never have to go through something like this again.

"I've gotta go," Jesse says, backing toward the door. "I'm on the ferry tonight. You waiting for Simon?"

I nod. I don't have a car. Truth be told, I never needed one in Manhattan. Renting one for a month felt excessive. Especially when I have a perfectly good lighthouse to hide in.

"You'll be waiting a while," Asher says. "I just saw him drive onto the ferry."

My mouth drops open. "What?"

Great. That means I'll be waiting at minimum an hour. Probably longer. Knowing Simon, he'll stop off for a sandwich and a nap before circling back.

"Sheesh," Jesse mutters. "I'd offer you a ride, but if I'm late again I'll get written up."

"I'll take you," Asher says.

Of course he will. In that stupid blue car. The one now burned into my memory as the scene of the crime. Or, more specifically, the scene of the orgasm.

"It's fine," I say quickly. "I'll walk."

He glances at the two massive suitcases at my feet. "It's two miles," he says flatly. "You're not walking."

God, I hate him.

Or at least I keep trying to.

I sigh loudly and dramatically, just so the universe knows that I'm not happy with this situation.

Then I look Asher straight in the eye.

"A ride would be great, thank you."

"Autumn tells me you're staying for a month," Asher says as we drive along the coast road toward the lighthouse.

"Yep." I keep my voice breezy. I've decided that being sullen in front of him is only playing into his hands. "I needed a break. Some fresh salty air is just the ticket."

I can feel him scrutinizing my face, but I refuse to look at him.

"How does your boyfriend feel about you being away for so long?" he asks.

Oh shoot. I'd forgotten all about the imaginary guy that's supposed to be providing me with security. "Um, he's fine. He's going to visit when he can," I say. "But mostly he wants me to relax. He's very lovely like that."

"Hmm." I don't like the way Asher says it. So I finally look over at him. Speaking of relaxed, he's so laid back he's practically horizontal. Dressed in a white shirt, no tie, sleeves rolled up, his hair perfectly tousled from the breeze coming in through his open window, he could be the lead in an ad for a high end car right now.

"What's that supposed to mean?" I ask him.

"Nothing."

"Oh come on, you can't make a noise like that and say it means nothing. If you have something to say, just say it."

He shifts gears, because of course he drives a stick shift. His movements are so fluid it's stupidly attractive.

"If a guy lets a woman out of his sights for a month it means one of two things," he says, like he's the source of all knowledge when it comes to men and relationships. "Either he's not that into her..." He trails off as he turns the corner onto the little road that leads to the lighthouse. It's rocky and bumpy and there's no suspension in this car so I find myself being jolted up and down like I'm riding a donkey.

"Of course he's into me," I say testily. Because if I'm going to have an imaginary boyfriend, I at least want him to adore me. It'd be awful if he was an asshole. "So what's the other thing it means, Einstein?"

His lips twitch at the nickname. It doesn't stop him from coming out with the killer blow though. "Or he doesn't exist." His voice is light, but his eyes are anything but. For a second, I see something fierce behind them. Possessive. Raw.

"Are you accusing me of lying?" I shoot back. "Maybe there's a third option, genius."

"What would that be?" he asks languidly. He comes to a stop outside the lighthouse, in the exact same spot he parked in last time.

My body shivers at the memory of how he touched me that night.

"That we're grownups who trust each other and know that the other person is busy."

Asher smirks. "I guess that's a possibility." He climbs out of the driver's side, and I pull at the handle of my own door because there's no way I'm going to let him open it for me. "So let's say... what did you say his name was again?" he asks.

"Nice try," I say as I climb out of the seat right as he reaches my side. "I'm not telling you, remember?"

"Well, when you think up a name, let me know," he says, walking to the trunk of his car to pull out my suitcases. The trunk space is small, and they're so tightly packed he has to yank the first one hard to get it out. He puts it on the ground and I reach for it before he lets go.

And immediately pull my hand away like it's on fire.

Asher lets out a sigh. "I don't have a disease. You don't have to panic about touching me." He reaches out and takes my hand. His palm is warm, his fingers soft as they curl around mine.

I'm not panicking. I'm just staring at those fingers and remembering. I let out a rough breath and bring my eyes up to his.

He looks at me like he can read my mind and knows exactly what I'm thinking about. My heart thuds against my chest as he slowly runs his thumb over my wrist.

"Does he know about us?" Asher asks, his voice low.

"There is no us." My voice is unsteady. Actually, my whole body is and I have no idea why. He's just holding my hand. He's not touching me anywhere else. He's certainly not twisting them inside of me like he did that night.

And yet, I'm as turned on as I was then. By a simple swipe of his thumb against my skin.

"I'm going to find out," he murmurs. "You do know that?"

"Find out what?" I ask him. God, his hand is big. I try to remember what they say about guys with big hands. Or is it big feet?

I look down. They are at least size thirteen. Maybe bigger. Dear Lord.

"Find out his name. Or that he doesn't exist." He gives me the cockiest smile.

"Well, while you're wasting your time, I'm going inside to call my boyfriend. He's planning our next date. Maybe you'll get to meet him then."

thirteen

FRANCIE

"Ryan," I mutter. "No, sounds too much like I'm copying Ryan Reynolds. Or Ryan Gosling." I let out a sigh. "Jack, that's a good name." I frown as I pour a cup of uncooked pasta into the boiling water. Autumn had arranged for the kitchen to be fully stocked for my arrival, and right now I'm making myself some macaroni and cheese because I need the comfort.

"Or Richard," I try the name out loud. It sounds aristocratic. The water starts to boil over, hissing as it hits the hot plate. "Dammit," I yell, turning the burner down. Stupid Asher and his stupid fingers.

I've spent most of the afternoon trying to think of a fake name for my fake boyfriend, when I should be writing, which means I'll be staying up all night to catch up on my word count.

That's if I don't spend the rest of the night thinking up a fake job for the fake man. Because my first thought – firefighter – is way too problematic. Not only is it overly sexy, but a firefighter in New York is probably easy to track down for Asher. He'll know I'm lying in about thirty seconds.

And I can't stand to think about how smug he's going to be when he's proved right.

Once upon a time, I loved that he knew everything. I was fourteen the first time I asked him for help with my math homework. I was visiting Liberty for Autumn's birthday, and I had an assignment I'd been putting off all week. I was in an advance math class even though I absolutely shouldn't have been, but to do anything else would have upset my family.

So I studied my ass off, but pre-calc was kicking that same ass. Until Asher found me crying in front of my textbook, and slowly and patiently explained sine, cosine, and tangents to me.

I blink at that memory. I haven't thought about it for years. I was fourteen and he was twenty-four. The kind of age when most guys would have been utterly selfish. He was in grad school by day and building his business by night. And yet when he'd found me crying because I was so sure I was going to fail, he'd grabbed a chair and sat down next to me.

"Come on," he'd said, nudging my shoulder with his. "It's just cosine. Nobody ever died from a triangle. *Probably.*"

It took two hours before everything he tried to explain finally sunk into my brain. And then Hudson, West, and Parker dragged him out to The Salty Dog because they were old enough to drink and I was still in braces with hair that was uncontrollable and a major crush on my best friend's older brother.

I let out a sigh. I don't want to think about all the ways

he was nice to me growing up. I want to think about how aggravating he is to me now. Instead of remembering the way his lips felt on mine. Or how thick and hard he was against my thigh as he made every muscle in my body feel like they were melting when he made me come.

My phone buzzes and I pick it up, hoping for some distraction.

You have a message.

It takes me a second to realize it's the dating app Charlie installed. Somebody actually looked at my profile? With that stupid photograph? I don't know whether to feel sorry for them or be afraid.

Still, I open it up and see what looks like a normal, thirty-something guy staring back at me. In photo form, thankfully. He doesn't look like a serial killer, but then neither did Ted Bundy.

He looks more like a surfer if I'm being honest. In his photo he's wearing a white, linen shirt, opened one button too far to reveal a smooth, tan chest. His hair is long, curling around his neck, and he has about a dozen necklaces on. He's grinning with the whitest teeth I think I've ever seen.

He's so completely not my type it's not even funny. I open the message anyway, because curiosity is my middle name.

Hey friend! How wild is it that we've matched out here in Liberty? It feels like the island has aligned us or something. I'm staying at the Grand Liberty Hotel holding space for a breath-work immersion at the hotel. Only here for a few days, but would love to vibe over a matcha or walk along the beach barefoot and just... be. No pressure. Just presence.

· · ·

Reed Marks. That's his name. I'm no virgin at dating apps. If a guy is 'just visiting it means one thing. He wants a no-strings night with you.

And I'm so not a one night no-strings girl. I start to write a gentle brush off to him – because I'm way too polite to ignore his message – when my phone starts to ring.

When I see Autumn's name flash up, I can't help but smile.

"What are you doing calling me at this time?" I ask her, checking my watch. "Isn't it the middle of the night in London?"

"It is." She sighs. "I can't sleep and Parker is snoring so I thought I'd call and see if you've settled in okay."

"I've settled in great," I tell her warmly, so happy to hear from her. Talking to Autumn always makes me feel better. "And thank you for all the goodies you left me. I feel like I'm staying in a luxury hotel."

"You deserve it. Plus I have an ulterior motive," she says, her voice low. I can hear the low hum of a television in the background. The poor girl really is having trouble sleeping.

"Of course," I tell her. "What do you need? Want me to sing you to sleep?"

She starts to laugh. "I need your words. Send what you've written to me. I can read them while Parker drives me crazy sounding like a steam train."

"I can't send you them yet. They're a mess." I frown. Though I guess I could clean them up. I need to read through it all anyway, to plan the third act of the book. "How about later this week?" I suggest. "I'll send you the first half."

I think about the scene I wrote yesterday with the heroine pinned between a wall and the man who shouldn't be touching her. And how maybe, *just maybe*, I wrote it with a certain dark-eyed security ass in the back of my mind.

"It's a deal." She sounds giddy. I love how supportive she is of my writing. I'm not sure I'd still be doing it without her. Back when we were teenagers and I was writing Kylo and Rey fanfiction, she was the only one I told about it. And then, when I got a following on Wattpad, and started writing original stories, she was the first to encourage me to publish them.

It's been four years since I uploaded my first book for sale. And she's been with me, as my first reader, my biggest supporter, and now she's essentially my patron, giving me somewhere to stay.

"So how's your trip going?" I ask her.

"It's horribly luxurious," she says. "Parker's a bigger draw here than I realized."

"He's hot, he's rich, and he's a professional athlete," I point out. "Of course he's a draw."

"Did you know they call it American Football over here?" she asks, giggling. "It annoys him to hell."

I grin, imagining Parker's grumpy reaction to that. "They call soccer, football, right?" I ask. I've only been to Europe once, back when I was eighteen and my brothers bought me a trip to Rome for my birthday. It was glorious and way too short. With this new book, my UK publishers are already planning a tour all over the UK next year. Which is another reason why I need to get the thing written and stop angsting over Autumn's brother.

"Yep. He's started calling it 'English Soccer' whenever anybody mentions American Football. That doesn't go down well." She lets out a sigh. "I miss you."

"I miss you too," I tell her. "I'm sorry I can't be there."

"It's not your fault. I still get to read your words soon,

which is almost as good as having you here. Tell me, did you write the group scene yet?"

I blush, because yes, I did, and it was hot. "Um…"

"You did. You dirty girl. You know I love those scenes the most." She laughs again. "And Parker always gets the benefit, if you know what I mean."

"Oh God, I don't need to know that." I wrinkle my nose.

"Speaking of grumpy asses, I spoke to my brother earlier."

"Which one?" I ask, ignoring the pang in my stomach.

"Asher. He said something about you dating somebody." She clears her throat, and I realize this is actually the purpose of her call. "Are you?" she asks. "Without telling me?"

She sounds genuinely hurt. My chest tightens because she always tells me everything. When she and Parker first started dating under the radar because neither of them wanted her brothers to find out, I was the only one she confided in.

"I'm not dating anybody," I say. "It's just something I said to get both of our brothers off my back." I tell her about the dinner with Myles and Asher. She giggles when I describe them both being so stupidly protective.

"You're like Rapunzel," she teases.

"The one who lived in a tower?"

"That's her. The one with the long hair. You're just like her, apart from the hair that is. I thought my brothers were bad, but yours are worse, I swear." She sounds relieved, like she was worried there was something coming between us. "So why didn't you come clean to Asher?"

I clear my throat. She doesn't need to know about what happened the stupid night when she got drunk at The Salty

Dog. "He's working with Myles, I can't risk him telling him. You know what Asher's like."

"That's true. He's so intense." She sighs. "He really started drilling me. I tried to blow him off, but you know what he's like. Talking to him is like being interrogated by the CIA."

Oh God, now he'll know for sure that I was lying. I hate this.

"Don't worry. It's not your fault. I'll come clean to him."

"Oh no, don't do that. You're absolutely right, Asher would definitely tell Myles. And then you'll have to deal with them not only being over protective but asking why you lied to them." She lets out a low breath. "And if they start sniffing around, they're bound to find out about your books."

"Oh God." The thought of any of my brothers discovering my books – and god forbid, reading the smutty scenes – sends my blood cold, but the memory of my discussion with Alice about marketing sends it colder. "You're right. Let's just hope they get busy with their security issues and forget about me."

A low voice rumbles in the background. I'm guessing it's Parker.

"You would tell me if you started dating somebody though?" she asks, sounding uncertain again. "I know we don't live together anymore, but we're still besties, right?"

"Of course we are. And of course I would," I promise. "Now go to bed."

She laughs softly. "Yes ma'am. And Francie?"

"Yep?"

"Don't forget to send those chapters."

"I won't," I promise. She hangs up, and I look at my phone again. Reed Marks is still beaming up at me, his golden retriever energy practically bursting through the screen.

Before I can think better of it, I start typing a reply to him. This is a good idea. Brilliant, even. Unless it backfires. But it won't. Probably.

Hi there Neighbor (for a few days)! How about a drink at The Salty Dog Beach Bar tomorrow night? I can meet you there at eight.

I have absolutely no doubt that word will get back to Asher that I've been seen with a guy, and he'll stop grilling everybody about my dating life.

I smile at my brilliant idea. Sometimes, I amaze myself. After all, what could possibly go wrong?

fourteen

FRANCIE

The following night at eight o'clock sharp I'm sitting at the bar of The Salty Dog, aware that I've made way more effort than a date at a beach bar – even a gorgeously renovated one like this – deserves.

I managed to get five thousand words written by two o'clock, then went for a walk along the cliff, trying to think through the next scene. After that, I spent over an hour getting ready for this non-date that only exists because Asher is so convinced I don't have a boyfriend.

And yes, he might be right, but I hate that he's always right. Sometimes I'd like the man to have egg on his face.

"Oh wow, you have the most grounded energy I've seen this year," a slightly-too-high-pitched voice says. I turn to see Reed Marks standing next to me. Or at least I think it's him – he looks at least ten years older than the photo on his profile.

"Hello." I smile. "And thank you." I think that's a compliment. "You're... very grounded too."

He pulls up a stool. He's wearing white linen pants that billow around his legs – slightly see-through, and I'm almost certain he's not wearing anything underneath. But worse than that? He's wearing those barefoot shoes with the individual toe compartments.

Oh no, I have the ick. And we've only exchanged one sentence.

"What can I get you?" Maud asks, eyeing him.

"Do you have chlorophyll shots?" he murmurs.

She gives him the side-eye. "We have tequila."

He sighs, like that's the most offensive thing he's ever heard. "Spring water, please. Alcohol is very bad for the chakras."

"I don't know them," Maud mutters, her brows crease. "Are they local?"

My lips twitch.

Maud brings over the water, and Reed unrolls a little hemp pouch, pulling out a glass straw. "Gotta take care of those dolphins," he says, inserting it with care.

I glance at my watch. This is already a disaster. Maud catches my eye with a frown.

"If you need anything," she says, emphasizing each word to me, "you call me over, okay?"

"Of course."

"Skyler might drop by later," she adds. "And Hudson."

Reed closes his eyes and inhales deeply, then opens them like he's about to give a TED talk. "This bar has weird energy. Probably the LED lighting mixed with unresolved trauma." He glances at Maud. "Have you tried saging the air?"

She looks affronted. "It's cleaned every morning. I think we use Clorox."

"I know a great eco-cleaning company. Want the number?"

"I'm just the barmaid." She backs away fast.

I turn back to Reed. If nothing else, he's great character inspiration. "So what brings you to Liberty?" I ask him, aware that if this gets back to Asher I at least need to look like I'm interested.

"I'm here for Eliana Markham."

I blink. "The actress?"

"She's healing from burnout. I'm her breathing consultant. She flew me in from California."

"On a private jet?" I raise an eyebrow, thinking about what animal that would impact.

He nods solemnly. "Obviously that's not ideal, environmentally speaking, but healing burnout is sacred work." He gives me a pained look. "My carbon guilt is part of her karmic release."

Right. I nod, checking my watch again. Maud's seen me here. That should be enough to get word around. Or at least to Asher.

"Have you tried breathwork?" Reed asks, glancing at my chest. I instantly regret my dress.

"Um, no?"

"You're tense. Breathe in." He hovers his hand over my chest. "Let the oxygen burn away the tension."

"Oh, I'm not tense. I'm fine."

"Francie?" Maud calls, holding out a white landline handset. "Can you come to the phone?"

I jump up. "Sorry about this," I tell Reed.

"Those things are poisonous," he mutters. "The rays are bad for the atmosphere."

Maud ushers me behind the bar. "Are you okay?" she half-whispers. "Who is that guy?"

"I'm fine," I promise.

"I called Skyler. She wants to talk to you."

I take the handset. Behind me, Reed is lifting his arms in the air like he's about to summon a weather system.

"Hey," I say, letting out a breath.

"Maud says you've got a man bun situation. Are you joining a cult?" Skyler asks.

I laugh. "He doesn't have a man bun. But he does have toe shoes."

"The barefoot ones? Ew."

"Right?"

Another voice murmurs in the background.

"Hudson says if he starts chanting, you have to run." She pauses for a beat. "Asher's here too."

My stomach tightens. Of course he is. This is good, right. Now he'll know I'm not a liar. Even if I am.

I clear my throat. "I should get back to my boyfriend." I whisper it so Reed can't hear. He probably already thinks I'm a psycho.

"Are you sure you're okay?" Skyler asks, sounding genuinely concerned.

I raise my voice a notch too high. "I'm good."

More murmuring.

"Asher wants to talk to you."

"No," I say. Too fast, too sharp. "I have to get back. Tell him I'm busy." Because yes, I'm doing this pantomime to get him off my case, but the man isn't stupid. A couple of pointed questions and he'll see right through me.

"Okay, okay." She pauses. "Call me later."

I hang up and hand Maud the phone. "Thanks," I say, then return to the bar where Reed is telling the man next to him that he once released ten years of trauma by screaming for eight days straight.

The man looks terrified.

"Hi," I say, still standing. "I'm so sorry, but I have to get home. An emergency."

Reed frowns. "That's sad. I really felt our energies could mesh."

I'm not sticking around to find out if that's code for tantric breath sex. Instead I smile and pull out my cell to dial Simon.

But he doesn't pick up. Of course he doesn't.

ASHER

"What do you mean she hung up?" I ask Skyler, frowning. "Did you tell her I wanted to talk to her?"

"Of course I did. I guess she was in a hurry to get back to her date. Who apparently is a lot older than her."

Skyler grins, glancing at Hudson who looks like he's also trying not to smile. Which is stupidly weird, because I know the man is as protective of Francie as I am. She's Autumn's friend. Part of our circle. We take care of those our loved ones love.

"How old?" I ask.

"Maud thinks he's forty. Maybe older. Says it's hard to tell because he dresses like a teenager. Anyway, Francie is fine. She just wanted to go back to her date."

So it's him. "What's his name?" I ask her.

"Dear lord, I don't know. I didn't ask his shoe size either." Skyler shakes her head and stretches her arms. "I'm heading up to bed." She kisses Hudson's cheek softly, and I see my brother melt at the sensation of her lips.

As soon as she's left, Hudson turns to look at me, eying me up like I'm something he doesn't quite understand. "What's going on between you and Francie?" he asks me.

"Nothing. She's Autumn's friend, and I'm worried about her."

He takes a deep breath, like he's trying to find the right words. "I know that Annalise screwed you over," he begins. It actually looks painful for him to say it. Fitzgerald men aren't deep talkers. We don't do emotions, we don't talk about our trauma. We just fight through it. From our childhood onward it's been the only way.

"It's okay," I say, patting his arm. "You can tell Skyler I'm fine." Because I know she's the one who put him up to saying something. "I was over Annalise a long time ago. She and her brother lost. I won. I'm glad to be out of it, and I'm very happy being single. I'm not planning on falling headfirst into a midlife crisis and start banging my much younger sister's best friend."

He presses his lips together and nods. "How did you know Skyler put me up to this?" he asks.

"Because I've known you all my life." If I'm uptight, Hudson is practically Victorian. "And I can see the physical pain in your face at asking. Just tell her we had the conversation and everything is fine. Now do you want a drink?"

He shakes his head. "I should probably head up to bed."

I don't take it personally that he prefers to spend time with his wife rather than me. That's how it should be. "Okay."

He goes to leave then turns around. "Do you think you could check out the security cameras at The Salty Dog?" he asks.

I hold my phone up. I have access to all the cameras we've installed throughout the island. Only on Fitzgerald property, of course, but that's the majority of the buildings. "Already on it."

I've also already sent a still photograph of the guy that Autumn's dating to my security team to run a search on him, but I don't tell Hudson that.

"Is she still there?" he asks, lingering.

I glance down at my phone, only to see her gathering up her purse and sweater. "She's leaving," I say tightly.

Our eyes meet. "Go to bed," I tell him. "I've got this."

He's not used to letting anybody else be in charge. But he nods anyway. "You're right. She's young. Sweet. Don't let him do anything to hurt her."

"Of course I won't." My jaw is tight. Any jealousy I felt has been replaced by genuine concern. I like Francie. And Hudson is completely correct. She's sweet, smart, too beautiful for her own good. Any guy would fall for her... if he wasn't already trying not to.

As he leaves the room, I head over to the computer on his desk that I used earlier to show him the progress on the security upgrade and switch it on, sitting down hard in the leather captain's chair as the three screens flicker to life.

A few taps of the keyboard allow every camera on that side of the island to be displayed. I hone in on the one outside The Salty Dog, just in time to see her leaving the bar, the asshole's hand resting on the small of her back like he owns her. My fingers tighten into a fist.

Mine, some primitive part of me growls. Then I shut it down, hard. She's not mine. Not even close.

But I still spend the next ten minutes tracking them all the way to the lighthouse.

fifteen

FRANCIE

"Thank you," I say hurriedly, tugging at the door handle like it's a lifeline. No way am I giving Toe-zilla the wrong idea. "You got me out of a real bind."

Simon and his stupid cab were nowhere to be found. Next time I'll walk home with a flashlight and a taser.

I close the door behind me and give him a quick, awkward wave, hoping against hope that he doesn't follow me. Then I power-walk toward the lighthouse, exhaustion setting in like someone hit the 'off' switch on my legs.

Behind me, a car door slams. My heart jumps.

Of course it does.

I turn slowly. Reed is headed my way, gliding silently in those freaky shoes like a ninja yogi.

"I'll just make sure you get in safely," he says.

"You can do that from your car," I offer helpfully, without stopping. Because there's no way I'm giving the man an in. I just want him gone.

"Yeah, but I'd kill for a coffee." He grins.

"Isn't caffeine a capitalist toxin or something?" I ask, quickening my pace. "Anyway, I'm going straight to bed. *Alone*. Thanks again. And good luck with... the breathing."

"I won't bite," he murmurs.

Men who won't take no for an answer are almost as annoying as the ones who push you away before you have a chance to say yes. Like a certain overprotective security expert who'd rather stare at a screen than at me.

Not that I'm thinking about *that* guy right now or anything.

"I'm good, really," I say, pasting on my brightest please leave me alone before I have to fake a seizure smile. "You've been super helpful tonight, but I'm going to dive straight into bed and pretend today never happened."

Reed doesn't move. He shifts his weight onto one freaky toe-shoe'd foot and gives me a look I think he believes is sultry. Needless to say, it's more pained than sexy.

"I could come in for just one," he says, pushing his lips into a pout. "We don't even have to talk. We could just... breathe."

"Tempting," I deadpan, "but I've hit my inhale quota for the day."

My phone buzzes in my hand. I glance down at the screen and nearly drop it.

Asher Fitzgerald appears across the glass. I don't know whether to be annoyed or stupidly relieved.

I decide to go for relieved and flash a smile at Captain Chakra. "Sorry, this is important," I tell him. "I need to take it." I swipe accept and lift the phone to my ear. "Hello?" I try to sound casual, like I'm not currently in the midst of batting off the advances of a breath-loving forty-something who is so not my type.

"Francie. You okay?"

I stiffen. "Why wouldn't I be?"

"Look behind you."

Something flickers down my spine. A mix of fear and something else I don't want to name. I do what he says, half expecting to see the man himself casually leaning against the front door of the lighthouse. But of course he's not there.

"Look up. Above the door."

My gaze lifts, and I see what he's talking about. There's a little black camera with a flashing red light. "Oh," I murmur.

"You look uncomfortable," Asher says. "Am I right?" There's the softest tone to his voice. Like he's trying to calm a frightened animal.

And I realize that's exactly what I must look like to him right now.

"Yes," I say, my stomach tightening.

"Pass the phone to him, please."

"What? Why?" I ask, because this whole situation has just turned even weirder on me.

"Francie." He still has that calming-frightened-rabbit tone. "Please just do it."

I sigh and hold the phone out. "Reed," I say, "it's for you."

He frowns. "Who is it?"

I shrug, because I have no idea how to explain my relationship to Asher. And quite frankly, I just want Reed to leave. He reluctantly takes my phone, lifting it to his ear while flashing me a confused look.

"Ah yeah?" Reed says, looking nonchalant.

There's a beat of silence, then Reed's brows furrow until

they form one perfectly hairy line. He nods, even though he doesn't know Asher can see him, then hands me back the phone like it's about to explode.

"I gotta go," he mutters, not catching my eye. "I have an early flight. And I can't miss my sunrise yoga." He stumbles over his words as he abruptly turns on those terrible shoes. "Peace out." He practically runs to his car, yanking the door open and flinging himself inside. I only take a single breath before he starts the engine and reverses like a bat out of hell down the driveway.

"Francie?"

I blink. Asher is still there.

"Are you okay?" he asks again. His voice is still gentle. And I like it. Way too much. More than the angry, accusing Asher that I seem to awaken every time we talk.

"What did you say to him?" I whisper.

"I might have misquoted Liam Neeson's speech from *Taken*," he admits.

"You told him you have a very particular set of skills?" I don't know whether to laugh or not.

"Something like that. Now go inside and lock the door behind you."

I do as he tells me, flicking the lights on, and taking a deep breath as I kick my shoes off, the weariness I felt earlier coming back tenfold.

"Can I check the lighthouse?" he asks me.

"What do you mean? You want me to put you on video?"

There's a gentle laugh. "No, I'm asking if I can turn on the cameras to check that you're safe."

"Wait, cameras? You've been watching me?" I ask him, shocked.

"No," he says quickly. "Not once. They've been off since Autumn left."

I can tell by the tone in his voice that he's telling the truth. "Okay. Then yes, please turn them on. Just to check. Then off again, right?"

"Right," he confirms. "I won't turn them on unless you ask me to."

"Thank you." I believe him. There's a silence, then I see a flashing light in the corner of the room. "Can you see me?"

"Yes," he murmurs. "You look anxious."

"That's because you're looking at me."

"Are you really okay?" he asks. His voice is so soft I feel like it's wrapping around me.

"I'm not sure," I murmur. "Is the rest of the lighthouse okay?"

"It's fine." There's a pause. "He's not your boyfriend, is he?"

"No," I admit. "I made that up to get you and Myles off my back." There's no point in hiding it now. Especially since he went to all this trouble to check on me. "I'm sorry."

"I'm sorry for making you feel like you had to." He takes a breath. "He looked like a dick."

I start to laugh. "He was. Those shoes..."

"Can you believe people wear them and still think they're gonna get laid?" he asks.

"Nope. I'm going to have nightmares about them tonight. Who wants to see toes like that?"

It's Asher's turn to laugh. "You're all clear. Alone. Safe."

I turn to look at the camera, knowing he's looking right back at me. It's weird, not being able to see him back. Yet there's still this weird sense of peace washing over me. "Thank you," I tell him, staring right at the lens.

He clears his throat. "You're welcome. And by the way, I just got notification that your ex-date is on the ferry."

"I thought he was staying at the hotel," I say, confused.

"He was. But I wanted him off the island. Away from you. I told him to head to the ferry and his things would follow. I thought you'd feel better with him gone."

My mouth drops open. That's weirdly sweet. In a stalker kind of way. "Did you really quote Liam Neeson?" I ask him. A wave of warmth washes over me.

"I didn't really quote. Just said something similar. I can't remember the exact words. I was a little..." he trails off like he's finding the right word. "*Annoyed* with him."

And I'm a little turned on. More than a little, if I'm being honest.

There's a silence. It's not awkward, more charged than anything. Like the space between lightning and thunder.

"I should go," I murmur, though I make no move toward the guest bedroom.

"Yeah," he says, but he doesn't hang up.

I stare at the blinking light above the camera. "Are you still looking at me?"

There's a beat of nothing.

"I haven't stopped."

Something flutters low in my belly. Stupid, traitorous thing.

"Goodnight, Francie," he says, his voice a tad rougher. "I'm going to turn the cameras off, okay? But call me if you need anything. Anything at all."

"I will," I whisper. "Goodnight." Though I'm pretty sure I won't be sleeping.

The flickering light stops right as I end the call, the screen going dark in my hand. But the warmth doesn't fade. Nor does the aching need deep inside of me.

And later, after I've showered and checked that all the cameras are indeed off, when I reach for my toy and press it against me, I don't even try to pretend it's not his name on my lips.

* * *

ASHER

I stare at the computer screen long after I've switched off the cameras. There's a still image of her on the screen, staring at me, her eyes hooded, her lips parted. I'm hard as a fucking rock and I can't look away.

Her hair is a little messy. Her cheeks are flushed. She looks like she's just whispered my name, and not in thanks.

I reach down to adjust my aching cock, but my hand lingers. The door to the study is closed, I'm all alone.

Just me and an image of the woman I shouldn't want. I imagine walking toward her, running my thumb over those swollen lips. Pushing it inside to feel the velvety warmth of her mouth.

My groan echoes in the quiet study as I unzip my pants, my need too strong to ignore. I curl my fist around myself, remembering that night I touched her. How soft her lips were against mine, how hot her breath was as I slid my fingers inside of her.

How fucking tight she was as she came around them.

What if she let me in? What if I didn't have to hide how much I want her?

When I reach my peak, I groan out her name, spilling my desire all over my stomach in long, achingly pleasurable pulses.

I'm not sure how long I can keep doing this. Watching. Waiting. Pretending I don't care.

I want her.

But I shouldn't. I know that. That's what stops me from calling her again. From ruining everything. From telling her the truth – that she's the only damn thing I want.

sixteen

ASHER

"Please repeat that," I say, my voice thick. I barely remember the phone ringing, let alone answering it, yet here it is against my ear, Brad's voice cutting through the fog.

"The police are on their way. It's a mess. I hate to do this to you, but you should probably come in."

Agitation claws at my gut. "What's a mess?"

"The office. The break in. Whoever it was really fucked it over. Half of our equipment is trashed, the stuff they didn't steal. And your office... it's not good. Really not good."

"Is it secure?"

"I called the first team in. They're all here."

"Good work." I'm wide awake now. Ripping the covers off, I sit up and slide my feet to the floor. "I'll be there as soon as I can. Keep this line open. I want constant updates."

"Understood."

Fuck. Any remaining exhaustion is gone, as I storm into the bathroom and turn the shower on, taking less than three minutes to clean myself before I put in my contacts and grab a crisp white shirt and dark suit from my closet. And all the time I have my assistant – who I woke up and now owe a huge bonus – on the phone with me, talking through the logistics of getting off this island in the middle of the night.

There are no ferries for at least two more hours. And all the charter owners will be fast asleep. Yes, I could wake them up, but Hudson recently installed a helipad just north of the hotel for the exclusive use of VIP guests, so my assistant manages to track down a pilot willing to fly a chopper from New York to pick me up.

I hate to think how much this is going to cost. Yes, I can afford it, but I'm furious anyway. I grab my phone and wallet, then slide my feet into my leather shoes, taking a second to check myself in the mirror, before I walk out into the hallway, ready to drive to the helipad.

"Asher?" Hudson walks out of the master bedroom. His hair is mussed up, and he's wearing a pair of sleep shorts and nothing else. If I had more time I'd rib him, but I don't.

"Sorry, didn't mean to wake you," I tell him, my voice low, because I don't want to wake the rest of his family.

"What's going on?" he asks, glancing at the smartwatch on his wrist. "It's the middle of the night."

"There's been a break in at my office," I tell him.

He winces. "Is it bad?"

"So I hear. I need to get there to sort things out. I've got a helicopter picking me up from the pad."

"Want me to drive you?" he asks, but I'm already shaking my head.

"No need. I'll drive myself. You go back to bed."

Our eyes catch. He knows what a break in means to a security company like mine. Not only are the optics terrible, but we house a lot of secrets in that building. "Call me when you get there," he says.

"It'll still be early. One of us should be getting some sleep."

"I want to help. Call me."

I nod, giving him a mirthless smile before I head out of the house and to my car. The air outside is cool, the aroma of salt and damp sand coming up from the ocean. I've always hated this time of day. It's quiet. Too quiet. And far too lonely. Like there's nobody else in the world except for me.

My worst nightmare.

Climbing into my car, I start up the engine and switch the stereo on to break the silence. Linkin Park comes on, and I put the car in drive, letting the anger take over as I drive to the helipad to wait for my ride to Manhattan. When I get there I check my phone – there's an update that the police have arrived and would like to talk to me when I get to the office, but nothing else.

It only takes twenty minutes for the helicopter to arrive, which is pretty impressive for this time of day. I stand back, feeling the wind rush through my hair and my clothes as the huge machine lands, waiting for the pilot to give me the all clear. As I climb into the cabin, he passes me a headset and shakes my hand.

"Pier 6, right?" he asks, referring to the Downtown Manhattan Helipad next to the East River. At this time of day it'll be less than a five minute drive to my building.

"Yes please."

Five minutes later we're taking off, hovering in the air for a moment before we start moving forward. Liberty shrinks beneath me as we pass over the hotel and the expanse of green, before I see the lighthouse beneath us.

Francie. Memories of last night rush through my mind. I let out a long breath. Was it only a few hours ago that I was telling that toe-socked asshole that if he didn't leave right away I'd be telling his wife and kids exactly what he's been doing?

Yes, he's married. I managed to find that out with a quick, targeted search. And no, I'm not telling Francie about that. No harm, no foul. She didn't know he's a cheating piece of shit when she accepted the date and I don't want her to feel bad.

I will be arranging for his wife to find out anyway, though.

The sun is rising over New York as we fly into Manhattan airspace. The streets are still fairly empty, though, save for the trash trucks and delivery vans that keep this place going. My car is waiting for me when we land, and as soon as I get the all clear, I run out of the helicopter to the waiting car door, where my driver gives me a wry smile.

"Sorry," I tell him, knowing he must have been woken up the same way as the rest of us. And yes, I'll compensate him fully for the inconvenience, but I know how annoying it is for a phone call to blast through your dreams.

"All in a day's work. I heard about the break in," he says, closing the door and climbing into the front seat. "Is it bad?"

"I believe so. I'm about to find out I guess." I sit back on the plush leather seat, checking my watch. Is it really only six? For a second my mind flits to Liberty. To her.

And then I bring it right back because I need all my energy on this shitshow. The car pulls away and I take a deep breath. We're a security company. We're going to find out who did this.

And when we do, I'm going to make them regret it.

* * *

FRANCIE

My thumb hovers over my phone, hesitating over the end call button. I've already left a voicemail. One more and I'll sound like a stalker.

Still, I let the message play through the speaker as I walk barefoot along the sand, the salty breeze lifting my hair. The sun's high, casting glitter on the waves, and the gulls overhead are crying like they have something to complain about. Maybe they know how hard it is to write a damn fight scene when your brain is stuck on the man who chased off your toe-shoed almost-date last night.

His voice comes through the speaker. It's smooth and unbothered.

"You've reached the voicemail of Asher Fitzgerald. If it's not urgent, leave a message. If you need an immediate response, call my assistant."

He rattles off a number I don't bother memorizing.

There's nothing overtly sexy in the words, but his voice... it hits me like a slow stroke down my spine. Confident. Controlled. I remember the way he said, "I haven't stopped," when I asked if he was still watching me. The softness in his voice. The heat behind it.

The way I'd wanted him to keep watching. To never stop.

"Hey!" Skyler's voice cuts through my thoughts as she

jogs toward me with Ayda in tow. Her ponytail bounces, and she's flushed from chasing a five-year-old down the beach. "So you haven't been abducted by a foot-worshipping cult?"

She rests a protective hand on her still-flat stomach. A subtle reminder that she's pregnant. Only three months along, and according to Autumn, Hudson is treating her like a princess. It's sweet. And kind of heartbreaking, in the best way.

I grin. "I couldn't even believe those."

"Mylene asked if they were real or an urban legend. I think she's considering a pair."

"If she buys some, I'm leaving the island."

Skyler laughs, then lowers her voice conspiratorially. "Hudson said Asher practically chased the guy off Liberty. Very lowkey *Taken* energy."

My heart skips. "He told me he might've misquoted Liam Neeson."

"So Hudson wasn't exaggerating." She smirks.

Ayda runs up and presses a small white shell into my hand. "This one's for you."

The shell is smooth and cool, like a tiny heartbeat in my palm. "Thank you, sweetheart."

Skyler watches Ayda with that soft look I've come to associate with her. "She's doing really well."

"She is," I say, voice warm. "She's talking again. That's because of you."

Skyler blinks, and I can see emotion bubbling beneath her surface. "Okay, no getting mushy," she says, shaking it off. "Let's go back to gossip. Did you hear about Asher?"

My smile falters. "What about him?"

"He left Liberty early this morning. Like, really early. Took a helicopter off the island."

I stop walking. "Why?"

She sighs. "There was a break-in at his office. Hudson said it was bad. They trashed the place. Equipment, documents, the works."

A cold wind blows straight through my gut. "Do they know who did it?"

"Not yet. Asher's there now, talking to the police." She gives me a pointed look. "Hudson says Asher's pissed. And embarrassed. I guess when you run a security company and get broken into... not great optics."

I nod slowly, heart thudding. He was watching over me last night – calming me down, chasing Reed off, making me feel safe – while his business was falling apart.

The guilt hits me fast. If he hadn't been babysitting me, maybe he would've noticed something was wrong. Maybe he could've stopped it.

"Do you know when he'll be back?"

Skyler shrugs. "No idea. He might be stuck in the city for a while."

I press the shell tighter in my hand, letting the sharp edge cut into my palm. I shouldn't feel disappointed. I shouldn't feel like someone's pulled a plug on the warmth building in my chest.

But I do. And I hate that I do.

"I tried to call him earlier," I say. "Just to say thanks. I didn't know..."

"I'm sure he appreciated it," Skyler says gently.

Ayda tugs on her hand. "Can we get a milkshake now?"

Skyler ruffles her hair. "You want to come with?" she asks me.

I should. But the fight scene is still staring at me like a challenge. And truthfully, I'm not sure I'll be good company right now.

"Can I take a raincheck?" I ask.

"It's a deal." She smiles, and I watch them walk off hand in hand, Ayda skipping ahead while Skyler matches her step.

I stay behind, watching the two of them shrink toward the edge of the beach, heading for downtown Liberty and its pastel-painted coffee shops and toe-shoe gossip.

I turn back to the ocean, the wind brushing my cheeks. The mainland is hazy in the distance, but I know he's there.

Asher.

He left. And I know it wasn't personal, but it still feels personal. Like he took something with him when he left. This unspoken thread between us, fragile and humming with potential.

Maybe it wouldn't feel so raw if I hadn't spent last night whispering his name into my pillow.

If I hadn't closed my eyes and imagined his hands, his mouth, his rough voice in my ear.

I know it's a crush, a passing fantasy. These past few days have been ridiculous. And not what I came here for.

I'm supposed to be writing a book. The biggest break of my career. The one my editor's waiting on. I told myself I could finish it if I just got away from the chaos at my apartment.

But somehow, Asher Fitzgerald has become the biggest distraction of them all.

I let out a breath, turning back toward the lighthouse, still thinking about how close he felt last night, even though he was on the phone.

There's nothing between us. There can't be.

But it doesn't stop me from wishing he was here.

ASHER

The office smells like scorched wires and bad decisions. Most of it is sectioned off, the crime scene unit collecting evidence as my team tries to explain what all the equipment does.

Brad, my second-in-command, is waiting for me. "Asher," he says, shooting me a pained look. "This is Detective Claire Russo, in charge of the investigation."

"I know Claire," I say, holding my hand out. "Thanks for being here."

"I know you, too," she replies, a wry smile on her lips. "And in case of any doubt, this is my investigation."

"Sure it is," I say agreeably. We both know I'll be running a parallel one. "What do you have so far?"

She walks with me down the hall, her boots crunching on broken glass. "Your server room was the target. Whoever did it knew exactly what to hit and how to get in. No alarms tripped, no entry logs. Just a fried firewall."

"Do you have any suspects?"

"I was hoping you could give me a list. Rivals, enemies, whoever."

"You don't think the motive was financial?" Fuck, I wish it was.

"Do you?"

No. But I'm not giving her everything. Discretion is what we sell. And I already have an idea of where to start.

She glances at her phone. "We just heard from the hospital. Shaun Morris is starting to regain consciousness."

I stop. "Wait, one of my employees was hurt?" I turn to Brad. "Why didn't you tell me?"

He winces. "I was going to, as soon as you got here. He was in the control room last night. Whoever did this had to get through him. He put up a fight."

Fury tightens my chest. "We're covering his care, right?"

Brad nods. "He has a private room, a top neurologist. We've spoken with his wife. She's there with their baby."

Jesus. They just had a kid.

I rake a hand through my hair. Shaun's lying in a hospital bed because of me. Because someone wanted to make a point.

"Send flowers, food, anything they need," I tell Brad. "Offer security if she wants it. A babysitter too."

He nods grimly. "Already on it."

I turn to Claire. "Once he's stable, I want to talk to him."

Her lips curl. "You planning to interview my witness?"

"I just want to make sure he's okay. If he remembers anything, you'll get it."

She gives me a pointed look. "Sure I will, Fitzgerald."

I ignore that. But I will speak to Shaun first.

My phone buzzes in my pocket. *Francie Salinger*. Just seeing her name punches the air from my lungs.

There's already a voicemail too. I shouldn't listen here. But my thumb hovers over the screen.

Even now, in the middle of all this wreckage, I want to hear her voice. To know she's okay after last night.

But I tuck the phone back in my pocket.

I can't listen yet. Because I know a phone call won't be enough. And right now, I can't have more.

* * *

It's late afternoon when I leave Shaun's hospital room, murmuring reassurances to his wife. I tell her not to worry about anything. I'll handle it all. Just focus on him. On their baby. But I'm carrying the guilt like a weight on my shoulders.

I head for the stairwell – six floors isn't much – but stop cold at the sign on the door.

Maintenance underway. Please use elevators.

I stare at it like it's mocking me. Of course. One more thing to make today worse.

I glance toward the elevator bank, silver doors gleaming under the fluorescent lights. One dings open. An orderly wheels out a cart, chatting with a nurse, like the walls aren't closing in.

My pulse spikes. Sweat prickles at the back of my neck.

This is ridiculous. I've run black-ops security for billionaires. Sat across tables from men who'd kill me for blinking wrong. But a metal box? That terrifies me.

It's the smallness. The stillness. The lack of escape.

I curse under my breath and step inside anyway, bracing myself against the back wall. Just one button to press. *G.* Ten seconds, maybe. But my chest's already tight.

The doors close. The elevator hums.

And suddenly I'm ten years old again, locked in the dark, listening to my father scream.

I hit the wall with my fist, pain flaring in my knuckles. It does nothing. The nausea's already rising.

When the doors open, I stagger out, adrenaline crashing. I barely make it to a planter outside before I'm retching, doubled over like I've been punched in the gut.

My legs give out. I sink to the concrete, back against the cool stone. Gasping. Waiting for the panic to fade.

But it won't.

Maybe nothing will.

Except... maybe someone can.

I pull out my phone. My fingers are already moving.

FRANCIE

The shrill ring of my phone makes me jump. I glance at the screen, expecting it to be a spam call, or Skyler. Or maybe – if I'm really unlucky – Captain Toe Shoes himself.

But it's Asher. And my heart skips a beat.

Lifting the phone, I slide my thumb against the glass to accept the call.

"Hey," I say, ignoring the thud of my heart against my chest. "I'm so sorry about the break in."

There's no reply. For a second I hear nothing, then heavy breathing. It reminds me of my youngest cousin who has asthma.

"Asher?" I say softly. "Are you okay?"

There's more ragged breathing, followed by a choked inhale. And then finally – his voice, rough and low, like it's been dragged through gravel.

"I'm okay," he manages. "I just... I couldn't breathe. I—"

He cuts off with a shuddering breath that sounds so far from okay it isn't funny.

Oh my God. I've never heard him like this before. I sit up straighter, my laptop and writing forgotten. "Where are you? Are you okay? What happened?"

A beat of silence. "I'm outside the hospital."

And just like that, my lunch starts to rise in my gut. Please let him be okay. "Why are you there? Are you hurt?"

"No." He inhales sharply. "Not me. One of my employees. He got a head injury during the break in."

I hate how relieved I feel that it's not him who's hurt. "I'm so sorry. Is he hurt badly?" I can't imagine what that must feel like.

"It's Shaun."

I blink. "Shaun who guarded me?" I ask, remembering the tall, young guy who was lurking outside my apartment all that time ago. For some reason it feels like a personal attack.

"Yeah." He sounds despondent.

My eyes widen. "Wasn't his wife about to have a baby?"

Asher's breathing is slowing. But not fast enough. I think he might be having a panic attack. "They had it. A girl. He's okay." Another moment of silence. "I'm sorry, I should go. You don't need to—"

"Stay," I tell him. "Stay with me. Talk to me. Try to slow down your breathing. We can do it together," I tell him. "I know a qualified breath consultant."

That joke does the opposite of what I intend. He starts to choke.

"Asher?"

"It's okay. I'm okay." I'm not sure who he's trying to convince, me or himself.

"And so is Shaun," I tell him. "This isn't your fault. It's nobody's fault except whoever hit him." I take a breath, trying to remember how to deal with a panic attack. There was a girl at school who used to get them regularly. "You're okay," I tell him. "Look around you. Try to find something green."

"There's a planter I just vomited in," he says sounding almost embarrassed. "Will that do?"

I bite down a smile, figuring I need to be normal for him. Especially after what he did for me last night.

He saved me. Maybe I can repay the favor.

"Nature can be healing, right?" I quip.

There's the faintest huff of a laugh from the other end. It sounds a little broke, a little raw. But it's there and it warms my heart.

"I can't remember the last time this happened to me," he murmurs. "Fuck, I thought I was past all this. I feel like I'm a kid again."

My breath catches. "You've had panic attacks before?"

"A very long time ago."

I hesitate. "Do you want to talk about it?" I ask softly. I have no idea how to make him feel better, but I want to keep him on the line. Hearing his voice makes my whole body feel like it's vibrating, but I also need to make sure he's okay.

I owe him that. And more than that, I want to do it.

There's a long pause before he speaks again. I hear his breathing – becoming less shuddery, more regular. There's the sound of cars and the occasional bird. I wish we were on video, but I don't think he'd like that.

Asher Fitzgerald is always so closed off. So in control. I'm not sure he'd ever show this side of him in normal circumstances. And I don't want to break the connection we somehow have right now, even though he's hundreds of miles away.

"I was stuck in a closet," he says. His voice is so low I have to concentrate to hear him. "I was ten. My dad owed the wrong people money. Shocking, I know."

I wince, because I know all about their dad's gambling addiction. He lost their home, their island, and their fortune after all. By that point, Hudson and Asher were older. They managed to keep the family going. But it affected Autumn and Eden and I saw it first hand.

"He used me to help him cheat," Asher confesses. "He figured out I was good at math and turned it to his advantage. Made me hang around the room when they had poker games. I had to count the cards."

Good at math is an understatement. The whole family knows that Asher is pretty much a math genius. Eden, their youngest sister, is too. Autumn used to regularly complain that the gene somehow skipped her, especially when it came to tests at school.

"He made you do it?" I ask.

"He'd intimidate me. Would tell me there'd be no food on the table if I didn't. Told me I was doing it for the family.

I was a kid, I..." He lets out a breath. "I should have said no. But I loved him, you know?"

My heart contracts. "Of course you did."

"One night we got caught," he tells me. "They locked me in a closet while they...handled him."

Oh god. The breath leaves my lungs like I've been punched. I press a hand to my chest, trying to calm myself.

"I sat in there for hours, listening to him get beat. Hearing him scream. Thinking that I'd be next and it was all my fault." He trails off, like he's done talking. "Since then small places... just mess with me."

It occurs to me that I've never seen him in an elevator. His office is on the second floor, his apartment on the third. He could afford the penthouse but...

"Asher." I have no idea what to say that doesn't sound hollow or useless. So I say the truth. "That's not something you just get over. No wonder you feel so bad."

He exhales. Not shaky this time. Just tired. The man's been up since God knows when. Dealing with a mess that could threaten his business. No wonder he's exhausted.

"I shouldn't have called you," he tells me.

"I'm glad you did," I say firmly. "You're allowed to not be perfect sometimes. You're allowed to lean on someone."

This time the silence isn't uncomfortable. It's heavy, but with something else. Something new.

"I have no idea how to do that," he admits.

"Well, you're making a pretty good attempt of it now," I tell him softly. I try to imagine him right now, slumped outside the hospital in his expensively designed suit. His hair a mess, his heart racing. The man who always holds everything together is finally letting someone see through the cracks.

And I'm the one he's letting in.

"My car is here," he murmurs. "I have to get back to the office."

"I'll stay on the line with you as long as you want," I whisper. "Even if we don't talk. I'm here."

He's quiet for a moment. I think he's standing up. I imagine him dusting himself off, running a hand through his hair to tame it.

"You make it hard to keep my distance," he says, his voice thick.

The words slip under my skin. Warm and electric.

"Then maybe," I say softly. "You should stop trying."

He doesn't say anything else. But I hear him breathe. Slow, steady.

And it feels like something between us has shifted.

* * *

Later that night, I can't sleep.

It's not because I'm not tired – I am. After talking to Asher, I spent the next few hours staring at the same blinking cursor. But now, in bed, every time I close my eyes I think of him. Of his voice. Of how raw he sounded on the phone, like something inside of him had cracked wide open.

And he let me see it.

The wind is whipping around outside, making the lighthouse groan in a way I'm starting to get used to. But it's not the weather that's keeping me up.

It's him.

I haven't heard from him since he arrived at the office, and I'm worried about him. Or at least that's what I tell myself as I grab my phone and pull up his name, my fingers quickly typing out a message.

. . .

Hey. Just checking in. Are you okay? – Francie

The dots appear almost instantly. Then disappear, before they finally come back again.

I'm fine. Just got back to my apartment and took a shower. Been a long day. – Asher

His third floor apartment. Easily reachable by taking the stairs. Which explains everything to me now. Another message appears.

I'm sorry about earlier. It was a bad time. It won't happen again. – Asher

And just like that, I can feel him pulling away. Slipping back into the cold, buttoned up version of him that keeps everybody at a distance.

I stare at the message. Then I type my reply before I can overthink it.

You don't have to do that, you know. – Francie

Do what? – Asher

. . .

My chest feels tight.

Pretend like it didn't mean something. It did. To me at least. – Francie

It feels awkward, putting myself out there. But I can't criticize him for being closed up if I'm doing the same thing. There's a long pause, where I'm second guessing all of my decisions. And then.

It meant something to me too. – Asher

I swallow hard, my skin prickling. Six words, yet it feels like I just won something I didn't even know I was competing for.

What you said earlier. About me making it hard for you to keep your distance. Were you just saying that because you were shaken up? – Francie

The seconds stretch.

No. I meant it. – Asher

. . .

I stare at the screen. The words glow like they've burned themselves into my chest.

He doesn't just want me physically. He trusted me. With a part of himself nobody else gets to see.

I sink back into the pillows. The sheets are cool against my skin, but everything inside of me feels overheated. Every nerve alive.

And it isn't just arousal.

It's him.

I bite my bottom lip, debating. This thing between us – whatever it is – is teetering on the edge of something dangerous. Something real.

I don't want to pull back. And I don't want him to, either. Not tonight.

I want to close the distance. I want to feel the weight of his eyes on me – even from miles away.

My fingers hover over the keyboard for a long moment before I type.

Do you still have access to the lighthouse cameras? – Francie

I haven't used them. I promised you I wouldn't. You don't have to worry about it. – Asher

My blood heats up as I read his message. Of course he hasn't used them. Because he's Asher. Even when he's unraveling, he still keeps his promise.

But I don't want distance tonight. I don't want promises or polite boundaries.

I want him.

I know you haven't. But I want you to now. Turn on the camera in the guest bedroom. – Francie

Another pause. Dots appear again.

Francie... - Asher

Turn it on. I want you to see me. – Francie

I close my eyes for a second, feeling the flutter in my stomach. The warmth blooming low down in my belly. This isn't about sex. This isn't about trust.

I want him to see me.

I open my eyes again, looking at my phone. For a moment, there's nothing. No reply. No dots. Just silence.

And then, in the top corner of the room, the tiniest red light blinks on.

The camera. My body tightens. He's watching.

I lie back slowly, letting the covers slip down my body. Revealing the tiny silk shorts and camisole I put on after my shower this evening. My hair is down, tumbling in waves across the pillow.

I lift my eyes, my thighs clenching as I look into the camera, hopefully connecting our gazes. My skin prickles with awareness.

It's like I'm not alone in this room. I'm not nervous. I'm not embarrassed. I feel empowered.

Because right now I feel like I'm his.

eighteen

ASHER

The moment the camera flickers to life on my laptop screen, I forget how to breathe.

She's there. Sprawled across the guest bed like something out of a dream I didn't know I could have. Her skin is glowing in the soft lamplight. The flimsy silk of her camisole clings to curves I've spent way too many nights trying not to imagine.

Her hair is a dark halo on her pillow.

She looks straight into the camera. Straight into me.

And in that moment, I'm no longer in my apartment. I'm not in New York, or in a crisis, or barely holding myself together by a thread.

I'm hers.

And she's going to fucking unravel me.

Her hands flutter, sliding across the silky camisole, brushing her breasts. I see her mouth something into the camera.

It looks like my name. I'm instantly hard.

I lean forward instinctively, like I can somehow get closer. Like the pixels between us aren't enough.

"Francie," I whisper, even though she can't hear me. Not through the camera. Only through the phone if I say it out loud.

I reach for it, fumbling for the call button before I can stop myself. It only rings once before she answers, sounding breathless.

"Asher..."

"Say my name again," I command her, knowing my voice is harsher than I intend. More desperate.

She shifts, her camisole sliding up, revealing her smooth, soft stomach. My hand clenches into a fist on my thigh.

"Asher," she breathes, and I swear I feel it everywhere. Like she's touching me with her words.

I stare at her, trying to hold onto the last thread of control I have left. "You're so fucking beautiful."

Her lips curve. "Do you like watching me?" she asks.

"I've never liked anything more."

She moves one hand between her thighs, dragging it slowly over the silk of her shorts. I nearly come undone.

"Tell me what to do," she murmurs.

I swallow hard, trying to form words with a mouth as dry as the desert. My whole body is lit up like a fuse.

"Touch yourself," I say hoarsely. "Touch that pretty pussy. I want to see you fall apart for me."

She doesn't hesitate. Her hand slides beneath the waistband of her shorts, and I catch the sharp hitch of her breath through the phone. My body tenses like a live wire, a pulse hammering in my throat as I watch her fingers move.

She's slow at first. Teasing. Drawing it out and torturing us both.

"I've thought about you. About this," she whispers. "So many times."

I groan, dragging my hand over my jaw. Trying to ground myself. Failing.

"Thought about what, baby? Tell me."

"You," she breathes. "Your voice. Your hands. How your fingers felt inside of me that night. How it would feel if it was more."

"Christ." My hips jerk forward before I can stop them. I reach down, palming the thick ache in my pants. "You have no idea what you do to me." She makes me want things I've never let myself hope for. Makes me forget the rules I built to keep people safe from me.

She lets out a whimper, her back arching slightly, her eyes flickering closed as her rhythm picks up.

"I like you watching me," she whispers. "I like imagining that you need me. Desperate for me."

"I am," I rasp. "I need you so fucking much."

The connection between us feels heavy. Pulsing with an emotion I'm not sure I can name.

Her breath starts to speed. Her lips part. She's so close I can almost smell her arousal.

I can't pull my eyes away. She's imprinted on my brain. All soft and full of desire and so achingly pretty.

I palm myself harder.

"I want to come for you," she whispers.

"Do it," I growl. "I want you to fall apart. I want you to scream my name."

I want to be there with her. To taste her. To be inside of her. My dick aches for her. God, I'm never going to recover from this. I'll never be able to go back. I'll never be able to stay away.

She cries out, soft and broken, her body tensing as the pleasure peaks. She lets out a cry, then says my name.

I'm on the edge of coming with her. But I stop. I want to concentrate on her.

Her hand slows as the waves pass over her. My eyes don't move. None of me does. Her own eyes lock on the camera like she's handing me something sacred.

And I take it. Gripping it with both hands like it's the only thing keeping me sane right now.

"Francie," I rasp. "You're killing me."

Her chest is rising and falling rapidly, her cheeks flushed, her body loose. Her eyes are shining as they stare at the camera.

"I wish you were here," she says. There's no seduction in her words. Just truth.

"I wish I was too." I'd spend the whole fucking night making her feel good, just to hear her say my name again.

She smiles softly. Sated. Her gaze is a little unfocused. She looks sleepy. Fuck, I want to hold her.

"Are you okay?" I ask, my voice low.

She nods slowly, still catching her breath. "Better than okay." There's that smile again. Soft, sweet. Just for me. "Are you?"

I swallow hard, emotion crawling up the back of my throat like a threat. "Yeah, I am now."

She blinks slowly, that hazy, satisfied look still softening her features.

"You should go to sleep," I tell her. If I were there, I'd hold her until the sun came up. Trace her skin until she fell asleep in my arms. I'd do anything to stay close.

"I know. But I'm scared you'll go all weird on me again."

"I won't," I promise. And then. "I'll turn off the camera."

"No," she murmurs. "Not yet."

Her words wrap around me, like a weighted blanket.

I don't say anything. I just sit there, watching her eyes flutter closed. The smile still on her lips as her chest starts to rise and fall in a steady rhythm.

And even though I'm alone in my apartment, exhausted and aching, I've never felt less alone.

* * *

"Have you slept *at all* this week?" Brad asks me, as we go over everything we've discovered in the last few days. One of the NYPD detectives called to say they've still found nothing. No fingerprints either digital or physical, no DNA, nada.

And our investigation has been similarly frustrating. I'm beyond annoyed but at least we've managed to get everything back online. The tech team has done an amazing job of rebuilding the infrastructure in the office from the ground up. We've re-secured every client file, scrubbed the backup servers, and tightened access protocols until even I need a thirty-two step authentication to unlock my own office.

We're back up. Running. On the surface, at least, everything looks fine.

But it's not.

Because whoever broke in didn't take anything. They left a message. One I still can't read.

We've been down every obvious path. Former employees. Old clients. We even checked out the guy who'd been eyeing Francie at the Ivory Club in case he was trying to get revenge for me warning him off, but no dice. And, then of course, there's Nathan.

My ex business partner's vindictive enough to do something like this. But he's clean. His alibi is tight, his bank records are clear. We even hacked his fucking phone but there's no sign of him being involved.

I don't know whether to be relieved or more pissed off.

But Brad's right, I've barely slept at all this week. Just not for the reasons he thinks.

All I can think about is *her*. Every night this week, she's been my lifeline. She calls me, I turn on the cameras.

And she lets me watch.

Even thinking about it makes my body heat up. Remembering that little smile she makes when I say her name. The way her voice trembles when she whispers mine. The soft, breathless way she looks into the camera, like I'm the only thing in the world she sees.

She likes me telling her what to do. And I like it, too. Way too much.

But I haven't let myself come. Not once. It feels like a test now. Maybe I'm not a perv if all I do is watch. Maybe I want to make it all about her.

All I know is that I won't do it, not until I'm with her in person.

I rake a hand through my hair, trying to refocus, but the image of her arching her back against the guest bed last night keeps bleeding through my mind. Her voice in my ear. Her body in my head.

I'm obsessed. She's all I can think about. And watching from a distance isn't enough.

I look at Brad. "Am I still needed here?" I ask him, waving my hand at the equipment. "Or have you got this?"

He lifts a brow. "You planning on leaving?"

"I'm halfway through the security upgrade on Liberty," I remind him. Though I think we both know it's a bullshit excuse.

He lifts a brow. He knows how anal I am. How hard it is for me to walk away from work. Or at least, how hard it has been. But he's still my employee. He nods slowly.

"We've got things under control for now," he says, though confusion still tinges his voice.

"Great." I send a message to my assistant, asking her to sort out a flight back to Liberty. "Call me if you hear anything at all. I want constant updates. If a fly lands on the fucking screen, I want to know about it, okay?"

His mouth twitches. "Yes, sir," he says, touching his fingers to his brow in a mock salute.

I ignore that, too busy thinking about her.

Because the next time she says my name, I'm determined to be close enough to feel it.

nineteen

FRANCIE

My daytimes are all about writing kick-ass heroines slaying their enemies while enthralling the dark and broody hero who can't take his eyes off her. My night times, though, have become something altogether different. More intimate.

Every night for the past week, I've slipped beneath my sheets and let Asher command me through the guest room security camera. My body heats up as he guides me with his low, commanding voice that I can only dream of capturing on the page.

And I do everything he tells me to. Slowly, deliberately, loving the way it makes his voice go ragged and his breath speed up. I become a breathless wreck too, whispering his name like a prayer.

But he doesn't touch himself. Not once. I hear the raw need in his strained voice as he tells me I'm his good girl, so beautiful, so perfect. And yes, I might be a strong woman with my own agency, but I like hearing him say those words. Sometimes, they're dirtier than the profanities he whispers as I arch my back from the mattress.

I don't know why he keeps holding himself back, but his restraint makes me feral. It makes me tease him, more and more, testing his boundaries.

I end up getting myself so worked up thinking about it, that after lunch, I take a run on the beach, needing an outlet to work off this buzzing energy that rushes through me every time I hear his name.

It's a warm fall day, the sun is high in the sky, but the temperatures have dropped from their summer high to a much more relaxing low sixties. I pull on my sneakers, swipe a hand over my messy bun, and step out of the light-house and head toward the cliff, taking the steps down to the golden beach below.

The beach is almost empty. The summer travelers – the out-of-towners, as the locals call them – are few and far between. It's the quiet season, the lull between the summer crowds and the winter visitors looking for the kind of magic you only find during the holiday season.

I jog along the shoreline, trying to plan my next scene, but my mind keeps drifting to Asher. To the dirty things he whispered last night. Maybe I should just skip to the sex scene. Get it all out on the page.

Sometimes being a writer means you can fulfil all your fantasies, if only in your imagination.

The breeze from the ocean scrubs my skin, drying the perspiration on my face and neck. By the time I make it back to the lighthouse – three miles later – all I can think about is a long, scalding shower and a cool drink. Kicking off my running shoes, I drop my keys in the bowl by the front door and peel off my running gear, heading straight for the bathroom on the first floor.

The room is tiny. Small enough to fit a toilet, basin, and shower. Every room in this lighthouse was specially designed by Autumn. The shower is round with a little porthole window looking out over the ocean. The white tiles are in a brick-style, and there's a built in bench with a wooden seat below the modern light-up rain style shower, which I turn on, closing my eyes and luxuriating beneath the firm spray.

It's heavenly. Hot enough to sting in all the right places, pounding against my skin like therapy. I lather up slowly, letting the suds slide down my thighs as the steam curls around the tiny room like a cat.

Then I hear a loud buzz.

I freeze, blinking water out of my eyes. Was that the doorbell? It can't be, nobody ever rings the doorbell here. I don't have any deliveries or packages, or even mail, coming here. It all goes to the hotel to be picked up at leisure.

I wipe my face with the palm of my hand, glancing at the bathroom door, but the sound doesn't repeat. Maybe it was a mistake. Or the wind. Turning back to the shower, I rinse the shampoo from my hair, then reach for the conditioner.

And that's when I see it.

A spider.

No, spider isn't a good enough description. This thing is a massive, eight-legged monster dangling from the corner of the shower like it's auditioning for a horror movie.

My heart immediately starts to pound. I can deal with dragons in my writing. With blood and gore and even snakes, when I have to.

But spiders are my nemesis. There's a reason I have exactly zero of them in my books.

"Oh hell no," I whisper, backing away. My hand grasps for the shower door, but I hit the bench instead. My calves catch on the wood, my feet skid forward, and I flail like a failing backup dancer before slamming my head against the glass.

Stars explode behind my eyelids as I land in an ungainly, compacted heap, on the shower floor.

And then I feel it.

A light, horrible tickle against my shoulder. The spider.

I open my mouth and unleash a scream so bloodcurdling it could shatter glass. What I don't expect is for the spider to say anything.

But it does. It says my name. So clearly that I think I must be hallucinating – either dead or on my way there, and the road to hell is filled with arachnids.

"Francie?" it shouts again.

I thrash, trying to bat it away, and catch the blurry outline of the shower door as I scramble to my knees. The eight-legged demon is still winning. I'm soaked, disoriented, and naked, but I manage to push the door open, which gives way too easily, making me sprawl half-in and half-out of the cubicle like a slippery, shrieking disaster.

Then a bang echoes through the house.

The front door. It takes a second for me to register that someone is inside.

Footsteps thunder down the hallway, fast, heavy, and furious, and then the bathroom door crashes open.

And he's there.

Asher Fitzgerald. His chest is heaving, his eyes are wild with panic, and he has one hand clenched like he's ready to throw a punch. He scans the room like he's seconds away from launching into a fight.

Until his gaze lands on me.

Naked, wet, shampoo in my eyes. Curled in the corner like a drowned gremlin. The fury slips from his face, replaced by confusion, and something that might be horror.

Because while I'm trying to figure out how to breathe again, he's staring at me like he walked into a crime scene and discovered the world's weirdest boudoir shoot.

I open my mouth.

He opens his.

And instead of asking what the hell is going on, or why I screamed like someone was being murdered, he says the worst possible thing.

"Is that a spider?"

* * *

ASHER

I freeze as I stare at the scene before me. I swear I thought she was being attacked.

The second I heard her scream, all I could think about was that asshole I forced off the island and the fact my office had been broken into and ransacked, and now this. It was like something primal detonated in my chest. I slammed my fingers against the emergency override on the front door and rushed into the lighthouse, because she was fucking screaming. She needed me.

But I wasn't expecting this.

Francie scrambles onto all fours, eyes wide, breath ragged, trying – and failing – to cover herself with her arms.

Water glistens across every inch of her bare skin, her hair clinging to her shoulders, her lips parted in shock.

I know I should look away.

But I can't.

I'm frozen. For the past week I've watched her through a camera. Heard her moan, seen her writhe, watched her fall apart with my name on her lips. But none of it prepared me for this. For the woman I've been fantasizing about in real life, flushed and wet, droplets of water trailing down her collarbone and sliding into the crevasse between her perfect breasts.

"Oh my God, don't look," she screeches.

I don't tell her it's a bit too late for that. Instead I grab a towel, holding it out to her, and she snatches it from me like it's a lifeline. Then something crawls across the tiles on the floor and she starts to scream again.

It took me a second to register what she's screaming about. Then I realized it's a spider. Casually strutting across the white tile like it owns the place. I reach down, scooping it into my hands.

"What are you doing?" she cries out. "Asher! No, don't touch it."

Ignoring her, I carry it to the front door, the soles of my shoes leaving wet marks as I walk. Opening the front door just wide enough, I release the little spider into the wild. It skitters off into the grass like it didn't just commit war crimes against the woman I'm obsessed with.

When I return to the bathroom, she's pressed into the corner, towel wrapped tight around her chest, her hair dripping down her back.

"I hate you," she mutters.

"For saving the spider?" Maybe I should have killed it. But I couldn't bring myself to.

She shakes her head. "For seeing me like this. This is *not* how our first encounter was supposed to go."

"It's hardly our first encounter," I point out. "I've known you for years."

"That's not what I mean." Her face screws up and I find it stupidly endearing.

A smile pulls at my lips. "I've seen you come," I point out. "Multiple times. And you're embarrassed about me seeing you naked?"

Her jaw drops.

"I've watched you beg for me," I say, my voice low. "Heard you moan my name. And now you're freaking out because I saw you wet and on the floor?" I'm not sure I'll ever fully understand the way a woman thinks.

Francie scowls, clutching the towel tighter. "It's not the same, Asher. You watched me on camera. This is different."

"Different how?"

She lets out a huff. "I had some dignity for one."

"You still have dignity," I say softly. I take a step toward her, letting myself look at her again. Her cheeks are flushed, there are damp strands of hair clinging to her neck. I go to reach for her, to comfort her, but then I see it.

A thin trail of blood slides down from her hairline, weaving its way toward her shoulder.

"Francie." I step forward, my tone changing. "You're bleeding."

She blinks. "What?"

She reaches up to touch it, and I catch the tremble in her fingers.

And for a moment, she's not the confident, teasing woman I've been watching all week.

She's vulnerable.

There's something in her eyes, raw and unguarded – like she's waiting for me to decide whether she matters.

And fuck, it undoes me faster than the spider ever could.

I reach out, brushing her wet hair gently aside, and see a small gash right behind her ear.

"Does it hurt?" I ask urgently. I've been first aid trained. We all have in the company. Security doesn't only mean fighting the bad guys, it means taking care of the good ones.

But all the training doesn't help the panic I feel at seeing blood running down her neck. "Jesus, we need to get you to the hospital."

"It's nothing," she tells me. "I'm not going to the hospital. They'll laugh me out of the ER."

"Sit," I tell her, nodding at the closed toilet lid. "I'll get the first aid kit." I know it's in the kitchen. Every time Autumn moves, I make sure it's stocked and up to date. With a determined step, I head toward the hallway, but right before I leave, I glance back.

Francie's sitting now. Her towel is hugged around her. Her eyes meet mine and I feel it. That need, that ache. That constant want that's taken me over.

My hands start to shake as I turn toward the hallway. Not because she's half naked. Or bleeding. Or looking at me like I'm the only thing that's keeping her together.

It's not because I care. Not because I feel like I'd burn the whole world down if anything happened to her.

No. It's just adrenaline. At least that's what I tell myself.

twenty

FRANCIE

This is not how I expected our first time to play out.

I'm flat on my back in bed, a bandage stuck to my scalp, a cup of lukewarm peppermint tea dying a slow death on my nightstand, with Asher Fitzgerald role playing nurse-maid like he's Florence Nightingale with a six-pack and a god complex.

After he cleaned up my cut, his jaw clenched like he was prepping for surgery instead of popping a Band-Aid on a glorified paper cut, he handed me a fresh pair of pajamas and ordered me to rest. And by ordered, I mean full-on alpha command.

He's been checking on me every hour like he's running a concussion protocol. Sticking his head around the door to ask things like "What day is it?" and "How many fingers am I holding up?" and "Do you feel dizzy?"

Yes, Doctor Doom, I feel dizzy. From your abrupt change from hot sex god to qualified head trauma surgeon.

Because what I haven't done is kiss him. Or touch him. Or scream his name while he's actually in my damn room instead of at the other end of a camera feed like the world's hottest voyeur.

The tension between us is suffocating. He's all chiseled restraint and clenched jaw and I'm one deep breath away from combusting.

So I sit up, rip off the unnecessary bandage, and shake out my hair, which now looks like I've lost a wrestling match with a sea witch.

And then I march straight into the living room.

But I don't get the chance to deliver my ultimatum. Because there he is, lounging on the sofa like a cover model for Moody Men Monthly, one ankle propped on his knee, his brows dipped in concentration as he flips a page.

Of my manuscript.

The one I printed earlier. The one that's supposed to be sitting on my desk, waiting for me to go through it with a red pen.

The one he's very much not supposed to know about, let alone reading.

I come to a stop, mid stomp, my heart doing a triple axel in my chest. "What are you doing?" I ask with a panicked voice. It's clearly not as intimidating as I'd hoped.

He doesn't even look up. Just turns another page and mutters, "This scene. Chapter sixteen. Is this guy supposed to be me?"

My jaw drops.

Oh god, he's reading *that* scene. The one with telepathy and her sending him dirty thoughts, showing him exactly how she touches herself while the brooding commander is away on maneuvers. He sends orders back. Commanding, filthy instructions laced with praise and control. But he never once touches himself.

I think I might die.

My cheeks start to flame as I step the rest of the way into the living room. "I can explain…" I tell him. Oh god. "It's just a story. Fiction. Completely made up." I'm babbling, trying to fix this. "And the similarities to anybody living or dead are entirely coincidental."

He lifts a brow. "Francie."

"Just because he has a jawline dangerously similar to yours means nothing. It's not like you're telepathic, is it? Unless you count the cameras as telepathy. Which they're not…"

"Francie." This time his voice is louder. More commanding. My body does weird things I'm not sure I'll ever get over.

But it does the trick. I stop talking.

He looks at me. Cool, steady, like he's cataloguing every inch of me. As if he's remembering exactly what I do when I'm alone at night with the lights off and one of his filthy little voice notes in my head.

"I've known about your books for a while," he says calmly.

My mouth opens, then closes. Heat prickles down my spine.

He's known? How long? For days. Weeks maybe. And I didn't know he knew. He watched me come undone every night and never said a damn thing.

It feels like being naked again. Not in the fun way.

"After everything that went down at the club, I needed to make sure you were safe. It came up in my checks."

I blink. "Why didn't you say anything?"

"It wasn't my business to say anything. Generally, if

people are hiding things and not hurting others by doing so, I assume there's a reason behind it."

A weird feeling comes over me. Guilt. I was so angry at him after that, yet he kept my secret. My heart feels so tender it might be bruised.

He leans back, the manuscript in his lap, looking entirely too comfortable considering I'm melting down.

"You don't think it's your business when your literary alter ego is telling my alter ego to touch herself in graphic detail?" I ask, trying to ground myself.

A corner of his mouth lifts. He's smirking, goddamn it.

"I do have a question for you, though," he murmurs. "Why do you keep it a secret? I'm guessing my sister knows."

"You didn't ask her?" I ask. Autumn would never be able to stay quiet under an Asher interrogation.

"As I said, not my secret."

I take a deep breath. "Yes, she knows. And my cousin Charlie. Plus my editor. That's it."

"The rest of your family doesn't know?" he asks, his brows knitting. "Why not?"

"I just..." I exhale softly, pushing my unbrushed-dried mess of hair from my face. "I guess at first I wanted to succeed under my own efforts. Not because I'm a Salinger, or because my brothers gave me a boost. Half of my family works in publishing. I hated the thought that I'd be viewed as a nepo baby. And then there's what I write." I sigh. "My brothers really don't need to read some of those scenes."

Asher says nothing. Just looks at me like I'm an algorithm for him to be studied and dissected.

I keep going, because the dam's cracked now. "The longer I kept it quiet, the harder it was to come clean. Now if they found out, they'd be hurt that I never told them. I guess I'm stuck."

His expression softens. "You know what I think?" he murmurs.

"No, but I'm guessing it's going to be wrapped in some gruff, emotionally unavailable big-brother type advice."

That earns me a faint smile.

"I think they'd be proud. I would be if it was one of my sisters. I'd be fucking delighted for her. I'd want to shout it from the rooftops. You've created a world, you delight your readers. I've read your reviews, Francie. You don't get those kind of raving reviews because you're a Salinger. You get them because you're damn good at what you do."

His honesty hits harder than I expect. It feels like he believes in me. Not because I'm a Salinger. Or because he's trying to get in my pants. But because he sees me. And that's scarier than anything.

Even the spider.

"You should tell them. It's not good to hide things. Not from those you love."

I push my emotions down, because I don't like how they make me feel. "That's kind of rich coming from you," I point out. "You're like Fort Knox when it comes to secrets."

"I am?" He tips his head to the side. Leaning forward, he lays the manuscript on the coffee table, then stands.

I have to lift my face to keep my gaze on his.

"You hide everything," I say softly. "Your feelings. Your past. Your real motivations."

He doesn't flinch. Just watches me, his jaw tight.

Then his eyes drop to my mouth, his voice a low rumble. "That's because I like to savor things, Francie. I don't rush what I know is going to wreck me."

My breath catches. He thinks I'm going to wreck him? Why does that feel so hot?

Without letting my brain overthink it, I roll onto the balls of my feet and press myself against him.

"Sometimes you need to stop savoring and start wrecking," I whisper.

His dark eyes lock on mine. His jaw flexes, his hand lifts like he's going to touch me, but then he freezes. His fingers hover inches from my face, his knuckles pale with tension.

"No," he says hoarsely. "You hit your head."

"I'm fine," I whisper. I look at him, my eyes wide and I swear he winces.

"You're not fine." He pulls back an inch, and I wince at the rejection. "The second I touch you I'm not going to be able to stop."

The air pulses between us. My body aches for him. *Kiss me, dammit.*

But instead he steps back, just enough for it to physically hurt, and turns away.

"You should lie down," he says, not looking at me anymore. "And I need to do some work. I'll use Parker's office. Shout if you need me."

And just like that he's gone.

But I'm not.

Not really.

Because if he thinks he can hold back forever, he doesn't know me at all.

And I've got just the plan to ruin him.

* * *

ASHER

. . .

An hour later, I'm on a video call with Brad, who's taking me through the server resilience upgrades, a dry subject at the best of times, but right now I can barely bring myself to care what he's saying about contingency improvements and the new three-tier protocol we've installed for client-side encryption.

I like my deputy, I really do, but right now all I can think about is *her*. Lying in bed in the next room. The way she looked at me an hour ago, like I was the only thing keeping her upright, makes me want to end this call and stride right in there. There's a tightness in my chest. It feels suspiciously like anger, but I'm not sure who I'm angry at. Her or me.

Maybe both.

All I know is that I'm a hair's breadth away from storming into her room and showing her just how fucking furious I am.

I take a breath. She's hurt. She needs to rest.

"So then we added the rolling back-up redundancy to the client side key vaults, just in case anyone tries to replicate the previous breach vector again..."

Brad's voice fades into static as my phone vibrates next to the keyboard. I glance down at it.

Turn the bedroom camera on. – Francie

My mouth goes dry. Every rational part of my brain says to ignore it. But rationality has taken a back seat ever since I walked through the lighthouse door. Hell, ever since she texted me that first night and shattered into a million pieces in front of my eyes.

I adjust myself in my seat. And of course I turn the fucking camera on.

Brad is still talking, but it sounds like background noise, competing with the sound of blood rushing through my ears.

"What do you think?" he asks.

"Right," I murmur, dragging my eyes away from the screen long enough to unmute myself. "We should definitely... yeah. Do that."

Like a magnet, my gaze is dragged back to the second window on my monitor. To her. In bed. Bare shoulders, hair mussed. She's staring straight at the camera again, those wide eyes that short-circuit every single coherent thought I've ever had.

She knows exactly what she's doing. And I'm falling for it like a rookie.

"I'll send over the test results by the end of day," Brad says. "And while I have you, I wanted to run through the revised reporting interface for—"

The covers fall from Francie's chest. Revealing her perfectly round breasts.

My throat locks. She's doing it on purpose, there's no doubt about that. She's challenging me. Teasing me. And every part of me wants to rise to the bait.

But Brad is still talking.

I hit the unmute button. "I have to go," I tell him, my voice thick. I can't even pretend I'm sane anymore. Especially when she removes the sheets from the rest of her body. Revealing her completely bare body in all of its glory. Fuck, I want to touch her. I want to do everything to her. Make her cheeks pink up and her breath shorten as I make her come, over and over again until she's an orgasmic mess.

Brad blinks, uncertainty pulling at his features. "Is everything okay?"

No, everything is a fucking disaster. My body's on fire. I'm seconds away from breaking my own rules, and the woman I can't stop thinking about is naked and challenging me through a goddamn security feed.

"It's a personal matter," I manage to bite out. "We'll circle back on this tomorrow."

I don't wait for him to reply before I end the call. And then I push back from the desk, feeling one breath away from losing control.

If she wants to play games, she'd better be ready for me to play.

Because I always win.

twenty-one

FRANCIE

His footsteps hit the hallway floor like thunder. There's no doubt in my mind, he's coming for me. It's the second time today he's stormed toward me like a one-man battalion, but this time I'm not naked and flailing on the floor while screaming at a spider.

This time I'm in control.

I lie back on the pillows, my smile wicked, because I know exactly what he's going to see when the door bursts open. I'm propped up on the pillows, my dark hair a contrast to the white silk. My body is bare, my nipples are pebbled, and I have to concentrate hard to remember how to breathe.

The door slams open and he barges in. There's a wildness to his eyes that makes my heart thud against my ribcage. He slides his gaze over my body and I feel it viscerally. He takes every inch of me in, his breath catching in his throat.

"Are you trying to drive me insane?" he asks me.

I shrug nonchalantly, a smile playing at my lips. "You seem very tense," I murmur. "I thought you might need a release."

He steps closer. There's no smile on *his* face. Just a taut jaw and dark eyes that make me feel like I'm the most beautiful woman on the planet. "You're supposed to be resting," he tells me.

My smile widens. Sometimes this man is so easy to rile up. "I can't rest," I moan, running my hand over my stomach, trailing my fingers just above where I need him. "I'm aching."

His lips part. He can't tear his eyes away from my hands. "Francie..."

"What?" I murmur. "Sir?"

Okay, maybe that was too much. But the way my body flushes says otherwise. Oh god, I want him to command me.

Just in bed. Nowhere else. My stomach fizzes with anticipation.

"Where does it hurt?" he asks. I don't know if he's playing along or genuinely interested. I guess I'm about to find out.

"Right here," I whisper. Sliding my finger down. Over myself. I'm so wet it isn't funny. "I ache for you."

He closes his eyes for a moment. He looks almost pained, like there's a battle waging inside him.

I hope bad Asher wins. I really do.

When he opens his eyes they're blazing. Heated. Dangerous.

"I'm the one in control here," he mutters. I'm not sure who he's trying to persuade – me or him.

"Are you?" I ask softly. I never knew flirting like this

could be so much fun. I love the way he reacts to me. It's addictively hot.

He doesn't answer me. Just stalks toward me, like a lion hunting a gazelle. There's a twitch in his jaw as he shakes his head. Before I can say anything else he suddenly drops to his knees, like he's going to say a prayer.

But instead of placing his palms together, he runs them slowly up my thighs, then pushes them apart firmly.

I'm bare to him. Completely and utterly. And he's staring at me, like a man gazing at a work of art. Appreciative. Coveting.

His breath starts to speed.

"You have such a pretty pussy," he murmurs. "All pink and glistening."

My cheeks pink up. I knew he liked to talk dirty. He's done it enough over the phone. But face to face, while he's touching me. It's a whole other orgasm-inducing level.

"Asher…"

"You don't say a fucking word," he tells me. He leans in, his eyes closing and he sniffs me.

Is that a thing? Do men sniff women? Nobody has ever done that to me before. Yet I think it might be the hottest thing I've ever experienced.

I add it to my list of micro tropes I have to put in my book before all thoughts of dragons and soldiers rush out of my head.

"Perfect," he mutters. His lips press to the inside of my thigh, hot and reverent. I shiver, already on the verge of breaking. Not from fear. From anticipation. From the sheer weight of his gaze on my skin. I feel every cell in my body vibrating. Waiting. Needing.

He kisses my other thigh, his lips teasingly warm, then he looks up at me through hooded eyes. "Do you know what it was like, watching you fall apart every night on my screen. Knowing I couldn't touch you?"

I shake my head breathlessly.

"It was torture, Francie. Pure agony. I wanted to taste you. To feel you. To make you come so much you'd be begging me to stop."

I can't remember how to breathe.

And then his tongue flicks out to taste me. Just a slow, single stroke, and I lose every coherent thought in my brain.

"Oh God," I gasp, my head falling back.

"He won't help you." For the first time a smile flickers across his lips. Like he knows the tables have turned. The hunter is being hunted.

And I've never wanted to be caught more in my life.

"You're already so wet for me," he says, running a finger along my opening. Then he presses it between his lips, his tongue flicking.

"Asher..." I need him. Oh god, I need him.

"What did I tell you? No talking."

It's a game. I know it. I love it. My body responds to it like it's a dance it has always known the steps to – a timeless waltz only we can follow.

His thumbs press gently into my skin, parting me wider. His mouth follows. I feel his warm breath on me, so tantalizingly close to what I need. Then he devours. Not gentle this time. Full of intent. Savoring, worshipping, fucking me. My fingers flutter down, raking through his silky hair, my nails scraping his scalp.

He groans out my name and it vibrates through me in the most pleasurable of ways.

I want to cry out. I want to say his name. I want to beg him. But I have to keep my lips clamped together to stop myself. *No talking.* Instead I let him take the lead, dragging pleasure out of me with every lash of his tongue.

And then he pushes a finger inside of me and groans again.

"So tight," he mutters. "Fuck."

It's too much. It's not enough. I'm being undone with every touch.

It's so clear by the way he uses one hand to press down my stomach, the other to tease me into oblivion, that I'm not in control anymore. Maybe I never was.

I arch against him, unable to stop the way my hips buck to meet every stroke of his tongue, every curl of his fingers. My thighs are trembling; my world is narrowing to nothing but the slick heat of his mouth and the filthy sounds he makes as he devours me like I'm his last ever meal.

He pushes a second finger in, cursing at my tightness, then curls them, just slightly, but enough for the delicious pressure in my belly to uncoil. Stars start to burst behind my eyelids. I'm one tongue lash away from climaxing.

And then he pulls back.

I whimper, the sudden emptiness making my eyes snap open.

He looks at me, his mouth wet with my slickness. "You don't get to come until I say so," he growls. "You gave me control. Don't think about taking it back now."

I open my mouth, not too proud to beg, but he shakes his head, reminding me that the game is still on. I'm still not allowed to speak.

And then he stands, unbuttoning his shirt, his eyes not leaving my face.

His chest is pure sin. Broad, sculpted. I follow every ridge of his muscles, my lips aching to trace the valleys beneath them. My gaze slides down, taking in the defined cut of his abs, the sharp vee of his hips. His biceps flex as he tosses the shirt to the floor like it's offended him.

He watches me watch him. It's his turn for a dirty half-smirk. He runs his tongue along his lips then reaches for the button of his pants.

Slowly. Like he knows how tortuous this is. This is payback, I realize. He's letting me look like he's looked at me all week. Letting me ache like he's ached. And God, I really do.

He drags the zipper down, his cock straining beneath the fabric. It's thick as it pushes against his black shorts. My mouth feels dry as I stare at him. As he pushes his pants down and steps out of them, before following suit with his shorts.

He's fully naked. And so fully aroused it makes my thighs clench.

I want to reach for him, but I know better.

Wrapping his hand around his cock, he fists it, slowly, firmly. And I swear I almost come from that sight alone.

"Now it's your turn to watch," he rasps. "Don't move. Don't speak. Just lay there and see what you do to me."

I can't tear my eyes away from him. He's like a marble statue, all perfect lines and impossible strength.

His hand moves again. Faster this time. Rougher. He's not teasing himself the way he teased me. This is furious, raw. Like every moment he held back from me is erupting from him.

"Look at you," he growls, his eyes locked on mine. "Lying there all wrecked and needy. You have no idea what it does to me."

I can't breathe. I can't speak. I curl my fingers into the sheets like they're the only thing keeping me grounded.

"I've been dreaming about this. About you. About tasting that sweet pussy."

He drags his hand harder along his cock. His muscles are taut, strained. Like he's holding back a detonation.

"I'm going to fuck you until you forget your own name," he rasps. "Until all you can say is mine. But not now. Not yet. It's your turn to watch."

I inhale raggedly. This man is coming undone in front of me. And I've never seen anything hotter in my life.

"You think you're in control? You think you've got me undone? Baby, I've been hanging by a thread since the first night you whispered my name."

I press my thighs together. Whimpering. I'm only seconds away from begging.

He sees it. Smirks. "You want to touch yourself so badly, don't you? You want to come while you watch me lose it."

I nod, because that's all I can do.

His smile widens. "Too fucking bad."

Then he groans out my name. It's loud and rough, like it's coming from the depths of him. And I know he's so close to coming.

"I'm going to cover you with me," he groans. "I'm going to mark you. So every time you touch yourself you'll remember this. Remember that you're mine."

I nod, though I'm already his. He has to know that. His thumb trails across the head of his cock, then he steps closer to me as he comes.

With a low, broken growl of my name, his body jerks. Spilling over my skin. His hips flex once, twice. The cords of his neck taut as he throws his head back and rides the wave. He looks feral. Untamed.

Mine.

I lie there, my breath caught in my throat, watching the

way his chest heaves, his hand still loosely wrapped around his cock, glistening from release.

And when he looks at me, there's no smugness. No victory. Just hunger. I reach down, wanting to touch his release on my skin. To feel the mark he's made on me. More permanent than any tattoo.

But he's not done. Not even close.

"I told you not to move," he says hoarsely, his voice wrecked from his release.

I don't speak. I don't dare. I want to play this game forever.

"Come here," he says, his gaze sliding down my body like he's already planning his next sin.

I blink at him. Confused for a second. But then I do as he tells me, scrambling to my knees and crawling across the bed to him. It doesn't feel demeaning, though. The way he stares at me makes me feel on top of the world.

He curls his fingers around my hair, fisting it, then pulls back until my face is tilted, looking at his.

And then he kisses me.

His kiss isn't dirty or demanding. It's reverent, like he's worshipping me with his mouth. His lips press against mine, slowly at first, as though he's trying to prolong the first touch, to memorize every curve, every sigh, every shiver that trembles from my body.

My hair is still in his hand, but he's not pulling anymore. He's holding. Steadying. Like I'm something precious he's afraid he might drop and break.

It makes my heart stutter.

My fingers curl around his shoulders, feeling the warmth of his skin. He's damp with sweat. Still tense. I feel the rise and fall of his breath as he tries to catch it.

Pulling back, he rests his brow against mine, our breaths mixing.

"You undo me," he whispers. And those three words hit harder than anything else. I stare up at him, feeling an ache in my chest that matches the one between my thighs.

Then, before I can even breathe in, it's like a switch has flipped. His grip tightens, his eyes darken. Bad Asher is back.

"Now," he rasps, voice raw as he climbs into bed next to me. "I want you on my face."

My breath catches. "What?" I whisper.

"You heard me. Ride me, Francie. I want to taste you again. Until you fall apart."

I hesitate for a beat. Not because I don't want it. I think I might cry if I don't come soon. But because nobody has ever asked for me like this. Like I'm the treat. Like I'm the one who deserves to be worshiped.

Asher sees the flicker of uncertainty in my eyes. And he shuts it down with one look.

"I'm the one in control," he murmurs, leaning back against the pillows and dragging me with him. "So don't you dare deny me this."

I climb over him slowly, planting one knee on either side of his head. My heart is beating like a war drum. Bracing my hands on the headboard, I try not to shake.

"You're perfect," he murmurs. "Now put your cunt on my face."

It should sound awful. So dirty. But somehow he makes it pretty. Like he's asking politely.

So I do it.

And he groans so deep it rumbles far into my bones.

His mouth finds me instantly. He's hungry, possessive, a man starved. There's no niceties, no soft beginnings. Just his lips and tongue taking me apart piece by piece. He groans like I'm his favorite flavor, his hands gripping my thighs, keeping me over his mouth since I can't help but rock against him.

I lose the rhythm quickly. My body's trembling, my arms shaking as I clutch the headboard like it's a life raft. He devours me like I'm his last meal. Like I was made just for him.

Maybe I was.

My thighs clench. My breath shatters. My vision blurs.

And when my orgasm hits, it's physical and emotional and shatters something deep inside of me. A sob catches in my throat as he holds me close, letting me ride the wave he's created.

And then I collapse. A warm, boneless heap on his perfect body.

He catches me easily, wrapping me in his strong arms, pulling me down beside him. I bury my face in the crook of his neck, pleasure still wracking my body.

Asher doesn't speak. He just holds me, one hand running along my spine, the other curled possessively around me.

The only sound in the room is our shared breath. And the steady thump of our hearts.

He presses a kiss to my temple. It's so sweet it makes my breath catch.

"That," he murmurs against my skin, "was worth every second I've waited for you."

And somehow, I know he's not only talking about tonight.

twenty-two

ASHER

Francie falls asleep about two minutes after I make her come, muttering about needing to feel me inside of her. Her hand is resting on my chest, her cheek pressed against my shoulder like I'm her favorite pillow. Her hair is tickling my skin but I don't give a shit.

She looks peaceful. Spent. Beautiful.

I brush a strand of hair off her face, letting my fingers linger at her temple. Her skin is warm, flushed from the orgasm. The soft flutter of her breath is rhythmic against my ribs, like the aftershock of a storm.

I should leave. I should never have come.

Fuck, I should never have watched her come every night for a week on the cameras for me. And I absolutely should never have done this.

And yet I can't bring myself to feel sorry about it.

She lets out a sigh against my skin, and it makes my cock swell. Her skin is still coated with me. The perfect mix of innocence and dirtiness does things to me that nobody else can.

I stare up at the ceiling, feeling the darkness coming. It always does, in the end. Memories press against my brain like an unhealed wound.

The stifling dark. The splintered wood. My father's screams echoing off the walls as I cowered inside that fucking closet. The way they merged with my own.

I swore I'd never let anybody hurt me again. Yet right now I feel more fucking vulnerable than that kid ever did, letting this woman burrow under my skin like she belongs there.

Like she couldn't break me apart if she wanted to.

I pull back from the edge of those memories, grounding myself in the softness of Francie's breath.

The sound of my phone buzzing in the pocket of my pants on the floor is a welcome relief from the dark thoughts in my head. I lean over carefully, grabbing it without disturbing her.

The screen is lit up with Hudson's name.

Shit.

I don't answer. Even I can't pull off an easy conversation with my brother while in bed with my sister's best friend. And I'm not in the mood for a Fitzgerald family interrogation.

A moment later, a message pops up.

Why are you back on Liberty? And why are you at the lighthouse? – Hudson

. . .

Of course he's tracking me. We all do it. From the first time we got smart phones we could follow each other. We protect each other. Take care of our own.

But now it feels like an intrusion.

I thumb out a quick reply.

Was heading back to work on the security system. Francie hurt her head. I'm keeping an eye on her in case of a concussion. – Asher

It's not even a lie. Not really.

Francie shifts against me with a soft sigh, stretching out like a cat. Her hand drifts lower, brushing my stomach, sending sparks through my nerves.

She blinks sleepily, her cheek still resting against my shoulder. "Was that your phone?"

I nod, glancing down at the screen as it lights up again. This time it's not a message – it's a FaceTime call. From Skyler. "For fuck's sake," I mutter, pressing decline. "Why don't they know when to stop?"

My phone buzzes *again*. I look over at Francie and she's trying hard not to laugh. I roll my eyes at her. The last thing I need is to FaceTime with my sister-in-law, while I'm naked in bed.

In Francie's bed.

I love Skyler to death, but the woman has no off button. The whole village would know in less than an hour.

Skyler says pick up. She wants to know if Francie is okay. – Hudson

. . .

I mutter a dark oath under my breath and Francie lifts a brow. "What's going on?" she asks, leaning over to read the message.

"Hudson wanted to know why I'm at the lighthouse," I tell her.

Francie's eyes widen. "How does he know you're here?"

"We can track each other." I shrug. "Anyway, I told them about you hurting your head and now they want proof of life, apparently."

Francie's phone starts to ring. She lifts it from the nightstand and starts to giggle, showing it to me.

Skyler. At least this time it's a call not FaceTime, thank fuck.

"I'm going to answer it," Francie tells me. "Before they send out a search party and find us like this."

I nod and she swipes it to answer.

"Hey, Skye."

I hear Skyler's voice immediately. Clipped and concerned. "Are you okay? Hudson said you hit your head. Why didn't you call me? Should I come over?"

Francie mouths *help*.

Welcome to my world, baby.

"I'm fine," she says, brushing her hair behind her ear. "It was just a bump."

"You sure?" Skyler presses. "Hudson said Asher's staying the night to keep an eye on you."

Francie shoots me a look that's one part panic and two parts amusement.

"Go with it," I mouth at her.

"Yeah," she says smoothly. "He was already on the island, and Autumn's not here, so it made sense."

"Mhmm." Skyler says, clearly not convinced but also not wanting to pick a fight with an injured woman. "Well okay. I'll stop by tomorrow to check on you. I'll bring you a coffee and croissant from Mylene's."

"You really don't have to," Francie says quickly.

"Too late," Skyler cuts in. "And tell Asher I said thank you. Be good."

She ends the call. "What's that supposed to mean?" she asks me as she puts her phone down. "She just told me to be good."

"I don't know," I say honestly. Trying to understand Skyler is a fool's game.

"Well, we have less than twelve hours before your sister-in-law turns up with coffee and questions."

"I like coffee," I murmur, dragging my fingers along her thigh. Because a lot can happen in twelve hours.

And I intend to make it count. Turning in bed, the phone calls forgotten, I catch her mouth with mine. But the rumble that comes from deep inside her has nothing to do with the delicious way our tongues tangle.

And everything to do with hunger of the food variety.

She starts to laugh against my lips, the sound warm but shaky. "I'm sorry. Apparently orgasms aren't a sustainable food group."

I grin, brushing her hair from her face. "Your body went through a workout. You need to eat."

"I can wait," she whispers, dragging her fingers down my chest. Her thigh shifts over mine, warm and insistent. "Please don't make me wait. I need you."

Fuck.

My entire body tightens. She doesn't know what she's asking. Or maybe she does. Either way, I'm seconds from giving in.

But I can't. Not yet.

I cup her face, kissing her gently. "If I take you now, it won't be slow, Francie. I've been holding back for longer than you can imagine. And you need food, not just me."

She groans, dropping her forehead to my shoulder like I just canceled Christmas. "This is torture."

"I'm trying to take care of you," I murmur against her hair. "You almost passed out earlier. Your head took a hit. And I promised myself that the first time I'm inside of you, you'll feel everything. No distractions. No weakness. Just us."

She lifts her head and glares at me, all flushed and glowing and gloriously naked. "You're lucky you're hot," she mutters.

I chuckle, rolling out of bed and reaching for my pants. "You have no idea how lucky you are that I'm being noble right now."

She props herself on her elbow, watching me with narrowed eyes. "This better be the fastest meal in history."

I glance over my shoulder, letting my gaze roam over her naked, still-glowing body. "It will be," I promise. "And after," I tell her, dragging my eyes across every inch of her flushed, satisfied skin, "I'm going to fuck you until you know exactly who you belong to."

* * *

FRANCIE

In the time it takes me to drag myself up and out of bed, Asher is already showered, dressed, and banging around in the kitchen like he's auditioning for Hot Chefs of Liberty

Island. His collar is damp from his hair, his jaw shadowed because he obviously forgot – or couldn't be bothered – to shave this morning, and his biceps flex every time he lifts a pan. He looks annoyingly put together.

Meanwhile, I look like I just crawled out of bed after being thoroughly debauched. Which, to be fair, I was.

I need to shower. But right now, I'm standing in the hallway, eyeing the bathroom like it might attack me at any minute.

I don't want a repeat of earlier. Getting caught naked and shrieking on the floor isn't exactly part of my seduction playbook.

If I had one, that is.

"You need backup?" Asher asks, amusement in his voice. He's standing in the kitchen doorway watching me. "You know I'm fully trained in spider relocation and post-trauma naked recovery."

Stupid smirky handsome guy. "You're not helping."

He lifts a brow. "That's not what you said earlier."

I stick my tongue out at him, because apparently I'm five years old, then push the bathroom door open like I'm storming a castle.

But of course, there's no spider there. He's long gone, freed by Asher the Magnificent. And now, of course, I'm thinking about the way he made me come. I definitely need a cold shower.

I clean myself faster than the speed of light, managing to wash my hair, body, and shave myself everywhere. When I'm dry, I dress in shorts and a soft tank top, finally feeling human again.

When I pad into the kitchen, Asher's at the stove, flipping what looks suspiciously like chocolate pancakes. My stomach growls in betrayal.

He looks over his shoulder, his gaze heated as he takes me in. "Took you long enough. I was about to send in a SWAT team."

I roll my eyes at him. "Why is it that I believe you would?"

He chuckles softly. God, I like this side of him. I'm not sure I've ever seen him look so... relaxed. Maybe when we were younger, I don't know. All I do know is that I like it. Way too much.

"Where did you find the pancake mix?" I ask. I can't remember seeing a box in the cupboard.

"In the egg carton, flour jar, and milk jug." He shakes his head.

"Oh, you're one of those people who think pre-made mixes are the devil." I lean over and grab one of the pancakes he's already stacked.

His head whips around. "You did not just steal my pancake," he growls.

I deliberately lift it to my mouth, my eyes on his as I take a ginormous bite. The adult equivalent of licking a stolen cookie. I let out a low groan. Damn, the man can cook.

"You say steal," I say through bites. "I say taste test."

"Put it back."

The way he says it sends a shiver down my spine. Like it enjoys his commanding voice way too much.

"I bit it. It's mine."

His grin is feral. "Give it back or I'll make you."

I take another bite. There's barely a morsel left, but I don't care. I hold it like a treasure.

"You wouldn't dare."

"Try me."

I take a step back, feeling protective of the tiny pancake

remains in my fingers. He turns off the burner and steps toward me, closing the gap between us in one easy stride.

Then he reaches for my hand.

I pull it away, ducking behind the tiny kitchen table, trying not to laugh. God, this is stupid. But riling Asher up is officially becoming my favorite pastime. "If you want it, you're going to have to catch me first," I tell him.

"We're in a lighthouse. You have nowhere to run." His voice is low. Teasing. My body heats up. He walks around the table, but I've already started to run, almost making it to the kitchen door before his arm wraps around my waist, spinning me around until my body slams against his.

I can feel every hard plane pressing into me. And a hard ridge, too. Heat pools inside me. "Remind me to teach you self-defense," he murmurs, running his nose along my neck like he's an animal, breathing me in.

I deliberately pull my head back and slide the last piece of pancake between my lips. "Mmm," I say. "Stolen pancakes taste the best."

He reaches behind him. "You forgot the maple syrup," he says, his voice teasing. He flicks the lid open with his thumb.

"Oh no, don't you dare." I try – and fail – to squirm from his hold.

But he does. He squeezes out a large dribble of syrup on my collarbone, watching with amusement as it trickles down my cleavage. Sticky and wet.

"Dammit, I just showered." I pout at him.

He leans his head down, licking a long, slow trail across my skin. His tongue follows the syrup's path like he's savoring every drop. I swear I have a mini-orgasm. I grab onto his shoulders to stay upright.

His mouth finds my neck. His tongue hot and purposeful. His hand feathers my side, his thumb right below my breast. My nipples press hard and needy against my top.

"Asher..."

He lowers his head, running his tongue over my nipple through the thin fabric. "Hush," he murmurs against my breast. "Take your punishment like a woman." His mouth closes around my nipple, wet heat soaking through my tank as he sucks gently, then bites. My knees nearly give out from pleasure.

"This isn't in the Geneva Convention," I mutter, my fingers digging into his shoulders.

He looks up, his eyes dark as they gaze into mine. I try to read his expression, but this man is a master at hiding them. He takes my chin in his palm, lifting his head to capture my mouth. He kisses me slowly, like he's savoring me. His tongue is soft, his lips warm, his hand gentle as he cups my neck and deepens our connection, his body pressing against mine.

"Fuck, you're beautiful," he rasps when we break for air.

I taste of pancake. There's a cut behind my ear and my hair is dripping water from my shower. And yet this man makes me feel like I'm the center of the universe.

Like I'm his.

He picks me up without warning, setting me on the kitchen counter like I weigh nothing. The cool granite against my bare thighs makes me shiver.

"Tell me if you're sore," he murmurs, kissing along my collarbone.

"From your fingers?" I ask breathlessly. "No. They're not that big."

His eyes flash, wicked heat sparking behind them. "Not exactly the words any man wants to hear," he says, but he's grinning.

I laugh, soft and warm, but there's something fluttering in my chest. I wrap my legs around his waist and touch his cheek, tracing the stubble along his jaw.

He leans into me, putting his weight against me, and for a moment, the playful tension shifts into something deeper. Something real. I swallow hard, the heaviness of it pressing on my chest as much as his body.

"Asher..."

He tips his head to the side, like the way I say his name does something to him.

I take a deep breath. "I'm not... I don't..." Well this is excruciating. "I'm not as experienced as you are."

He watches me like I just handed him something priceless.

"Are you a virgin?" There's a softness to his voice. Like he's only now finding out something he should have known all along.

I shake my head. "No. But I haven't... done it often. And it's been a long time." I swallow, feeling suddenly vulnerable. "I just need you to know."

He lifts his hands to cup my face. "We don't have to do anything you don't want to do," he says.

"Oh god, no. I want to," I say so quickly my words stumble over each other. "I really want to. I'm just worried I might not please you."

He looks at me silently. Like he's assessing me. Then his thumbs stroke my cheeks, his gaze on mine. "Francie," he says, low and rough. "You please me just by looking at me the way you do. You saw me come apart just by touching myself. That was due to you. All of you. You might not have been touching me, but every part of my body could feel you."

He presses his brow to mine. "You've been the only

thing I could think about all week. The only person that got me through my days. I couldn't fucking wait to get home and watch you." He takes a breath, like his confession is making him just as vulnerable. "You say you're inexperienced, but I am too. In this. In being obsessed by something other than work." He shakes his head. "You have no idea what you do to me, do you?"

The way the hard ridge of him presses against me, I'm starting to figure that one out.

"If you need gentle," he murmurs, kissing my neck. "I'll be so fucking gentle it'll make you sigh."

I drag my fingers through his hair, his lips against my throat making me shiver.

"I don't want gentle," I whisper. "I want you. All of you. Everywhere. I want you inside of me, fucking me. Making me come so hard I forget my own name."

He smiles against my skin, lifting his head. Food forgotten, his hands slide around my waist as he hitches me up, my legs wrapping around his waist like an overexcited monkey, carrying me back to the bedroom.

The bed is unmade, the sheets kicked to the floor, but I don't care. He lays me down like I'm precious, then straightens upright, his eyes locked on mine as he unbuttons his shirt – slowly and deliberately – like he knows he's baring a masterpiece and wants me to admire every stroke.

I pull my tank over my head and shimmy out of my shorts, my breath catching at the way he watches me. Like I'm a piece of art he's outbid everybody in the room on.

"Francie," he says hoarsely, stripping off the last of his clothes. My eyes drop, and I swear I forget how to breathe. The thick ridge of him strains against his shorts. Every part of me clenches in nervous anticipation. I've never had anyone this big. I'm not even sure we'll fit together.

But how I want to try.

"Yes?"

"Birth control. I have condoms. Latex. You're not allergic, right?"

"No I'm not."

He nods, grabbing his wallet, taking out a silver disc. Then he pulls down his shorts, revealing that stupidly sexy, magnificent cock. Slowly, he rolls the condom on, and I can't take my eyes away.

When he climbs onto the bed, he immediately seeks out my mouth, kissing me, his hand brushing back my hair. "If it hurts you tell me."

"It's fine. You're fine."

His mouth takes mine again, slower this time, like he's trying to memorize the way I taste. He covers my body with his, warm and heavy, but he doesn't rush. One hand cups my cheek as he settles between my thighs, the other slides down between us, seeking me out, teasing me until I'm arching against him.

"You're so wet for me," he murmurs, his voice reverent and filthy all at once. "I'm not even inside of you yet, and here you are, dripping."

He flicks his fingers against me and I moan, unembarrassed by my response to him. "Please," I murmur, spreading my legs wider.

Asher groans, rubbing the head of his cock against me, teasing me, torturing me. "You want me to fill this pretty little pussy? Stretch you open with my cock."

God, he knows how to talk dirty. My whole body heats at his words.

"Yes please."

"Say my name."

"Yes, Asher. I want you inside of me."

He stares down at me like I've handed him a secret. And maybe I have.

He shifts, lining himself up, but before I can feel the blessed relief of him he pauses to kiss me again. "So fucking beautiful. The way you look at me."

And then he starts to push inside.

My breath catches in my throat as he slides into me inch by slow inch. My body stretches around him, the delicious burn making my toes curl.

He stills once he's fully seated, his brow pressed against mine. "Fuck," he groans. "You feel like heaven. So fucking tight." His eyelashes flicker against mine. "Tell me you're okay."

I kiss him, his breath warming my lips. "I'm more than okay." I'm not sure there are words to describe just how okay I am with Asher inside of me.

His mouth curves against mine. "Told you I'd go slow."

But he doesn't. Not really. Once he starts to move, with long, deep thrusts that press every inch of him right where I need him the most, my body forgets everything except him. The way he makes me feel so full. The way he kisses me when I gasp. The way he starts muttering against my skin.

My nails dig into his back. My hips rise to meet every thrust. He's everywhere, inside of me, around me, breaking me apart in all the ways I never knew I wanted.

And when he snakes a hand between us and presses a finger against me, it's over. I spiral, my whole body shaking as I unravel, crying out his name, my orgasm crashing through me like a tidal wave. He holds me through it, his rhythm faltering as I clench around him.

And in that moment, he owns me. Heart, body, and soul.

"Fuck, Francie," he groans, his voice cracking. He buries

himself deep, shuddering as he comes, his head tucked into the crook of my neck. Every muscle in his body tightens as he spills inside of me.

For a moment, we don't speak. We just lie there, tangled and breathless, our bodies still connected, our skin sticky with sweat and syrup and everything that just passed between us. My heart pounds against his in the quiet aftermath. Like it's trying to match his rhythm.

When he finally lifts his head, there's an expression on his face I can't quite read. Something tender. Something open.

"You okay?" he asks, voice raw.

I nod, too wrecked to find the words.

He leans in and presses a soft kiss to the corner of my mouth. Like a promise. Like a beginning.

Then he lowers his forehead to mine, our noses brushing. His hand finds mine on the bed, lacing our fingers together.

"I've never..." He trails off, his throat working. "That was—"

He shakes his head, like the words aren't coming. But I understand. I feel it too.

The shift. A quiet weight of something that might matter.

I squeeze his hand. "Yeah," I whisper. "Me too."

We stay like that for a moment longer, just breathing each other in. No teasing. No tension. Just him and me and this fragile bubble we've created.

He pulls the sheet over us, holding me tighter than before. "Whatever this is," he murmurs, "it's not going away."

And neither am I.

twenty-three

FRANCIE

When I shuffle into the kitchen the next morning, I feel like I've aged forty years overnight. Everything aches. My thighs, my hips, and about a dozen muscles I didn't even know existed. I blame Asher Fitzgerald and his magic wand of a cock. That thing should come with a warning label.

May cause spontaneous acrobatics and full body exhaustion.

The man himself, the cause of this pain, left an hour ago to meet Hudson at the hotel, freshly showered, shaved, and looking like a walking sex fantasy in his open-collared shirt and navy pants. At some point during the night, while I was in an orgasm-induced coma after our fourth time, he must have slipped out and gotten his travel bag ready for the morning.

He didn't say when I'd see him again. But I'm pretty sure it'll be soon. Or I hope so anyway. This island is tiny, after all.

I look over at the stove where he cooked pancakes that

we never managed to eat last night. It's pristine, just like the rest of the kitchen. He must have cleaned that up, too.

I bet if CSI walked in here right now, there'd be no evidence he was ever here. And it shouldn't bother me. This was never meant to be anything, but the silence he left behind feels bigger than the room. Like an echo I can't quiet.

He hasn't texted or called since he left, either. Not that I expected him to. I know he's busy, but the quiet hum of my phone on the counter feels louder than it should.

The doorbell rings, bringing me out of my thoughts. I take a steadying breath, forcing the ache in my chest down. It's probably Skyler, but for one foolish second, I let myself wish it were him.

When I pull the door open, Skyler stands there in full small-town FBI mode, wearing a pretty flowing skirt and a crop top, beneath a beaten up denim jacket. She's holding a coffee in one hand and what looks like an herbal tea in the other, plus a bag from Mylene's coffee shop. "Chamomile," she says, nodding at the tea. "Baby doesn't like caffeine. Or anything fun, apparently."

She follows me into the kitchen. "You look like shit," she says, pulling no punches as we walk to the kitchen. "Let me see the damage."

I touch my head. I'd forgotten I'd hurt myself until she mentioned it. "It's nothing."

But she insists, pulling my hair back, her eyes narrow as she inspects it closely. "Hmm," she says. "Just as I thought."

I blink. "What?" I ask. I can smell the pastries in the bag and my stomach growls at them.

"You smell of sex. *Fitzgerald* sex."

I roll my eyes. "If you're talking about Asher, he was a perfect gentleman," I tell her. I'm not sure I'm ready to talk about this with her. Or anybody. I also know that if Autumn finds out I've told somebody else first, it'll cause problems.

Skyler raises an eyebrow and gives me a long, meaningful look. "Uh huh. So you're walking like a baby deer on a frozen lake because he held your hand too firmly?"

"I pulled something when I fell," I mutter, lifting the coffee to my lips while I think of a better excuse. But what excuse is there for the way I'm walking like a girl who rode a horse for hours?

Skyler pulls the pastries out of the bag and hands me one. There's no judgment in her eyes. Of all the people on the island, she probably understands me the most. Like me, she didn't grow up here. But she and Hudson fell in love and now Liberty's her home.

We're still both technically out-of-towners. And I guess we've also now both slept with a Fitzgerald brother.

My heart tightens at that thought. I already miss being in his arms. More than I want to admit. And I don't want to admit it. Because that would mean this is something. That he might matter.

"Look," Skyler says softly, "I'm not trying to judge. Asher's a good guy underneath all that buttoned-up repression. But I promised Autumn I'd take care of you, and I need to know that you're okay."

I blink a little too fast. I don't know how to explain the way he made me feel, like I am something worthy. Like he saw all the parts of me I try to keep hidden and didn't flinch.

Guilt washes over me at the mention of Autumn's name. I'm standing in my best friend's house. The one she so generously said I could stay in while I try to finish my book. And instead of writing, I spent last night in every position imaginable with her brother.

Tearing a corner from the croissant, I pop it into my mouth. The buttery pastry melts on my tongue, but it doesn't quite chase away the unease curling in my stomach.

Skyler is looking at me like she knows exactly what's going through my mind. There's concern there, mixed with understanding. And maybe a little curiosity.

Okay, a lot. This is an island. Nothing exciting ever happens here, unless you count Mylene and Eileen's eternal blood feud. Skyler loves to gossip. It's not a sin.

And the truth is, I'm not sure if I can keep this inside me much longer.

"If Autumn finds out she'll kill me," I finally say. "Please don't tell her."

Skyler puts her own pastry down, her chamomile tea untouched, like I'm much more exciting than buttery layers of goodness. "Oh. My. God. You two did it!" She claps her hands together. "But why wouldn't you tell Autumn? She's your best friend, isn't she?"

"Of course she is. And I will tell her. Depending on what happens between me and Asher. But I want to do it face to face. She knows me too well. She'll know that it wasn't just one night. There's backstory. I need to find a way to break it to her that doesn't have her thinking I've been lying to her."

"I love backstory," Skyler says. "Gimme." Then she frowns. "Oh no. Maybe don't gimme. If I find out any more, I'm going to end up spilling my guts to Hudson. Then everybody's going to find out. Damn it." She pouts like I've just ruined her favorite game.

"You don't have to know everything," I tell her, feeling sorry for her because I hate being left in the dark, too. It happened too many times in my childhood. I was too young and innocent to be involved in family business. It used to drive me wild. "Just know that I'm fine. Apart from every muscle in my body aching because Asher's dick is completely addictive."

Skyler chokes on her tea. "Jesus, Francie."

I grin. "Sorry, did I say that out loud?"

Dabbing at her mouth with a napkin, Skyler looks me in the eye. "Don't say sorry. I just wasn't prepared for it from you. You have this innocent look about you." She shakes her head. "Tell me, is he good?"

"Amazing."

And then, because I'm a glutton for punishment and it feels like we're bonding, I tell her about the book I'm writing. About my secret life and the way not many people know I'm an author.

"Oh god, I think I'm going to die," Skyler says when she's finished grilling me, and has promised me she'll keep my secret. "This is the best thing to happen to me since I discovered Hudson's high school yearbook. Let's just say the man cannot rock a mullet." She grins.

I laugh at the image that conjures up. "I don't remember him having a mullet." Though that was probably before I met Autumn.

"He didn't. I just scanned the photo and photoshopped him one. Then stuck copies everywhere around the house." She wrinkles her nose. "I might have wanted to trigger him into teaching me a lesson."

"And did he?"

"Oh yes." Her eyes go a little dreamy. "Angry Hudson is the best Hudson."

Our gazes lock. There's a knowing look between them. Because I'm pretty hot for furious Asher, too.

"You're glowing," she says. "I don't know how you think you're going to hide all these secrets from everybody. One look at you and they're all going to know."

"Good thing I'll be staying here at the lighthouse and hiding away," I say lightly. And possibly hoping that Asher comes back to check on my very real sex injuries this evening.

She frowns. "You can't do that. You have to come to my dinner party this evening."

"I'm what?" I ask. "What dinner party? I never agreed to that."

Letting out a sigh, Skyler gives me a puppy dog look. "Hudson's having guests over. Boring ones. It'll be all business talk and repressed New York boredom. You have to come keep me company. It's your duty."

"I'm supposed to be writing my book," I point out. And having sex with Asher. I don't say that one out loud, but I think she gets the point.

"Okay, fine. I'll tell Hudson you're too busy rubbing uglies with his brother to spend time with the loneliest girl on the island." She's joking. At least I think she's joking. But I get the point.

And I do get it. Business dinners are the most boring things in the world. I've been through enough of them while growing up to know that. Small talk and one-upmanship, mixed with a splash of passive-aggressive bragging and the occasional 'my kid got into Yale' humblebrag. It's not exactly my idea of a fun night out.

Sensing weakness, Skyler bats her eyelashes at me. "Martin is catering. And he's making a chocolate volcano dessert."

I groan at the thought of Martin's cooking. The hotel chef has worked in Michelin-starred restaurants all over the world. "Fine, I'll come. But only because you bribed me."

She beams. "I knew chocolate would tip the scales." She grabs my hand. "Thank you. I might not die of boredom tonight after all." She shrugs. "And if you want to put Hudson off your sex scent, you can be all flirty and giggly with his guests."

I narrow my eyes. "I'm not flirting with anybody." That wasn't in the agreement. And I can't flirt anyway. I'm more likely to end up looking like a scary stalker.

"Not even a little?" she asks slyly. "Just a flash of thigh and a toss of your hair to keep Hudson distracted?"

"I'm not tossing anything. Especially not my hair. In case you didn't notice, I can barely walk."

She sips her tea, entirely unbothered. "Limp seductively. Just enough to sell the 'I'm totally *not* having hot secret sex with your brother' lie."

I swallow hard. "You're going to completely spill the beans to Hudson."

"I'm not," she promises. "I just need your help to keep my mouth shut. Distract me. Entertain me."

"I'll be there," I tell her. "But no hair tossing, limping, or flirting."

"Of course not." She grins. "You're a star. This is going to be so much fun."

ASHER

"Are you okay?" Hudson asks. "You seem distracted."

I've been working from his office all day, trying to focus on the upgrade. We'll run the new system overnight Sunday, their quietest time for the hotel. In between, I've been getting constant updates from Brad. Once the system's live, we'll manage it remotely from New York.

Not that I'm in any rush to get back.

New York feels like another lifetime, even though I left it yesterday. Here on the island, everything is quieter, calmer. Or maybe it's not the island at all. Maybe it's her.

Francie.

Not that I'm going to explain that to Hudson.

I shrug. "I didn't sleep well."

He gives me a dry look. "Yeah, I kind of figured. Playing nurse to your kid sister's best friend isn't exactly restful." He grins. "You're a good guy."

My mouth goes dry. I'm not the good guy. I'm the one who can't keep his hands off the one woman he should stay away from. But I can't stop.

Hudson checks his watch. "I gotta go. Skyler's already pissed I'm late for dinner. Everyone else is there. She's threatening to feed my dinner to the dog." He wrinkles his nose. "On the plus side, at least you're off the hook tonight. Francie's at ours for dinner with the others."

"The others?" My voice tightens.

She's not waiting at the lighthouse, not curled up on the couch where I left her, not texting me, because I didn't text her. I buried myself in work all day like it would keep me from thinking about her, and now I'm checking my phone like she owes me something. Like I didn't vanish the second I walked out the door this morning.

"You're having a dinner party?" I ask.

He rolls his eyes. "Yes, I told you earlier. I asked if you were coming and you said no. Why doesn't anybody in my life ever listen to me?"

"You didn't say Francie was going to be there." I try to keep my tone light, but the words come out sharper than I intend.

Hudson grabs his jacket, oblivious. "Yeah, Skyler

insisted. Said she was worried about her. She wants to make sure she's okay."

He pauses. "And then she said something about one of my associates being the perfect guy for Francie. You remember Ben? She's trying to matchmake them or something."

Ben.

Of course I remember him. Works in Hudson's New York office. Ambitious, polished.

Fake as hell.

And maybe Francie would like that. Safe, predictable. Not someone like me who can't even send her a damn text because I'm too twisted up in my own head.

"Actually, I'm feeling pretty hungry," I say suddenly. "Maybe I'll join you after all."

Hudson pauses, eyeing me. "You sure? A minute ago, you said you'd be working through the night."

"Yeah, well, plans change." I grab my phone and jacket, already heading for the door.

He gives me a long look, like he's trying to figure out what he's missing. Then he shrugs. "Suit yourself. But you have to tell Skyler she needs to place an extra setting at the table."

"No problem."

Because Skyler definitely isn't the problem.

Reminding Francie who she belongs to, that's the only thing on my mind.

twenty-four

FRANCIE

I've been sitting at Skyler and Hudson's massive, reclaimed wood dining table for the last thirty minutes, sipping a glass of wine and nodding like I care about the NASDAQ and share prices and whatever else they're all talking about.

Ben, Hudson's latest wunderkind from the New York office, is holding court like he's on a TED stage. He can't be any older than twenty-five and is painfully enthusiastic.

"So I told Hudson that we really need to shift the equity position if we want to maximize yields across all verticals," he says. "And boom, one week later the numbers prove me right."

"Boom," I repeat, deadpan. I down another mouthful of wine. I'm not sure how much more of this I can take.

Next to me, Skyler keeps looking furiously out of the window at the driveway. She picked me up earlier, plied me with pre-dinner drinks and gossip, and right now she's on the edge of losing it over Hudson's lateness.

"I swear to God," she mutters under her breath, "if he's not home in the next five minutes I'm going to cut his balls off and tell his associates they're a new delicacy."

I try not to grin. "Now that would be a maximum yield."

She snorts into her water glass. "Exactly."

"It's just about making bold moves, you know?" Ben continues. "I told Hudson, if we want to stay ahead of the curve, we need to be the curve."

"Scratch that," I murmur to Skye. "You can feed them to Ben while they're still attached to Hudson. I think he'd like that."

"Hudson or Ben?" she asks, giggling.

I shrug. "Ben, for sure."

Before we can be even ruder about her guests, Hudson's car pulls into the driveway. He drives around to the back of the house to the garage, and Skyler wrinkles her nose.

"I guess his balls stay on. And un-Benned."

"Maybe next time," I say, soothingly.

The door to the dining room opens, and Hudson walks in, as cool and composed as if he hadn't abandoned his wife to entertain his associates. She shoots him a dirty look. He shoots an even dirtier one back.

Oh, they're absolutely going to have angry sex tonight. I shift in my chair.

"There's the man!" Ben says, shooting upright like he's a jack-in-the-box. He rushes to shake Hudson's hand. "I was just telling everybody about the curve we need to make."

His words fade into nothing, because Hudson isn't alone.

Asher steps in behind him, tall and devastating in a

fitted dress shirt. His sleeves are rolled up to his elbows, his jacket is in his hand.

His gaze lands on me, sharp and narrow, then moves to the chair Ben recently vacated and narrows even more. Like he's trying to figure out how I ended up sitting next to him.

"You brought Asher," Skyler says, her voice lifting like a woman on the edge. "You told me he wasn't coming."

Asher gives her a devastating smile. "That's all my fault. I changed my mind at the last minute." His gaze locks with mine again. "Don't worry, I checked in with Martin. He's making an extra plate."

Skyler's already standing up. "Let me grab you a chair."

"No need," Asher cuts in smoothly. He crosses to the end of the dining room and grabs a spare chair from the corner like a man on a mission, swinging it around to slide it in next to Hudson. Then, without hesitation, he slides into Ben's seat like he can't stand the thought of another man being close to me for one more minute.

"That one was taken," Skyler points out. She gives me a sly look.

"Ben can sit with Hudson," Asher says mildly. "Looks like they have a lot to catch up on."

Ben is currently talking off Hudson's ear about something. The man himself keeps looking at the table like he's trying to find an out from a conversation that most certainly contains every buzzword in the finance bro book.

Hudson murmurs something I can't hear, and Ben nods earnestly. He comes back to sit back in his chair and does a double take when he sees Asher sitting there.

"Oh. Uh, that was my seat."

Asher looks at him with an infuriating calm expression. "It was, but I figured Hudson would love you to sit next to him. He was telling me all about your work on..."

"Equity yields," Ben tells him, looking delighted.

"That's it. He was telling me how he could listen to you talking about them all night."

Skyler snorts into her sparkling water. Ben blinks, then turns to look at Hudson.

"Great, I have a lot of things I need to run past him."

Before he's even taken his new seat, Ben is rambling away at Hudson, who glances at Asher, frowning. He's trying to work out what's going on. Skyler looks at us all delighted, seeing Hudson starting to get payback for being late.

Asher pulls out his phone, grinning when he reads the screen. He turns it so I can see it.

Remind me why I invited you? – Hudson

Asher taps out a reply, still letting me watch.

Technically, I invited myself. – Asher

Sliding his phone back into his pocket, he lets his leg brush against mine. I lift a brow at him. We're supposed to be playing it cool here.

But he smiles back, leans in, and whispers low enough so only I can hear:

"Missed you."

Just two words. But they knock the air out of me more than any teasing touch.

"Dinner is served," Martin says, opening the door to the

dining room. He's in his chef's whites, that have somehow remained unsullied despite cooking for hours. Two of the wait staff from the hotel carry in the plates.

"Oh Ben," Skyler says, leaning forward. "Tell Hudson about that podcast you listened to the other day," she says brightly. "How long was it?"

"Three hours, but worth it." He turns to Hudson. "It's really hard to condense into a short soundbite." He laughs. "This may take some time."

Hudson pinches the bridge of his nose between his fingers, then picks up his silverware and starts attacking his dinner like it's his prey.

I lift my glass of wine to my lips, trying to figure out how to get this scene into a book when Asher's hand finds my bare thigh under the table. He squeezes softly, almost like he's grounding himself. Then he trails a finger along the edge of my panties and I start to choke.

Red wine splatters from my mouth all over Skyler's pristine tablecloth. Before I can even try to breathe, Skyler is slamming her hand against my back like I'm her worst enemy, making me choke so hard my eyes start to bulge and tears fall down my cheeks.

Hudson shoots to his feet. "Are you okay? Do you need water? CPR?"

"I'm still breathing," I manage to say.

"She's fine," Skyler says, shaking her head at Asher. "Probably amazed that Ben knows so much about finance at such a young age.

Though she's not really a finance girl," Skyler continues smoothly, smiling at Ben. "She's more of a creative."

Ben perks up. "Oh yeah? What kind of creative?"

I roll my eyes at Skyler. Hello? My job is supposed to be a secret.

"She freelances," Skyler says. "Design. Media." She leans forward. "And of course she models."

Ben's eyes scan me like I'm on a conveyor belt. "You're a model?" he says, like that's just upped my worth.

I kick Skyler under the table. She smiles sweetly back.

"You live in New York, right?" Ben asks. "We should go out sometime."

"I'm not sure her brothers would like that," Asher says, giving Ben the side eye.

"Brothers. Salinger." Ben's eyes light up. "Wait, are your brothers with Salinger Enterprises?"

"Mmhmm," I murmur.

"Wow. That's amazing. I've been trying to get a meeting with Myles and Liam for months. Do you think maybe you can—"

"No," Asher says smoothly. "She can't."

Ben frowns. "I was just going to—"

"Francie is Hudson's guest. She's not here to talk shop or be a secretary for her brothers. So maybe let her finish her wine without being propositioned."

Well that was hot. I rub my thigh against Asher's. He covers it with his palm.

Ben blinks. "Maybe I could drive you home later? We could talk... creatively."

Asher slams his fork down. "She's already got a ride home."

Ben frowns. "Skyler picked her up. I figured..."

"And I'm taking her home," Asher says. "She hit her head yesterday. And you've been drinking. Probably not great for you to be navigating unfamiliar, dark roads with a buzz on."

The way he says it makes me think he means hard-on.

I clear my throat. Amused and turned on. I'm not used

to being fought over. Not that there's any doubt who will win.

Hudson frowns. "Wait, I thought Skyler was driving Francie home."

"I was," Skyler says breezily. "But I'm pregnant and tired and Asher is a dear." She yawns theatrically.

I bite my lip to stop from laughing. Hudson stares, then stabs a piece of broccoli. The table dissolves into silence.

Asher squeezes my thigh. And doesn't remove his hand.

The rest of dinner passes quickly. Ben finds his voice again after dessert, but all I can think about is Asher's finger tracing my thigh. I don't dare drink. I barely eat.

"Everything okay?" Skyler asks.

"She looks peaky," Asher says. "I should probably take her home."

"But we have coffee coming," Skyler protests. "Is your head hurting?"

"Coffee is very bad for concussions," Asher murmurs.

Skyler frowns. "I brought her coffee this morning. She seemed fine."

"He's very passionate about concussions," I say. "Very… thorough."

Asher smirks. His hand gives my thigh one last squeeze before pulling away. Thankfully, before I combust.

"Well, far be it from me to stand in the way of healing," Skyler drawls. "Just make sure she rests."

"Rest is the plan," Asher says, giving me a look that says it very much isn't.

I slip my arms into my cardigan. "Thanks for dinner," I say to Skyler. Then to Hudson, "Have a good night."

"I'm pretty sure yours will be better," Skyler says, brows lifting.

Hudson looks at Asher for a long moment, but Asher's

face remains neutral. I can almost see the clock in his brain ticking.

Before he can speak, Asher is pulling out my chair. When I stand, he puts his warm hand along the curve of my back, propelling me to the dining room door.

"Hey, are you doing New York Fashion Week? We should exchange numbers," Ben says, jumping up with his phone. "So we can—"

"No," Asher says firmly, grabbing my hand and pulling me into the hallway. In no time we are out into the night, the cool air a welcome relief to my flushed skin. Sliding his hand around my waist, he leads me to his car, pulling the passenger door open. But before I can sit inside, his mouth is at my ear, his body pressed against my hip.

"You don't give your number to men like Ben, sweetheart. Not when you're mine."

twenty-five

FRANCIE

"Why didn't you tell me you were going to Hudson's for dinner?" Asher asks, pulling out of the driveway and onto the road that leads to the lighthouse. There's an edge to his voice that sends a shiver down my spine.

Glancing out of the window, I can see the moonlight glimmering on the inky black ocean. "You didn't call me all day," I remind him. "When was I supposed to tell you?"

"I was with Hudson all day," he replies. A frown plays at his lips. "Did you want me to call you? Why didn't you say so?"

"Because maybe I wanted you to want to call me without any prompting," I say.

For a second he says nothing. Like he's trying to take the words in. I'm not trying to argue with him, but this is all very new and I'm not sure why he's suddenly so mad with me.

"Of course I wanted to call you," he finally says. "I

didn't want to leave your fucking bed this morning. I was thinking about you all damn day. And then…"

"Then what?" I ask, genuinely interested.

"And then I find you flirting with another guy."

I turn to him, my brows raised. "Flirting? Are you serious? Did I look like I was entranced by his bro words?"

His knuckles are white as he grips the steering wheel. "He wanted your number. I nearly hit the guy. I spent most of last night inside of you for fuck's sake."

Is he jealous? Of Ben?

"This is stupid. I didn't give it to him. And I absolutely didn't flirt with him."

He veers left, onto the tiny road that leads to the lighthouse.

I glance at him, then out the window, and bite my lip. "I missed you today," I admit, my voice soft. "More than I wanted to."

He glances over, and for a moment the tension breaks. His grip loosens on the wheel, the muscle in his jaw unclenches.

"I couldn't stop thinking about you either," he admits.

But then, almost like he can't help himself, the steel returns. "But that guy—"

"What did you think I was going to do?" I cut in. "Flirt my way to a dinner date with the first man who used a series of buzzwords? Just because you went radio silent like a ghost with a day job?"

His jaw twitches. "That's not what I meant."

I fold my arms. "Then what did you mean?"

He doesn't answer for a beat. The silence feels thick between us, the only sound is the crunch of tires against the gravel. He pulls up outside the lighthouse and puts on the handbrake.

"You're mine, that's what I meant. And I don't want to watch some finance prick try to slide into your DMs because he thinks you're a fucking model with a family who might give him a boost in life."

You're mine. There it is again. I hate how annoyingly hot that makes me feel.

"You don't own me," I point out.

He shuts the engine off, then pinches the bridge of his nose, like he's in genuine pain. "I know that." His voice is low. "You think I don't know that? Maybe it's the other way around. Maybe you own me."

Oh. My heart slams against my chest.

Finally he looks at me, his gaze catching mine. "I don't own you, Francie, but I don't like to share."

The way he says it, so intensely, makes my thighs clench.

"I'm not looking to be shared," I murmur. "But this is all so... new. I still don't know how you really feel. And I'm worried. About Autumn, about my brothers. You think they won't care if they find out that I'm seeing somebody older than me? Because they will." The thought of it makes my stomach tighten.

"Is that what this is about?" he asks. "Your family? You keep so many damn secrets from them." He looks at me like he's trying to understand. "Why?"

I don't know that I'm ready to talk about this. I know for a fact he won't understand. He's older. A brother. He has no idea how stifling my life can be.

"I'm the little sister, the baby," I say, trying to find the right words. "I've spent a lifetime being coddled. Never taken seriously. Once I tell them about my books, they'll become... I don't know, jaded. Not mine anymore. Like everything else, they'll want to take over. And I can't bear that."

His voice softens. "Francie," he murmurs. "If it was my sister I'd want to know. I'd be so damn proud of her."

I look him square in the eye. We both know his sisters. Yes, Autumn is my best friend, but I love Eden too.

"And how would you feel if they were sleeping with an older man?" I ask.

"Autumn's married to Parker. He's older."

"And Hudson gave him hell for it. You did too," I point out, because I had a front row seat to that shitshow.

"And now we accept it. Because he loves her and makes her happy. So yeah, I'd want to know what brings my sisters joy."

I stare out of the windshield at the lighthouse. The white stucco looks almost gray in the moonlight.

"Maybe I just want something that's only mine," I say.

He unbuckles his seatbelt. "Am I that something?" he asks.

I swallow hard. "It felt like you were last night."

He leans in, his face close enough that his breath tickles my cheek. This close, I can see the fire in his eyes.

"I've been yours for a lot longer than last night, sweetheart."

Before I can respond, his hand is on my jaw, tipping my face toward his. His mouth crashes into mine, hot, hungry, and full of frustration. Like he's starving. I gasp into him, grabbing at his shirt as his hands tangle in my hair. All the tension, bickering, heat, and emotion explodes into that kiss.

I'm dizzy by the time he breaks away, only far enough for our eyes to lock.

"I didn't call," he says softly, "because I knew if I did, I'd lose it and come straight back here. And I didn't think you'd want that. You have a book to write."

"Maybe I do want that," I whisper. "Maybe that's all I want. Maybe I thought about you all day, thought about touching myself, but I knew nothing could feel as good as you do inside of me."

He growls low in his throat, opening his door and speeding around to mine.

"Inside," he says, holding out his hand. The gentlemanly act contrasts perfectly with his expression, which is definitely ungentlemanlike. "Now, before I fuck you in this car."

I let him pull me up, breathless as his hand curls around mine and he leads me to the front of the lighthouse, spinning me around until my back is pressed against the door.

His lips brush my ear, his hand taking mine, pushing it down until I'm cupping him. Feeling the hardness of his desire against my palm.

"You want something that's yours?" he says. "Good, because every inch of me is yours tonight."

* * *

ASHER

She stares up at me, her eyes wide, her lips softly parted, and I realize that I'm already a goner for this woman. I can't think properly, I can't do anything but want her.

Maybe it's the way she talked to me when I was losing it outside the hospital. Or the way she intuitively knows how to make me feel better.

All I know is that I can't stand the thought of another man touching her.

Her chest is rising and falling fast, and the way she looks at me, like I'm a fucking god, sends heat straight down to my cock.

"I don't want to fight with you anymore," she murmurs.

Before I can tell her that I feel the same way, she grabs my face and kisses me.

It's hard. Raw. My mouth slants across hers like I've been waiting all day for this, and I have. Her lips part as she grasps onto me, her fingers curling into the front of my shirt, dragging me closer. I nudge her head back with mine, and push her against the door, one hand braced behind her head, the other tight around her waist.

She moans when I press all of me against her. "Inside," I rasp.

"No." She shakes her head, her hands sliding down to my belt. "I can't wait that long."

Her fingers make quick work of my buckle, as she loosens my pants and slides her hand inside. Her warm palm wraps around me.

"Francie," I growl against her mouth. "Are you trying to kill me?"

She grins wickedly. "I'll make it a pleasurable end."

She runs her hand up and down, her thumb rubbing against the bead of precum already forming on my dick. She drops to her knees, and for a second, the heat in my chest mixes with something deeper. The trust in her eyes, the way she looks at me like I'm already hers. It makes me feel fucking invincible.

Then her mouth envelops me, warm and velvety, her tongue teasingly trailing along the length of me.

"Christ." My head tips back, my hand cups the back of

her head. She finds a rhythm, her sweet lips making every nerve ending in my body vibrate.

It doesn't take long for me to feel that familiar pull deep in my belly. Her flickering tongue, her insistent mouth, the way she looks up at me, bats her eyelashes, shows me she owns me even while she's knelt at my feet. And then I tangle my fingers in her hair, my voice urgent as I tell her to stop.

"I don't want to come in your mouth," I tell her. "I need to come in you."

I pull her back up and kiss her, showing her my appreciation, my hand slipping beneath her dress to find her warm, wet heat. I slide my finger beneath her panties, dragging it against her before I push it inside of her without any preamble. Her head slams against the door, her body clenching around me like she's already close.

"This is mine," I tell her.

Her eyes flash. She likes it. Fuck, I like it too. We both know it's a lie. I'm the owned one here. But if my girl wants to feel my possession, I'll give that to her. I slide a second finger inside of her, my cock delighting in her tightness.

"Yes," she gasps. "Yours. Just yours."

I can't wait. I don't want to. I yank her dress up higher, fist my cock, and she wraps her leg around my waist like she was made to do it.

"You want this?" I ask her, my voice rough as I drag myself against her. "You want me to fuck you against the door like you've been aching for me all day?"

Her eyes burn into mine. "Oh God yes."

I push into her with one deep thrust and we both cry out. Her nails dig into my shoulders, her mouth falling open, her eyes full of heat. I capture her lips with mine.

"You like this, baby?" I murmur against her. "You like being fucked like you're owned?"

She nods, her grip on my shoulders tightening, like she needs this as badly as I do.

"More," she begs. "Harder."

"Ask nicely," I murmur, thrusting into her again.

"Please," she moans. "God, Asher, please."

The way she says my name almost makes me come. I kiss her again, devouring the sounds from her mouth. Her body shudders with every thrust of my hips. I feel her getting closer, feel the flutter of her walls around my cock.

"I'm gonna... I can't... *Asher*..." she cries out.

"You can," I rasp, slipping my hand between us to rub her clit. "Come all over my cock, baby. Let me feel it."

She splinters into pieces, her legs trembling, her mouth moaning against my neck. She squeezes around me and I lose it, pounding into her one last time as I come hard, spilling inside of her in long, hot bursts, her name a growl on my lips. It's so fucking exquisite I see white stars behind my eyes. It's never felt this good. This raw.

The motion light flickers on above us, casting our shadows long and wide across the porch.

We're both panting, slick with sweat and sex, using the door to hold us up, when I go to pull out.

And fuck. "I'm not wearing a condom." My eyes widen. How the fuck could I be so irresponsible? "Jesus, Francie. I'm sorry. I—"

She smiles at me, looking all soft and sated. "It's okay. I'm on birth control. And I'm clean."

But it's not okay. I'm a thirty-six year old man. I never have sex without a condom. Fucking hell, protection is my job. The very least I can do is practice safe sex with the woman who steals my breath away.

"I'm clean too," I murmur, brushing the hair from her face. "Next time I'll remember."

"Next time you'll remember that I like you just like this," she whispers. "I want all of you."

My heart does a double thud against my ribcage. But I don't argue. What this woman wants, she gets, that's the honest truth of it.

And she already has all of me.

* * *

ASHER

I'm leaning over the security console at the hotel the next day when my phone vibrates with a message. And because I've decided to actually stop being an asshole and answer Francie's messages when she sends them, I pull it out right away, only partly grimacing when I realize it's the Fitzgerald family group chat.

AUTUMN:

I'm messaging you live from Venice 📖 Parker just tried to row a gondola. It did not go well. There's currently a very angry woman yelling at us in Italian.

ZACH:

Is she hot?

. . .

AUTUMN:

Zachary!

ZACH:

What? If you're going to get yelled at, it might as well be by a woman with good cheekbones and kissable lips.

HUDSON:

Please don't harass the locals. And tell Parker to stop trying to row things. He's a thrower not a rower.

AUTUMN:

I've tried. Believe me. Anyway, how are you all? I miss you. How's Liberty?

HUDSON:

Same old same old. We're all good. Asher is being a pain in the ass though.

AUTUMN:

Wait, Asher is on Liberty?

I roll my eyes. Even as a kid Autumn loved to be at the center of everything. And she hated to be the last to know a secret. I also remember how easily distracted she is.

• • •

ASHER:

Yes I'm on Liberty. Doing some work for Hudson. By the way, has anybody heard from Eden? I'm kind of worried about her.

There, that should do it. The last thing I need is Autumn asking me questions about Francie.

AUTUMN:

Not since the last chat.

HUDSON:

I swear to God if she's been arrested again—

My lips curl, because I know just how to throw a grenade into the works.

ASHER:

I'll ask one of my team to track her down. It shouldn't take too long.

I smirk because that's a lie, it would take a lot of time. The CIA could learn some tricks from Eden. She knows how to hide.

. . .

EDEN:

Oh my God, chill Asher! I'm fine. I just have really bad reception. We're working on a project in the mountains and I can be without signal for days.

ZACH:

She lives!

HUDSON:

Glad you're all right. Just try to check in more regularly, please.

EDEN:

I can't make any promises. The world needs me. But no tracking me down, Asher. I'm serious.

ASHER:

Noted.

EDEN:

Talking of unresponsive. Where's Wyatt? I don't see you all going crazy over him going radio silent. It's very sexist, you know?

WYATT:

· · ·

HUDSON:

See, he's fine.

EDEN:

So if I just checked in with an emoji, that would be okay?

WYATT:

👍

HUDSON:

NO

ZACH:

Definitely not.

AUTUMN:

That's a no from me, too, sis.

Before they can ask my opinion, I shake my head and close the chat, a smile playing on my lips. Yes, my family drives me around the twist, but there's something nice about us all checking in.

And to be honest, I'm just constantly in a good mood right now. Spending the night with Francie will do that to a man. So if they want to be chatty, let them.

Just as long as they don't start asking me too many questions about why I'm hanging around the Lighthouse so much.

twenty-six

FRANCIE

"I swear to God this was your hottest scene yet," Autumn tells me breathlessly, as we talk on the phone. "I had to jump on Parker as soon as he walked into the hotel room. The poor guy didn't know what hit him. Especially when I started begging him to pretend to be a Dragon Rider."

"Does he even know what a Dragon Rider is?" I ask her. I'm feeling kind of smug at how well the writing is going. For the past week I've been on fire. I write all day, then Asher comes to see me after working at the hotel, and we pretty much spend the night tangled in my bed.

I'm starting to get too used to it, truth be told. Which probably means I'm in trouble.

"Well, no. At first he thought I was supposed to be the dragon. But we talked it through and he got the gist. Three times."

I snort. "You've been drinking, haven't you?"

"Only three mimosas. And a glass of champagne. Please

tell me there's no third act breakup. I don't know that I can take it. Can't you just write the whole book full of hot sex?"

"I think my editor might have something to say about that," I tell her. "But I'm glad you liked it."

"Not as glad as Parker." She lets out a sigh. "It felt different though."

"Different *how*?" I ask, feeling the worries creep in. Different sounds bad. Am I going to have to re-write it? Ugh.

"I don't know. It's just... that scene. The throat holding. The whispering. The dirty talking." There's a pause. "It's like you've found your inner slut."

"Thanks." I try not to laugh. Drunk Autumn has no filter.

"Have you been having dirty dragon rider sex with somebody?" she asks me, taking me by surprise.

I cough. "Excuse me?"

"You heard me. Who is it? Jesse? Mylene? Or a random guest from the hotel? Don't tell me Captain Toe Shoes has made it back to the island."

I wince. "You're never going to let me live that down, are you?"

"Nope." She sounds gleeful.

"Well lucky for you I just have a good imagination," I tell her. "And access to the internet." Most of the time. Kind of.

"Liar," Autumn singsongs. "That internet connection is terrible. And don't try to kid a kidder. Remember when I was having hate sex with Parker when I was forced to live in the apartment next to his? You sound exactly like I did then."

I frown, remembering how she and Parker got together. He's Hudson's best friend, and wouldn't go near her. Until those weeks when the two of them were living next to each other on the island while Autumn oversaw the renovations of the Grand Liberty Hotel while Hudson was overseas fighting for custody of his daughter.

"It's nothing like that," I protest. I *will* tell her about this. Eventually. When she's back on the island and I can explain everything to her. That's if there's anything to explain. Yes, I've been spending all my non-writing time with Asher, but I also know from the phone calls I overhear that he needs to get back to New York. I don't know what will happen then.

And I don't really want to think about it.

But maybe there'll be nothing to tell Autumn by the time she's back here.

I tell myself that, even though something inside of me aches at the thought.

There's a pause, but then she sighs. "Fine, I'll let it go for now. But if I find out it's someone sketchy, I reserve the right to call your brothers and demand a full-scale inter-vention."

The laugh gets caught in my throat. "About that..."

"About what?" She sounds confused. But this is something I want to run past my best friend. She's been part of my life for so long. She knows the way I think, and I need her now.

For a moment there's silence. "Wait, seriously?"

She knows how adamant I've been about them not finding out about my writing. And I can't tell her why I've been thinking about it. Those words Asher said to me, that night in the car. That he'd want to know. That he'd be proud.

And I know they'll be hurt, too. That I didn't tell them from the start.

"I think it might be time," I say, feeling every word thump with the tightness of my chest. "I hate hiding it. But also, I'm terrified to come clean." I lean back on the sofa and look up at the ceiling. "Once they know, they'll all have opinions. Liam will want to see the financials, Myles will want to talk to my publishers. And then there's the sex." I wrinkle my nose.

"The steaming hot sex scenes," Autumn adds.

"Exactly. Those." Nobody likes to think about their family reading the smut they wrote. "I'm not sure they'll ever look at me the same way again."

Autumn clears her throat, like she knows I need her advice right now. "But maybe they shouldn't," she says. "Maybe it's time that they see you as a grown up. Somebody with a career, a gift. You're right, it's time to let them in a little. They love you, you know that."

"They do," I say softly.

"Good. Then we're agreed. Operation come clean is go." Her voice lowers. "Now back to the important stuff. Throat holding. Have you done that? Because Parker won't and I'm not happy about it."

I'm about to laugh when the front door opens and Asher steps in. I've told him to stop knocking and use the spare key – mostly so he doesn't disturb me when I'm writing.

I shoot him a wide-eyed look and quickly wiggle the phone at him.

He raises a brow. "Who is it?" he mouths.

"Autumn," I mouth back.

He rolls his eyes. Then he crosses the room slowly, with that lazy predatory stroll he does when he knows he's about to wreck me. He kneels between my legs where I'm curled on the couch and presses his mouth to my bare knee.

I swat him away, but he ignores me, a grin on his lips.

"It's your sister," I mouth.

"Tell her you're busy." He doesn't mouth that one. Says it loud enough for me to glare at him.

"Are you watching TV or something?" Autumn asks.

"Yep," I lie. "I'll turn it down. Anyway, how's Parker handling things? Is he enjoying commentating?"

"He is, but to be honest, I'm a little distracted whenever he's on the screen. All the British announcers sound like sexy Bond villains. But when I ask him to mimic their accent he refuses."

I snort. Then gasp as Asher kisses along the inside of my thigh. Damn him for making this feel like more than just sex. "Well that's not fair."

"I know, right? I had a dirty dream about one of them last night. Between the Bond guys and the dragon riders, Parker's being a little overworked."

"What's that?" I ask, loudly for Asher's benefit. "You've been having lots of hot sex with Parker."

Asher wrinkles his nose. Haha, gotcha. No guy wants to hear about his sister's love life.

I lift a brow at him. Checkmate.

"Obviously," she says. "That's not news." She laughs softly. "I'd better go. Parker will be home any minute. I'm going to see if I can get him to say *bees knees* by giving him a blow job. Love you, babe. Talk soon."

"Love you too," I choke out, hanging up quickly.

Asher looks at me. "Never, ever let me hear about my sister's love life again." But he's smiling, leaning in to kiss me, like he's missed me all day.

The same way I've missed him.

"Then don't touch me when I'm on the phone with her," I say reasonably.

"It's hard not to touch you when you're looking so beautiful," he tells me. The softness in his eyes mixes with heat.

"Sweet talker." I tip my head to the side, feeling my body respond to him.

"I mean every word I say," He leans forward, pressing his mouth to mine again. This time, his kiss is full of intent.

I kiss him back, pulling him closer, until his body is pressed against mine, our legs tangled, our hands seeking each other.

"Good," I tell him. "Now touch me again."

ASHER

"Is this what you do now?" Hudson asks, walking into the security room at the hotel with two cups of coffee. "Run software tests all day like you're a trainee at your own company and not the CEO?"

"You'll thank me for it later," I murmur, closing my laptop quickly. "This place is going to be like Fort Knox. Nobody will get onto the island without your knowledge."

I know how much he wants to keep his family safe. Skyler, Ayda. And the new baby on the way.

Leaning against the wall, Hudson sips his drink, his gaze firmly on me. "How many overnight tests do you have to run?" he asks. "Isn't this the third one this week? You can run them during the day, I told you that. Instead of staying here all night watching a damn screen."

There's a half smirk in his voice, like he knows I've been lying through my teeth. Of course I haven't been watching a screen all night. I've been fucking Francie. Holding her. Teasing her for her Clark Kent fetish while she practically melts at the sight of my glasses.

I've been living a life I never thought I'd have.

"Do you want the system to have vulnerabilities?" I ask him. "Or are you gonna let me do my job?"

"I want to know why you say you're working here all night, except when I came to the hotel last night there was no sign of you," he says.

"You came here last night?" I frown. "Why?"

"Because your emergency contact lenses arrived from the mainland and I assumed you might need them." He points at the box I found this morning. "But apparently, you're fine without them."

I ran out two days ago. I've been wearing my glasses since then, and I hate it. Francie, on the other hand, acts like I'm walking sex in them. She kept tugging at the frames last night while she straddled me. Told me I look like a dirty professor.

Not that I mind the comparison.

Hudson lifts a brow. "If you're not staying at the hotel, where are you sleeping?"

"I have a feeling you know the answer to that."

"Well, I saw your car outside the lighthouse," he says slowly. "Our sister's house."

Jesus. When did my brother become such a prude? "What do you want me to say?" It's a serious question. He's caught me. If he wants to know, he can know. But I'm not sure he really wants to.

Plausible deniability is a beautiful thing.

"You're messing around with Francie." There's pain in his voice when he says it. Like he really doesn't want to have this conversation.

"Messing around makes it sound like something it's not. I'm seeing her. Yes."

"Every night? All night?"

"You want a blow by blow account?"

He squeezes his eyes shut. "Fuck's sake. First Parker, now you. Why can't you find some nice girl in New York and keep me out of this? She's Autumn's friend. Skyler's too. You mess things up and they're gonna get pissed at me."

"Why would they get pissed at you?"

"Because they'll know I know. And they'll ask me why I didn't stop you. And now I'm talking to you and the expression on your face makes it really fucking clear that you're not going to stop doing this thing that's going to cause me to get shouted at. And possibly make me involuntarily celibate for the foreseeable future." His words came out fast and uncontrolled, and his face is pink.

I stare at him for a moment as he finally calms down.

"Do you feel better?" I ask, a grin in my voice.

"No." He shakes his head. "I feel worse."

"What if I promise not to mess things up?"

"Not really." He sighs. "I promised Skyler I wouldn't mess things up and I did." He sinks down into one of the office chairs. "Why did you have to tell me?"

"I didn't," I point out. "I asked you if you really wanted to know and you said it out loud. I gave you an out. You didn't take it."

He glares at me. "Do you like her?"

"Very much." My throat tightens.

There's a beat of silence. A long, loaded pause.

"How long has it been going on?" he finally asks. "I assume it was you who made her cough wine out at the dinner party."

My mouth twitches at the memory of that night. "It was."

"And before that?"

"It's been… building." I won't be telling him about the sex club. Or the surveillance feeds. Some things are sacred.

"Now, do you want to know what she does when I pin her wrists above her head and call her my good girl, or can I get on with my job?"

He winces. "Just… do it." He waves at my laptop. "And please never, ever say those words to me again."

My grin is pure provocation. "I'll try. But it'll be hard. She's very vocal when she's being good."

Hudson groans and rubs a hand over his face like he's trying to erase the last two minutes of his life. "I hate you."

"You love me." I reach for my bag. "But if you don't leave, I'm going to keep torturing you."

He's halfway out the door when I toss one last barb at him. "And maybe tell your staff to avoid reviewing camera four unless they're prepared for a very educational experience."

That one's a lie. But the horror on his face is worth it.

"Jesus Christ," he mutters under his breath. "I need a fucking therapist."

When the door shuts behind him, I finally let the smile drop.

I should feel triumphant. But instead there's this dull ache in my chest. A creeping dread I can't quite explain. I'm staying on the island longer than I need to. Delaying meetings. Ignoring decisions. Because for the first time in my life, someone sees all of me and doesn't flinch.

That should scare me. Maybe it already does. Everything I touch eventually falls apart. I know that better than anyone.

I pull out my phone.

I'm on my way over. I'll pick up some dinner. And wear my glasses. – Asher

My mouth twitches as I hit send.

It feels good, this quiet domestic rhythm we've fallen into.

Too good.

I grab my things and the dinner I ordered, then make my way outside, breathing in the salty air, already imagining her opening the door with that sleepy little smile she gives me.

But then my phone rings.

And just like that, the whole damn world shifts.

twenty-seven

ASHER

By the time I step outside the hotel, insulated dinner bag in one hand and phone wedged between my shoulder and ear, Brad's already dropping a bomb.

"There's been another breach," he says. My stomach immediately drops.

"How can that be?" I frown. "We tightened the security so much even I can barely get in."

I head toward my car in the growing twilight, the salty breeze tugging at my clothes. The hotel chef packed Francie's favorite dinner, and I was smiling as I left the kitchen. But now my jaw is tight.

"We think whoever broke in left some kind of back door," Brad says. "We can't find it, but it's there."

"Christ." I run my hand through my hair. "I thought we had this locked down. I don't suppose you have any idea who it is?"

"We're trying. But whoever they are, they made sure to

leave very little trace. We've been over the whole codebase to see what's changed, and there's nothing."

"There has to be something." I open the trunk, set the bag inside, and slide into the driver's seat. "Go through it again."

"We already are. I've authorized the team to work overnight. I hope that's okay."

"Of course." I hit the button to start the engine. "I'm assuming you haven't heard anything from the police."

"Not a word. You?"

"Nothing." Which is good. Because whatever's going on in our systems, I want to be able to deal with it fast. Without the law looking over our shoulders. "You checked on Nathan again?"

"He's out of the country. Apparently on the bender to end all benders."

With the money I paid him. I wrinkle my nose.

"Doesn't mean it isn't him."

"I know that. We have him under twenty-four hour surveillance. The man's done nothing to raise suspicion. He's too drunk and drugged up to do anything but sleep it off. Either he's the world's best actor, or he's not involved."

I run my tongue over my dry lips. "I'll be back first thing tomorrow." Even I know when I'm defeated. And truth be told, I never should have come back here after the break in. I wouldn't have, except for her.

"We'll be here," Brad says, sounding relieved. I know I've asked too much of him. I shouldn't be here when the business is under attack. And yet I haven't been able to stay away either.

Guilt pulls at my gut. If I'd been in New York these past few days, would I have found the breach sooner? It was there all along. Whoever broke into the office almost certainly used it as a cover up for creating a backdoor into our systems.

And I flew back to Liberty and let them walk right in. Because my dick did the thinking.

Pulling out of the hotel parking lot, I take a right, seeing the lighthouse rising into the sky in the distance. For some reason it immediately calms me. Knowing she's there. Knowing I'll see her in a few minutes.

That I'll be able to touch her. My body relaxes at the thought of holding her. Kissing her. Making her come.

For the first time in years, maybe longer, I've felt... steady. Like I belong somewhere. With someone.

I hook another right, the tires crunching against the loose gravel, each rotation sending a soft scatter of stones beneath the wheels. It sounds like home, which is such a fucking stupid thing to think. But I do anyway. I park, grab the insulated bag, and those fucking contacts that Hudson was so desperate to give me, and stride to the front door.

Francie is waiting for me when I unlock the door, her smile lighting up her whole face. She's barefoot, wearing one of those oversized sweaters that hangs off her shoulders. Her hair is in a loose topknot, strands spilling from it.

Her legs are also bare. My eyes drink them in.

"Hi honey, how was your day," she says, her voice low and sexy.

"Better now." I put the bag on the entry table and pull her into my arms. She smells of flowers, like she's freshly showered. For me.

My dick immediately goes hard.

"What's wrong?" she asks, like she can sense my mood.

I brush the loose strands of hair from her face. She's not wearing makeup. Fuck, I want this woman.

"Brad called right as I left the hotel. There's been another breach in our system."

She frowns, looking up at me. There's so much concern in her eyes that it makes my chest tighten. "Another one?" she asks softly. "I thought everything was okay now."

"We think somebody left a backdoor in the system after the break in. We can't find it yet. But it means I have to go back to New York."

"Oh." I hate the way she sounds disappointed, even though she's obviously trying to hide it. "Of course you do. When do you leave?"

"I need to take the first ferry to the mainland in the morning. I'll get a flight from there."

"No helicopter swooping onto Liberty this time?" she teases.

"I think I'll go for a less dramatic exit." I follow her to the living room, where she's obviously been writing all day. Her laptop is open, there are handwritten notes scattered on the coffee table. "Did I interrupt you?"

"No. I've finished for the day. Just gotta tidy up." She shuffles the papers into a loose pile. "So, tonight is our last night," she says. "I guess we need to make it count."

"It's not our last night," I say. She's bent over the coffee table, and the oversized sweater has ridden up to reveal her panties. I reach for her hips, pulling her ass against my front. Her breath hitches.

"What were you writing today?" I murmur, kissing the back of her neck.

She lets out a contented sigh. "A fight scene."

"Not a sex scene?" I ask. "Shame." She wrote one the other day and I came home and reaped the benefits.

"That's next week's job. The last one. The makeup sex." She turns to look at me, her gaze warm. "I was hoping you'd be here for inspiration, but I guess I'll have to use my imagination."

"I have something that might help." I remember what I found on my laptop earlier.

"What?"

I pull up my phone, accessing the system. "Turn on the television."

She gives me a curious look, but does it anyway. Then I log in to my own private access, the part of the security system that I know is beyond locked down. I scroll down with my thumb until I find what I need.

Then I Chromecast it to the seventy-inch screen.

It flickers, as the video comes to life. And what appears is a blurry image, especially blown up that big, but the view of the lighthouse door is clear. Even at night.

"What is this?" she asks. "Have you been spying on me?"

I shake my head and fast forward the footage. Two people come into view. *Us.* The me on the video feed spins her around, slams her back against the front door. We say some words that can't be heard, then she grabs my face, kissing me hard and deep.

"Oh my God, Asher," the real Francie whispers. Her cheeks are pink as she watches me deepen the kiss. We both look angry. Probably because we were. "It's the night of the dinner party," she murmurs.

"Yeah."

She's still against me. Her back to my front. I absent-mindedly start to caress her stomach as video-Francie drops to her knees and starts to run her tongue over my dick.

My body heats, like it can feel the softness of her tongue. Francie watches, her breath speeding.

Then the screen-me pulls her up and hooks her leg around my hip as I thrust inside her so hard it makes her head fall back.

The real her gasps. I run my hands up her body, under the sweater, groaning when I find that she's not wearing a bra. Her breasts are soft, her nipples hard. Her breath catches as I start to play with them.

"See how beautiful you are?" I murmur in her ear. "When I found this, I nearly fucking came in my pants. I was supposed to be working."

We start to fuck harder on the screen. All I can look at is her face though. The way it's flushed, so close to pleasure.

She's the most beautiful woman I've ever met.

"Asher," the real her whispers. She rocks against my back and I get the message. Sliding my hand down, I hook my fingers beneath the waistband of her panties.

And then I find her warm wetness waiting for me. One touch of her clit and she lets out a cry.

On screen, she drops her head against my neck, and I know that she's close. It's the same in real life. I slide a finger inside of her, my thumb rubbing gentle circles on her clit as she rests her head against me.

"Look how pretty you are when you're letting me inside you," I whisper in her ear. "Look how close you are to coming."

"I'm so close," she whispers.

I know it. My girl has tells. Her breath shortens, her pussy tightens around my fingers. I can feel her clit, swollen and needy, against my thumb.

And then the screen-her starts to come. I'm so hard from watching that, I'm aching. I increase the pressure on her clit, and the real her starts to peak.

"Asher…"

"Let it go, baby," I murmur, curling my fingers inside of her. "Look at you. Both of you. Coming and glorious. I'm going to think about this every night when I'm away."

She starts to shatter, her breath harsh, her body tight. I wrap my arm around her waist to keep her standing.

She's trembling in my arms, her release washing over her in deep, pulsing waves. I hold her close, my lips kissing her ear, her throat, her cheek as I whisper what a good girl she is for me.

With my free hand, I pick up the remote and click it off. There's only so much I can take. I'm already on the edge.

I rest my hand on her belly, warm and sated beneath my touch.

"You're so perfect," I murmur.

She lets out a soft laugh, her breath still shaky. But then she stiffens in my arms.

"Wait." She twists in my grip to face me. Her eyes are wide. "That footage. If it recorded that, what else did it record?"

"I locked the lighthouse cameras the minute you asked me to watch you," I tell her. I'd already anticipated this. "Nobody has access to them apart from me. Not my team, nobody."

Her hands go to her cheeks. "But what if somebody did see? Parker or Autumn. Oh my God, they could have—"

"They didn't." I reach for her face, tilting her chin so she's looking at me. "Francie, I swear. I told them I'd keep an eye on everything so they could relax while they're away. It's completely locked down. Far away from any eyes. This is isolated on the local system. For our eyes only."

She swallows hard. "You're sure."

I nod, giving her a smile. "It's my job, remember?" I kiss her jaw, my lips soft. "Come to New York with me. You can write at my place." There's a twist in my stomach at the thought of being away from her.

"I can't."

"Why not?"

"Well, I have this book to finish for one." She traces her finger along my bottom lip. "You may not know this, but you and your magic fingers can be very distracting." She takes a deep breath. "But also, I need to go to Virginia."

"Is everything okay?" Her parents live on a huge estate in Virginia. And her father is old. I immediately start thinking the worst.

"Everything is fine. It's just that my brothers are all going to be there and I want to talk to them." She pulls her lip between her teeth. "What you said the other day, about telling them the truth. I've been thinking about it, and all the marketing that's going to come soon. I need to tell them about my writing. Before they find out from social media."

I blink, surprised that she actually listened to me. It had been a throwaway comment. But something warm grows in my stomach at the thought that she's ready to move forward with this.

"I'm so proud of you, baby."

She grins. "Thank you." Then she lets out a long breath. "I can't believe you have to leave. I'm going to miss you. It feels like the end of the best summer ever."

"It's fall already," I point out.

"I know. But I still don't want it to end."

I tighten my arms around her, my mouth against her ear. "It's not the end, sweetheart."

She lets out a breath, leaning against me. "It feels like it."

"It's not." My voice is firmer now. "You're going to go to Virginia to tell your family the truth. I'm going to head to

New York to sort out my own issues. It's a pause, nothing else."

"And what happens when we un-pause?" She looks up at me.

"We'll come back together. I'll come to you, you come to me, we both come here. Whatever. We'll work it out."

"Maybe I'll get my book finished too. Assuming I can work out the ending."

"I already know the end," I say, kissing her softly.

"You do? Can you tell me please?" she teases.

"Guy gets the girl." My lips claim hers again. "And the guy never lets her go."

She shakes her head, amused at my poor attempts to plot her book. "It needs a cliffhanger. That's part of the contract."

"This is why I'm a security guy, not a writer. But our ending, baby. That's not coming. This? You and me? We're just getting started."

twenty-eight

FRANCIE

When I wake up the next morning, Asher has already left. The sheets are cold, but the pillow next to mine still smells faintly of his skin. Clean and sharp, with a hint of spice. It makes my stomach tighten, the way it always does when it comes to Asher Fitzgerald.

Deciding that I can't just lie here and mope – because I have a book to write, damn it – I force myself to sit up, my hand reaching to the nightstand for my phone. That's when I see them. His glasses. Folded neatly beside the lamp. He must have forgotten them in his rush to catch the first ferry to the mainland.

A pang slices through my chest. It's like a little piece of him is still here. And the man isn't going to be able to see for shit tonight, not once he takes his contacts out. And he's definitely going to struggle when I tell him to switch the cameras on later this evening to tease him like I plan to.

. . .

You forgot something. Your glasses. Or, as I like to call them, your 'I'm about to ruin your life' disguise. – Francie x

I barely hit send before I see the typing icon come up on the app. A moment later his reply lands.

Shit, did I? Guess I was too busy ruining your life to notice. – Asher ;)

Getting a winky emoji from Asher Fitzgerald feels like winning the world cup. I didn't know he even knew how to wink.

You're going to have to squint at your spreadsheets all night like a sexy mole. I'm picturing it now. Getting a little turned on to be honest. – Francie x

Are moles sexy? – Asher

Only when they wear five-thousand-dollar suits and whisper filthy things in your ear until your legs buckle. Which, to be clear, is my entire fantasy now. So thanks for that, Moley. – Francie x

. . .

It cost three thousand actually. And keep the glasses. You can model them for me. – Asher

Only if you wear the suit. Just the suit. Nothing else. – Francie x

I smile, finally swinging my legs out of bed. Just messaging with him has already made me feel better. I miss him and his sexy-nerd glasses more than I care to admit. That end-of-summer feeling is still there, pulling at me, but maybe, *just maybe,* going back to metaphorical school won't be so bad after all.

Don't play with me. I'm about two seconds from turning around and coming back to get you. – Asher

A smile pulls at my lips. I really need to get in the shower and get some caffeine in my body, because I'm so close to finishing this book. I slide my feet onto the floor and grab my bathrobe, wrinkling my nose because despite it being Asher-certified spider free, I'm still not the biggest fan of the guest bathroom.

What are you wearing right now? – Asher

I laugh out loud. He might have expensive suits and a flash car, but he can be such a *boy.* I glance down at my overworn robe. It's white, but has turned a little gray, threadbare in spots, and has a faded hotel logo from the place I stole it from four years ago, though I left housekeeping the biggest tip.

It's also the most comfortable thing I've ever worn. I think I'd give up my sanity before I give up this robe.

Nothing. – Francie x

I stare at my phone but there's nothing. No typing bubble either. Then it appears.

Jesus, Francie. I'm in a meeting. If I have to stand up anytime soon, I'm going to get arrested. The things I'm gonna do to you when I get back to you. – Asher

Laughter bubbles in my throat. I pad into the bathroom and start the – thankfully spider-free – shower running. The pipes groan, as though they're as reluctant as I am to start the day. Just as I shuck off my robe, my phone vibrates again.

I need visual confirmation. – Asher

Yep, he's definitely a boy.

. . .

Send me a photo of you first. I can add it to my suit porn collection. – Francie

I wish I could. But Brad just walked in, and we have a system audit going. Later. I promise. – Asher

I twist my hair into a messy bun and step into the shower, groaning as the water mists up my body. Before I close the door, I grab my phone, making sure it doesn't get wet as I hold it as far out as my arm can reach, turning to the side so there are no full frontals. Just the curve of my waist, the swell of my hip, and water beading against my skin.

Steam curls around me, softening everything, making it look like a still from an adult movie.

A very *adult* one.

I take the shot then I check it. It's cropped just right. Suggestive without giving anything away. It says 'I want you', not 'here's my annual physical'.

Or at least I hope it does.

Before I can think it through and hesitate, I press send and put my phone on the vanity, stepping back under the spray and letting it soothe every muscle in my body.

And when I get out there's a message from him.

You're beautiful. And I'm hard as fucking steel. And I'm supposed to be concentrating on screens full of code. You're going to pay for this when I see you again. – Asher

· · ·

Lucky me. I look forward to it. – Francie

I stare at the screen for a second too long, the ache in my chest surprising me. Maybe this is just texting. Maybe it's not. But God, I want him back.

Not as much as I will. Now get to work before I start losing my mind. – Asher

* * *

ASHER

"You look way too happy for someone who's had another breach," Brad says, looking up from his laptop to find me smiling like a loon at my phone.

I turn the messaging app off. I'll look at the photograph more carefully later. When I'm alone.

And yeah, maybe I'll even send her one of me in my suit like she asked. I'm all about quid pro quo.

"Apparently I left my glasses on Liberty," I murmur. And yeah, it's a pain because now I'm going to have to either live with my spare pair, which are about two prescriptions-ago too weak, or get my assistant to look into ordering me another pair. I decide on the latter, quickly sending a message to her before I slide my phone in my pocket.

But still, there's a weird tingling in my body. Like she still has a piece of me, which is way too Hallmark movie-esque for my tastes, but there it is. I push the thought away. Another thing to ponder on later.

"So?" I ask. Brad's just run the final protocol. He looks like crap, having worked through the night trying to find where the breach came from. And when I arrived this morning, he was still neck deep in code.

"It's just not there," he mutters. "We're watertight. There's no way somebody can get in." He looks up at me. "I don't understand it."

My stomach twists. There's a sick taste at the back of my throat. I want there to be another answer. Any other answer.

Because we both know what this means. Even if we don't want to admit it. But if we're still going to have a business by the end of this week, somebody has to say it out loud.

"An inside job," I murmur.

Brad blanches. "It can't be. I trust every man who works for me with my life."

That's the painful part. So do I. The only person I don't trust is Nathan. And we've looked into him so many times it fucking hurts. He's way too blasted to be this sophisticated.

And he was never a coding kind of guy. There's no way he left a trojan horse in the system when he left. We would have found it by now.

"There are no clues to who it could be?" I ask him, hoping against hope that the answer is somewhere in the code.

Brad shakes his head. "No. There's not even any clues to what it is. We just know it's there, feeding information." His jaw tightens. "If word gets around that we've been breached again..."

We'll be screwed. Completely. "We need to get this shut down as soon as possible. Get answers the old-fashioned way."

Brad nods. "I'll start interviewing everybody. Go through every single employee with a fine-tooth comb." I can tell how much he hates having to do this by the way he's talking. Like he wants to be sick.

We're a tight knit company. The thought of somebody betraying us feels as painful as if they stabbed us in the chest.

"It's going to take more than the two of us. Who do we trust completely?" I ask. Francie's face flashes in my mind. The way she looked last night, flushed and soft and completely mine.

I don't want her anywhere near this mess. I don't want to bring this poison back to her door.

"We'll need a team of at least five to get this done as quickly as possible," I point out.

"Marie, Ryan, and Sam," he reels off. I nod, because they would be my picks too. But we need two more at the very minimum.

"Dan?" I suggest.

Brad shakes his head. "His father's sick. He could be vulnerable to blackmail."

"What kind of sick?" Another thing I didn't know about my employees.

"Pancreatic cancer."

I swallow hard. I really don't know anything about my employees. Yes, I've been paying for everything for Shaun, but that's the very least I could do.

He's paying the price for whoever's betrayed me, after all.

"Sanjay then."

"Absolutely." Brad nods. "And Kelly."

"Yes, I completely agree. Call them all in for a meeting.

Make it clear this is completely confidential. We'll do it off site. Any ideas?"

"My house," Brad says. "Your apartment has been empty. Which makes it vulnerable, too."

I wince. He's right, but I don't want to hear it.

"Okay. Call them in. And get someone to sweep my place." I'll also do it, but the more eyes I have on it the better.

"Already on it." Brad pulls out a burner phone from the drawer. We typically have a lot of them on hand for sensitive situations. He hands one to me. "All communications between us are on these," he says. "But preferably face to face."

"How do we know these haven't been compromised?" I ask him, turning the old-fashioned Nokia around in my hand. Jesus, I haven't used one of these since I was a kid. It's only one step away from a pager. For a moment I wonder if it still has snake installed.

"Because I bought these ones this morning." Brad lifts a brow. He's one step ahead of me, which is unusual. But I've been a little distracted. "Enough for the whole team."

I give him a nod, reminding myself to give the man the biggest bonus of his life when this is all over. "We maintain business as usual on all other channels," I say. "As far as the rest of the company knows, we're carrying merrily along, with no idea that one of them is a snake in the grass."

"Exactly." Brad nods.

I stand, feeling the weight of my smartphone in my pocket as I slide the Nokia in beside it. And I'm thinking of Francie again. My throat tightens as I realize she's one of the very few people I can trust. And my biggest vulnerability.

Someone's inside my company, playing a game I didn't agree to.

And when I track them down, they'll discover exactly what I do to people who break my trust.

twenty-nine

FRANCIE

I'm hunched over my laptop in the corner table at Mylene's coffee shop, my fingers flying across the keyboard as I write the groveling scene, where my hero has to beg the heroine for forgiveness.

These are always my favorite parts. Mostly because I've noticed that in real life men so rarely grovel. They say 'I'm sorry' with a grunt. Or worse, a shrug. And what are we supposed to do, just melt?

Not in my books. Right now, the commander is bleeding and crawling in an attempt to show her how penitent he is. She won't listen to him with her mind, so he'll find a way to make her listen with her heart.

And I'm going to enjoy it all the way.

But just as I'm about to make him walk barefoot across a burning path, the door to the café flings open.

I look up, my eyes widening. Eileen is standing in the doorway, her expression full of fury. There's a letter clutched in her hand. She's holding it so tightly, her knuckles are as white as snow.

The entire coffee shop turns silent. Even the out-of-towners who are visiting for the day must sense there's something very wrong, because their chatter dies down almost immediately. I look around, desperate for somebody I know to be in here, because this moment is... momentous. Seriously, the two of them have never been this close since forever.

Everybody on the island does their best to keep them apart. My heart starts to slam against my chest. Should I be recording this for Autumn? She's going to be so pissed she's missed it.

Eileen steps forward, her mouth pinched so tight it could slice through an iron girder. Without a word, she slams the letter down on the counter in front of Mylene.

"This," she hisses, stabbing an accusing finger at the paper, "arrived in my mailbox this morning. Care to explain why the Better Business Bureau is investigating me for false advertising?"

Oh, this is just too delicious. I grab my phone and message Autumn, because I can't go through this alone.

Eileen's being investigated by the BBB. She just accused Mylene of reporting her. It's high noon in Liberty. I can't breathe! – Francie

"You started serving blueberry pancakes for breakfast," Mylene says, as though it's an everyday occurrence for her estranged twin of forty years to come into her coffee shop. "And claiming them as your secret recipe."

.   .   .

***Oh. My. God. I need pictures. Video. I can't believe I'm
missing this. – Autumn***

"Who told you that?" Eileen asks. She looks suddenly
shifty.

"I have my sources. And I know exactly what's in those
pancakes. That's my recipe. You stole it." Mylene calmly
pours a latte, passing it to the unlucky customer at the
counter.

"It was Mother's recipe," Eileen retorts. "And you
accuse me of having rats in the kitchen."

"It's the truth. I'm looking at the rat." Mylene wrinkles
her nose like there's a bad smell in the room.

Eileen's shoulders square up.

"You've always been jealous of me. My success. You
hate that my Tripadvisor reviews are higher than yours."
Eileen leans forward, her voice low and deadly. "You're
going to pay for this."

"What are you going to do?" Mylene asks, looking
amused. "Put a hex on me?"

"Are you calling me a witch?"

Mylene shrugs. "If the pointy black hat fits."

Eileen lets out a low rumbling sound, suspiciously like a
growl, then snatches up the letter. "This isn't over," she
warns. "By the time I'm through with you, you'll regret the
day you were born. Second, by the way."

Before Mylene can think up a pithy retort, Eileen turns
on her heel and flounces – as much as she can on her
unsteady legs – out of the coffee shop, slamming the door

closed behind her so hard the glass is in danger of shattering.

For a moment, nobody says a word. Then Mylene sighs and looks at the next customer. "What can I get you, sweetheart?"

My phone buzzes. Autumn again.

What's happening? I need details. You're supposed to be a writer. – Autumn

I smile. I'd hate being out of the loop too.

I'll call you later. Fill you in on everything. Once I'm out of Mylene's earshot. – Francie

You'd better. – Autumn

Before I put my phone away so I can go back to the hero groveling, my phone buzzes again. An unknown number.

I frown, because I hate talking to strangers. But I'm supposed to be a grown up so I answer anyway, trying not to sound too pissed off.

"Francie?"

"Asher?" I blink at his voice.

"It's me," he continues. "This is the only number I want you to use from now on. Just in case. Save it."

I'm confused and sure it is reflecting on my face. "Are

you okay?" I ask him. It's not like him to sound like he's in the middle of a heist movie.

"I'm fine. Just taking precautions after the breach."

"For a second I thought you might have lost your phone as well as your glasses." I smile softly, so happy to hear his voice. "You just need to misplace your wallet then you'll have the full trifecta."

"About the glasses," he murmurs. "I'm going to send someone over to pick them up."

"Oh. Okay." I try to hide my disappointment. For some reason, having them here with me felt like he would definitely be coming back soon. And now... I don't know. I feel disappointed, I guess.

"The driver will be at the lighthouse at five. Does that work?" he asks.

I check my watch. A couple of hours. "Yeah, that's fine."

There's a pause. I try to find something to say. Of course he needs his glasses. He's blind without them. But I still feel strange.

"Does that give you enough time?" he asks.

"To get back to the lighthouse?" I let out a soft laugh, even though I'm not feeling amused. "The island isn't that large. I'm only at the coffee shop, so yes."

"I mean do you have enough time to pack?"

"Pack?" I frown. "Why would I pack?"

"Because the driver's going to pick up the glasses – and you – and bring you both to the helipad. I want to take you out. Tonight. In New York."

I let out a breath. This time my laugh is genuine. "Are you feeling okay?" I ask him.

"Never better," he drawls. "Can you be ready when he gets there?"

"Yes," I squeak.

"Good. Now I've got to get back to work. I'll be waiting for you." He hangs up, and I stare at my phone for a moment.

Oh. My. God. We haven't even been apart for a day, and he's gone all James Bond on me.

And I'm so here for it.

* * *

ASHER

I'm waiting at the helipad for Francie to arrive when my phone vibrates. I sigh as I read the screen.

You have ten unread messages from the Fitzgerald Family Chat. Ten? Jesus. I quickly skim through the messages to make sure nobody is dying, because tonight all my attention is going to be on *her*.

ZACH:

Has anybody heard from Asher? I tried calling him and he hasn't answered?

I roll my eyes, because really? I don't need them gossiping about me right now. Especially when my business is falling apart and I intend to seek solace with the one woman who knows how to soothe me.

HUDSON:

He's in New York. Dealing with the break-in.

. . .

There's a string of messages where Hudson fills them in on what's happened. Which is kind of a good thing I guess, because it saves me a job. Still, there's a weird lump in my throat as I read it, because this whole thing is such a mess.

AUTUMN:

I guess that explains why he's been so weird lately.

ZACH:

Weird, how?

AUTUMN:

I don't know. Just different. He has this tone... I guess the only way I can explain it is he sounds like Hudson did when Skyler first came to the island.

ZACH:

You think a woman's involved?

AUTUMN:

On Liberty? No. But maybe in New York. The break in could be a convenient excuse

WYATT:

· · ·

ZACH:

Wyatt agrees. That means it's irrefutable.

I let out a sigh and finally type a reply, because they're driving me crazy. And the last thing I need is them figuring out who is heading to New York right now.

ASHER:

I'm fine. And you all need to find some hobbies. Speaking of which, anybody heard from Eden?

HUDSON:

Not me. No. Anybody else?

Bingo. Job done. I make a mental reminder to send my youngest sister a big box of chocolates some time. Yes, it needed to be done to give myself some damn peace from them all, but Eden being the sacrificial lamb deserves some kind of payment.

AUTUMN:

She texted me a selfie yesterday. Said she was "heading up the mountain" and hasn't responded since.

ZACH:

Didn't she say that the time she got stuck in a monastery with no cell signal?

HUDSON:

I swear if she's sleeping in a hammock above a ravine again—

EDEN:

Chill. I'm alive. Just busy saving the planet and occasionally stealing Wi-Fi. Miss you weirdos.

A smile curves at my lips and I shove my phone into my pocket just as the helicopter comes into land, climbing out of the backseat to greet the woman who's always the best part of my day.

* * *

FRANCIE

Asher and his car are waiting for me on the ground when the helicopter lands on Pier 6 in New York. It's not my first time on a helicopter, but it's also not my preferred method of travel. So by the time I climb out my legs are feeling a little wobbly.

He strides forward, looking almost impatient, as I pull out his glasses.

"There you go," I say chirpily, putting them in his hand. "I'll see you later." I turn around like I'm about to throw myself back into the death trap, but before I can move his warm hands curl around my hips, pulling me toward him.

I'm wearing a short red dress. Because Mr. Control Freak sent me instructions every hour or so throughout the afternoon.

It's getting chilly in New York. Remember to pack a jacket.

We're going to head straight to dinner when I pick you up. The dress code is business casual.

But don't wear heels in the helicopter. If there's an emergency tennis shoes would be better.

And, my very favorite of all, because it perfectly highlights his demanding ways.

Make sure you listen to the safety instructions. Helicopters can be dangerous.

"You're not going anywhere," he murmurs in my ear.

"Well, unless you want me to walk around naked, I'll need my suitcase," I point out.

Asher looks over my shoulder, his brows furrowing as the pilot rolls my suitcase across the blacktop. It's not quite big enough to fit a body in it, but it's close.

"Are you planning on moving in with me?" he asks,

reaching out to take the case from the pilot. They shake hands and we turn, walking to the black town car that takes Asher everywhere when he's in Manhattan. "Not that I'd mind," he adds.

That makes my chest feel tight.

"Not unless you want me to move the entire Salinger clan in," I say lightly. "I'm going to see my brothers, remember? For D-day. I thought I'd head straight to Virginia from here."

Something flickers in his eyes, but he doesn't say anything. Just loads my luggage into the trunk like it's nothing, ignoring his driver's protests.

Then he opens the car door for me, sliding in next to me as the driver starts the engine.

As we pull out of the lot, I glance over at him. He's still wearing his suit, but he's lost his tie. And he looks tired.

"How was your day?" I ask him.

"Long." He sighs.

I nod, hating how exhausted he looks. "Any more news on the breach?"

He winces, like I've asked the wrong question. Then he drops his head back against the leather seat. "Can we talk about literally anything else?" he asks. He doesn't sound annoyed, just weary. "I've spent the whole day swimming in paranoia. Right now I want to lose myself in you."

I slide my hand into his and squeeze it. "Want me to distract you?" I ask him.

He glances at the driver. The screen is down.

"Not like that." My lips twitch. I prefer to save my exhibitionism for when there are only cameras on me. "I mean, do you want to hear about the big thing that happened between Mylene and Eileen?"

"You found out why they don't talk?" he asks, looking

suddenly awake. Because everybody from Liberty wants to know why they're estranged.

"No. But I was at the coffee shop today and Eileen stormed in. The two of them had a showdown right in front of my eyes."

He tips his head while I tell him about the letter from the BBB and the complaint. And then his mouth curls into laughter when I tell him about the witch insult.

"God, I need this," he says. "Keep going."

"I wish I could, but Eileen stormed out and I've no idea what's going to happen next. And now I'm here."

He lets out a sigh.

I'm still grinning when my phone buzzes. But as I look down, I groan.

Autumn. Damn. I was supposed to call her and fill her in, but then this whole James Bond date distracted me.

I lift my brow and look at Asher. "It's your sister."

He gestures for me to go ahead.

"Hey," I answer.

"Don't hey me, where's my call? I've been waiting on tenterhooks to find out if Eileen burned the whole island down."

"It's okay," I tell her. "It's still standing. And I'm sorry. I was writing a groveling scene. I got kind of hooked."

"They're the best," she says excitedly. "Can you send it to me? I love seeing grown men reduced to bumbling idiots."

Asher's hand slides over my bare thigh, right under the hem of my dress. My breath hitches.

"What was that?" Autumn asks sharply. "Where are you?"

"At the lighthouse," I lie. "I thought I saw another spider."

Asher's fingers inch higher. My thighs clench around his hand. I can see the smirk on his lips from the corner of my eye.

"Oh God, we should call an exterminator. Did I ever tell you about Parker and the bats we found?"

Bats? She never told me that. I frown, wondering if I'm scared of them too.

Asher's fingers trace the edge of my panties. "Ah, yeah." I can't think straight. I shoot him a dirty look.

"Is there something wrong?" my best friend asks me. "You sound weird."

Yes, yes I do. Because my very hot, very determined secret boyfriend is currently attempting to slide his finger inside my panties while his sister is chirping on about bats.

I grab his hand, stopping his movements. So he leans forward to kiss my neck instead.

Oh god. He knows all the places to make me sigh.

"Everything's fine," I manage. "My food is ready though. Microwave meal. It just pinged."

Autumn sighs. "Okay, I'll let you go. But I expect a full update later. Or else I'm sending my brothers after you."

Asher's smirk widens.

"I promise," I manage. "Speak soon." Then I hang up and turn to glare at him.

"Asher Fitzgerald, you're an asshole."

He brushes his lips against my ear, sending a shiver down my spine. "You could have told her the truth," he murmurs. And it makes my heart do a weird flip.

"Not over the phone," I say. "Not like that."

He sits back, his head to the side, like he's trying to read me. "She's going to find out eventually. I'm pretty sure she suspects something where I'm concerned. She and the others were talking about me in their group chat. It's only a matter of time before they put two and two together."

I hear the silent implication beneath it. This isn't going to end well. And it makes my heart race even more.

"I know. But I want to tell her properly. Face to face. Not while I'm a liar on the phone." I roll my eyes at him.

He smiles, like he gets me. "We can do it together. When she and Parker get back from Europe."

It hits me somewhere deep. Like he's letting me see the man behind the armor, if only for a second. Not the CEO. Not the control freak. Just Asher.

And I'm not ready. Except I am. Maybe I've been ready since the moment he kissed me in the kitchen.

And for the next few minutes, we're silent, my hand in his, as he keeps leaning over to kiss me. On the mouth, the neck, my jaw.

When we pull up outside the glittering lights of an uptown restaurant, he doesn't wait for the driver to get out. He's already opening the door, then holding his hand out for me.

"Ready for our first date?" he asks. And I smile because I've done almost everything with this man.

Except go out in public.

"Only if you promise not to touch me under the table."

His smile is pure heat. "No promises."

thirty

ASHER

As soon as we arrive at the restaurant, the maître d' greets us and escorts us to our rooftop table, tucked in the far corner of the terrace beneath a canopy of glowing lanterns and trailing ivy. It's private and quiet, with a view of the river, and I wonder how many strings my PA had to pull to make this happen.

He pulls out Francie's chair, next to the heater that's needed for an October night. Despite the warmth radiating from it, Francie shivers and I immediately shrug off my jacket and wrap it around her shoulders.

It's a shame to block the view of that red dress, but at least she doesn't protest. I'm way too tired and wrung out for arguments. I just want a nice evening with my girl.

"What does groveling mean?" I ask her.

She blinks. "You don't know?"

"In your book," I clarify. "You said you were writing a groveling scene. What is that?"

"Oh." Her face lights up, like I've hit on her favorite subject. "It's when the guy messes up big time and has to win the heroine back. But she's tough and won't take his shit, so he has to work over time."

I frown, not getting it. "And you like that?" I ask, remembering how Autumn squealed when Francie mentioned it. "Why?"

She leans in, resting her elbows on the table as her fingers toy with the stem of her water glass. "Because it's satisfying," she says with a grin. "You've got this big powerful guy who usually controls everything. Life, business, even the heroine's emotions. And suddenly he's flat on his back. Figuratively. Or sometimes literally. He's bleeding for her. Begging for her forgiveness. And finally he realizes that love means vulnerability."

I frown, taking her words in. "So you want your heroes… *bloody*?"

That makes her laugh out loud. "I want them to be humble. And honest. Maybe a little desperate." Her eyes twinkle and I realize that this was a mistake. We should be at home, at my house. Fuck, I'd be humble for her.

Just before I made her scream my name.

"It's not about punishing them," she murmurs softly. "It's about showing the heroine she's worth fighting for."

I trace my thumb across my jaw, thoughtful. "Doesn't she know that already?"

She shrugs. "I guess we all like to be reminded."

"I'm happy to take you home and remind you right now."

"Why?" she asks me. "Do you need to grovel about something?"

I lift a brow, taking in her glowing complexion. Trying

to ignore the fact that I can't be away from her for a day without missing her.

"The night is still young," I tell her and she laughs again.

I feel it in my chest. The easy comfort between us. The soft edges of something real taking shape. Today has been the biggest shit show of my life, yet somehow, she makes everything better.

The waiter arrives with some wine, and we let the conversation drift. She tells me about her plans to visit Misty Lakes, the estate her family owns in Virginia, where she'll come clean to her brothers about her writing.

I tell her about the time I lost a bet with Hudson and had to swim naked in the Atlantic in the middle of December.

"In December?" she winces. "How did I never hear about this?"

"It was before you and Autumn met." I lift a brow. "And no man wants to recount the time his balls shriveled up so far they reached his sternum." I blanch at the memory. Fuck, it was cold. "I swear I got hypothermia."

She tips her head, clearly amused. "Was this before or after you became obsessed with security and control?"

I meet her warm gaze. "Before. It's one of the formative disasters that turned me into the well-adjusted person I am today."

Her mouth twitches. I reach out to touch it with my thumb, dragging it along her bottom lip. The tension that's been coiled in my chest all day loosens.

"That explains the helicopter safety texts," she murmurs.

"I just needed to see you. And I needed you safe." And

yeah, I feel a little sheepish because this woman doesn't need me to take care of her. She's fully capable of doing it herself.

Truth is, I like doing it. I like the dynamic. I have a knight-in-shining armor complex and I have no idea how to suppress it.

"And here I am." She lifts my hand to her mouth, kissing my palm. It sends a shot of desire right through me. "But I wouldn't say I'm safe." She tips her head to the side, like she's studying me. "By the way, the naked swimming thing would have been a great grovel."

I chuckle. "Feel free to use my humiliation as fodder for your books."

"I'm already using your psychic sex. What's a little ball shrivel between friends?"

I capture her hand. "We're not just friends. We already established this." I run my thumb along the delicate skin on her wrist and her breath catches. Just the smallest hitch.

It's enough to tell me she hears the truth behind my words. That this isn't just friends fucking.

It's something else. Something more. I may not be able to say the words yet, but I know what I feel.

When our food arrives – scallops for her, a rare steak for me – we fall into a low, easy murmur of conversation that only happens when everything fits. I find myself watching her instead of eating, soaking in the way she tucks her hair behind her ear, how she wrinkles her nose when she tells me a secret.

How I'm falling for this woman, hook, line, and sinker.

And then I feel it. A prickling sensation on the back of my neck. Like I'm being watched.

A moment later, a shadow shifts in the corner of my vision.

"Asher."

The voice is low. There's an edge to it that pulls at my chest despite the owner of the words.

Francie turns her head to look at the woman standing next to her, staring at her like she's my mistress and I'm a cheater.

"Annalise," I say. *Fuck.* Just when I thought today was getting better.

She looks at Francie expectantly, as though she's waiting for me to introduce them. But before I can say anything, Francie lifts her hand.

"Hi," she says, smiling. "I'm Francie."

Annalise blinks, disarmed. "So you're the latest then?"

Francie doesn't miss a beat. "The latest what?"

Annalise opens her mouth to reply, but thinks better of it and closes it again. And I'm reminded of just how much I like Francie Salinger. I squeeze her hand tightly.

Annalise runs her tongue along her bottom lip. "How are you?" she asks me.

"I'm fine." My voice is tight. "And you?"

She inhales softly. "Nathan hasn't been well," she says. "The doctors think it could be serious."

I swallow hard at the mention of my ex-business partner. Not that I'm surprised he's unwell. You can only snort so much coke before it messes up everything in your life.

Francie looks from me to Annalise, like she's working out who Annalise is. Her hand squeezes mine and damn it feels good.

"He overdosed a week ago. He's in the hospital in Aruba." Annalise looks at me like it's my fault. "He's only just regained consciousness."

The words hit harder than I expect. Not because I feel sorry for him. Nathan Vale knew exactly what kind of game he was playing when he tried to gut our company from the inside. But because it means something else.

If he's been unconscious for a week, he's definitely not behind the breach. And there goes my last hope that it isn't somebody I trust.

"I hope he recovers," I say, because it's the right thing. But I don't miss the way Francie's thumb strokes gently along the side of my hand.

Like she knows I need her.

Seeing the way I don't let her hand go, Annalise nods tightly. Christ, I don't want to hurt the woman, even though she gave Nathan information on me. Information that helped him nearly steal the company from me. But I need her gone.

"Have a good evening," I tell her. It's a dismissal. She's not stupid, she gets that. With one more sweeping look, she gazes at Francie with equal parts curiosity and disdain, then turns on her heel and disappears back behind the huge pots of trees that are artfully laid out to give each table some privacy.

Once I know she's gone, I let out a low breath and rake my free hand through my hair.

For a second neither of us says anything. Then we both talk at once.

"I'm sorry. I wasn't—"

"She's something." Francie lifts a brow. But there's no edge to her words. Just warmth. "She's the sister of your ex business partner, right?"

I nod. "Yeah."

"And you two had a thing?" Her eyes lock on mine. She's not stupid, she can pick up cues. But I still hate that my sordid past and my perfect present are clashing.

There's a tightness in my chest as I nod. "We dated for a while. Before Nathan screwed me over."

"And then?"

"I found out she'd been reading my emails while I was asleep," I tell her. "Is this the part where I need to grovel?" Because no woman wants to come face to face with their date's ex. Especially not when she's flown in to spend time with him.

But, because she's Francie, she blows me away.

"You don't need to grovel about having a past, Asher." Her eyes meet mine, her gaze unwavering. "I care about you," she adds, her voice soft. "Whatever drama came before me, it's not going to scare me off." She wrinkles her nose. "Even if she did have the perfect shoes."

My lips twitch, remembering the flats I insisted Francie wear.

"I like yours better."

We both know I'm not talking about the shoes. But her words land squarely in my chest, hitting deeper than they should. I don't deserve her. But I'm keeping her anyway.

She tips her head, a small smile playing at her lips. "You're looking at me funny."

My brow knits. "Funny how?"

"I don't know," she murmurs. "Like you're trying to figure me out."

"I'm trying to figure out if you'll be annoyed if I cancel dinner and haul you back to my place," I murmur."

She grins, slow and wicked. "I thought you'd never ask."

Our eyes lock. That slow burn between us flares like a flame to dry leaves. The restaurant around us fades to a blur. All I see is her.

"Want to get out of here?" I put it into words. My intentions very clear.

She doesn't even hesitate. Just folds her napkin and puts it on the table. "So much."

The waiter appears. "Just the check," I tell him.

"Can't we tempt you with dessert?" he asks, looking at our half-eaten plates.

I glance at Francie. Her eyes are still on mine, her cheeks flushed, lips parted like she's already imagining what comes next.

"I've got dessert covered," I say roughly. Francie's lips twitch like she can read my mind.

The waiter blinks then nods and disappears, returning only moments later with the check. I don't want to wait for him to run my credit card, so I throw a bunch of fifties on the table and reach for her hand. And as we walk away from the heater into the cool Manhattan night, she leans against me, her hair tickling my face.

"Just so you know, I really wanted dessert."

My lips curl as I lean in close, brushing my mouth against the shell of her ear.

"You're getting it," I murmur. "At least three times."

She lets out a laugh that makes my whole damn body tighten. And as the driver pulls up and I lead her to my car, I know exactly how this evening is going to end.

Not with groveling.

But with me showing her how I really feel. Even if I can't say it yet.

* * *

FRANCIE

"Asher…"

My voice is breathless and ragged, like the sound is being pulled from somewhere deep inside of me. My back arches off the sheets as he thrusts again, slow, but unrelenting. The drag of his body inside mine is stealing every coherent thought from my head.

I don't care that his ex turned up at our first date. Or that I'll be facing my family with the truth very soon. I don't even care that I'm going to have to tell Autumn the truth when she's back.

All I can think about is that he's holding me like I'm a goddess. He's under my skin, etched into the softest parts of me.

He shifts slightly, the angle changing, but he's still holding me like I'm something precious. My own hands scramble for purchase on his damp back, my nails grazing his skin. He kisses me. My mouth, my jaw, the slope of my neck. Like he's starving and I'm the only thing on the menu.

He slides back against me, sending a shot of pleasure through my body.

"I can feel you everywhere," I whisper, because it's true.

His lips brush my ear. "That's the point."

And when he slides his fingers between us, finding my achiest place, every cell inside of me cries out in response. My legs tremble around his hips as he moves again, deep and deliberate, like he's trying to memorize the shape of me. His fingers don't rush, they just stroke and circle, coaxing me higher until I'm so close I can't breathe.

But he doesn't let me go there. Not yet.

Instead, he slows.

His forehead presses to mine, and I open my eyes to find him staring down at me. Those inky blue irises, so sharp and clear, feel like they're looking straight into my soul.

"You're killing me," I whisper.

His mouth curves. But it's not playful. It's reverent.

"No," he murmurs. "I'm loving you."

The words hit like a blow to my chest. I don't know if he means it. If he even realizes he's said it. But my heart clenches so tight I can barely speak.

"Asher." It's a murmur. But I need to say it out loud, to make sure this is real.

He kisses me again. Slower this time. Tenderly. Like the kind of kiss you give somebody you don't want to lose.

He starts to move again. Slow at first, like he's savoring every second. The rhythm builds gradually, the way a song does when it's about to hit that perfect, devastating note. My hips lift to meet his, greedy for every inch, every stroke.

And when his thumb brushes over my clit again, I shatter.

It's not a quiet, gentle kind of orgasm. It's a full-body unraveling. A cry rips from my throat as he drives me straight into oblivion. My hands cling to him like he's the only thing anchoring me to this world.

Maybe he is.

Because even as I'm falling apart he's still here. His voice in my ear, telling me how beautiful I am. How perfect.

I'm still tightening around him as he groans.

"Francie. I can't. Fuck, I'm so close."

I cup his face, needing him to join me. "Let go," I manage to whisper.

And he does.

With a final thrust he buries his face in my neck, his breath hot and ragged against my skin. He comes in thick, long, aching bursts, spilling deep inside of me.

We lie there tangled. Our hearts racing, our bodies slick with sweat. Aftershocks rush through me, making him groan every time I contract.

His voice is hot against my ear. "You're mine," he tells me.

It isn't quite him declaring himself. But it's close. And he's right. I *am* his. I've been his for a long time. And I'm not sure I know how to be anything else.

thirty-one

ASHER

She falls asleep almost immediately. I barely get a chance to clean her up – or offer her a real dessert – before she's sprawled across my sheets like she belongs here. Her hair is a wild halo on the pillow, one hand curled beneath her cheek and the other resting where I can feel the warmth of her on my chest.

I should be sleeping too. God knows I need it. But instead I lie here watching her, unable to look away.

I brush a strand of hair from her face, letting my fingers linger just long enough to memorize the softness of her cheek.

She sighs in her sleep, turning toward me like she knows I'm here and she needs me closer.

My chest tightens.

Before I can pull her against me, my phone buzzes from the nightstand, cutting through the silence. I slide out of bed and reach for it, the screen glowing in the dark.

Brad's name is written in black.

Stepping into the hallway in only a pair of shorts, I answer quietly, pulling the door closed behind me.

They've been working all night. That's what he said they'd do when he pushed me out of his house to go pick up Francie.

"Keep it normal. Don't let anybody think you know we have a breach," he'd told me. *"We don't want them to panic and hide."*

"What's up?" I murmur, looking at the clock on the hallway wall. It's past midnight. They all need to go home and get some sleep.

"We've found them," Brad says. "The mole. We know who it is."

FRANCIE

A pair of soft lips press against my mouth and I groan, my eyelids fluttering open to see Asher leaning over me. He's fully dressed, in a suit and tie. And from the way his hair is damp he's showered too.

"What time is it?" I murmur. The room is still dark, but I have no idea whether that's due to some expensive blinds, or the fact that it's not morning.

"Just before one." He brushes a lock of hair out of my face. "I have to go to the office. Go back to sleep."

I sit up. "Is something wrong?" I ask him.

He hesitates. Then lets out a soft breath. "Brad's found something. He wants to take me through it."

"And it can't wait until morning?" My stomach tightens

at the expression on his face. It's tense. Like he's trying not to boil over.

"No." He shakes his head. "What time are you leaving for Virginia?"

"Eleven," I tell him, trying not to show my nervousness. Yes, I love my brothers but I'm so scared they're going to take my revelation poorly. "Will you be back before then?"

He shakes his head. "I don't think so." His phone vibrates. It's only when he pulls it out that I realize it's an old flip phone. Not a smart phone, just a handset that can make calls and send texts. He looks at whatever is on the small screen and winces. "My driver will take you to Virginia."

"It's okay. I have a ride."

"I'd rather know you got there safely," he says.

I force a smile onto my face, because he seems so different from the man who opened himself up to me only hours ago. "It's fine. I'll text you when I get there."

He nods, but the crease in his brow doesn't ease. He leans down to kiss me again, slower this time, his lips lingering like he's trying to memorize the feel of mine.

When he finally straightens, I lace our fingers together.

"Are you sure you're okay?" I'm worried about him. "Maybe I shouldn't have come here."

I'm a distraction. I know that. And he has so much going on.

"I'm fine," he says a little too fast. "Just need to deal with this shit."

The breach. I open my mouth to ask him about it, but then his words from earlier in the night flash back into my memory.

I want to lose myself in you.

Everybody makes demands of him. His employees, his

family, and whoever is trying to ruin his business. I don't want to be that person. Yes, I want him to talk to me, but if there's one thing I know about this man it's that he'll open up when he's ready.

So I swallow the questions I have about what's going on and nod.

"I'll call you tonight," I say instead. "To give you the low down on how my brothers take it."

"Are you worried about their reaction?" he asks.

I shrug, trying to be nonchalant. "It's far beyond time they found out. I'm a romance author, not a serial killer. I don't know why I built it up in my head for so long." And it helps that Charlie's coming along with me. He's my ride.

He thinks it's hilarious that I'm finally coming clean.

Asher nods, but there's still that distant look on his face.

"Don't worry," I add, wondering if he's worried about me disclosing our relationship as well. "I'm not planning on overwhelming them with too many revelations at once. I'll start with the writing before easing them into the idea of us. I'm not sure that 'by the way, I'm dating this older guy I met at a sex club' will go down well." I smile at him.

"Thanks for the PR strategy," he says dryly.

"You're welcome." I sit up and reach for him.

He leans in instinctively, his arms wrapping around me, his mouth claiming mine. His kiss isn't gentle. It's hungry and hard and sends shots of desire through my body that have no place being there when he needs to leave.

But I kiss him back anyway. I don't want to forget this. Don't want to forget the way he feels. Not when I have to go face my family and tell them I'm not who they think I am.

When he pulls away, he stares at me for a moment, his breath soft against my cheek. I close my eyes and think about earlier. The way he felt as we made love, because that's what it was.

The way he moved inside of me like he never wanted to stop.

The way he told me he was loving me.

I'm still not sure he realizes what he said. But those words are imprinted on my brain.

I'm falling in love with him. Or, let's face it, I've fallen. I can't be without him anymore.

And I don't want to try.

I let out a ragged breath. I want to tell him how I feel. But it's so not the right time. "Why does it always feel like we're saying goodbye?" I ask.

Asher's gaze holds mine. Then he leans in and presses his mouth against my brow, lingering for a beat too long.

Like it hurts to pull away.

"It's not goodbye," he says quietly. "We both have things to sort out. You're going to face your brothers and finish your book. I've got to handle this shit with the breach. And then we'll be together again."

"Where?" It comes out before I can stop it. I hate feeling needy, but that's what I am right now.

"Here," he says. "Or Liberty. I don't care. But we'll be together. And we'll make some plans."

His words wrap around my heart like a promise.

"You'd better be there when I type *the end*," I tell him. "I'll want to celebrate."

His lips curl into a genuine smile. "I'll be there," he promises. "I'm planning on giving you some ideas for the sequel."

His phone buzzes again. He rolls his eyes, and I smile at him. "Good luck."

He gives me a wink. "Right back at you. Let me know when you get to Virginia."

"I will," I promise.

He kisses me again, and then he's gone. The door clicks behind him and I let myself fall back on the mattress, turning my head to his pillow. It's still dented. Still smells of him.

Tomorrow is going to be interesting. But suddenly I'm not scared of my brothers' reactions.

Because I finally know exactly what I want.

thirty-two

ASHER

I stare at the large screen in the monitor room at my office, watching the same blurry video for the third time. There's complete silence in the room, despite seven of us being here.

Brad stands with his arms crossed beside me, his jaw locked tight. Sanjay, our analyst, sits at the console, his fingers poised over the keyboard like he's bracing for impact.

The footage plays in slow motion. It's grainy and color-less, captured by one of the cameras that had been corrupted during the breach. It was deleted, but a trace remained, and once Brad and his team knew what they were looking for, they managed to recover enough for us to see exactly who was involved in the break in.

The date stamp is from a week before the office was ransacked. The rooms are quiet, save for the on duty guard making his regular patrol. He stands from his position at the monitor – the same monitor we're all huddled around – and moves toward the hallway. The image switches, as Shaun moves with confidence, swiping his badge to access the high security server alone.

He shows no hesitation at all. Like he's a man on a mission.

"There," Sanjay murmurs, tapping a key to freeze the frame. He zooms in on the monitor beside him, his fingers flying across the keyboard. A script window opens, lines of code flashing for a brief moment before the camera blacks out completely.

"That's the trojan," Brad says, like he still can't believe it himself. "Shaun installed the backdoor himself."

My stomach twists. Of all the people I expected to be involved in this, the man lying in a hospital bed with a head injury – *on my dime* – is the last person I thought would be the mole.

I try to push the feeling of betrayal down, as Sanjay brings up another clip.

It's of the outside of the building. The date stamp shows the night of the break in.

"Where did you get this?" I ask. When we went through all the security videos the night of, they'd been deleted.

"We hacked into our own servers," Kelly murmurs. "The trojan was supposed to stop us, but we managed to recover this from an old backup. Once we realized what the trojan was, it made it simpler."

The screen shows the hallway outside the office suite. The door opens and Shaun walks out, then stops. Two men approach him, their faces obscured with balaclavas. For a moment the three of them talk. Then he lets them into the office, into the security room. Shaun points at something, the server room maybe?

And then one of the men punches Shaun. *Hard.*

Another takes what looks like a piece of piping out and slams it against Shaun's head.

Shaun doesn't fight back. He doesn't even flinch. He submits. Like taking the beating is part of the plan.

Probably because it was.

Nausea rises inside me as blood drips from his temple and he slides to the ground, one of the attackers crouching beside him like he's checking for a pulse.

Then the screen goes dark.

"We think that's when they started breaking things in the room," Brad says. "After that we can't recover anything else."

I pinch the bridge of my nose, the image of Shaun's bleeding head in my memory. For a moment, all I can think of is my dad's beating that day I was locked in the closet.

The way he screamed. The way he bled.

"He staged it," I finally say, my voice hoarse. "The break-in. The injuries. All of it."

Brad nods. "It was a cover. So he wouldn't be suspected. It was only a matter of time before we discovered the breach. This way, they could stop us from finding the trojan, or at least from blaming him."

"The beating he took was pretty brutal," I murmur, my stomach churning at the sight.

"Yeah, I suspect he wasn't expecting them to cause that level of damage," Brad agrees. "It's kind of poetic justice at least."

"Has anybody called the hospital?" I ask him.

"He was discharged two days ago," Brad says, his eyes meeting mine. "But the good news is, he's at home. I sent a guard over as soon as we found the footage. He's not going anywhere."

"And you're sure the guard is uncompromised?"

"Absolutely." Brad nods. "What do you want to do?"

"Bring him in." My voice is low.

Brad straightens. "You want to talk to him yourself?"

"I want him in my office before the end of the day." I meet his gaze. "And I want to know who he's working with."

We know of at least two accomplices. I need their identities. And if anybody else is involved.

Brad hesitates. Just enough to make the hairs on the back of my neck lift.

"There's something else," he tells me, reaching for the remote and clicking to a new folder on the screen. "It wasn't only the Manhattan office that was compromised."

He can't quite meet my eye.

I frown. "What are you talking about?"

He brings up some more code. "Your phone and laptop. Shaun accessed them a week before the break-in. Just a couple of log entries at first. Then a full system sync."

My stomach turns to stone.

"You're telling me he had access to my personal communications?" I rasp. It takes a moment to remember to breathe.

Brad nods. "Yeah. I'm sorry, man."

My mind flashes to all the things that are on my laptop. The security cameras for the lighthouse. My messages with Francie.

The video of her touching herself for me. I fucked her against the lighthouse door. All on camera. Available for Shaun to see. And whoever he's working with.

Fuck.

"How much could he see?" I ask, barely able to get the words out.

"We don't know yet," Brad says carefully. "We're pulling logs and backups. But if he mirrored the drives and the SD card…"

He doesn't finish the sentence. He doesn't need to.

Because I already know exactly what's at stake.

And if those videos are out there. Christ, I can't think about that. Think about him seeing her at her most vulnerable. Think about who else has.

I promised her she was safe. That it was only me watching. That I had the cameras locked down.

She trusted me.

And I failed her.

A cold sweat breaks out along my spine. It dampens my shirt, making it stick to my skin, a contrast to the storm building inside of me.

Brad's still talking. Something about data packets and encrypted fragments, but it's a dull buzz against the roar in my head.

I see her face. Her smile. The way she looked at me like I was worth something. Like I made her feel safe. Free.

And I might have brought her world tumbling down.

"Drag him in here if you have to," I say, my voice thick. "We need to know what he knows. Are the systems safe now?"

"Yep." Brad nods. "As well as your laptop and phone. We've recoded them. Nobody can get in."

"Bring him to my office when he gets here," I say, needing to be alone. Which is fucking ironic, because I've never felt so lonely right now.

I can't tell her. Not when she trusted me to keep her safe. Not when I'm the one who failed.

I just need to make this go away.

* * *

FRANCIE

Charlie can't hide his grin as his car turns onto the sweeping driveway that leads to our family estate.

"Home sweet ridiculously oversized home," he says, eyeing the mansion ahead like it personally offends his minimalist aesthetic. "So." He taps his fingers against the wheel. "You ready for your big confession?"

It's the third time he's asked since we hit the Virginia state line. And at least the twelfth since we left Manhattan.

I narrow my eyes at him. "If I say no, will you turn the car around?"

He leans dramatically toward the windshield. "Too late. We've crossed the point of no return. Cue the ominous music and emotionally stunted brother stares."

He's been like this for the entire seven-hour drive. Peppering me with not-so-subtle questions about why I had him pick me up outside Asher's apartment building. Not that he knows it's Asher's. But Charlie has instincts like a bloodhound with a gossip addiction.

Unfortunately for him, but very fortunately for me, I've learned how to handle Charlie-level nosiness: weaponized distraction.

So I spent most of the drive getting him to talk about his new TikTok channel, where he gives financial advice to broke Gen-Zers. He's gone viral twice, much to his glee. Once for explaining compound interest using Starbucks cups, and again for a video titled *Buy Your Avocado Toast AND Retire at 60.*

He has the golden touch, not that I'll ever tell him that.

And he's also completely obsessed with his new channel, luckily for me.

But now we're here. And he's vibrating with glee at the prospect of me dropping a literary bombshell on my six older brothers.

"Don't look so excited," I mutter.

"Oh please." He adjusts his sunglasses with the flair of someone born for drama. "You're about to tell the most macho men in Virginia that you've spent the last five years secretly writing hot, sexy, wildly successful romance novels. This is the Super Bowl of family confessions."

"Do not say the word 'hot' in front of your dad or uncles," I warn him.

"I would never," he promises me solemnly. "Unless it comes up naturally."

The car hums along the gravel road that leads to the family home, winding beneath a canopy of towering trees that arch overhead. Shafts of sunlight flicker over the windshield as we drive deeper into the heart of Misty Lakes, and then, as if summoned, the trees part and the view explodes into technicolor.

It's breathtaking.

Rolling green hills, manicured lawns, and our family home, perched like a crown on top of it all. It's an elegant, sprawling stone and glass mansion that wouldn't look out of place in *Architectural Digest*. And beyond the hills, to the left, peeking out is a glint of blue. The first of the lakes the estate is named after. Though we can't see them from here, the lake is surrounded by six cabins. Each belonging to one of my brothers. When they reached the age of eighteen, it was a rite of passage that they built their own home along the lake.

Over the years they've added to their buildings as they

added to their families. Now they're all full of luxuries, and their homes-away-from home.

Charlie gives a low whistle as we pull up outside the main house. "Here we are," he says. "The promised land. Where strong men build cabins and emotionally repressed women write romance novels in secret."

He reaches to pull open the door.

"Oh no you don't," I say. "You're not coming in."

His eyes widen. "What? Why not? I've been living for this drama."

"I messaged your mom. She's expecting you. She's made dinner." I give him a wide grin. I love him – and I owe him for driving me, but this revelation is between my brothers and me. No onlookers invited.

Charlie groans. "I can't believe you're making me miss the fireworks. This is emotional sabotage." There's teasing in his voice though. He's never one to hold a grudge.

"You'll survive," I tell him, grabbing my purse from the backseat. "Besides, I'll give you the full play-by-play once the dust settles."

He narrows his eyes. "I expect voice memos. With tone. And at least one dramatic reenactment."

I nod, trying not to grin. "Deal."

Then I lean in to kiss his cheek and he grins like an idiot. "Go get em, Hemingway."

"Wrong genre."

"Nora Roberts then."

"Much better."

Once I've grabbed my ridiculously sized suitcase from the trunk, Charlie drives off, his arm out of the window, his playlist thumping some overloud rap music he happily mouths along to.

Then I turn toward the house.

The front door opens before I even get there. Six tall men walk out, looking ridiculously handsome, despite their age. And before I can lift my suitcase to carry it up the stairs, my brother Linc – the second youngest, runs down to grab it from me.

But it's Myles that always makes me feel a little panicky. My oldest, most responsible, and most likely to interrogate me under a spotlight brother, walks over to hug me.

"Francine," he murmurs. "How was your drive?"

"It was good," I say, trying to hide my nervousness. "Charlie didn't kill me so I call that a win." I look over my shoulder, seeing his car in the distance. "He's heading to meet up with Ava." Myles' wife. Charlie's mom. "Said he'd see you there tomorrow."

As soon as I walk into the huge, echoing hallway with its marble floors and wood paneled walls I feel it. The loneliness that used to come over me despite the fact that I was part of a huge family.

Growing up here, with a father that was older than most of my friends' grandfathers, and a mother who saw her responsibility as taking care of him more than spending time with me, shaped me into the woman I am today.

Strong, yes, or at least I hope so. Independent for sure. But also closed off. Because I learned from an early age that showing weakness and emotions made my family feel uncomfortable.

I know my brothers would hate to know that I always felt left out. They tried to include me in everything. But they were so tight, the six of them. And completely grown up, with wives and families of their own before I was out of elementary school.

I didn't belong with them, and I didn't belong in this

house either. Which was why I spent so much of my time escaping into books. Pretending to be somewhere else.

Like he can read my mind, and he knows I'm feeling vulnerable, a message arrives from Asher on my phone.

Did you arrive safely? – Asher

It's brief, unemotional, but completely understandable. He's got messes of his own to clear up.

I did, despite Charlie's driving. With my brothers now. I'm going to freshen up then hit them with it. Wish me luck. – Francie x

Less than a heartbeat later, a reply flashes up.

You don't need luck. You've got this. I'll call you later and you can tell me all about it. – Asher

"You want a drink?" Linc shouts out to me when I walk into the kitchen. He's at the breakfast bar mixing cocktails. Behind him is a huge picture window with a view of the rolling green hills that stretch down to the lake.

"No she doesn't," Myles replies to him, always the biggest, most overprotective brother.

Linc rolls his eyes at me, making me smile. "I'll get you a soda," Linc tells me with a wink. "With vodka in it."

I laugh, because it's barely five o'clock. "It's okay. I'm going to freshen up and then I'll grab something. Are you all staying for dinner?"

Myles nods. "Yes. There's something we need to talk to you about."

Immediately my blood runs cold. Do they know about my writing already? Yes, it would save me having to tell them, but they'll be super mad I didn't come clean first.

And they don't seem super mad.

"I'll be back soon," I say, though none of them look like they're going to be mad if I take my time. Linc is pouring out what looks like paint stripper from the cocktail shaker, Brooks and Hudson are in a deep discussion about God knows what, and Liam and Myles are looking at their phones. Eli, on the other hand, already turned on the television in the kitchen and is scrolling through the sports channels.

Some things never change.

I miss you – Francie x

I type it out quickly and send it to him. Because when he's around, even in my texts, I feel less alone.

So much, baby. – Asher

And that's the last I hear from him as I walk upstairs to my childhood bedroom and unpack my toiletry bag, ready for a shower, to make myself ready for the big reveal.

thirty-three

FRANCIE

By the time I come back downstairs, freshly showered and wearing linen pants and a t-shirt, the smell of something delicious is wafting from the kitchen. I peek in to find Linc and Brooks bickering over pasta.

"Finally," Linc says, grinning. "I need your help. You're a woman of taste. Pasta should always be underdone, right?"

"Al dente." I nod. "With a bite."

The oversized table is set for seven, with linen napkins, crystal glasses, and the kind of silverware that only comes out when Mom's hosting.

"Is all this for me?" I ask. Because my brothers aren't usually ones for such pretense.

"Of course." Myles says, sweeping in. "You've come home. It's something worth celebrating."

There's a stupid lump in my throat that no swallow will get rid of. I let out a breath. "Thank you."

"Always," he says softly.

"Dinner's up," Linc calls out, always the domesticated one. When his son was born – Rowan who's now twenty and breaking hearts at college – he took a sabbatical and became a house husband. "Brooks, take the salad and bread over. Myles, can you pour the wine? Everybody else, help me serve."

For a minute or two, there's complete mayhem. The kind you can only get in a big family, six of whom are all over six foot two. But finally we're sitting down, eating Linc's delicious carbonara, groans of appreciation echoing around the room.

I eat politely, carefully twirling the spaghetti around my fork the way my mom taught me, but my brothers eat like a pack of wolves who've been fasting for a year. And I can't help smiling as they banter and bicker and steal food off each others' plates.

It's loud, warm, and just a little overwhelming. And it makes me feel like I'm part of something that I haven't been for a long time.

Which makes it harder to bring up the thing I have to bring up. *Ugh*.

So I don't. Not for a while. Instead we talk about everything and nothing. Eli's coaching schedule, Liam's new house project, the fact that their kids are growing up and making their gray hairs turn steely.

The food disappears faster than I thought humanly possible, and by the time I go to clear the plates – and am swatted away by Linc – the air is thick with satisfied sighs and the sound of wine glasses being refilled.

Then Myles clears his throat and my stomach tightens.

He's at the head of the table, his posture straight, his hands clasped together like he's chairing a meeting.

Which technically, he is, even if he doesn't know it. I know I need to tell them. But right now, I feel like the food is sitting heavy in my stomach, my nerves twisting tighter with every laugh and bite.

"We should raise a toast to Francie." He lifts his glass to me. "It's good to see you."

"To Francie," my brothers say, lifting their glasses.

I give him a smile. "Thank you."

"We wanted to talk to you about something," Myles says once they've all swallowed down their wine. He glances around at the others. Every single one of them goes suddenly silent.

The hairs on the back of my neck prickle.

I look over at Linc. My pal. My closest brother. "This isn't an ambush," he tells me quickly, as though he can sense my unease. "It's just... we've been talking. About you."

"And we realized we've made some mistakes," Myles says. "You've always been our little sister. But I think we forgot you're also a grown up. A woman with her own dreams. And... we would like to be part of that. If you'll let us."

I open my mouth. This is it. "I can explain," I say quickly. But Myles holds his hands up.

"It's not your fault," he says. "It's all ours. We should have realized how excluded you felt. How hard it was to talk to us."

"But I..."

"We want to help you build a cabin," Linc blurts out.

I blink.

"What?" I look around at them. "Is that what you think this is about?"

"We all built our own cabins. Helped each other. Just as

soon as we became adults." Myles gaze catches mine. "You should have one, too. We didn't even think about it. And that's our faults. So we want to do that for you. As soon as possible. Work on designs, order the materials. Do it together."

I'm not sure what I expected when I walked in here today, but it wasn't this. A table set for me, a toast in my honor. And now this. An offer to be their actual sibling. Their equal.

To have my own place around the lake.

As a kid, I longed to be part of their tight knit group. They were all so much fun, so grown up. But also so much older than me, they were my dads more than my brothers.

But this offer. To build something permanent. Something mine.

Something they want to share with me.

It's making me want to cry.

"Are you sure?" I whisper, the lump in my throat back with a vengeance.

"Of course." Myles blinks. Because my brothers are many things. Overbearing, loud, mildly allergic to emotions. But they've never been disingenuous. And the way they're all looking at me now, like they're excited to make me part of this...

It makes my chest feel full.

I bite my lip because the last thing they need is for me to cry. They can only cope with so much emotion.

"Thank you," I manage. "That means a lot."

Linc gives me the softest of smiles. "We miss you. Whenever we're together it feels like there's something missing because you're not there. We want you to have your own space. One that we can help you build. It's important to all of us."

I nod. "I love that, I really do."

And then I pause, my finger tracing the rim of my wine glass. Because they're being so open with me. They deserve the same respect.

"But there's something you should know," I say, taking a deep breath.

Linc's face immediately falls. "Shit, are you pregnant?"

My mouth drops open. "What? Where did that come from? No. It's not that."

"It wouldn't matter if she was," Brooks points out. "She's an adult, she can do whatever she likes."

They start talking over each other again, and I have to pick up my spoon and hit it against my glass to get their attention.

"Can you all shut up?" I ask them. "I'm trying to talk here."

They all have the good grace to do exactly that.

And then I do it. I look at them, the brothers who've always felt so distant but who feel so close right now.

"I've been lying to you all. I'm not a barista," I tell them. "I'm a published writer. I write romance books. I've been publishing under a pen name for the last five years."

There's complete silence.

The kind you can only get in a room full of men who have absolutely no idea how to process what you've just said. I can see Myles' fingers twitching, like he's desperate to call his wife for advice.

"Wait," Linc says. "Why didn't you tell us?"

I pull my lip between my teeth. It's so difficult to put it in a way they'll understand. "I guess at first I was afraid I might fail. And I didn't want anybody knowing if I did. And then, when they became popular, I was worried..." That they'd interfere. But I can't tell them that. "I just wanted something that was mine, I suppose. Then the lie grew and it got too big to tell you." I look at them. "I'm sorry."

Myles winces. "No, I'm sorry," he says. "That you didn't trust us enough. That's on us, not you."

Linc blinks at me. "What kind of romance?"

I turn to look at him. "Fantasy. Romantasy, they call it."

Linc nods. "Zoe is into those," he says, talking about his stepdaughter. "I read one of them on a flight." He looks at Brooks. "It was dirty as hell." He starts to laugh and then trails off. "Wait. Are your books spicy?"

It's so Linc that he even knows the term for sexy books. "Um, kind of," I admit. "I guess they're in the middle. But they're about to get spicier."

"In the middle?" Myles echoes. "What does that mean? And what the hell is spicy? Are there chilies in it?"

My lips twitch.

"It means it's dirty," Linc says, winking at me.

I roll my eyes back at him. He's really not helping. So I turn to Myles.

"It means my romantic scenes don't fade to black, but I also don't write super sexy, descriptive books." Until now. But we'll deal with that later.

Brooks snorts into his wine.

"You know we're going to read them now, right?" Holden asks me. "*All* of them."

"God help us," Eli mutters.

"My books aren't exactly written for men your age," I say, trying to imagine them reading *those* parts.

"That's ageist," Linc says. "And possibly sexist."

"I'm just warning you. You might not see me in the same little sister light anymore." I then explain to them about the new book, that unlike the others it'll be in bookshops.

Myles face lights up. "Twisted Publishing?" he murmurs. "I know Alice DuChamps. Maybe I should..."

I narrow my eyes. "No. Absolutely not. If you interfere I will burn this house down."

Myles lifts his hands in mock surrender. "Fine. But if you ever need help..."

I take a deep breath. I know it comes from a place of love. "Thank you," I tell him. "But I have a great agent and I have this."

He nods. "Okay." And then he smiles at me. "I'm so damn proud of you."

Oh. That sends a shot of happiness straight through me.

"Thank you." I nod. "That means a lot."

Linc clears his throat. "So is that it? The big confession? Or is there anything else? A secret baby? A secret boyfriend? Or are you planning on running off with a hot dragon?"

Oh god, he really has been reading books like mine.

"Not tonight," I say lightly. "One shock to the system is enough."

They laugh, and the moment feels warm and real. Like I'm part of something I've always longed for.

I can't wait to tell Asher how well it went. To hear his voice.

I know I'll have to tell my brothers about him soon. But not tonight.

We're not there yet, but we're getting close.

I'm not hiding anymore, and it's a good feeling.

* * *

ASHER

. . .

"What do you mean he's gone?" I ask Brad, a frown pulling at my lips. "We had eyes on him. Twenty-four seven."

Brad's face is tight. "I know that. But the guard took a bathroom break and..." He shakes his head. "Don't worry, I'm dealing with him."

"And he left? Just like that?" Fuck, I need to talk to Shaun like I need air. He could barely stand two days ago. Where the hell would he even go that fast? "What about his wife, what does she say?"

Brad shakes his head. "She's gone too. And the baby. They must have been tipped off. Abandoned everything. His car is still in the driveway. He had to have it planned."

"Credit cards?" I ask, because we both know that's the easiest way to track somebody.

"Wiped."

"Fuck."

"I know." Brad winces. "I'm sorry. This is my fault."

I put my hand up. "It's nobody's fault except Shaun's. And whoever he's working with." I take a deep breath, tension knotting in my spine. "What about his background? We vetted him when we took him on, right? Ran a full check?"

Brad shakes his head. "That's the thing. It's like he never existed. All the HR files are corrupted. Even the stuff we had on hard copy is missing. I had Sanjay search everything, and it's just... gone."

A beat of silence stretches between us.

"But he no longer has access to our servers, right?"

"They're locked down so tight it hurts. But that doesn't mean he didn't make a copy of everything before we found out what was happening."

I swallow hard. Because that includes the videos I had on my laptop.

"We also found this," Brad says, placing a piece of paper on my desk. "It was in the middle of his dining room table. I have no idea why."

It's a printout of a still image. Grainy, blown up. Slightly pixelated.

But I'd know that face anywhere.

It's Francie. My stomach tightens as I take in her expression. Her head is tilted back, her lips parted, her eyes half lidded. You can't see her body but I know exactly what she's doing.

It's a still image from one of the nights she touched herself for me.

Rage crackles through my chest. This isn't just a threat, it's a declaration. He knows. He watched. He has her, even if only on screen. And he's telling me he's not done.

Fuck.

I run a hand over my mouth, pressing my fingers hard enough to hurt.

"It's getting late," I say, my voice tight. "We can't do anymore today. Send everybody home and I'll lock up."

Brad catches my eye. Like he wants to say more. But then he thinks better of it and nods.

He leaves and I sit at my desk for a long moment. Staring at the printed image before turning it over and sliding it into the drawer.

When I hear them all leave, I stand and grab my coat, pushing through the empty corridor to the main door. Making sure it's locked up and the alarms are on – even though it feels pointless right now – I head for the stairwell and outside into the cool night air.

I close my eyes for a second, trying to breathe through the pressure building in my chest. Then I reach for my phone. I need to hear her voice.

Just for a minute. To remember what she sounds like when she doesn't know what a fucking idiot I am.

The line connects after the second ring.

"Hey you." Her voice is soft and warm and makes my chest ache. "How was your day?"

Of course she'd ask about me first. "Tiring. But more importantly how did yours go? Are your brothers still talking to you?" My car pulls up at the sidewalk and I hop in, giving the driver a nod.

"They took it really well, actually," she says. "Even Myles. Who now knows what spicy means and wishes he didn't." She laughs and I want to join in. I want to trace her lips with my fingers.

I want to disappear in her.

I let out a quiet breath that might almost pass for a laugh. "I bet that was interesting. And I'm not surprised they took it well. They love you."

"Still," she says. "It was scary. But… kind of amazing. For the first time I felt like I belonged."

My throat tightens. I want to tell her everything. About Shaun. About the cameras and the image.

But instead I say, "I'm proud of you."

And I mean it.

There's a pause. Then her voice drops. "I miss you," she tells me.

God, I miss her too. The scent of her hair against my face. The sound she makes when she's half asleep and I brush her skin with my fingertips.

The way she looks at me like I'm not the dipshit I know I am.

She keeps talking, telling me about her brothers' offer to help her build a cabin by the lake, and how happy and free she feels now that everything is in the open. Her voice soothes me as the car drives me to my apartment building, as she tells me they're all having brunch tomorrow before her brothers have to leave.

"So I'll head back to New York instead of Liberty," she says. "I can write there as easily as anywhere else, especially now that my apartment is back to normal."

"You should head back to Liberty," I say, my voice thick. "Things are still... going on here. It's going to take a few days for me to straighten things out."

"Oh." She sounds sad. But the thought of her being here, so close to everything that's going on, makes my stomach sick.

There's a soft pause on the line. Then, "Okay, Liberty it is. I'll head back to the lighthouse and finish the book."

"We can celebrate when you're done," I murmur.

"We'd better."

I huff a quiet laugh. "And Francie?"

"Yeah?"

"I miss you more."

She doesn't reply right away. But I can hear her breathing, feel her presence like a thread pulling me to her across the miles. "Go to bed and get some sleep," she says gently. "You sound wrecked."

I feel it, too. "I'll call you tomorrow," I promise her. We say our goodbyes and she hangs up right as the driver parks outside my apartment.

We arrange for him to pick me up first thing in the morning and say our goodbyes. Then I slide my phone into my pocket and step out of the car.

The city hums around me, the breeze cool against my face. The car pulls away from the curb, its red tail lights disappearing into the night.

And that's when I feel it.

A prickle at the back of my neck.

Then a figure steps out from the shadows. And just like that, the night turns colder.

thirty-four

ASHER

For a moment I assume it's a coincidence as the lamplight hits the face of the last person I want to see as she takes a step toward me.

"What do you want, Annalise?" I'm unable to hold back the sigh of frustration I feel at not being able to walk back into my apartment and go to fucking sleep.

She's wearing a black dress and the kind of high heels that look awkward as hell to walk in. But somehow she does, taking another step toward me.

Enough for me to see the shadows under her eyes. The way her skin looks sallow.

And for one moment, I actually feel sorry for her.

"We need to talk," she says softly. Like she doesn't want anybody else to hear.

I frown. "There's nothing to talk about." And then I remember the other night. The way she looked when she saw me with Francie at the restaurant. Christ, I don't have the bandwidth for this kind of drama.

"Nathan's insurance refused to pay his hospital bills," she tells me.

"I'm sorry to hear that." But it's not my fucking problem. I don't add the last bit. I'm not the biggest asshole in the world. Not yet. "Maybe he can use some of the money I paid him."

"You don't look sorry. And it's your fault. If you hadn't thrown him out of his own company…"

I put my hand up, annoyed. I don't have time for this. "Look, Annalise, whatever Nathan has done, including snorting all that money up his own nose, is his own fault. I'm sorry he's sick, I really am, but it has nothing to do with me. I'm tired, I'm cranky, and I have no idea why you came here to say this."

"Because I have these." She pulls an envelope out of her purse, her expression somehow triumphant. It reminds me of the days my dad would win at poker. When he thought he was the king of the world.

My stomach tightens as she passes it to me. And against my better judgment, I take it, knowing that no good can come of this. The envelope feels warm against my fingers as I slowly lift the unglued flap.

There are prints inside. The glossy type, like you used to get before selfies were a thing and memories were forever.

And then I see what's on them.

Francie.

Her eyes closed. Her lips parted. The same picture we found in Shaun's house. But in a much, much better resolution.

"She's very… expressive, isn't she?" Annalise says.

I narrow my eyes at her. "How did you get this?" Did

Shaun sell the stills to her? How did he even know about her?

She shrugs. "Let's just say your security breach was more thorough than you realized."

"You know about the breach?" My voice is low. I'm trying not to let the fury overwhelm me.

"I *am* the breach." She gives me the softest of smiles. "Did you really think you could get away with screwing me over?"

I look at that picture again. At Francie. All I can think about is how happy she sounded on the phone.

"I have the videos, too, of course." She wrinkles her nose. "Those weren't my kind of fun to watch. Of course, you don't seem to have lost your touch."

I say nothing.

"And backups. I'm not an amateur here. Shaun was very detailed."

"You paid him?"

"Shaun's an old friend." She lifts a brow. "Not that his name is really Shaun. But I think you know that already."

There's a crushing feeling on my chest. Like the world is trying to push against me. Box me in. That kid being pushed into the cupboard, hearing his father screaming out in pain.

Knowing he's responsible.

My head starts to pound.

"What do you want from me?" I grit my teeth so hard my jaw aches.

Her knowing eyes catch mine. "An apology would be a good start," she tells me.

"An apology for what?" I can't stop looking at the photograph. It's like every mistake I've ever made, pixelated and formed into the face of the woman I love.

"For treating me like shit. You didn't have to throw me to the wolves when Nathan tried to remove you from the company."

"You were feeding him information," I remind her. "You were in my bed while your brother worked to gut my company."

"It was his company too," she says, like I didn't already know that. "And family's complicated. You of all people should know that."

"Ethics aren't."

"Don't be so dramatic," she replies, her voice light. "You always took things so personally. That was part of the problem."

Something twists in my gut. The same hollow, scraping feeling that's been following me for days. The same one I got when I found out that my dad had started to use Eden to cheat at poker, the exact same way he'd used me.

And I hadn't protected her.

Annalise tilts her head. "But none of that really matters anymore. What matters is those videos," she tells me. "And what I intend to do with them."

My jaw tightens. "If you do anything at all to expose these I'll fucking slay you."

Her lip curls. "I'm not planning to do anything at all. As long as you do what you're told. I want you to walk away. From the company. Transfer fifty percent of your shares to Nathan and fifty percent to me. Quietly. No fanfare. No scandals. You just... walk away."

"And if I don't?" I lift a brow.

Her smile is ice cold. "Then I upload these photographs and the world can see your little girlfriend playing show and tell."

Something inside me snaps. "I swear to God if you hurt her..."

"I'm not the kinky asshole who recorded her. That's all you. All of this is you." Her eyes catch mine and I can see how deadly serious she is. "You handed her to me on a silver platter, Asher. You get to decide what happens next."

The roaring in my ears reaches a crescendo. She's right. This is me. My carelessness. I thought I could control everything.

I was wrong. And now history is repeating itself, giving me the worst déjà vu.

I'm the common denominator.

"Leave," I tell her, my voice cold.

She looks delighted. "Gladly. But I'll need your answer soon. Or these videos go viral." She tips her head. "And we both know how far you'll go to protect the people you care about." She lifts her hand to wave goodbye, then turns on her heels to walk away.

I stare down at the envelope and the fucking pictures of all the mistakes I've made.

The thing is, she's right.

I fucked up. Big time. And the woman I care about is going to get hurt.

* * *

"You fucking idiot," Hudson says. But there's no malice in his voice. If anything there's sympathy.

He knows I know better than to do something this stupid. I'm a security expert for fuck's sake. I committed the cardinal sin of thinking I was in control.

And I never have been. Not since that moment I saw *her* on the security cameras of the Ivory Rooms. Every part of my body has been doing the thinking for me. My dick, my heart.

But not my head.

We're sitting in his office, because we don't know if mine is compromised. We don't know if my house is compromised, either. I've even switched phones again, but Francie's phone could be compromised, so I can't even talk to her.

Brad is doing another sweep of everything. And I haven't told him the exact details because the less people who know about this the better. But the two men in front of me know everything.

Because I trust them with my life.

Hudson flew in first thing this morning. And West was already in Manhattan for a meeting with a client, so he's come to strategize, because if anybody knows how to deal with assholes it's West. He does it for a living as a media lawyer and general troubleshooter in Hollywood.

"Okay," West murmurs. "Let's go through this again. From the very beginning."

I grit my teeth, because I don't want to. We've already done this once and I'm ready to take action. But there's no action I can take that doesn't involve compromising the woman I promised to protect.

"The Ivory Rooms," he says. "There could be evidence of you both being there, correct?"

"There are no photographs of that in any of the black-mail she provided," I tell him. "I think it was too early. She doesn't know about that."

West lifts a brow. "You should still assume she has details of that. So we have that, the... videos of yours and Francie's..." he trails off and I wince.

"Of her completely exposed," Hudson adds, lifting a brow at me.

Message received. I'm a dick. But at least he agreed to be here to help.

"And then of you two outside the lighthouse," West adds.

I nod.

"Anything else?"

"No." I shake my head, because I've wracked my brain and can't think of anything else.

"But all Annalise showed you were stills. So how can we be sure she has the videos?" Hudson asks.

I turn my laptop around to show him the email I received this morning. "There's a video attached," I tell him. "It shows everything."

It's Hudson's turn to wince. "Christ."

"Yeah," I nod. "I know."

"And Francie? What does she say?" West asks me.

"I haven't told her. I asked her to head straight for Liberty." I look at my watch. "She should be arriving any time now." Because of course I chartered a plane for her. And arranged for a car to take her to the ferry." I look at Hudson. "Skyler knows to pick her up and take her to your place, right?"

Hudson nods. He, of all people, knows that I need her to be safe right now. And Liberty is the safest place I can think of. Plus, there are no security cameras at Hudson's house. And we can monitor everybody that goes on and off the island.

And knowing the woman I care about is safe – at least for now – is everything.

"I still think you should tell her," Hudson says. "Nothing good comes from hiding things."

I lift a brow at him. "Pot meet kettle." The man has more secrets than the Illuminati. "You didn't exactly follow your own advice with Skyler."

"And I'm trying to teach you from my mistakes," he points out, but he looks resigned.

"She can't find out. She's got enough going on. She has to finish her book, she's just reconciling with her brothers. I can't endanger any of that."

Neither of them says out loud what I know they're both thinking. I already have.

"So that's it, you're just going to capitulate?" Hudson asks. "Give the shares to Annalise and Nathan?"

I swallow hard. "I don't have another choice."

"And what if they renege? What if she uploads them anyway out of spite?" West asks. "A woman scorned and all that..."

"My lawyer is already drawing up an ironclad agreement."

"Like the last one?" Hudson lifts a brow. And he has a point. Nathan and I signed a legal contract.

But I'm still on the verge of losing everything.

I look my brother straight in the eye. He looks as messed up as I feel. But he doesn't say anything. He doesn't need to. I can already hear the echo of my own thoughts bouncing off his skull.

I'm a fucking idiot. It's not the first time I've hurt the people I love.

But it has to be the last. I can't keep doing this.

"The contract will have contingencies," I tell him. "It'll be so tight they could strangle a lawyer." I lift a brow at West. "Present company excluded."

"I'll check it over too," he offers. "Make sure that if she

releases anything she'll go down with it. And she'll know it. That's the important thing."

"You really think she cares about going down?" Hudson asks, leaning back in his chair. "She's not stupid, she's vindictive. That's worse."

For a moment none of us speak. Hudson knows all about vindictive exes. His daughter's mother stole their child and took her to a different continent, after all.

He might have his daughter back now, but the scars remain. And the law did nothing to help him until it was too late.

"I have no fucking idea what else to do," I admit. "She's desperate. Her brother's dying, her life's imploding, and she wants someone to burn for it. If giving her the company keeps Francie safe, then that's what I have to do. Let her burn me instead."

"You're giving her control over you," West murmurs. "You're going to lose everything. All the years you've worked on this. Your intellectual property. It'll all be gone."

I drain the last of the water in the glass on Hudson's desk. And let out a long breath.

"What else can I do?" I ask them.

They exchange a glance.

"No. I'm not talking to Francie. You know how she'll react. She'll try to dissuade me. And I'm not going to let her do that. Annalise can destroy me, that's fine. I've been destroyed before. But I won't let them destroy Francie."

Rubbing the back of his neck, Hudson looks as resigned as I feel. "I'll stand by you. Of course I will. No matter how this shakes out."

"Thank you." My voice is hoarse.

"Same." West nods. "You'll get through this."

I give them a weak smile. "I hope so."

And yeah, I probably will. But will she? If I lose her because of this...

I can't even finish that thought. I'm between a rock and a hard place. Either I lie and protect her, or tell her the truth and throw her to the wolves.

Neither of them says a word. But I can read the expressions on their faces. I'm well and truly fucked.

Francie deserves better than this. Better than secrets and manipulations and some twisted white-knight fantasy where I martyr myself for her safety.

But I don't know how to stop.

"I need to go to my lawyer's office," I say hoarsely.

Hudson nods.

West stands up. "You want me to come with you?"

I shake my head. I love them both. But this is my mess, not theirs.

"But I'll keep you updated."

"And you'll send me the draft agreement, right?" West asks. I nod, grateful for his support. Knowing I don't deserve it.

Then I look at Hudson. "Are you going back to Liberty today?"

"I have a few meetings tomorrow. I'll go after those."

I let out a breath. I need him to be there. To make sure she's safe.

Before I can tell him that, my Nokia buzzes and a text message appears in black across the tiny screen.

Made it to the ferry. When will you be back? I need some writing inspiration, Asher style. – Francie x

Her words feel like a fist around my throat, squeezing tight.

My thumbs hover over the keypad. I could lie. I could

tell her I'm coming back now. That we'll celebrate with wine and words and that thing she does with her tongue that makes my brain short-circuit. But I don't. Because lies might feel like comfort, but they're still fucking lies.

Instead, I slide the phone back into my pocket and say nothing.

She still thinks I'm the hero of her story, but instead I've turned into the fucking villain.

thirty-five

FRANCIE

"Welcome home, stranger," Skyler says, hugging me tight as I step off the ferry. "I missed you."

"It's only been three days," I point out, but I'm still smiling because it's so good to see her.

After I left Misty Lakes – promising to return soon so that my brothers and I can start working on my brand new cabin – I took a charter plane from Virginia to the local airport, where a car was waiting to whisk me onto the ferry.

And now Skyler is here, her face beaming, and it feels like everything is slotting into place.

I get into her car, and as she drives out of Main Street and into the country lanes that weave to the middle of the island, I tell her about my revelations to my brothers, and how well it went. She tells me about Ayda's latest obsession with unicorns, and how she wants to be one when she grows up, when I realize she's taken a wrong turn.

"You missed the road to the lighthouse," I tell her, smiling.

"You're coming to the Captain's House," she says. "Didn't Asher tell you?"

I frown, because no, Asher didn't tell me. In fact, he hasn't replied to any of my messages.

I assumed his Nokia needed charging. Or he's busy trying to sort out the breach. Just because I've managed to sail through my issues with my brothers, doesn't mean I should expect him to be at my beck and call.

But I miss him. And I wish he was here.

"Did he say why?"

Skyler shrugs. "No idea. Hudson just said it was important, and I should make sure you're comfortable and fed." She rolls her eyes. "That's his way of telling me to be hospitable, I think. Which I am because I put a bottle of wine into the refrigerator as soon as I heard you were coming, which is good of me since I can't drink any. So I'm completely hospitable."

I smile at her. "It's only three in the afternoon."

"It's six o'clock somewhere."

I look at my phone again, feeling my stomach dip. "Is there something wrong with Asher?" I ask her, because if Hudson is asking her to bring me home with her there has to be a reason, doesn't there?

She frowns. "Not that I know. Why?"

"He hasn't replied to my messages today. And now this. It feels… like somebody's about to give me bad news."

Skyler pulls into the road that leads to the Captain's House. The white stuccoed building complete with a nineteenth century cupola appears in the windshield. "As far as I know, Asher is okay." She frowns. "He called this morning, Hudson said he had to go to New York, then later he called me and told me to pick you up. I don't know if you know, but he knows all about you and Asher. I mentioned something – because pregnancy brain – and he told me he already knew." She parks and looks at me. "Fuck, they're doing that thing aren't they?"

"What thing?" I frown, because I have no idea what she's talking about. Skyler has a habit of jumping about three thoughts ahead of everybody else.

She sighs. "The 'keep the women safe while the big, bad men run around making terrible decisions' thing. Hudson does it all the time, thinking he knows better than me. Or he did, until I started locking him out of the bedroom."

Oh *that*.

We exchange glances. I know exactly what she means. My brothers are the kings of doing it. Or they were until the last few days, when I showed them I was just as good as they are at keeping secrets.

"Shit," she says. "I'm going to kill Hudson. That conniving asshole. 'Look after Francie, have some fun. Put on some face masks.'"

I try not to smile at her impression of Hudson. And then the urge disappears, because it's replaced by a thought.

What's going on that Asher wants me here, cooped up at the Captain's house. Why won't he reply to my messages?

"I'm going to call Asher."

"Good. They can't get away with this macho bullshit." She narrows her eyes as I pull up his number and hit the call button. Then narrows them even more when I put his voicemail on speaker.

"Don't leave a message," she tells me. "If they're going to ignore us, two can play at that game."

I don't point out that Hudson isn't ignoring her, he's

just misinforming her, because it's nice to have somebody on my side.

"I guess this is what it feels like to be ghosted," I say.

She sighs dramatically, reaching for the door handle. "They'd just prefer we go all faint and lie back on our chaise lounges while they fight the dragons."

"Do you have any chaise lounges?" I ask her. Because truthfully, lying on one of those sounds pretty good right now.

She shakes her head sadly. "No."

"Shame."

For a second neither of us say anything. Then she looks at me, her eyes twinkling. "You know what I do have though?"

"What?"

"A car."

I blink in confusion. Because yes, I know that. We're sitting in it. "Um, well done?"

She pushes my arm. "I mean, we have a car. We don't have to sit around and act all faint. We can do something. Like drive to New York and find out what the hell our emotionally constipated men are up to."

My mouth twitches. "You want to storm the city?"

She grins. "It beats waiting at home like a good little wife appliance."

I'm not sure who she's describing, because Skyler in no way fits the phrase wife appliance. Unless you're talking about a washing machine that not only refuses to do laundry but also organizes all the other domestic appliances to rise up against the patriarchy, because white goods have feelings too.

But she also has a point.

"It really does." I've been from Liberty to New York to

Virginia and then back to Liberty in the past few days. What's another few hundred miles between friends?

I look down at my phone again. Still no reply.

I raise my brows. "You sure you're up for a five-hour road trip?'"

Skyler shrugs. "The baby's fine with it. It's my bladder that's the problem."

"Okay," I say. "But you need to drive. I'm a menace on the roads. Plus I'm a writer on a deadline, remember?"

"Absolutely. You can write a death scene from the passenger seat," she tells me. "Preferably involving two brothers who think they know better than anybody else." She pulls out her phone. "Let me just call Jesse and ask if he can keep Ayda overnight."

Jesse is Skyler's half-brother. And Ayda is in love with him. I'm pretty sure the feeling's mutual. "I'll tell him we're channeling our inner Thelma and Louise."

"Without the death scene," I remind her.

"Obviously." Skyler looks so buzzed she's practically vibrating in her seat. "Unless Asher or Hudson try to pull more of their macho-man nonsense, in which case all bets are off.

"I'm totally fine with that," I tell her, unbuckling my seat belt.

While she calls Jesse, who agrees with equanimity because the man doesn't have a bad bone in his body, I climb out of the car and slip my phone behind the big ceramic plant pot by her front door.

She catches me as I'm climbing back in. "What did you do with your phone?"

I shrug. "I figure if Asher decides to use his stupid technology and track me, he'll think I'm chilling here."

"Ooh, you're a devious little genius." She grins widely. "I love it."

It takes her a few minutes to run inside and pack an overnight bag for herself and Ayda. Then we swing by Jesse's place. He's waiting on the porch with Ayda clinging to one hand, the other holding out his phone like he's about to defuse a bomb.

"Thanks," Skyler says, squeezing Ayda tight, then swapping phones with Jesse. "Text me if she starts climbing the walls."

"I have no idea why you're making me use your phone," he mutters as he slides hers into his pocket. "I'm too scared to ask."

"In case we're tracked," Skyler says, like we're in the middle of a spy movie. "We're going full-on *Mission Impossible*."

Jesse blinks. "Right. Obviously."

Before he can ask any more questions we peel out of the driveway, making a quick stop at Mylene's for coffee because Skyler claims she can't launch a rescue mission without caffeine.

"I need fuel, even if it's only decaf. What if I have to chase a man down?" she asks as we walk up to Mylene's counter.

Mylene raises an eyebrow. "Should I even ask?"

I wrinkle my nose. "Probably not."

But Skyler is way too excited to keep quiet. "We're going to pick a fight with the patriarchy," she says. "Maybe stage an emotional intervention. Depends on traffic."

Mylene nods as though this is perfectly normal. Which it kind of is around here.

Five minutes later, we're back in the car with two large

coffees – decaffeinated for Skyler – along with a bag of emergency muffins.

Skyler starts the engine. "You ready for this?"

I pull my laptop out of the sleeve at my feet, ready to write on our way to New York as we head down the road toward the ferry, where the gates are open for us.

"I'm ready," I confirm. "And I'm putting a horrific death in chapter thirty."

Skyler glances at me. "Asher or Hudson?"

I look at the manuscript. I'm so close to the end. "I'm not sure. Possibly both of them in one amazing blaze of glory."

She grins, putting her foot on the gas as the ferry captain beckons us forward. "Remind me to stay on your good side."

"You're always on my good side, Thelma," I promise her. We're really doing this. Going full rogue. While writing a book and without our phones.

It's the twenty-first century version of *The Heroine's Journey*. And I'm here for it. Even if my heart feels one beat out of sync the whole way there.

ASHER

West and Hudson stare at the draft agreement that my lawyer sent over for my approval, scowls pulling at both of their lips.

"There has to be another way," Hudson says. He looks at West who just lifts his brows.

Because he knows as well as I do that there isn't any

other way. If I want to stop those videos from becoming public property, I have to give Annalise what she wants.

"I'm signing it tomorrow," I tell him, my voice final. Even saying it feels like I'm cutting out a piece of my own heart. This company is everything I've built, everything I've bled for. And I'm giving it away. For a woman who doesn't even know I'm protecting her.

Hudson mutters something that sounds suspiciously like 'dumbass' then pulls out his phone. "Whatever, I'm calling Skyler. She's been quiet all day."

"Maybe she's enjoying her break from you," West says, without looking up from the contract. "Not everybody wants a status check from you every fifteen minutes."

Hudson ignores him, pointedly putting the call on speaker. It rings. Then rings some more.

And then Jesse answers, his voice sounding weirdly tremulous. "Hello?"

"Hey." Hudson frowns. "Where's Sky?"

"Oh. Ah. She's um… resting. You know. Napping. Because of the baby. Doctor said rest is important and, uh, no phones. Very restful. Lots of pillows." He sounds almost frightened.

"Are you at my place?" Hudson asks.

"Um no," Jesse replies. "At mine."

"She's napping in your guest bed?" Hudson says, looking more confused than ever.

"That's it. Yep. I'd hate to disturb her, you know how cranky she gets." Jesse gives a half-laugh.

"Is Ayda there too?" Hudson asks. He's starting to look panicky.

"Yep. She is. Say hi to daddy, Ayda."

"Hi Daddy."

The relief that washes over Hudson's face is palpable. It

wasn't that long ago when he came to New York for a meeting and his daughter disappeared, after all. "Hey baby. You okay?"

"Yep, Uncle Jesse let me have unicorn poop ice cream."

West lifts an eyebrow, but carries on reading. He gets his pen and strikes through a clause, writing something so small I can't read it.

"That's good. How about Mommy? Is she okay?"

"Yup. She and Aunt Francie looked super funny when they started shouting at Uncle Jesse."

I look at Hudson's phone. "She got there okay?" I ask.

There's a little kerfuffle. Jesse comes back on the line. "Sorry, gotta go. Unicorn poop emergency." The call disconnects and Hudson frowns.

"Did he say if Francie was there with Skyler?" I ask Hudson, trying to figure out where she is.

He shrugs. "I've no idea."

There've been no more calls or messages since she arrived. There's a pang in my stomach that she must think I'm ignoring her. I wish I could just pick up the phone. Tell her the truth. But the truth might break her, and I'd rather it break me instead.

Still, just for my own peace of mind, I pull open my laptop and triangulate her cell.

"What are you doing?" Hudson asks.

"Tracking Francie." Relief washes over me when I see she's at the Captain's House, as promised.

"Does she know you do that?" West murmurs. "Because that's not stalkerish at all."

"It's the first time I've ever done it. So no." I glare at him. "And I'm not planning on making a habit of it."

Hudson leans in, squinting at the laptop screen. "Wait, that's her phone? At my place?"

"Yep."

"So why is Skyler at Jesse's?" he asks, more to himself than to me. "When I asked her to bring Francie home she promised she wouldn't leave her alone. And now she's left her there without telling me?"

"I don't know," I murmur. Our eyes meet. And for the first time today, I try calling Francie.

And of course it goes straight to voicemail. She's probably trying to get back at me for the radio silence and I don't blame her.

"There's something fishy about this," Hudson murmurs. "I'm going to call Jesse again."

"Wait," West says, looking almost annoyed with us. "Do you still have a tracker on your car?" he asks Hudson.

"Yes." Hudson nods. "It's an expensive car."

"So look it up, if it's at Jesse's then Francie probably is too. Now can I finish going through this without you two gossiping like it's your job, please?"

Hudson is already pulling up the tracker on his phone.

It loads up and his eyes narrow, a frown pulling at his brow. "That can't be right," he mutters.

"What is it?" I demand, leaning over to stare at his phone.

And then I see it. The little dot, moving like it's Pac-Man trying to escape the ghost gang. And nowhere near Liberty.

"Why's my SUV on the mainland?" Hudson asks.

My stomach tightens.

"They left the goddamned island," I mutter.

West leans back on his chair with a self-satisfied smirk that makes me want to throw something at him.

"This is what happens when you tell lies," he says like he's a school teacher.

Hudson looks at me. "Skyler and Jesse swapped phones," he says. "To throw us off."

West actually starts to laugh. The asshole.

I look at his phone again. There's no doubt about it. That dot is still moving and it's getting closer.

Skyler – and possibly Francie – are heading toward New York.

Hudson lets out a low whistle. "Skyler's going to kill me," he says. "For not telling her what's going on. And I'm going to kill her for doing this with our baby inside of her."

West finally puts his pen down, grinning like it's Christmas morning.

"Well this should be fun," he says.

Fun isn't exactly the word I'd use.

Disaster would work better. Catastrophe even more.

I rub a hand down my face, the truth of the situation hitting me like a sucker punch to the gut.

I can feel it. Francie's coming here to New York.

And she's going to find out everything.

About the videos. The blackmail.

The fact I lied to her face.

God, what if she walks away? What if I lose her?

Not because of the breach, or the videos, or Annalise's bullshit. But because I was too much of a coward to let her in.

I stare at the moving dot once more. It's coming straight for me.

And so is she.

thirty-six

FRANCIE

"What do you mean you think Hudson knows about us?" Skyler demands, one hand on her hip, the other holding her phone like she's about to bludgeon it into submission. We're on our third rest break of the trip. Turns out a gallon full of coffee and small bladders don't mix.

On the other end of the call, Jesse starts stammering. "He just... asked a lot of questions. You know what he's like. It's like being grilled by the Spanish Inquisition. Except worse. And more Hudson like."

"So what did you tell him?" Skyler asks.

"Nothing. But he knows. I know he knows. He knows I know he knows..."

I wince, because there are way too many knows in that sentence. It needs a good editor.

Skyler lets out a sigh. "Is Ayda okay?"

"Having the time of her life. I just let her paint my nails."

"That's nice. What color?" she asks, like we're not on a two-woman mission to stop the idiots we love from doing idiot things.

Whatever they are.

"Purple glitter. With stickers," Jesse tells her.

Her expression softens and I can see in her eyes that whatever irritation she's feeling is no match for her love for Ayda. Or her brother, for that matter. "Tell her I love them already," she tells Jesse. "And that I love her. And I want a manicure when I get home."

"You got it." Jesse pauses. "Be careful, okay? I love you, sis."

"Love you more." She hangs up and blows out a breath, her expression still warm as she tucks her phone into the side pocket of her purse. "Okay, so my child is blissfully unaware that her stepmother is on a secret mission. But Jessie is apparently cracking under the pressure, and Hudson is playing dumb like it's an Olympic sport."

I pass her another coffee, because yes, we like to refill after we've emptied. "So what now, Thelma? Shall we turn left to the Grand Canyon?"

She lifts it to her mouth and takes a sip. "Not yet. But we need to know what's waiting for us. I'm going to call Hudson and grill him until he starts to squeal. And if he comes clean on what's happening, I might only mildly ruin his life."

I grin. "You're all heart."

She pulls out Jesse's phone, grimacing as she types the code in wrong twice before it unlocks. And I lean against the hood of her car and stare at the horizon like it might offer me a clue.

I hate that I don't have a phone to check. That mine is

currently hanging out in a Liberty Island plant pot, living it's best Captain's House-adjacent life.

I wish I hadn't left it there. It's like I left my heart behind.

Because if Asher has texted, I won't know. If he's called, left a message – it's all the same.

Maybe he isn't ignoring me.

But deep down, I know he is.

And I'm halfway across the state chasing a man who might not want to be caught.

Skyler pulls up Hudson's contact and presses call, and we both look at each other as it connects.

"Jesse? Skyler?" He sounds almost frantic.

I smile grimly at that. Because I'm starting to feel the same way.

"It's me," Skyler says, her voice ominously low. "Where are you right now?"

"Shouldn't I be asking you that question?" he asks, sounding annoyed.

Skyler lets out a laugh that sounds somewhere between sweet and homicidal. "Oh baby, you can ask me whatever you want. But unless you want to spend the next six months sleeping on the sofa, I suggest you answer mine first."

Hudson groans. "Sky..."

"Don't you Sky me." She catches my eye and I can see she's enjoying this. "What's going on? Why did you make me intercept Francie? Why isn't Asher picking up when she calls?"

"Why don't you ask Asher that?" He has the voice of a man on the edge. One who knows he's about to be interrogated and really doesn't want it.

"He won't answer his phone," Skyler tells him. "Seriously, we're coming for you. And you should be super scared."

"Believe me, I am," Hudson mutters.

"Good. So spill. Why did you hot tail it to New York so fast? Why is Asher acting like a ghost with commitment issues?"

There's a long pause. I can practically hear Hudson chewing on whether he wants to live to see another day.

Skyler takes a noisy slurp of her coffee.

"It's complicated," Hudson says finally.

Skyler snorts and I swear I see some coffee fly out of her nose. Like a caffeinated dragon. "Assembling IKEA furniture is complicated. Talking to your wife should be easy."

"Baby, I…"

"Oh no. Not the babies." She shifts her feet. "I hate it when you bring those out." She looks at me. "You might want to close your ears for this," she whispers, holding her hand over the phone mic.

I lift a brow. I'm not going anywhere. This is more fun than watching a rerun of *Friends*.

"I'll give you five seconds to tell me what's going on," Skyler says to him sweetly. "And if you do, I'll do that thing you like. With the whipped cream and bedless sex."

There's a spluttering noise on the other end. "Sky! Jesus, people are listening."

"I warned Francie to close her ears." She winks at me. "But she's still here, probably taking notes. So what's it gonna be, *baby*? Gorgeous bedless sex or six months of celibacy and me throwing every left sock you have away."

Wait. *Socks have sides?* She just shrugs at me. And I have to press my lips together to stop from laughing. In this whole, stupid mess, I think I've found my new heroine.

She's terrifying when she wants something.

Another beat of silence follows. Then Hudson groans like a man who knows he's lost. "Okay, fine, I'll tell you. But you have to swear not to kill anyone."

"No promises," Skyler mutters.

But it's clear he's about to cave. I lean in, my heart slamming against my ribcage, a thousand different scenarios running through my brain.

And not a single one of them prepares me for the truth I'm about to hear.

Hudson sighs so loudly it sounds like there's a hurricane rushing through New York City. "Asher's being blackmailed."

Skyler stills. I do too.

"What?" I ask, my voice sharp enough for Hudson to hear.

His voice is low and scratchy, like it physically hurts him to reply. "It's his ex. Annalise. You know her brother is the one who tried to steal the business from Asher."

"And Annalise helped him," I say. "While she was supposed to be in love with Asher." I roll my eyes, because that bitch needs a slap.

Hudson grunts. "Yeah, well it turns out she's behind the breach. She paid Shaun to infiltrate the business."

Wait. *What?* "Shaun? As in Shaun the security guard?"

"Yep."

The one with the baby. Who begged me to help him keep his job. I feel sick.

"She has videos of you, Francie," Hudson says, taking my mind off sneaky Shaun and back to the issue at hand.

"Of me?" I repeat.

Hudson clears his throat, like he'd rather be anywhere other than having this conversation. "She somehow got access to the security servers. And all of Asher's private files."

Oh God. *Those videos.* My cheeks start to burn.

"She's threatening to release them unless Asher signs the company over to her and her brother. He's already got the agreement drawn up. The transaction happens tomorrow morning."

I blink. "He's giving away his company?" That doesn't sound right. It's everything to him. "He can't do that."

"He's doing it to protect you." Hudson sighs again. "It's what he does. Takes everything on himself. Thinks he can solve every problem in the world."

I feel the weight of what he's done crack inside of me. Knowing that part of him still doesn't believe I'd choose him if I knew the whole truth.

I can't even speak. The rage. The hurt. It's like a vice tightening in my chest. The memory of her coming up to speak to us in the restaurant flashes through my brain. What a bitch. I should have slapped her.

"Why didn't he tell me?" I say, trying to keep a hold on my emotions.

"He thinks he's doing the right thing, I guess."

Skyler snorts. "Of course he does. That's so stupidly Fitzgerald. You idiots always do this. You clam up the moment things get hard, like your vocal chords have unionized. This isn't chivalry, Hudson. It's stupidity."

There's a long silence. I'm pretty sure Hudson knows better than to say anything else. Then, because she's as frustrated as I am, she ends the call without saying goodbye.

And all I can think about is that Asher is going to lose everything, because he won't talk to me. Won't tell me the truth.

Like I'm some kind of delicate flower who can't handle it.

I take a deep breath. "Skyler, we're going," I say.

She glances at me. "Where? Home?"

I shake my head. "To Manhattan."

Skyler does a fist bump. "Hell yes!"

"I'm done being protected," I say, tossing my cold coffee. "If Asher wants to play the noble hero, he can do it with someone who likes that bullshit, because I don't."

She slides behind the wheel, then pauses. "Wait. Tracker."

A second later she's crouched with her phone flashlight, triumphant as she flings a tiny black device into the grass. "Suck it, Hudson Fitzgerald."

She looks at me as the engine growls to life.

"Let's go educate our men on what happens when you try to outmaneuver women with a vat full of coffee and a grudge."

We peel out of the lot. Fueled by caffeine, fury, and just enough heartbreak to make it dangerous.

I grit my teeth, thinking about the video, the lies, the way Asher treats me like I'm breakable.

Like my brothers always did.

But I'm done playing the damsel. And Asher Fitzgerald is about to find out exactly what happens when you underestimate the heroine.

* * *

ASHER

. . .

"Come on," Hudson mutters, staring at his phone. "Move, damn you." He looks at me. "I don't suppose you can hack into the security cameras at the rest stop?"

I shake my head. "That's not how this works. I'm a security expert, not James Bond."

Hudson groans and tilts the screen toward me. The little tracker dot of his SUV is still in the same place twenty minutes after Skyler hung up on him. At a rest stop some-where off I-95.

"She threw the tracker, didn't she?" he mutters.

West, who's been unusually quiet since Skyler's tele-phone rant, finally opens his mouth. "Of course she did. Maybe those two should be running a security company, instead of you idiots."

"I don't run a security company," Hudson says. I notice he doesn't deny that he's an idiot, though.

Nor do I, come to that.

I let out a sigh and take Hudson's phone.

"What are you doing?" There's still that note of hope in his voice that I'm somehow going to be able to follow every security camera between I-95 and here.

"I'm calling them back," I say. Because somebody needs to stop this lunacy. I'm hanging on by my last thread of sanity here. I never should have told Hudson about this. He's weak when it comes to his wife. One look from her and he folds like a deck of cards.

The phone rings once, twice.

"Hello?" Francie's voice is sharp. Tired. It makes my stomach twist.

Christ, I miss her.

"It's me," I say softly. "Don't hang up."

"Why would I hang up?" she asks. Oh, she's pissed. "I'm

not the one who ignores messages and calls and thinks they can fix everything by playing Batman in a business suit."

I close my eyes. "I wasn't trying to ignore you. I just…"

"What were you trying to do then, Asher? Because from where I'm sitting it felt a lot like you didn't trust me with details about my own life."

"I was trying to protect you," I tell her, and even I can hear how weak it sounds.

She lets out a laugh. It's not funny. It's sharp and brittle and cuts right through me. "Wow, you and my brothers should form a club. You could call it 'People who think Francie can't handle her own shit.' Meetings every Monday. Matching jackets optional."

I put on my best cajoling voice. "Francie."

"Just stop talking," she tells me. "Here's what you don't understand. I don't want to be protected. I want to be trusted. Your equal in everything. And I thought you felt the same." Her voice catches. "I really believed you understood me."

I try to swallow, but my throat is too dry. There are a thousand things I want to say, but not one of them feels like enough.

"I never meant to hurt you," I say softly.

"But you did."

Those words feel like a punch to the center of my gut. I hurt her. When all I wanted to do was make sure she was safe.

I open my mouth then close it again, because I can't think of a single thing to say to make this right.

Skyler murmurs something that I can't hear. Then Francie's low voice comes back on the line.

"I'm hanging up now," she tells me. "But just so we're

clear, if you sign that agreement, or let that woman win, you'll be losing me as well as your company."

Before I can respond, she hangs up. I stare at the phone for a minute, willing it to ring again. Wanting to call her back.

Hudson whistles low under his breath. "Well that went well."

West leans back in his chair, arms folded. "I hate to say I told you so but..."

I don't answer.

Because I'm all out of words. And I have no idea how I'm going to make this right.

thirty-seven

FRANCIE

"This is it," I murmur, as Skyler comes to a stop outside an expensive five-storied brownstone apartment building on the Upper East Side. Annalise's address was easy enough to find out. One phone call to Jesse, who looked at Skyler's contacts on her phone as he muttered, "remind me never to get on your bad side," and two seconds later we had the intel.

Now we're staring at the kind of building where the air smells faintly of Christian Dior and generational wealth.

And I should know.

"Are you sure you don't want backup?" Skyler asks, peering through the windshield like she wants to storm the place herself. "I can play the muscle. Or the getaway driver." She gives me a soft smile. "Or the wildly supportive friend who stands in the background and mutters passive aggressive commentary."

"You wouldn't mutter," I tell her. "You'd scream it."

"You know me so well. And that's why I love you."

I reach out to squeeze her hand. "Thank you for all your support. But this one is mine."

"Shall I stay here? Circle the block? Wait at the corner like a mom on a school run?" she asks.

I shake my head. "Go over to Hudson's. Make him grovel. I'll grab a cab when I'm done."

Skyler looks more than a little disappointed. But she's also a good friend, so she nods. "Fine, but call me as soon as you're out of there. I need proof of life."

"I will," I promise, reaching for the door handle. I'm trying not to show how scared I am. How confronting Annalise feels like I'm heading back to high school and standing up to my bullies. But I have to do this. And do it alone.

She has videos of me. She was using them to blackmail Asher. And I can't let her win.

I climb out of the car and go to close the door. "Hey Francie," Skyler says. She's giving me a serious look.

"Yes?"

"Don't let her get in your head."

"I won't," I promise.

And with that, I close the door and step into enemy territory.

The doorman looks at me as soon as I walk onto the path. "Can I help you?" he asks.

I put on my best rich-girl smile. Because if I've learned one thing growing up with money, it's that bluffing is so much easier when you're confident and not afraid.

"I'm here to see Annalise Vale. She's expecting me." I pretend to tap out on my phone then smile. "I'll let her know I'm here." I wink. "Ugh, she's in the bathroom.

Urinary infection, probably best not to call over the intercom."

He shifts his feet, looking distinctly uncomfortable. "She's on the top floor."

I give a light laugh. "I know that, silly."

He hesitates for a beat. Probably weighing whether he wants to deal with Annalise in full diva mode if I'm telling the truth. But then he steps aside and pushes the door open.

"Have a nice day," he murmurs.

I smile as I breeze past like I own the place, then feel the cool rush of air as the door closes behind me.

The lobby is all marble floors and fresh flowers. The kind of place where the furniture costs more than most people's annual salaries. I press the old-fashioned elevator button, and watch the wooden doors whisper open before I step inside.

My heart starts to speed as it smoothly rises up. I try to get my thoughts straight in my head.

When the elevator arrives on the top floor – directly opposite her door – I step out and rap my knuckles against the oak. Steeling myself for what happens next.

Within moments the door is flung open.

And there she is.

Annalise. The woman Asher used to love. I try to ignore the clench of jealousy in my stomach because I don't want to be that girl. The one who gets annoyed that her boyfriend has a past. And she is the past.

Whatever he's doing, he's not cheating on me. He's just being an idiot.

Barefoot, wearing a floor-length cashmere cardigan over what looks like extremely expensive loungewear. Her gaze rakes over my face. Her expression is a mixture of shock and pure Upper East Side disdain.

"Oh my," she says slowly, like she's trying to decide if I'm just a bad dream. "I wasn't expecting a trash collection today."

I smile sweetly. "Figured I'd drop by and say hi. Since you seem so obsessed by me."

Her jaw tightens. "I'm just trying to figure out what Asher sees in you. You're so... *messy*."

I step inside without being invited, because manners are wasted on people like her. "I'm here because you're blackmailing somebody I care about. And you've crossed a line."

Her brows shoot up. "Blackmail is such an ugly word," she says lightly. "Besides, it's not my fault you two decided to turn his security system into your own version of Only Fans."

My cheeks heat up but I don't blink. "If you liked them that much, maybe you're the one who should be paying for them."

Her eyes narrow. "Oh sweetheart," she says. "You think this is about you? I had him first. I know his body better than my own. He used to wake me up with his mouth between my thighs." She tips her head to the side. "He never made me do it myself, not like you."

I take a long breath in. *Don't let her get in your head.*

She wants me flustered. Off balance. Small.

Too bad for her I'm done feeling that way.

"You really think this is about sex?" I ask, taking a step closer. "That what you had with Asher even comes close to what we have?"

Something flickers behind her eyes. I press on.

"Maybe you had his body. But you never had him. And that's why this is eating you alive."

She scoffs, but it's tight. Defensive.

"You really want to do this?" she asks, flicking her hair behind her shoulders. "Because I have those videos. The ones where you're mouthing his name like a bad lip-syncer. Imagine what people will think. Your family, your friends. Your employer."

She doesn't even know who I am, I realize. She doesn't know me at all.

And that's her problem.

I stare at her for a beat then laugh. Actually laugh. It bubbles out before I can stop it.

"Do it. Release them. Set up a TikTok channel. Go full influencer if you want. Because I don't care. I don't care who sees them. They were made for the man I love and if people don't understand that, then that's their problem." I swallow hard. "That's the difference between you and me. I don't build my self-worth on other people's destruction. I know who I am. I know what I've done. And I know who loves me."

Her lips twist. "You'll regret this."

I shake my head. "No, I really don't think I will. But you will. You're standing in a glass palace full of nothing but lies and bitterness. And you built it yourself. How does it feel? To know that nobody cares?"

She blinks. But says nothing.

So I give her a smile. The kind women reserve for other women who try to destroy them.

Then I walk out of the door, head high, heart hammering.

And I don't look back.

* * *

ASHER

Hudson paces his office like a caged tiger, his phone to his ear, his jaw clenched so tight I can hear his teeth grinding.

"I don't care if she's not answering," he barks. "Try again. Try everywhere."

I'm right behind him, calling Jesse for the third time while I review every security log I can find, desperate to figure out what the hell Francie and Skyler are up to.

But Jesse isn't picking up either now. I throw my phone down, annoyance rising inside me.

West, on the other hand, is leaning back in his chair, his legs crossed, sipping a glass of water like he's got front row tickets at the theater.

Hudson slams his fist on the desk and West's lips curl.

"Have either of you considered," he says casually, "that you're not the main characters in this particular episode."

My eyes lock with Hudson's. Yeah, we both pretty much want to kill his best friend right now.

Before we can decide on our weapon of choice, the office door bursts open like it's been kicked.

Skyler strides in, her eyes narrow.

All the air rushes out of Hudson like a pricked balloon. "Sky…"

She puts her hand up, like she's trying to block him. "Don't try to sweet talk me," she says. "Unless your next sentence is 'here's a chilled glass of lemonade and a full confession."

"Where's Francie?" I ask, looking behind her. I'm already rushing to the door, desperate to see her.

Skyler doesn't answer at first. Just looks at me like I'm even more of an idiot than her husband.

"She's not here," she tells me, like I haven't already gathered that.

"Then *where* is she?" My jaw tightens.

Skyler sighs, walking further into the office and sitting down on the corner of Hudson's desk. She suddenly notices West.

"Oh hi," she says, like it's a goddamned tea party. "How are you?"

"Completely entertained," West says, deadpan.

"Hello?" They're unbelievable. "Francie? You were going to tell me where she is."

"Oh, I dropped her off at Annalise's place."

Silence fills the room. What the fuck?

Hudson swears under his breath. I feel the floor tilt beneath my feet.

"What?" My voice is too sharp. Too loud. But I can't help it.

"She wanted to talk to her, woman to woman. About the blackmail." Skyler's eyes meet mine. "Since you and Hudson have this whole vow of silence thing going on, she decided to go straight to the source."

"You let her go there alone?" I ask, my voice thick. I'm not sure I can breathe.

Skyler tilts her head. "I offered to be her wingman, but she said no. Because – *shocker* – she's not a damsel in distress, Asher. She's a grown ass woman who's sick of being treated like she's breakable." She looks at Hudson. "And don't think you're getting away with this."

"I'm damn sure I'm not," Hudson mutters.

But I'm already grabbing my phone and keys. Then realizing I don't have my car here, I grab Hudson's.

"Upper East Side?" I ask Skyler.

"Yep. I dropped her off fifteen minutes ago."

My throat tightens as I storm off, shoving the door open.

Then I'm gone, sprinting down the stairwell like my life depends on it.

Because it does.

* * *

I take the corner too fast. Tires squeal. A horn blares. And I don't give a flying fuck. Hudson's ridiculously expensive sports car growls beneath me like it's made for moments like this.

My whole body is tense. My blood is heated, full of emergency-level, heart-pounding, punch-a-wall panic.

My fingers tighten on the steering wheel as I pull up outside the familiar brownstone apartment building.

And then I see *her*.

Francie is standing on the sidewalk, trying to hail a cab like she doesn't have a care in the world. Her expression is unreadable but her eyes...

God, they slice straight through me as I climb out of the car, abandoning it in a no parking zone.

Relief rushes through me as I realize she's not hurt. And then it's immediately swallowed by something hotter. Darker.

Rage.

"What the hell were you thinking?" I snap, slamming the car door behind me. "Going to see Annalise alone? Do you know what she's capable of?"

Francie doesn't flinch. Doesn't even blink. She just stares at me like I'm the one losing my mind.

"Yes," Francie says calmly. "I know exactly what she's capable of. Because I'm a grown adult who knows how to talk. Which is exactly what I did with her, instead of appeasing her threats like you planned to."

My chest heaves. "She's dangerous."

"And I'm not helpless." Her voice is clipped. "But thanks for making it crystal clear that you think I am."

I take a step toward her. I want to hold her. To keep her safe. To never let her go. "I don't think you're helpless."

Her eyes lock on mine. I can see the hurt there. The anger, too. "Then why didn't you tell me what was going on?"

I blink, raking my hand through my hair. Hating the way she's looking at me like I'm nothing more than another man who let her down.

I reach for her and she takes a step back, breaking my heart in fucking two.

"I'm sorry," I whisper. "I wasn't trying to hurt you."

"No," she says, her eyes so sad it hurts. "You were just trying to control me. You didn't trust me with the truth. You treated me like some liability you have to keep protected while you make all the decisions."

"That's not what I intended."

"But it's what you did." Her jaw tightens. "You lied to me, Asher. You ignored my calls, my messages. You let me sit there and feel like you were ignoring me. Like I didn't matter. While you were the big man making all the decisions and shutting me out completely."

I grit my teeth. "I was trying to protect you."

"From what?" She lets out a low, humorless laugh. "The truth? From being an actual partner in our relationship?" She takes a deep breath. "You know what's really messed up? You called me brave. Smart. Fierce. And I believed you."

She doesn't understand. I just need to explain it better. I realize that.

"I was scared," I admit, my voice raw. "I've hurt people before. I needed to…"

"Well maybe I'm scared too. But I don't punish the people I care about because of it. You think you're the only one with scars? I've got a lifetime of people making decisions for me. Walking into the room and assuming they know better. You think I need you to do that too?"

Her words hit like a blade. But she doesn't stop.

"I never wanted a hero, Asher. I wanted a partner. An equal. Someone who chose me, not only when it was easy, but when things got ugly and hard and real."

Silence stretches between us. She stares at me, unflinching.

"And just so you know, I told Annalise to do whatever she wants with those damn videos. But you won't be giving her anything. I'm not a pawn for you both to bargain over."

The hollow feeling in my chest expands.

She doesn't wait for me to reply. Just steps back, turning toward the street like the conversation's over.

"Wait." I reach for her but she shakes my hand off.

"I'm tired. And I have a book to write," she says, still not looking at me. "I need to go."

She turns away, her stride measured and even, like my heart isn't smashed on the floor, ragged and breaking. I start to walk after her.

"Sir?"

A sharp voice cuts through the air. I glance over my shoulder to see a pair of NYPD officers approaching, their eyes immediately zeroing in on the sleek sports car half on the curb, hazard lights blinking.

"Is that your vehicle?" one of them asks, his hand on his belt. "You can't park it there."

My hands clench into fists. "Yeah, I'm moving it now," I murmur. But my eyes are still on her. She pauses at the end of the block. For one impossible second I think she might look back.

But she doesn't.

She keeps walking, her head held high, as the officers keep talking. And all I can do is stand there, surrounded by noise and blue uniforms and a goddamn Lamborghini that's become the world's most expensive shackle.

I could leave it, piss Hudson off and chase after her.

But she's made it clear, she doesn't want to be chased. She doesn't want me making the decisions for her.

"Sir, are you listening?"

So instead I watch her disappear into the city like I never mattered at all.

thirty-eight

ASHER

The bar is almost empty. Mid-afternoon sunlight filters through the tall windows, catching on the amber swirl of whiskey in my glass. It's the kind of place that charges twenty bucks for a drink and another fifty for your regrets. Hudson's nursing a beer and watching me like I'm a ticking bomb, which to be fair, isn't far off.

"She's back in Liberty," he says, breaking the silence. "Jesse told Skyler this morning."

I nod. I already know. But knowing where Francie is doesn't fix the fact that she won't speak to me. Won't answer my messages. And for the first time in weeks I haven't checked the lighthouse security feed. I can't. Because if I see her... and she looks like she's better off without me, I don't know what I'll do.

"How are things with Skyler?" I ask, because to top everything else off, my decisions have caused problems in

Hudson's marriage. *I pulled Skyler into this mess when she's already dealing with enough.*

"Furious." His lips twitch. "And it's so damn hard to make it up to a woman who can't be bought with flowers or jewelry. I've spent the last two hours searching through a record store in the village for an original copy of Stevie Nicks and Lindsay Buckingham's first album."

I give him a sympathetic look. Skyler is a huge Fleetwood Mac – and Stevie Nicks – fan. I make myself a note to apologize to her for involving her in this mess.

Hudson takes a slow sip of his beer. "So are we going to talk about this, or are you just going to brood into that glass like Batman on a bender?"

I let out a humorless laugh. "You ever think maybe I'm not built for this?"

"For what?" he frowns.

"Relationships. My last girlfriend tried to steal my business from me. And my current – or possibly past one – thinks I'm the world's biggest screw up."

"You are."

"Thanks."

We exchange glances. Hudson lets out a sigh.

"I know you were only trying to protect her."

"I was." I nod.

"But you can't go around thinking you can protect everybody and everything." He runs his hand through his hair. "I learned that the hard way."

When he pushed Skyler away after nearly losing his daughter. I remember it well. He was lost. Broken.

The way I feel right now.

"Yeah, well when you grow up learning that people either control you or leave you, it makes you choose the first one real fast." My voice is thick.

"You're talking about Dad." His face softens. "I hate what he did to you."

"To all of us."

"But especially you. He exploited you. Used you. Left you in the dark, literally."

I swallow hard, the panic of that day rising inside me again.

"He's been dead a long time," I say. "I can't keep blaming him for my decisions."

"You can if you let him be that voice in your head." Hudson gives me a knowing look. "Three years of therapy taught me that. He hurt you. I know that. And that was on him. But this?" He shakes his head. "The decisions you make now are on you. Either you face up to it, or you lose what you care about."

"I'm scared I've already lost her," I admit. And there it is. The sick thud in my chest. The realization that it's all my fault.

Not Francie's. Not Shaun's. Not even Annalise's.

I could have told Francie what was going on. I could have involved her. Treated her like the strong woman she is. Like an equal.

Instead I was afraid. That little kid in the dark closet, willing to do anything to get out.

Hudson lets the silence settle for a moment, like he knows I need the space to breathe through it. To let the past roll over me one more time before I finally let it go.

"The way dad treated you wasn't your fault," he finally says.

"I know."

"And the way he used Eden. That wasn't your fault either." His voice is firm.

I look at him. I want to believe him, but I let our sister

down. I should have protected her. I knew what he was capable of. But instead I got out of Liberty as fast as I could.

And she paid the price.

"You know what sucks?" I say, my voice rough. "I spent my whole life building walls to keep people out. And then I met Francie and all I want to do is let her in. But I have no idea how. I don't know how to stop myself from shutting down, locking her out."

He nods. I know he gets me. But it's not enough.

"Remember the day Autumn, Eden, and Francie dressed up as the Spice Girls for the Liberty Nineties Karaoke fundraiser?" I ask, my lips twitching despite everything.

Hudson groans. "Don't remind me. Autumn had glitter in her hair for a week. And Francie..."

"Was Sporty Spice. She wore those god awful track pants and started talking with a British accent. And then she did that roundhouse and kicked Mylene's cake display over."

Hudson chuckles. "Now *that* was girl power."

My chest tightens. Even then, she knew what she wanted. And for a brief while, that was me.

I was the luckiest man in the world. And I'm so in love with her it hurts.

But love can't be about controlling somebody. Or sacrificing in the dark. It's about knowing when to let somebody knock the cake table over and still cheering for them.

"Autumn called this morning," Hudson says, breaking my thoughts. "I didn't tell her anything. But..."

Another person I've pushed away. My stomach tightens.

"I'll tell her."

Our eyes lock.

It's time to start cleaning up the mess I made. And fighting for what I want. In the light, in the open.

Where she can see me.

And where – if I'm really lucky – she'll choose me.

* * *

FRANCIE

I'm sitting at my desk in the lighthouse, staring at my laptop screen, wishing the words would appear from nowhere so I can finish this book and go back to brooding.

It's been two days since I got back to Liberty. Two days of trying to write, of dodging concerned texts from my brothers, and ignoring every single message Asher's sent.

I took the ferry alone. Watched the island come into view through eyes that felt raw from holding back tears. And when Jesse picked me up at the dock, I smiled and told him I was fine, even though we both knew I was full of crap.

I've barely left the lighthouse since.

I told myself I needed space to write, but really, I needed space to breathe. To untangle the mess inside me. To stop hearing his voice every time I close my eyes.

The phone rings, and I almost don't answer. But when I see Autumn's name flash across the screen, something inside me shifts. She deserves more than silence. She always has.

I press accept and lift the phone to my ear. "Hey."

"About time," Autumn says, her voice warm and wry. "I was starting to think you'd ghosted me for good."

The way she says it reminds me of Asher. The way he ignored me.

And I realize I've been doing the same to her. Avoiding talking to her, telling her what was happening.

I accused him of not thinking about what I want. But I've done exactly the same to Autumn. My best friend would want to know what's happening. To be in the loop.

Instead, I excluded her.

"I was going to call you," I say. "I just... there's something I need to tell you." Because even if this is all a mess right now, she deserves to know. I'm done hiding. And if she hates me for a while, so be it.

I'll make it up to her somehow.

"Let me guess. It has to do with Asher." Her voice is gentle, like she knows I'm feeling vulnerable right now. And this is why I love her.

"How do you know?" I rasp. Tears pool in my eyes. What a mess I've made of things.

"Oh sweetie, you sound like a wreck. Just like him. I figured something was up when you ghosted me harder than a bad Tinder date. But I didn't think it was my big brother making you do it."

"You've spoken to Asher?" Hope immediately rises in my chest.

"I did. I wasn't supposed to say anything because he's worried you'll be upset that he told me. But honey, he's broken. Seriously, I've never seen him so low."

I press my lips together, trying to ignore the lump in my throat. "He shut me out."

"I know," she says. "And you were right to be angry. He knows that. But Francie, my brother cares for you in a way that terrifies him. He's spent his whole life protecting people because nobody ever protected him."

I close my eyes, her words hitting something deep inside me. She's right. She's always right.

"I'm sorry," I whisper. "For not calling. For not telling you what's going on. I shut you out and you didn't deserve that."

"No, I didn't. And you owe me big time. When I get back to Liberty I'll think of a way you can repay me." There's warmth in her voice that makes my heart feel like it might heal. "And trust me, I get it. Things get messy fast. But next time, just tell me. I have ice cream and bad decision wine, and I know how to use them."

A watery laugh escapes my lips. "It's a deal."

But I'm still cringing on the inside.

I blamed Asher for keeping me in the dark, but I did the exact same thing to the person who's been my anchor since I was twelve years old.

"Will you talk to him? When you're ready?" she asks me.

My heart thuds against my ribcage. "I miss him," I whisper. It's like every corner of this place echoes with him. I can't sleep in bed without imagining him beside me. Smiling that soft smile.

"You love him," she says, like she can read my mind. Maybe after all these years she can.

Tears burn in my eyes. "I do."

There's a quiet moment between us. Then she clears her throat.

"He loves you too, Francie. Enough to break himself wide open. But maybe it's time he let you help put him back together."

My heart twists. The thought of him hurting makes me want to throw something. "How do you always know what to say?"

"It's a gift. Now go finish that book, and when you're done, finish your own story."

I nod even though she can't see me. "I will," I promise.

We hang up and I set my phone down beside the laptop. A breeze flutters through the open window, lifting the edge of a sticky note Asher left me weeks ago.

You've got this.

It's in his messy all-caps scrawl.

I smile. And then I hear it. The crunch of tires on gravel.

And when I look out of the window, there he is. Asher Fitzgerald, driving up the makeshift road in a black SUV.

And for the first time in days my heart doesn't ache. It beats.

Maybe, *just maybe*, our story isn't finished yet.

thirty-nine

FRANCIE

The SUV comes around to the front of the lighthouse and the engine cuts off. A moment later, there's a knock at the front door.

It isn't loud. Not urgent. Just a soft, rhythmic tap, like he knows I need time.

I stand up from the desk, my muscles knotted from sitting here for too long, and pad to the front door.

But when I pull it open there's nobody there. Just a cup of coffee with cream and a sprinkle of cinnamon – the way I like it – and a bag full of muffins with a note written across the brown paper.

Finish your book. Then come and find me. I'll be waiting. Always. A x

. . .

I pick them up with trembling fingers. And as I glance up I see the SUV is parked at the end of the graveled lane. And even though I can't see him through the reflection of the sun on the windshield I know he's there. Waiting like he said he would.

I close the door with a soft click and pad back across the floor to my desk. As I put the coffee and the muffins down, my laptop screen glows with the half-finished sentence I've been working on all morning.

But now there's a tremble in my hands that has nothing to do with writer's block.

I pick up my phone and before I can second-guess myself I open our message thread. The one I haven't touched since I got back to Liberty.

And I send him a message.

What if it takes a few days for me to finish this book? Are you going to sit out there forever? – Francie

For a moment there's no reply. Then the typing icon appears.

Then I'll bring more coffee tomorrow. And the day after that. And if you still need time, I'll open my own coffee shop. Can't promise I'll make them as good as Mylene does. – Asher

A small helpless laugh bubbles up inside me.

. . .

That's dedication. How about showers – are you just going to stink? What if you need to pee? – Francie

You're a romance writer. You know the hero never needs the bathroom. – Asher

I roll my eyes even as my throat tightens. Then I put my phone down and turn my gaze to my laptop screen. We're at the darkest moment. Just before the dawn. Everything is lost and yet... there's still hope.

Maybe that's what love is. Not a perfect arc or fairy-tale ending. But the grit to keep showing up when things get hard. To wait outside in the cold, to bring coffee and cinnamon muffins, because you have to believe the story isn't over yet.

I take a long sip of the drink he left. It's warm and sweet. Then I turn to the keyboard.

One more chapter to go. My fingers tap on the keys, so ready to write.

Because the real happy ending isn't going to be in this book. It's waiting in the SUV parked at the end of the driveway.

* * *

ASHER

It feels like forever since I pulled up outside the lighthouse. It's been at least nine hours, long enough for the sun to arc across the horizon and dip low toward the ocean behind the lighthouse, leaving the sky inky black. My back aches from this stupid seat, and I'm pretty sure I've read the same line of this email from Brad five times without actually taking any of it in.

But I don't move. I don't check the cameras. I don't message her. I don't knock on the door again. Because this time, I'm not here to fix things on my terms.

I'm here to wait. For as long as it takes.

I ate my last muffin hours ago. My stomach is growling when the soft creak of a door opening breaks the silence. I lift my eyes from the phone and there she is.

Francie.

Her hair is tied up. She's barefoot in a pair of yoga pants with a sweater hanging off her shoulder like she doesn't even realize how heartbreakingly beautiful she looks.

I open the car door and climb out, sliding my phone into my pocket, striding toward the lighthouse, my shoes crunching on the gravel.

And when I get close, she takes a few steps toward me, only stopping when the concrete meets the gravel and she remembers she's barefoot.

The porch light behind her casts a halo around her head. And even though I'm cold and aching and nervous as hell, I swear to God I've never felt warmer.

"I'm finished," she says softly when only a few feet from her.

My chest tightens. "Yeah?"

She nods. "It's messy. And raw. And might get me disowned by my editor. But it's done."

"It sounds perfect," I murmur. "And we need to celebrate. I brought champagne." I look back at the SUV, remembering the bottle I brought with me. "I'll go and get it."

She shivers.

"Meet me inside," I tell her. "That's if it's okay for me to come in."

She nods and I go back to the SUV, pulling out the bottle from the cooler. She left the door to the lighthouse open for me, and I walk in, finding her in the kitchen, pulling out two champagne flutes.

"I brought cups," I say, pulling out the two paper cups I stole from Mylene.

"Classy," Francie says with a soft smile.

"I aim to impress." I pop the cork, pour the bubbly liquid into the glasses, and hand her one.

Her fingers brush mine as she takes it. "I can't believe you waited in your car all day."

"I told you I would."

"I know." There's the smallest smile on her lips. "You must ache like hell from being cramped up."

"It was worth it," I tell her truthfully. And then, I take a deep breath. "I'm so sorry. For not talking to you. For not trusting you with what was going on. I'm working on it. I promise. And I won't block you out. If you just give me... *us*, another chance."

Her lips part. "You nearly lost everything."

"I nearly lost you." I pull my phone out of my pocket. "I started writing a short story while I was in the car. Would you like to see it?"

She blinks, somewhere between confused and amused. "Okay."

I open the notes app and pass it to her. And she starts reading it out loud.

. . .

"He realized he'd lost the best thing that ever happened to him. And he groveled. For the rest of his life. The end."

She looks up, her eyes crinkling. "You're such a nerd."

"I'm your nerd," I murmur. "If you'll have me back."

Her breath hitches. "I'm so mad at you."

"I know."

"You hurt me." Her voice cracks and it fractures something inside me too. But this is my fault. And I need to make amends.

"I know that too. And I'll keep apologizing every day until you believe how sorry I am."

A beat of silence follows. Then her voice softens. "But I'm so stupidly in love with you it hurts to be without you even more."

The air leaves my lungs. "God, Francie, I love you. So damn much."

Then she's in my arms, our mouths meeting in a kiss that tastes like champagne and second chances. It's wild and warm and filled with everything we haven't said.

The bottle tips over somewhere behind us, champagne hissing as it meets the counter. My elbow knocks over one of the glasses. But we ignore it, my hands in her hair, hers tugging at my shirt buttons like we're both desperate to make up for lost time.

She pulls back long enough to whisper, "Take me to bed. Now."

And I don't need telling twice.

* * *

ASHER

Francie lays in my arms, softly sleeping as I stare at the ceiling, my chest feeling so damn light I swear I could float up there if I wanted to.

It's been a long time since I've felt this content. Maybe I never have, I don't know. All I do know is that being with this woman feels like coming home and being on vacation at the same time. She's the best of everything. Definitely the best of me.

And she's forgiven me for lying to her.

Thank God. It already feels like months ago, the pain of watching her walk away, even though it's hardly been a week. The ache in my heart of knowing I'd messed up the best thing that had ever happened to me.

My phone starts to vibrate on the table beside me, and without moving Francie, I reach for it, ready to silence it. But there's a message from Zach. Some stupid meme of a cat wearing a bandana. I like it and go to turn off the screen, but of course I've unleashed the fucking Kraken. Because now the family chat notifications are buzzing.

And yes, the old Asher would be annoyed and turn it off. But I'm not the old Asher. I'm fucking happy and content and if my family wants to chat, let them.

ZACH:

Asher just liked a meme I sent him. At 10:47 p.m. On a Saturday.

. . .

HUDSON:

What meme was it? Skyler wants to know.

ZACH:

It was a cat wearing a crown that said "when he's secretly soft but also dangerous."

HUDSON:

She says that's basically Asher in a nutshell.

ZACH:

So the reconciliation worked then? The man is definitely in love.

AUTUMN:

Guys, it's the middle of the night here. If you're going to wake me up with gossip, you could at least send coffee. And I have ALL the details about the groveling. Our boy did good. I'm proud of him.

ASHER:

Can you all please stop talking about me now?

AUTUMN:

Shut up. You love it. And you love my best friend.

· · ·

I lift a brow.

ASHER: I do.

AUTUMN: Squee! He admits it. Oh god, I'm hyperventilating. Somebody send oxygen!

ZACH:
    It's sweet. We love to see it.

HUDSON:
    Seriously, though. We're happy for you, Ash. Just don't screw it up again.

ASHER:
    I don't intend to.

ZACH:
    Ah, my big brother is self-reflective! Now that's what I call character development. What is this, THREE of you in functional relationships? Who would have thought it?

AUTUMN:
    I know. It's weird. I'm scared. Hold me.

• • •

ZACH:

I'm telling you, if Eden ends up with someone, I'm going to need a therapist. I liked us all being dysfunctional. It took the heat off me.

HUDSON:

It's okay. Eden hates romantic entanglements. Right.

HUDSON:

RIGHT?

EDEN:

Hi everyone! And yes I do. I don't belong to anybody. Except mother earth.

HUDSON:

Good, let's keep it that way.

EDEN:

Not that I'd tell you if I WAS attracted to somebody. Especially not if he was completely the wrong somebody for me...

AUTUMN:

Ooh, that's oddly specific. Let's take this to the Fitzgerald girl's only chat.

. . .

HUDSON:

Wait. What? You have a side chat?

AUTUMN:

Of course we have a side chat. Do you know nothing about women?

ZACH:

Can I join?

AUTUMN:

Hell no.

HUDSON:

Eden, add me in.

EDEN:

Gotta go, battery's dying. LOVE YA FAM! 🌿 ✌️

WYATT:

👍

Just as I go to close the chat, Francie blinks awake, her lashes lifting slow. "You're smiling," she murmurs, her voice sleep-rough, like she's been dreaming of somewhere warm. "I like it when you smile."

I huff a laugh and tilt my phone toward her. "I've been reading the Fitzgerald Family chat. They all know we're together. It's chaos in there."

Her mouth curves, like she understands. "The good kind?"

"The best kind." I set the phone aside and let my hand trace her cheek, my thumb brushing the soft curve like I'm committing it to memory. "Almost as good as this."

Her gaze holds mine, steady and sure. "You look happy," she says quietly, like she's trying to put a name to something she's never seen in me before.

"That's because I am." My voice feels different when I say it. Hell, *I* feel different. Lighter. Like a softer version of who I used to be. "You make me that way," I murmur, leaning down to press my lips against her brow.

The lighthouse is quiet except for the faint hum of the sea through the open window. But everything else falls away.

She shifts, slow and deliberate, sliding over until she's straddling my hips. My hands find her waist, instinctively tightening, pulling her closer.

"You know," she says, her smile turning wicked, "we never did finish celebrating meeting my book deadline."

I lift a brow. "You finished twice, as I recall," I murmur, my voice dropping low, "But I'm not against celebrating all over again."

Her laugh is low, full of promise. She leans in, brushing her mouth over mine once, twice, until my patience snaps and I kiss her the way I've been wanting to all damn day.

The world can wait. The family chat can wait.

Because this woman? She's mine, and I'm determined to keep it that way.

So I circle my hands around her waist, and flip us over

until she's beneath me, her eyes wide with excitement, her lips parted with anticipation.

Yep, she's definitely mine.

And I'm never letting her go.

THE FOLLOWING YEAR...

FRANCIE

If you'd told me a year ago that I'd be standing in a seaside bookstore with my name splashed across the covers of actual books, signing them with a pink Sharpie while my overprotective brothers hovered like secret service agents and my boyfriend whispered utterly inappropriate things in my ear between well-wishers...

Well, I would've laughed. Then probably tripped over something. And definitely spilled coffee down my front.

But here I am.

Books by the Sea is exactly what a bookstore on Liberty Island should be. It's tucked between the pier and the village green, with whitewashed clapboard siding, big ocean-facing windows, and the salty scent of the ocean drifting in every time the door opens. Fairy lights twist around the ceiling beams. Shelves made from reclaimed driftwood line the walls, packed with bestsellers and beach reads, plus a local authors display – or rather local author, because I'm the only one – that makes me blush every time I glance at it.

There's a reading nook in the back with two overstuffed armchairs and a faded Persian rug. A big hand-painted sign behind the counter reads, *Books are magic, and so are you.*

Sadie, the new owner, opened the shop only three months ago. Nobody really knows her history, or why she decided to open a bookstore here on Liberty. But she's absolutely in her element, wearing a maxi dress covered in tiny books, tucking pencils behind both ears, and organizing themed displays with military strictness. She bustles around like a caffeinated book fairy, refilling the display table, chatting with customers, and sending up silent thank-yous to the book gods every time another ferry of readers arrives from the mainland.

"You're single-handedly funding my caffeine habit," she tells me under her breath, sliding another stack of my novels across the table.

"I aim to support small businesses," I reply solemnly, adding a heart to my signature.

Outside, the line of readers curls down the sidewalk and out of view. Autumn, who's taken on the role of unofficial publicist, content creator, and proud best friend, is filming the chaos for TikTok, cackling about views and engagement as she pans across the crowd.

From my spot behind the table, I see Mylene pacing on the sidewalk like a woman on a mission. She's flatly refusing to enter because Eileen is here, standing smugly at the front of the line, a copy of my book clutched to her chest like it's a rare diamond.

Sadie ducks behind a nearby display like Mylene might breathe fire. "She's convinced Eileen's going to buy the last signed copy," she whispers.

"I think we're safe," I murmur, eyeing the piles waiting to be signed.

"Francie!" Charlie's voice cuts through the buzz, loud and cheerful and unmistakably him. He materializes at my side, sunglasses perched on his head like a crown, carrying a coffee in one hand and a chocolate croissant in the other. "Just wanted to say thank you. It's not every day a man gets immortalized as the charming rogue in a romance novel."

"You're not in the book."

He winks. "That's what *you* think."

Sadie chokes on a laugh as Charlie flips open a copy and dramatically fans himself. "Page 263. You're welcome, America."

"Please stop," I mutter, my cheeks flushing.

Before I can catch my breath, Alice, my editor, strides in from outside, looking both chic and vaguely chaotic, her vape tucked behind one ear and her phone clutched like it's a glass of champagne. She stops beside my table, grinning like the cat who got the publishing deal.

"You're viral on TikTok," she announces, tapping her screen. "Advance readers are losing their minds."

"Oh god," I say, bracing myself. "Is it the cliffhanger?"

"Nope. It's your sex scenes. Listen to this."

She clears her throat dramatically and reads aloud, *"This book melted my Kindle. I had to put it in the freezer. My husband thinks I've been electrocuted."*

Sadie snorts from behind the display. Charlie fist-pumps. Myles chokes on his iced coffee, his face turning the color of beets.

Alice just beams. "Congratulations. You're officially

causing household drama. How quickly can you write the next book?"

I bury my face in my hands. "I swear to God."

And then I feel it. Warm fingers brushing the back of my neck. The quiet hum of Asher's presence sliding in behind me like gravity. Alice leaves my side, making a beeline for Myles who looks like he'd rather be anywhere but here.

"Your brothers are planning their next interrogation," Asher murmurs to me, his voice low and delicious against my ear. "If I don't make it out alive, tell Parker he can have my fishing rod."

"Don't," I say, turning just enough to meet his eyes. "I like watching them squirm when you touch me."

"They're terrifying."

"They should be."

Which is a lie, of course. They've warmed up to him. *Mostly.* Liam still refers to him as "that security guy," and Brooks pretends he's not impressed by the billionaire who brought muffins to woo their little sister. But they showed up today, with gruff hugs and soft smiles and their families in tow.

And it means everything.

Asher's family is here, too. Skyler, glowing and delighted to no longer be pregnant, is carefully navigating the stacks with a coffee in hand, pausing to pose for Autumn's camera. Hudson is holding their baby daughter, brow furrowed like he's assessing the shop for structural weaknesses. Jesse and Parker are deep in conversation about fishing rods, and Eden is curled up in the back corner with my book open, already a quarter of the way through.

Across the room, I catch West glancing at her, before quickly looking away.

Interesting.

One person who is thankfully not here is Annalise. For obvious reasons. After Asher handed everything over to the authorities, she was arrested last fall. The charges included hacking, conspiracy, and my personal favorite, obstruction with malice. She turned down a plea deal, so she's headed to trial.

Brad, on the other hand, is thriving. He's now COO of Asher's company, running the New York office like a dream, while Asher works mostly from Liberty. We're living in one of the newly renovated fishermen's cottages while we build something of our own.

And the book, the one I finished during a week that nearly broke me, is out in the world. It ends on a cliffhanger that's caused mild online chaos. People are posting reaction videos, theorizing over who survives the final scene, and preorders for book two are already through the roof. Even though it's not written.

And Alice is desperate for me to get back to my writing nook.

But not tonight.

Tonight, we celebrate.

Autumn turned the lighthouse lawn into a wonderland of fairy lights, paper lanterns, and a banner that reads From Cliffhangers to Happily Ever Afters. There's a chocolate fountain, an open bar, and, because this is my life now, a professional Fabio lookalike who's posing for photos with a plastic sword.

Everyone I love is here. My family. Asher's family. Half the island. Maybe more.

And later, when the lights dim and the crowd thins and the stars burn bright above the cliffs, I'll get him to myself.

The man who waited outside with muffins. Who sees

every part of me, even the broken pieces, and loves me anyway.

Tonight, I don't have to write a happy ending.

Because I get to live it.

* * *

ASHER

The evening is sultry, the lawns lit with fairy lights, as I stand with the velvet ring box in my pocket, trying to ignore the way Francie's brothers are staring at me like they're deciding what size casket they'll need to buy for me.

Autumn catches my eye from across the yard. She's wearing a vintage chiffon dress and a hopeful smile, nudging Eden in the side and gesturing at me like she's the conductor and I'm first violin.

She's known about my plan since I ordered the ring a month ago. And she's been dropping hints ever since. Her best one yet is the banner she strung up from the lighthouse.

From Cliffhangers to Happily Ever Afters is written in huge silver foil letters, stretched over a chocolate fountain that the kids are clustered around, next to the Fabio lookalike the women of Liberty are trying very hard not to drool over.

But the only thing I can't take my eyes off is Francie.

She's across the garden, head tipped back in laughter, holding a glass of champagne as she talks to Skyler and Jesse. Her red dress hugs her like it was made just for her. Bold and soft. Fiery and elegant. Just like her.

And when she turns and catches my eye, the whole party fades to black.

The ring box is burning a hole in my pocket, but I force myself to breathe. To wait. Because this moment? It's all hers.

Francie walks across the grass toward me, hips swaying, bare shoulders glowing under the lights. Her eyes lock with mine and my chest tightens with every step she takes.

I hold out my hand and she slips hers into it without hesitation. The moment our fingers lace, my body relaxes.

With my other hand, I reach into my pocket and pull out a folded piece of paper. Not my phone this time. This story is handwritten, the ink smudged in the corner where my thumb pressed too hard.

"I wrote this while you were signing books today," I murmur. "You were talking to readers, laughing, completely in your element. And all I could think was how lucky I am to be part of your story."

She unfolds the note carefully, smoothing it between her fingers before she begins to read.

She didn't need a hero. She never had.
She needed someone who would stand beside her in the storm,
Let her burn bright without dimming her fire,
And love her, not for who she might become, but for exactly who she is.
He'd never stop learning how to do that.
This is our chapter one. Here's where we begin.

Francie blinks hard, tears catching on her lashes. She clutches the paper to her chest and opens her mouth, but no words come out.

So I do what I've been waiting all day to do. I drop to one knee.

There's a breathless beat of silence. Her eyes widen, lips parting like she's trying to breathe and think all at once. And I swear my heart's about to pound through my chest.

"I'm so in love with you," I say, my voice rough. "I've been in love with you for longer than you can even imagine. And if you say yes, I'll spend the rest of my life learning how to deserve you."

She doesn't answer right away.

Instead, she lets the note float from her fingers to the ground, cups my face in her hands, and pulls me up. Just like she did the first time she kissed me outside the lighthouse.

Only this time, she's not uncertain. She's mine.

And then, with her mouth against mine, she whispers, "Yes. Obviously."

Cheers erupt around us. Autumn lets out a full-on scream. Eden jumps up and down beside her, grinning so hard her cheeks look sore. Hudson mutters something that sounds a lot like "finally" under his breath. One of Francie's brothers swears, loudly. Might have been Myles. Might have been Brooks. I'm not looking. And I don't care.

Because she said yes.

The lighthouse beam arcs over us, catching the tips of her hair like a halo. The breeze smells like salt and summer and home.

From the corner of my eye, I catch Eden talking to West. There's the strangest look on his face, like he's trying – and failing – to keep his calm. She rolls her eyes, and he immediately looks away, suddenly very captivated by a string of lights.

Interesting.

But right now, I've got more important things to think about. Francie's hand finds mine again, squeezing tight.

Whatever our future holds, we'll be plotting it together.

And deep in my heart I know, it'll be the best story I ever get to tell.

THE END

dear reader

Thank you so much for reading IN CASE YOU DIDN'T KNOW. If you enjoyed it and you get a chance, I'd be so grateful if you can leave a review. And don't forget to check out my free bonus epilogue which you can download by typing in this URL: **https://dl.bookfunnel.com/ m70b4fsfgr**

The next book in the series is Eden's and West's steamy age gap marriage of convenience romance - join them and all the Fitzgeralds in JUST UNTIL YOU LOVE ME.

I can't wait to share more stories with you.

Yours,
Carrie xx

THE FITZGERALDS

Must Have Been Love

In Case You Didn't Know

Just Until You Love Me

THE SALINGER BROTHERS SERIES

Strictly Business

Strictly Pleasure

Strictly For Now

Strictly Not Yours

Strictly The Worst

Strictly Pretend

THE HEARTBREAK BROTHERS NEXT GENERATION SERIES

That One Regret

That One Touch

That One Heartbreak

That One Night

THE WINTERVILLE SERIES

Welcome to Winterville

Hearts In Winter

Leave Me Breathless

Memories Of Mistletoe

Every Shade Of Winter

Mine For The Winter

ANGEL SANDS SERIES

Let Me Burn

She's Like the Wind

Sweet Little Lies

Just A Kiss

Baby I'm Yours

Pieces Of Us

Chasing The Sun

Heart And Soul

Lost In Him

THE HEARTBREAK BROTHERS SERIES

Take Me Home

Still The One

A Better Man

Somebody Like You

When We Touch

THE SHAKESPEARE SISTERS SERIES

Summer's Lease

A Winter's Tale

Absent in the Spring

By Virtue Fall

THE LOVE IN LONDON SERIES

Coming Down

Broken Chords

Canada Square

STANDALONE

Fix You